Holly Wainwright is a writer, editor and broadcaster who lives on the south coast of New South Wales with her partner and their young family. She's the Head of Content at women's media company Mamamia. *The Couple Upstairs* is her fourth novel.

Also by Holly Wainwright

The Mummy Bloggers
How to Be Perfect
I Give My Marriage A Year

The Couple Upstairs

HOLLY WAINWRIGHT

MACMILLAN
Pan Macmillan Australia

Pan Macmillan acknowledges the Traditional Custodians of country throughout Australia and their connections to lands, waters and communities. We pay our respect to Elders past and present and extend that respect to all Aboriginal and Torres Strait Islander peoples today. We honour more than sixty thousand years of storytelling, art and culture.

This is a work of fiction. Characters, institutions and organisations mentioned in this novel are either the product of the author's imagination or, if real, used fictitiously without any intent to describe actual conduct.

First published 2022 in Macmillan by Pan Macmillan Australia Pty Ltd
1 Market Street, Sydney, New South Wales, Australia, 2000

Reprinted 2022 (twice)

A catalogue record for this book is available from the National Library of Australia

Typeset in 12/16.5 Adobe Garamond Pro by Midland Typesetters, Australia

Printed by IVE

The author and the publisher have made every effort to contact copyright holders for material used in this book. Any person or organisation that may have been overlooked should contact the publisher.

The paper in this book is FSC° certified. FSC° promotes environmentally responsible, socially beneficial and economically viable management of the world's forests.

For Brent McKean.
Not my type.

Prologue

January: Mel

Mel didn't believe in ghosts, but there was one living upstairs. Tonight she heard his bare feet stepping across her ceiling. Heard his distinctive ghost voice falling through his open window into hers. Heard him ghost singing. Heard him having ghost sex.

In the evenings while she was likely sitting on her couch, a squirming child between her knees, a nit comb in hand, an over-wrought talent show blaring on the television, she could sense ghost man upstairs. He was strumming the guitar. He was playing chess with his girlfriend. They were talking, always.

When Mel was in her kitchen, making Eddie's bland, brown pasta sauce, the ghost was upstairs frying aromatic chillies and garlic, flicking off bottle tops, pulling corks, clinking glasses.

On summer nights like tonight, the windows were always open. It made the barriers between the six different households in Mel's sturdy art-deco block particularly porous. They were all floating in and out of each other's orbits.

'Are they dancing again, Mum?' asked Ava, lying in Mel's big bed, sheets kicked away, sweating in the heat, both of them tormented

1

by the infuriating whine of a lazy mozzie and the rhythmic gasps drifting down from the upstairs window.

'Go back to your own bed, darling,' Mel whispered to her girl.

'I won't be able to sleep there either,' moaned Ava. 'It's hot and noisy in with Eddie, too.'

'I'll turn the fan up.' Mel swung her legs out of the bed. 'Come on.'

Ava looked like she was heading for the door, but then abruptly turned and fell, face first, onto Mel's bed. A dead weight.

Mel's exhausted irritation surged. 'Ava, *bed*, or you won't be seeing a screen tomorrow.'

It was the kind of negotiation Mel knew the ghost wasn't having. The ghost and Lori, the young woman who shared his home, didn't have to do anything they didn't want to do. Fan on, fan off. Sleep, don't sleep. Work, don't work. Stay home, go out. They didn't even seem to think the ever-shifting rules that told everyone else where to stand and who to touch had anything to do with them. They certainly weren't having their nights co-opted by a sensitive tween whose primary motivation was wheedling permission for more YouTube time.

Mel knew this because the woman upstairs had, earlier, been downstairs, in Mel's apartment. Lori had become her regular baby-sitter this summer, as Mel had navigated school holidays and work and single parenthood, all in one big, fresh mess.

That morning, Lori had walked into a low-level war sparked by denied requests for ice cream.

'You know the wonderful thing about being a grown-up?' she'd said to Ava and Eddie, squatting to their level in her terry-towelling playsuit and her bare, tanned feet. It was exactly what Mel might have worn when she was her children's age, rather than the mini-adult ensembles Ava and Eddie wore – skinny jeans and camo shorts and tiny T-shirts bearing '90s band logos.

'When you're a grown-up, you can eat ice cream whenever you want,' Lori said. 'As much as you want. For as long as you want.'

Can you? Mel thought but didn't say. *That's not the information I've been given.*

'Being an adult is *so* boring, *so* dull,' Lori went on, 'there have to be perks. Your lives are still brilliant and interesting enough not to need sweetening with chocolate ice cream.'

Eddie and Ava were too old to fall for such rubbish, but there was something about Lori that made their eyes and smiles widen.

Lori always spoke to the kids like this, as if she was dropping them exciting little secrets and revelations. To the children, she was lightness and sparkle, a regular Mary Poppins – if Mary Poppins was a twenty-one-year-old backpacker from southern England which, let's face it, was a much more likely scenario these days.

Lori had straightened up, pushed her heavy fringe out of her face and looked at Mel. 'So where you off to, Mum?'

Mel tried not to flinch. Despite their talks over hot and cold drinks, despite the porous walls, despite everything Lori had shared with Mel about the ghost, Mel was still a mum, before anything else.

'Work,' she'd said. 'I'm going into the office to finish something.'

'Kids! Mum's going to the office.' Lori pulled at handfuls of her hair theatrically. 'There are so many more exciting places to go, right?'

Mel's children shrugged. They didn't much care where 'Mum' was if she wasn't with them. Even this past year, when their worlds had changed beyond recognition – between their dad moving out and the virus moving in – they were mostly focused on their imme-diate needs. Mel suspected that when she set foot outside the house, she ceased to exist for them.

But Mel had pushed the ball of irritation back down into her chest and picked up her laptop bag. 'Feed them whatever you can find in the fridge, we're low on supplies,' she'd said.

At the front door, Mel had stopped and turned quickly. 'Oh, and don't take them upstairs, okay?'

Lori had looked up from the kids, who were already pulling her down the hallway towards the lounge room and their Nintendo. Her eyes met Mel's for a moment and Mel thought she looked irritated, like the request was petty.

'Sure,' said Lori, with an almost imperceptible nod. Then she followed the kids, singing out to them as if they were all toddlers, 'Waaaaaait for me . . .'

Now, fourteen hours later, Mel was in her bed, and the babysitter's breathless gasps were keeping her awake in the sticky night.

For a moment Mel imagined herself on that tousled futon upstairs. Saw herself under the ghost's blunt fingers, felt the weight of his body, his hot breath on her neck. She knew how it would feel. How consuming it would be.

Sleep, she told herself. No need to wake any ghosts tonight.

It was the last night Lori's sighs would keep her from sleeping. The next morning, with its usual rushed routine of packing lunches, gulping coffee and scanning work calls, would mark the end of this strange summer tangle her household had found itself in with the stranded young people upstairs.

Lori wouldn't be babysitting anymore. Wouldn't be 'popping in' to share a cup of Mel's Yorkshire tea, a salve for homesickness and ghost trouble. Wouldn't be unsettling Mel with that casual familiarity she always fell into.

Because by tomorrow, the ghost would be saying that Lori had gone. Vanished. Her backpack pushed into the IKEA wardrobe, her clothes draped over chairs salvaged from roadsides. Her phone lying on the scuffed floorboards beside the bed, under the fairy lights she'd strung up to sprinkle a little magic.

Five days from now, Mel would have done things she didn't ordinarily do. Things she had only ever seen on screens.

She would have been interviewed by a policewoman who seemed no older than Lori herself. She'd have printed out pictures of her babysitter from Lori's crowded social media accounts and pasted them to lampposts. Pinned posters on cafe noticeboards next to the urgings to socially distance and wash your hands.

And lied.

Mel would have lied quite a lot.

Part One

1

October: Mel

Mel first saw the ghost six months after she'd told her husband to leave.

It was an unseasonably hot Friday afternoon and she'd spent thirty minutes trying to find a parking spot near home. The ghost was standing at the door to her building with his back to the street and a box in his arms. A backpack had been thrown on the tiled steps, alongside a scuffed guitar case and some bulging black bin bags. He was looking through the smudgy glass door, craning a little, waiting for someone who wasn't yet there.

Mel was reaching about in her sack of a bag, the one that suddenly seemed ridiculously large. It was the bag of a woman who always had to have everything to hand – water bottles and face masks and wet wipes and rice-cracker snacks and sunscreen. Except today she didn't, because it was the first time she'd dropped the kids with Simon for more than one night and now the weekend stretched ahead like a big empty space and she needed a smaller bag.

Everything was wrong today. She'd driven Eddie and Ava to Simon's, whose new place was nicer than it should be. His face on seeing them was a giant split of a smile and the kids had run to him, throwing a wave in Mel's direction as she'd called after them, 'I'll miss you two! Be good!'

It was exactly as it should be and it was absolutely devastating.

'Tell your mum you don't have to be good at Daddy's,' Simon had said, to the kids, not to her, and Mel had laughed too loudly and walked back to her car, arms empty of small, bright backpacks, her nausea rising.

As she looked up from her too-empty bag and walked towards the stranger's square-shouldered back, Mel was thinking it wasn't a day for chit-chat. It was a day to get inside her flat and feel its emptiness, hear the silence. To decide what to do with space.

She went to step around the stranger, silently cursing Simon's new place with its off-street parking, cursing the heat and the absence of the high-pitched soundtrack of nonsense kid-chatter.

The man at the door turned around and smiled. 'Can you get the door, please?' he asked, nodding at the box in his arms. 'Bit caught up here.'

Mel knew instantly he was a ghost, because she knew his face, which was absolutely impossible because that face was long, long gone.

She was so thrown that she literally fell – like some poorly sketched woman in a romantic comedy – tripping over her running shoes and stumbling backwards, down the second and first steps. Except Mel wasn't a character in a charming comedy, she was a forty-year-old woman, sweaty and agitated from a difficult day, with activewear that was straining across her thighs and a halo of frizz around her pulled-back hair.

She tried to self-correct by twisting one leg behind the other, pretzel-like, leaving her clinging to the peeling wrought-iron fence at the bottom of the steps, her giant bag swinging.

'You okay?' said the ghost, but he didn't put his box down. When Mel looked up, his eyes were creased in concern, but also, ever so slightly, in irritation. The box was heavy, it was hot, he didn't have his keys yet. Mel knew all these things, instantly.

'Are you . . .' She straightened up, one hand still on the rail, smoothing her damp hair with the other. 'Upstairs?' was all she could manage.

He nodded. 'Emily's stuck down south, she's left the keys upstairs for me,' he said, in his deep ghost voice. 'I'm subletting, but maybe I shouldn't say that.' He scrunched his face in a mini-frown, pressed his mouth into a line.

Mel obviously looked like the kind of neighbour who would call Emily's landlord, or who *was* Emily's landlord.

He quickly stopped talking and looked down at his feet. Or maybe he just decided that she didn't need to know his business. They were different, after all. Decades apart.

Mel was probably staring. Staring at the green-brown eyes and the cropped dark hair and the full lips. Staring at how his mouth twitched up at one corner and how his brows jutted like a shelf as he lowered them to squint at her. And she was likely staring at the hands that held the box with their long, strong fingers, wide palms, bare forearms with prominent veins. How was this person *here*?

Lowering her eyes, Mel stared at the spot where his baggy board shorts were riding low on his hips. The strip between his faded T-shirt and the frayed, elasticated waistband. She looked up again.

Mel couldn't help but say it out loud, just once. 'Dom?'

The ghost looked confused, shook his head. 'Flynn.' He looked from her to his box, again. 'Can you . . .'

Mel stepped up with her key in hand and edged past this Flynn. 'I should be wearing a mask,' she found herself saying, conscious of the momentary narrowing of distance between them.

'Why?' he said. 'It's fine with me.'

Finally, the door was open. He smelled of fresh sweat and musky soap as he passed her.

'Is guessing names your thing?' he asked, as he started up the stairs. His face was in full smirk. She had seen it before.

Her mouth was dry. 'You just remind me of someone,' she said. 'Sorry, long day.'

'Cool. Well, hello neighbour.' He smiled, and then started walking again.

'We won't be too loud!' he called down as he turned the corner to the next flight. 'Maybe a little moving-in party.'

No-one anywhere had had a party in six months.

Prickles of anxiety chased up her neck and into her scalp as she pushed open the heavy door to her unit. *Goosebumps. The neighbour's given me goosebumps.*

Inside, Mel leaned against the door, a light sweat sticking her back to the cool wood. She exhaled, and reached into her bag to fish out her phone.

'I've just seen Dom,' she said, the second her sister answered. 'He's moving in upstairs.'

'Darling, Dom's dead.'

'I know. But I just stood next to him, in broad daylight.'

'Dom looked like a lot of handsome young men, Mel. He was beautiful.'

'I fell over.' Mel straightened her legs, pushing her back harder into the door, letting her bag drop to the floor. 'It was mortifying.'

'You're an idiot.'

'Yes, I am.'

'The kids are at Simon's, right? Are you okay?'

Mel thought about it. The empty weekend, the ghost.

'Clearly not.'

There was a pause. On the other end, beyond Izzy's breathing, Mel could hear the whirr of a coffee machine, the muttering of TV news, a video game blaring.

'What time is it there? Can you have a wine?' Izzy sounded hopeful.

'I'd better not. I'm already seeing ghosts.'

'I wish I was there, duck.'

'Me too.'

'No, I really, really wish I was there. Everything here is awful. At least there you can stand next to a strange ghost in the daylight.'

'Yeah. We're very grateful.'

In two decades, Mel had never considered the time difference when she picked up the phone to call Izzy. Whether it was nine hours or twelve, neither sister had ever let it inhibit communication. There was never any consideration of children's bedtimes, dinner plans, sobriety status, sleep, sex. It had driven Simon mad, the conversations at all hours, some only a few seconds long, some devouring precious chunks of Mel's time.

'Maybe I should go up there, go ghost-hunting.'

'Terrible idea.'

'I know. Maybe I won't.'

'He's not Dom, Mel. He's just a guy. And you're just his old, downstairs neighbour.'

'Ouch. Thanks.'

'Tough love. You came to the right place.'

'Thanks a lot, Oprah. Talk later.'

'I'll be here,' Izzy said.

Mel had opened the window of the front room and leaned out, gulping in the early spring evening air and craning her neck to look back to the front door. The ghost's bags had gone.

She pulled the window closed and looked around her silent flat. Her computer, her papers, her ringed tea-mug. The mess of discarded kids' drawings, their kicked-off shoes, scattered remotes and too many chargers for too many screens.

I need to go out tonight. See if Fi wants to have a wine at the beach.

And that's when she heard it. The music from upstairs.

At first, Mel couldn't make out the tune. Then every goosebump her sister's voice had chased away was back, a ripple of prickles all the way up her arms.

The ghost upstairs was playing her wedding song.

2

October: Mel

Nick Cave hadn't been Simon's idea. He didn't even like 'miserable music', as he called it. But Simon hadn't really been that interested in the details of his own wedding.

The guest list, yes. The drinks list, yes. The holiday afterwards, definitely. But songs and menus and flowers? Not that bothered. Mel pretended to be irritated by his indifference, but really, she was grateful for it.

So he'd gone along with the song. Bear-hugged a frazzled Mel around the dancefloor of the local surf club to a sad, happy ballad he didn't really know.

Mel still hadn't told him why she chose it. Not that it mattered now.

Izzy, of course, had known.

'I can't believe you chose your ex's song for your wedding dance,' she'd hissed at Mel in the toilet cubicle, her fists full of white taffeta as she held her sister's dress away from the lightly slimy floor. 'I thought I'd vetoed it.'

'I didn't!' Mel had insisted, not entirely truthfully. 'You're thinking of a different one.'

'Come off it, Mel.'

Izzy had still been jet-lagged, more than a little snippy, and not quite the gushing, accommodating maid of honour Mel had fantasised about. 'As if Simon even knows who Nick Cave is.'

'You just met him.' Mel had reached for the toilet paper. One of the many strange things about living on the other side of the world from your family was the real possibility they might only meet the man you were going to marry in the week you were going to marry him. 'What would you know?'

'I know,' Izzy had said. 'He's sporty. Completely different genre.'

The song drifting down from upstairs had taken Mel back to that bathroom, with its faded green tiles, peeling Formica doors and basins stained like tea. Back to her sister's face, telling her off in a tiny cubicle, hands full of wedding dress. Knowing her so well.

Which was telling, Mel knew, considering it should really take her back to the dancefloor, Simon's arms around her waist, her tired head on his shoulder, and his proud smile.

But Izzy had been right. It wasn't Simon's song.

It was Dominic's.

Mel needed to get out. Call Fiona, make a break for it.

She looked around the flat. The endless bits of paper scribbled with half-drawings. A started but abandoned jigsaw of a humpback whale. Plates with crumbs and IKEA glasses scattered with sticky fingerprints. A shoe. A T-shirt. Another shoe. All the signs of Ava and Eddie, without any of the accompanying noise. Or any of the endless requests for snacks. Or the constant fighting.

For fuck's sake, Mel. She could hear her sister's voice in her head. *Get your shit together.*

Mel found her phone, blocked out the muffled wedding song, and called for help.

3

October: Mel

Sea salt. Fried food. Stale beer.

Those were the smells of Mel's neighbourhood.

It took four minutes to walk from her building to the beach. Across a road streaming with giant, shiny SUVs, past a massage shop with a tiny Buddha offering at the door and a sign that guaranteed a $39.99 special from masked and sanitised staff. Past a fried chicken shop trailing black crosses that marked where people should stand to wait for their burgers and shakes. Past a coffee shop selling acai bowls and spinach smoothies. Past an ice creamery that reliably pumped out the candied smell of caramel waffles, whether waffles were currently grilling or not. Past a giant pub that was sometimes open, sometimes closed, dependent on case numbers and confidence. Past benches scrawled with teenage graffiti, rubbish bins piled high with the greased paper and cardboard flip-top boxes of endless takeaway food.

At the end of the strip of shops there was a sandstone wall that had stood far longer than any of them. And over that, a short drop down to the wide expanse of beach.

The kids had toddled, scootered or sprinted their way alongside this wall almost every day of their lives. In the early morning, trailed by a pie-eyed, sleep-deprived parent. And at golden hour, to tire them out before bed. On stunning summer mornings to swim before the crowds descended. On crisp winter afternoons to chase a ball around the sand. Soon, Mel knew, Ava and Eddie wouldn't be happy to tag along on her daily ocean-side errands – coming down here for coffee and conversation, shopping on the way home, the kids whirling around her as she stopped and talked with whichever familiar face was passing, 1.5 metres apart.

The sea was a different mood each day, but always there, breathing in, breathing out. Deterring or beckoning, depending on the day. Pouring into the pools at both ends – sanctuaries for those who wanted to avoid the waves. And the sharks.

It was Mel's mum's fault that she couldn't look at the ocean without thinking about sharks. All those years ago, Liz had put *Jaws* on the DVD player, pulled on her coat and shoes and said she was just nipping next door for a drink with Alva.

It had taken Mel about six months to get back in the local swimming pool.

When little Mel, in the north of England, thought about Australia at all, she thought of sharks. Australians must be *crazy brave*, Mel and Izzy used to say. To still go swimming when you knew there might be monsters in the water.

Twenty years on, Mel swam in the sea for six months of the year, but she never went out beyond where her feet could touch the sandy bottom. She watched the morning shoals of point-to-point swimmers with awe, even now. *Crazy brave.*

When you lived next to a city beach, the best time of day to be there was early, and late. Autumn and winter. Never in prime time. It was spring now, and the crowds of visitors loitered a little later each day with their ice creams and their cans and their portable speakers. The quiet days were numbered.

The early evening, when the sun was sitting low and the litter-pocked sand was more golden than yellow, was Mel's favourite time at the beach.

Following the sandstone wall now without scooting kids, Mel left behind the song, the ghost, the empty flat. She kept her head up, looking ahead, as every guru always said you should. Keep looking forward, not back.

The sharky sea was the silvery blue it turned just before the sun dropped and Mel could see Fiona waiting near the steps, a suspiciously large bag over her shoulder, hiding a contraband bottle, no doubt. She turned, saw Mel and waved.

Mel quickened her pace, almost trotting towards her friend, suddenly flooded with relief at seeing someone real.

'Well, how does it feel?' Fi called, as Mel got within earshot. 'Are you alright?'

Mel clutched her chest as if she'd been shot. 'Hurts a bit, but I'll be fine,' she called back. She lifted her own heavy bag. 'Brought a sundowner to ease transition.'

'It had to happen some day,' Fi said, as they walked down to their spot.

For a moment, Mel thought she meant Dom's ghost, but of course she meant Simon taking the kids for two straight nights. Alternate weekends. The new normal.

'I know. Simon was going to get his shit together sooner or later,' she said. 'And plenty of people tell me I'll enjoy having weekends to myself, eventually.'

'Like when you start dating?' Fi leaned hard on the word, making it sound as ridiculous as it did in Mel's head. 'I am so here for that day.'

A strange but predictable thing had happened to Mel's social circle since Simon had left. The invites and messages from their 'couple friends', the families they'd spent almost every weekend with for years, had grown quieter, less frequent. But as they'd faded, a group Mel barely knew existed had come into sharp focus. It had started with Fi, who had stopped Mel at the school gate and said, straight up, 'You need to meet me, Mel.'

Mel had thought she'd already met Fi. In the same way she'd met lots of other parents from school. She knew, broadly speaking, the names of the kids who were the same age as hers, and could possibly pick their parents out of a line-up. She even knew Fi, whose son Will was in Ava's class, from the soccer sidelines the previous winter. They'd grimaced at each other over their take-away coffee cups, theatrically shivered at the morning cold and rolled their eyes at the parents who yelled at the referee. She knew Fi.

So at the school gate that day, she'd raised her eyebrows. 'What do you mean, Fi? I've met you.'

Fi, who was tall and imposing, with lots of curly dark hair and a flat-footed confidence that suggested wherever she was standing was exactly where she was supposed to be, shook her head and laughed. 'You haven't. Not really.'

She'd leaned in and stage-whispered behind her hand, 'There are plenty of us, you know, and you're going to need us. Your married friends,' Fi gestured around with an outstretched arm, 'they don't get it.'

At the time, just weeks after Simon had moved out, Mel had thought this was bullshit. There was no way that the people she and Simon had shared so much with for so long wouldn't find a way to support them both and remain impartial. They were smart people, after all. Kind people.

But now, months later, it was undeniable – what Mel had needed was not what her married friends could give her, even with their good intentions. What Mel had needed was Fi, and Tess and Roland – her 'single parent' buddies – and the bonds they'd formed fast on sanctioned walks and picnics. People who understood without explanation, people who weren't inhibited by loyalty. People who were happy to hear Mel let rip about the bullshit injustices of separation without feeling a constant need to smooth it over, to make it okay, to mould it into a story that both 'sides' could be comfortable with.

'I'm not ready for all your dating apps,' Mel told Fi, as they headed towards the ocean pool where they could sit with their backs against the rocks as the last of the sun's warmth faded out. 'My head is too full of other things,' she added as they found their spot and settled, wriggling their bums down into the sand.

'Other things?'

'Other people,' Mel said, like a confession. 'Other stories, other times. There's no room for anything new yet.'

Fi nodded, squeezed Mel's knee with the hand that wasn't holding the pink wine she had poured from the open bottle in her bag. Only with your nearest beach-drinking friends was it acceptable to turn up with a half-empty bottle from your fridge.

'Sometimes what really forces people out of your head is thrusting some other person in.'

'You really had to say thrusting, didn't you?'

Fi had been right that day at the school gate, Mel really did need to meet her. Especially once she'd heard her story – a story that Ava had been sitting next to in class for the best part of a year, for four years, in fact, with absolutely no idea.

Fi seemed indomitable because she was. In the last ten years she'd survived IVF, two miscarriages, a traumatic birth, a breast cancer diagnosis, the loss of her catering business and the discovery that her husband, Will's father, was the kind of despicable narcissist who would cheat on his wife while she was recovering from chemo.

All that, and yet she was still standing on those bloody grounded feet. A force as warm and powerful as a stiff northerly, changing the atmosphere, shifting people around.

'The first weekend Will went to Johan's, I thought I might die,' Fi said now, leaning her head back against their favourite rock. 'I spent the whole of Saturday convinced Will was crying for me, and his dad wouldn't let him call. I hardly slept. I thought Will would come home miserable and starving and cling to me like a shipwreck.'

'Not being melodramatic at all, then,' said Mel, returning Fi's knee squeeze.

Fi laughed a short, hard laugh. 'Will came home on a sugar high, with a bloody Apple watch and stories of how they'd spent the day at Luna Park, and then a night at that flashy new hotel at Darling Harbour. They'd had pizza at the pool bar and room service ice-cream sundaes watching *The Avengers* until midnight.'

'The bastard.'

'Yep. I was so fucking angry, but Will was bloody beside himself. He told me that his dad had made him feel special, and important, and it was just what he needed.'

'That little shit.' Mel laughed.

'Right?' Fi raised a dramatic fist. 'Damn you, Disneyland Dad.'

'Luckily, I know Simon is too tight to do that,' said Mel. 'And surely Johan couldn't keep that up?'

'He didn't. It settled down. The treats kept coming for a month or so and then he told Will he was getting too spoiled, and so they spent the weekend grouting tiles in the new ensuite. Will came home that Sunday and said he wished Dad didn't have so many bathrooms, and I could have kissed him.'

Mel tried to picture Ava and Eddie coming back. What they'd tell her about life at Dad's. What they wouldn't.

'So,' Mel began, 'are you used to it now?'

'I'll never be used to weekends without Will,' Fi said, draining her glass. 'But I've learned to see the advantages of having some "time off", as all the bloody married mums call it.'

'Like, time on the apps.'

'Exactly!' Fi pulled her phone from her bag. 'Come on, let's look together. You know you want to.'

'I do not,' Mel told her. 'I'm social distancing,' she said. 'That's why I'm a forty-year-old woman sitting on a beach drinking wine out of a plastic cup.'

In reality, Mel knew exactly what waited for her on the apps. Because she'd spent several nights on her lounge, flicking through pictures of middle-aged men who all looked vaguely familiar, and who, in a curiously high number, thought that holding a large dead fish was the way to a woman's heart. That or a barbecue spatula. Or a giant fish and a barbecue spatula.

She knew that, after a few minutes of feeling disheartened by who the algorithm thought she was, the algorithm would finally prove it did know what Mel wanted, or, at least, what she'd once wanted, and show her a picture of Simon. The father of her children, the man she'd slept next to for a decade. The man she was still married to.

Simon's profile said that he was looking for someone kind and fit. Mel only just snuck into his permitted age cut-off, despite him being five years older than her. It also said he was open to dating women with kids, cracking open the possibility of a future blended family that hurt Mel's heart, just a little. There was no fish in the picture he'd chosen, or, more likely, his sister had chosen for him. He'd been smiling, in a button-down collared shirt, holding a bottle that looked like a beer but was actually a kombucha in a tinted brown bottle.

The picture had been taken at his forty-fourth birthday barbecue. Mel had bought the kombuchas for him, because Simon wasn't drinking that summer. And she'd bought that shirt. In fact, she had been standing beside him, with her arm around Eddie, when Simon's sister took the picture. Eddie had been pulling one of his infuriating photo faces, the one where he rolled his eyes back in his head and pushed his tongue between his teeth. Mel remembered that the sun was in her eyes.

It didn't make Mel sad to think that she and Eddie had been trimmed out of the photo Simon was using as bait for someone new. Someone fit and kind. Someone no older than forty. It just made her tired.

'Really, Fi, thank you, but I'm not ready for the apps today.'

Fiona returned her phone to her bag, leaned back against the rock, and they both sat in silence for a moment, looking out at the sea.

'I'm glad I met you,' said Mel. 'You know, properly.'

'Me too,' said Fi. 'We need as many fucking people to call on as we can in these weird times. And you're so far from so many of yours.'

'It's okay,' Mel said, as a reflex. She gave Fi's knee another squeeze. 'You've been through worse.'

'True,' said Fi, with a cackle. 'True.'

Mel wriggled her toes in the cooling sand and for a few moments was grateful this was her life.

4

October: Lori

Lori's head bumped hard against the glass and she jolted awake.

She brought a hand to her mouth. Was she drooling? Sleeping in front of other people was always a risk. Was there now a photo of her lolling head against a dirty car window, a slither of spit trickling from her open mouth? Was it already online?

Looking around at the others in the car – new friends, almost strangers – Lori looked for quick clues.

The driver, whose name was either Ben or Rob but right now her foggy head couldn't quite remember, was nodding along to the ska-pop playing through the station wagon's dusty speakers. The other guy, George, next to her across the back seat, was engrossed in something on his phone. She could only see the top of the tilted head of the girl, Kat, in the passenger seat, but she was clearly looking down. Was it at a picture of Lori snoring? Was she typing a caption? *When your hitchhiker passes out. #droolbitch.*

Lori wiped the back of her hand across her mouth and sat up, smoothing her hair.

'I was tired,' she said, in a small voice.

'Obviously,' said George, not looking up from his phone.

What did that mean? Did that mean that, moments before, he'd tapped the others on the shoulder and they'd all turned, sneering?

'Hey,' said Kat from the front seat. 'Welcome back.'

It didn't sound sarcastic – it sounded friendly.

'Hey.'

Lori looked out of the window at the green, and the blue. The scenery looked the same as it had when she'd fallen asleep. Trees and sky. Trees and sky.

'Where are we?' she asked. 'Are we far?'

'Far from where?' replied Ben/Rob. 'That's the question, right?' And he'd let out a short, braying laugh.

That's right. Ben/Rob was a dick.

Lori's mouth was dry and she needed to pee. She leaned forward and reached for the phone she'd left charging between the two front seats, but someone had disconnected it, the cord was plugged into Ben/Rob's phone now. Hers was still dead.

How long had it been since they'd stopped? How long until they stopped again?

'We're not far,' Kat said. 'We've heard there's a hostel open in Merimbula, thought we'd try it.'

'A hostel,' the driver humphed. 'Fuck that.'

'Shut up Rob,' (*Rob!*) Kat said. 'I'm not sleeping another night on some random's floor. It's keep going or a hot shower, that's it.'

'How far from Sydney are we?' Lori asked. 'And can I please plug in . . .' She waved her phone.

'Still about another six hours,' Kat started.

'I'm done with driving in the dark,' said Rob. 'Before any of you get any ideas.'

'Soft,' breathed George, not looking up from his game.

If he heard it, Rob let it go. Lori suspected he didn't want to admit he'd be in a lot of trouble if he crashed this car. 'If the hostel has space, I'll eat the tyre.'

Six hours. Nothing really, in this vast, weird country. Lori felt like she'd been moving for days, weeks. But were they really moving at all? Never-changing scenery. Reluctant drivers. All conspiring to hold her back from where she wanted to be, where she needed to be.

The plates on the car said Western Australia. Which was a good thing, George had told her, last night, when she was lying next to him, with as many clothes on her body as she could stand to wear and still sleep, in someone's brother's mate's house in what they'd all called the High Country.

'If we had Vic plates, we'd probably never make it to Sydney. Bloody virus control would get us for sure,' he'd said, beer and weed on his breath. 'We've got to outrun those fuckers.'

Lori had lain there in the dark, comforted by the glow of her phone.

All these young men have outlaw complexes, she'd typed. *Running from the man.*

A beat.

How many young men are we talkin about? came the reply. And Lori smiled to herself.

George, Rob and Kat were driving from Perth to Sydney in a station wagon that looked like it belonged to a suburban family who appreciated the extra boot space for the Saturday morning sports run. On the back window, someone had tried to peel off a sticker of what looked like a fancy school crest.

These boys might have ironic mullets and deliberately sketchy tattoos, but Lori had already clocked the credit card in what was definitely a mum's name when George had paid for petrol, and she could tell that Rob had gone to exactly the right kind of school, by the way words like *first eleven* and *Italy exchange* slipped into his monologues. Lori recognised her own people, even if they'd grown up on the opposite side of the world.

George hadn't tried to touch Lori last night, which answered one of the anxieties she'd been carrying since Adelaide. She'd felt a little sick when Rob's brother's mate had pulled a saggy spare mattress out from under a bed, thrown a blanket over it and left them to it, giving George a wink that he hadn't meant Lori to see. But she'd also clocked that the wink had embarrassed George, and he'd made no eye contact with her as he stepped out of his jeans and fell onto the mattress in his shorts. The actual bed belonged to an absent housemate, who may or may not come home in the night, they'd been told. Lori had spent the night lying on the far edge of the mattress in her sweatshirt and leggings, staring at the spiderwebbed ceiling beams in the soupy dark, shivering a little, phone clutched to her chest as she imagined the sound of a car crunching towards the house, and listened to the gentle whistle of a sleeping George.

A hostel tonight would be great.

Lori had met her car-mates in Adelaide. Well, she'd 'met' them in the Travelmate Facebook group. They'd been the first people who'd answered her callout.

Need ride from Adelaide to Sydney. Happy to share the driving, provide epic playlist, not make small talk.

After a meet-up for all parties to assess 'serial killer vibes', and a texted agreement about sharing petrol money, they'd now been in the station wagon for almost three days, as they took what Rob called the 'scenic way' to Sydney. Lori wasn't allowed to drive, and no-one had asked for her playlist, but the small talk had been kept to a minimum. She thought maybe Kat and Rob were a couple, from last night's sleeping arrangements, but there were no obvious signs of connection. No in-jokes, no incidental contact, no secret smiles. Maybe she was wrong.

She leaned forward again, yanked out Rob's phone and put hers in the charger. 'You're full,' she said, with a smile.

Lori the student from Dorking did not get into cars with strangers. But traveller Lori did. In the past year she'd done all kinds of things that she'd never dreamt of doing before, like swimming with rays in a warm, translucent tropical ocean. Scrubbing caked-on shit from the toilets of a five-star resort. Dancing barefoot in thick red dirt under upside-down stars. Fighting off the groping hands of a middle-aged hotel manager. Sleeping in something called a swag. Drinking vinegary wine from a silver balloon. Learning words from languages older than nations. Picking fruit under a blistering sun. Singing cheesy songs at the top of her lungs on the flat back of a speeding truck. Having a leg-shuddering orgasm in a waterfall in broad daylight.

Falling in love.

This is what it feels like, she'd written, two weeks ago, in her journal. *It's overwhelming. And I can't do anything about it. Its pull is inevitable. It's drawing me across this country like a magnet, like a gravitational force.*

To Sydney.

Only six more hours away.

5

October: Lori

Rob was wrong.

The hostel in Merimbula had beds.

'No bugger's travelling,' the tired-looking woman at the hostel's bare front desk had told them. 'So take your pick.'

Kat had looked at Rob and raised an eyebrow. 'See?'

Their 'pick' was the option to have separate beds in single-sex dormitories, or to share a cabin of their own, for less. They chose the cabin, even though at this point Lori would happily have handed over her upper card limit to have some alone time.

How long was it since Lori had been in a room on her own, with a door that shut?

At the very beginning of her trip, she and Jools had booked a twin room in every place they stayed, but as they'd made their way north from Perth, at every stop the ocean getting bluer, the earth getting ruddier, the towns getting smaller and stranger, their fellow travellers getting more unkempt, they'd begun to realise that this was a long haul, and the money they'd scrambled together for this adventure needed to stretch. Hostels were built around community, not privacy, and the whole bloody point was to meet people anyway. Wasn't it?

But Lori was tired of meeting people now. Tired of the same list of questions: *Where are you from? How old are you? How long have you been travelling? Are you going to go home?*

These days Lori would love nothing more than to be around people she didn't have to explain herself to. Since Jools had left her, Lori hadn't spent time with anyone who'd known her for more than a handful of days. Well, with one notable exception.

But then he'd left, too.

The intimacy people formed at speed on the road was abandoned just as quickly. Lori's phone was already full of travellers she'd met, befriended but now barely remembered, their faces now more familiar from Instagram, where she followed their next adventures to compare them with her own.

'Who's where?' asked George, when they walked into the cabin with their backpacks. One double. Two singles. Seashell-patterned bedcovers. The air was musty, like ocean trapped in a cupboard.

The fact that George asked was the reason Lori felt safer in his presence.

Rob threw himself on the double, his long, pasty-pale legs dangling their Nike slides off the edge. 'Driver's privileges,' he said, putting his hands behind his head and directing a leer at Kat. 'Hey, Kat?'

'No way,' Kat said. 'Never again.'

Not a couple. A fling of convenience. That made a little more sense. Kat, tall and strong, was self-assured in every movement. Her confidence was evident from the way she pushed the passenger seat all the way back and rested her shell-pink, pedi-ed toes on the dashboard. It was there in the way she walked into a petrol station five minutes after Rob and dropped her chip packets and fizzy water in front of him just as he pulled out his card.

'I think,' Kat said slowly, looking straight at Rob, 'that the girls should get the double tonight.'

Rob rolled his eyes and got off the bed. 'Whatever.'

Neither version of Lori, the student or the traveller, could pull off Kat's level of authority. How did Kat know that people would do what she wanted? That she wouldn't be forced into a prickly confrontation?

Either way, Lori was grateful. An actual bed and a night spent without fear of an uninvited hand was more welcome than she'd realised. It was exhausting always being on high alert.

She'd felt that thrum of anxiety in hostels with mixed dorms. On camping trips in shared tents. On buses and in shared cars. Over the past eight months, she'd sharpened her instincts, like a twitchy gazelle in a David Attenborough doco.

Lori wanted to feel safe again.

'I'm going for a shower,' she said, dropping her backpack on the double bed.

'Me too,' said Kat, quickly, and another moment of alone time vanished.

In the shared bathroom, Lori watched Kat at the next hazy mirror along from hers, combing out her long, black hair, eyes steady on her reflection.

She decided to ask. 'How do you know Rob and George?'

'I don't really,' said Kat. 'They kind of know an old friend of mine. Not that he would have anything to do with them.' Kat gave a little snort and produced a small bottle of something creamy from her washbag, tapped it out onto her hands and pressed it into her face. 'I needed a ride and I heard they were going.'

'So you and Rob, you're not –'

'No!' Kat looked quickly at Lori. 'I mean,' Kat went on, as if she could tell Lori was remembering last night's stopover, the configuration of mattresses. 'I was horny the other night, but these guys are useless. They were meant to be on their gap year, yeah? Can't you just see them on a Contiki tour?'

Lori had no idea what a Contiki tour was, but obviously it was something that guys like Rob and George would do, but Kat would not.

'I just need to get to Sydney,' Kat said, producing an eyeliner and expertly tracing her top lash line. 'There's a job there for me.'

'Me too,' said Lori. 'Not a job . . . just, Sydney.'

'Six more hours,' Kat said. She dropped the eye pencil back in her bag and zipped it shut.

Lori thought about the face she wanted to see. Was going to see tomorrow.

Something in her expression must have intrigued Kat because she leaned on the sink and turned to look at her properly for perhaps the first time. She was older, Lori realised, maybe by a few years.

'What's in Sydney for you?' Kat asked.

Lori knew she was flushing pink under such a direct gaze. 'Just someone I met travelling.' She zipped up her washbag, too.

'A *someone* someone?'

'I think so.' Lori shrugged. *I really hope so.* 'He was, back in Broome.'

'Broome!' Kat smiled a big, knowing smile. 'Everyone hooks up in Broome. What happened?'

It was too simple a question. Lori knew that 'holiday romance' was a cliché, that young people moving around the country were going to bump up against each other, and that local guys, with their Chris Hemsworth accents, had the pick of travellers, thanks to their ability to do things European boys could not – like build a beach bonfire, change a flat tyre in forty-degree heat, and take you swimming at a gorge so breathtaking, with its soaring red walls and its cool, clean water, that its magic could not even be ruined by a throwaway gag that its traditional name translated as 'Knicker-dropper'.

She knew all that. But what had happened between them, out there, was different. Important.

Lori bent over to wrap her towel around her head and then straightened up. 'Nothing happened,' she said. 'We were together, then he had to go.'

'So you're following him?'

Lori didn't like the way that sounded. Her legs started to itch.

'I was always going to Sydney eventually, anyway, just . . . we thought, why wait, you know.'

As if she could sense the overreach in that 'we', Kat held her gaze for so long that Lori wondered if she had something on her forehead. She even lifted her hand to wipe the imaginary something off.

'Of course,' said Kat, eventually. 'Well, you're nearly there.'

Lori nodded. *Yes*, she wanted to say. Kat got it. She wanted to add, *Let's go and have a drink, let's go and watch the sea and eat some hot vinegary chips that will remind me of home.*

But she just said, 'What do you want to do? Do you want to hang out, or . . .'

And Kat smiled a wicked kind of smile. 'Or what?'

Lori shrugged, feeling silly now, itchy legs again. 'I don't know.'

Kat laughed. 'Yes, absolutely, let's.'

6

October: Lori

It's not that Lori hadn't thought about going home when the world changed. It's just, at the time, she'd been distracted.

It was difficult to reconcile that a catastrophe was looming when you were crushing tiny shells under your bare feet on the very edge of Western Australia.

And then, it seemed contrary to flee to a place where the inferno was blazing, when you were so far away you could barely smell a whiff of smoke on the warm breeze.

She felt the same sitting here, by the water at Merimbula. It was practically suburban compared to some of the places she'd travelled to in the past few months, but still, she felt another world away from the messages she was getting from back home. Her mum's messages, so desperate for her return at the start, had morphed into 'Stay there, you're safer there.'

Lori agreed, and pretended she was taking her mother's advice. But she wasn't. She was just chasing the new her.

Apparently, they didn't get sunsets on this side of Australia. Not like the ones she'd watched in Broome, sitting on her ratty towel in between Flynn's legs, listening to some overconfident young guy with a guitar and feeling like the chosen one.

Of all these other travelling girls, all glowing like night lights at golden hour, he had picked her to share his towel, and his van, and his bed. At the end of those days the sinking sun had been a spectacle, and the opening act.

And now Lori had been chosen again, this time by cool Kat, as a worthy companion for a takeaway dinner on a bench, watching the light change on this last night on the road.

'You're running away,' Lori's mum had told her. 'And it won't work.' She was right. And she was wrong.

One slip of the finger had made it untenable for Lori to stay where she was, at home in Dorking. Her finger pressing Post, instead of Send. Such a small thing. Such a monumental thing, when what you were posting was a picture of someone doing something they were not meant to be doing. With you.

It had been Jools who'd convinced her that this was the perfect time to run. That it would pass, this storm which started in Lori's phone but quickly spilled over into pubs and shops and student cafeterias, morphing from tags and vomit emojis and sharp four-letter comments into whispers and looks, unreturned hellos and backs swiftly turned. It would pass, but it might be best to take that long-talked about trip now, while the cyclone rolled through.

'By the time we get back,' Jools had said, 'this will all be over. There's never been a better time to exit, stage left.'

Jools was right. Every passing day validated the decision and the timing.

'There are so many more hours in the day when you're travelling,' Lori said, dipping a chip in the tomato sauce she'd squeezed onto the edge of the takeaway box. Vinegar had been a step too far for Australian Kat.

Kat looked up from her phone. 'You mean it's boring.'

'Not boring, just . . .' Lori fiddled with the edge of her sauce packet. 'The guy I met, he said being on the road was full of poss-ibility, that every day was an "anything can happen" day, and that's how life should always be, but it isn't.'

'Now you've mentioned him, you can't stop mentioning him,' Kat said, smiling in a way that Lori wasn't certain was kind.

'He just said interesting things,' Lori said, into her chips. 'He's different.'

Kat laughed. 'Why? Because he lived in a van and was allergic to shirts? I've met lots of those.'

'Oh, he's not like that.' But Lori didn't look up. She'd rarely seen Flynn in a shirt.

'It's okay,' Kat said, some warmth in her voice. 'I can be a sucker for shoulders, too. Do you think Rob and George have gone to the pub? Neither of them are messaging me back.'

Lori shrugged. She didn't much care where they were. Her stomach was rolling with impatience, and irritation. She just wanted to go to bed and look at her phone. And then for it to be tomorrow, and to be driving to Sydney.

She licked her fingers of the last of the salt and the fat. Kat was staring down at her screen again, poking at it sharply. Lori glanced down at her own phone, but she knew what she was looking for wasn't there.

I might be in Sydney tomorrow, Lori had typed, before they'd left the hostel.

There had been no answer. Yet.

'I might go back,' Lori said.

Kat nodded, still looking at her phone, and stood up. 'Me too.'

The hostel was in the grounds of a caravan park. In England, it would be called a campsite. But in England, Lori would never have set foot in a place like this. Camping and caravanning wasn't something the Harings did. No way. She'd spent her holidays in musty rented farmhouses in France and Italy.

But this last year, Lori had embraced living in the kinds of places she'd never been before, with communal shower blocks and barbecue areas with laminated signs warning everyone to clean up their own mess and, for God's sake, recycle. And now here she was, leading an actual Australian back to their room in a strange town as the sky darkened around them.

Lori had set out to reinvent herself, to no longer be the girl who'd exposed her soft underbelly – literally and figuratively – to a whole town. And maybe she had.

As soon as she tapped the code into the park's gate, she and Kat immediately knew where Rob and George were.

The sound of drinking men drifted across the sparse grid of campsites all the way to the gate. A wall of loud, braying barks, punctuated with shouting laughs and yells of 'Naaaaah, mate!', an undercurrent of EDM beats pulsing from a tinny cylinder speaker.

Rob and George had found friends.

'Shit,' said Kat, and at first Lori thought she was echoing her immediate reaction. *Shit, they're going to be drunk. Shit, I just want to go to bed.*

'Shit, that's so rude,' Kat said. 'They didn't tell us there was a party.'

Kat pulled at the hem of her blue cotton dress and started the walk across the campground towards the men's backs. One of the men they didn't know turned, saw Kat, and immediately let out a sort of guttural whoop that turned the others' heads, including Rob's, whose face split into a smug smile.

'Come on,' Kat said, turning back towards Lori.

But Lori's stomach was churning. 'I'm going to bed,' she said quietly, aware that it still wasn't completely dark yet. There was nothing about this that felt safe to her.

Kat looked at Lori for a long second before giving a tiny, almost invisible shrug. 'Sure, then.'

'Will you be alright?' Lori called after her.

But Kat was already walking towards the men, shoulders back, hair swinging. Looking for all the world like the most confident of women, she raised a hand to wave off Lori's worry and there was just the tiniest trace of a tremor in her fingers.

7

October: Lori

When she felt the hands on her legs, Lori wasn't shocked. In the split second between sleep and not-sleep, she found herself thinking, *Here we go. Here it is. This is when it happens.*

The hands were firm, pushing their way up her thighs, fingers searching, presumably, for the elasticated top of the tracksuit pants she'd put on before she'd climbed into bed. Tracksuit pants, a sweat-shirt and socks. It hadn't been cold.

How had she fallen asleep? That was the thought that came immediately after registering the hands. She'd lain there, just like the night before, vigilant, still. She'd heard Kat come in, hiss at her in the dark, 'Are you awake, Looooooori?' In the hazy grey she'd watched Kat's back as she pulled her dress over her head and fell into bed beside Lori. It must have made her feel safe, knowing Kat was next to her, and the last thing Lori could remember registering was the glow of Kat's phone and then it falling, dim, to her chest, and her breathing changing, slowing, deepening. Sleeping. No-one else had come back, Lori was sure of it, but she must have fallen asleep, because . . . here were the hands.

'Get off me,' she said into the dark mass, and jumped up, pushing against the pressure. The figure fell, but forwards, rather than back, towards her, not away. Lori's head bumped something, another head, and a rush of hot, beery breath was coming at her, along with the weight of someone taller, broader than her.

'For fuck's sake,' said the figure. Rob. Was it only Rob? The room was coming into focus. Kat wasn't next to her anymore, she could see an empty white space where the cover was pulled back. She couldn't tell if there was anyone else in the room at all, other than this wall of a man right in front of her. She pushed again, and Rob stumbled back a step, not so steady on his feet.

'Calm down,' the dark mass of Rob said, and his hands were on her shoulders, not pushing, exactly, but heavy. 'Just sit down.'

Lori's mind was on the door. She knew exactly where it was. Only four steps to her left, but the rest of the bed was between her and it. The window, next to the door, had a thin, blue gingham curtain hanging over it, and it glowed with the light of the outside lamp that marked each cabin, a promise of safety. In the seconds that she registered this, Rob had righted himself and was leaning in again.

'Come on, Laura,' he said, his voice thick and irritated. 'What's the matter?'

For a second Lori thought she was mistaken, that maybe he was just trying to wake her up to ask where the others were. But then he lunged, those hands out again, pushing against her shoulders, and Lori fell backwards. She knew she was going to hit the bed, and that he was going to land on top of her, and then she would be pinned. But surely she was quicker, especially with those beers in him. So she twisted and threw herself, face first, towards the other side of the bed. Towards the door. She just had to get to the door.

Rob grabbed her leg and his breathing changed – heavier, and faster.

Lori's palms were on the floor, and her body was in the air but her legs were on the damn bed and he was holding on to them.

It felt like forever, this moment. Of course. This is what was always going to happen.

Why did you think it wouldn't? This is what your instincts have been trying to tell you. Why didn't you just go and get a bloody bed in a bloody dorm away from these people? What is it you're trying to prove, Lori? That you won't be held back? Well, you're being held back now.

'Come *on*,' said Rob, pulling at her legs again. He sounded much more powerful than she'd thought he was. The private school boy from the suburbs who was driving the family station wagon, who had wanted Kat to want him, who wouldn't let anyone else behind the wheel, in case he got in trouble from his mum.

Lori took a deep breath. And screamed. It was higher than she'd expected it to sound. Ear-splitting. She screamed again.

'Fuck!' Rob shouted. He let go of her legs, perhaps only to change his grip. But Lori slid forward, onto the floor, and as she drew breath to scream again, the door flew open, a rectangle of light leaping into the room, illuminating her on the scratchy linoleum, her track-suit pants pulled down to mid-thigh, her mouth wide open, ready to howl.

It was Kat, back in her blue cotton dress, the buttons undone to her breasts, her long hair over her face. She flicked on the light, and Lori squeezed her eyes closed, and scrambled towards Kat's feet, pulling up her pants.

'What the fuck?'

Lori turned to look at what Kat was staring at. Rob, still on the other side of the bed, on his knees, his hands up, his arms bent, in an 'okay, you got me' gesture. He was swaying slightly, backwards and forwards. His eyes were half closed. And he was smiling. A broad, sheepish grin.

'I didn't do anything,' he said, his voice muddled with alcohol and indignation. 'She's fucking . . .' he raised his eyes to Lori's face, 'crazy. She's fucking batshit.'

'You're a dog,' said Kat, and she pushed Lori behind her and out of the door. 'You're a piss-weak dog.'

There was movement outside. Lori was suddenly aware of her heart. It was beating at a ridiculous speed, and she raised her hand to it, pushing against her sweatshirt, as if to quiet it. It was dark all around but lights were coming on in some of the cabins, it must have been her scream, and there was someone walking heavily along the concrete path towards them. George.

'I've got to . . .' Lori wanted to get away from the doorway, from these men, but she also wanted her phone, to call someone, anyone who knew her, who could look at this situation and tell her it would be fine. That she was fine.

Kat was in front of her, hands on her shoulders, looking into her face. 'Lori,' she was saying. 'Are you alright? What did he *do*?'

Lori's mouth was dry, there were no words coming. 'He . . .'

There was a noise from the room. A strange, loud noise.

Laughter.

They both looked into the cabin. Rob was still swaying on his knees next to the bed. Laughing. His eyes were closed and his head was lolling back.

Then something was pushing Lori away. George. He had shoved past Lori and Kat into the room, filling the doorframe for a second. Both Rob and George were bigger than Lori had given them credit for. She'd thought of them as boys. But they weren't. They were men.

George crossed the room at speed and grabbed Rob's T-shirt, pulling him to his feet.

'What?' sputtered Rob. He wasn't laughing now, but the white light from the cheap bulb above showed the lopsided grin on his face.

There was a moment as the four of them – car buddies, strangers, mates – stood, as lights flicked on around them and the air filled with mutters and the sound of tents being unzipped.

Kat broke the moment. She left Lori at the door and, in her cotton dress with nothing underneath, her tangle of hair hanging down her back, crossed the floor and shouldered George out of the way.

Kat looked over to the door, to Lori. Their eyes met and then Kat pulled back her arm and slammed her fist into Rob's face.

8

October: Mel

'**A**re you alright down there?'

Shit. He'd heard everything.

By everything, Mel meant the screaming she'd been doing at her children for the last ten minutes.

The screaming that, taken out of context of everything else she did for them, of love, and patience, and a half-bitten tongue, could sound like the angry cries of a mother on the edge. A stressed mother. A bad mother.

'We're fine!' Mel called back towards the top of the stairs. She forced a bright giggle into her voice. 'Just a bit of a morning, you know.'

The ghost's head appeared over the top railing. His close-cropped hair glistened a little. With what? Shower water? Workout sweat? *Hair gel?*

Stop it, Mel.

'As long as you're okay,' he said.

Mel was standing at the door of her unit with the empty recycling bin in her hand. She had asked Eddie possibly a hundred times over the past two hours if he would take it out, before finally doing it herself. When she'd upended the tub into the bin out on the pavement, tin-juice had splashed back at her, splattering her in watered-down tuna oil, baked bean sauce and the remnants of days-old Thai delivery.

'We'll try to keep it down,' she said, forcing the half-laugh again. 'I'm sure it should be you saying that to me.' Mel was horrified to realise she was gesturing to herself, and to him, with her bin hand.

But Flynn's expression told her he had already stopped listening and had moved on to another thought.

'Do you have any jobs that need doing?' he said.

Mel didn't know what to say.

'I've noticed,' said the ghost, in his deep, otherworldly tone, 'that you're on your own.'

'Well, I'm not exactly –'

'My mum was a single mum, too.' Flynn had pulled his arms up onto the banister, folding them as if settling in for a chat.

It had been two weeks since the ghost had arrived at the front door with his box, guitar case and bags. If fourteen days of living a few metres above her head had told Flynn that she was a woman who needed help, what had she learned about him from living a few metres below?

She had learned that he came with friends, and the hours they kept suggested people who did not have to be on 8 a.m. conference calls, or travel to work by any prescribed time. Although, Mel remembered, there had been times in her life when she had worked productive days from a baseline of four hours' sleep – the years when she'd stayed up drinking and talking and dancing, and the years when she'd had tiny babies who, like the people upstairs, didn't see the point of conventional time-keeping, and wanted feeding and patting and stroking on the hour, every hour, no matter what the light looked like outside, or what time was glaring from a glowing clock.

She had learned that many of these friends of Flynn's were from somewhere else. The accents she heard alongside the footsteps travelling down the hall and up the stairs reminded her of her home, her travels.

'They're us,' she'd told her sister the day before. 'They're us, decades apart.'

'No, they're not,' said Izzy. 'They're nothing like us. The whole experience of being young is unrecognisable now.'

Izzy had sounded like she was driving. The muffled thrum of air passing the window, her voice echoing in a large, confined space.

'Where are you going?'

'I'm going to pick Tom up from his appointment,' she'd said, the click-click of the indicator just audible. 'You know, trying to duck in and out of hell scot-free. It's our weekly excitement.'

Mel had breathed out. 'Is it driving you mad, me calling you about my sad divorce and my upstairs neighbours when you've got, you know, real problems?'

'Ha.' It was a word, not an involuntary sound. 'Not at all. I need to think about something outside my four walls. Your disintegrating sanity is light relief.'

Izzy was so funny. So cutting. She sounded like home.

'Okay, then.' Mel had laughed. 'Back to me. They *are* like us, Iz. They're free, and selfish and beautiful.'

'Oh, really? You were so beautiful?' It sounded like, on the other side of the world, it had started to rain. Water on the windscreen, skimming under the tyres.

'I know I was.'

'You know you're thinking about him way too much, right? Mum would say it's avoidance.'

'She would.'

'Would she be right?'

'You mean, I should be focusing on my real life?' Mel had asked. 'Like what the hell to do with myself now I'm single again? Whether Simon should get the fifty-fifty custody he wants? What's best for the kids? Where we might live? When I might get to see you again? Whether I can get a job that I actually like? And how likely it is that we'll all make it through this mess alive? You mean I'm avoiding all *that*?'

'By obsessing about your hot young neighbour? Yes.'

'I am *not* obsessing. And he's not hot. That's just embarrassing.'

'Yes, yes it is.' Izzy had arrived. Mel could tell that the movement on the wet road had stopped. She pictured her sister sitting in the hospital car park, not turning off the engine just yet. Her hands on the steering wheel, her eyes on the entrance checkpoint. Masks. Clear face shields. Green coveralls. The thin rubber of disposable gloves.

'Do you have to go in to get him?'

Izzy hadn't answered for a moment. There was just the faint noise of rain on the glass. The sound of other cars, a distant siren, growing louder.

'I'm not allowed,' she'd said, finally. 'But he's not allowed to go home alone. So they come to the entrance, and kind of hand him over.'

'I bet Tom loves that.'

'Yeah.'

Another pause. Izzy still hadn't turned off the car. 'I wish I was there, you know,' Mel had said.

'No, you don't.'

Her sister had turned off the engine. Mel could still just hear the rain. The faint, almost half-hearted drizzle that was ever-present in her hometown. Just enough rain to ruin your day.

'No,' Mel had said. 'I don't. But I wish I was with you.'

There was a pause but when Izzy had spoken again she was short, cold. 'Stop it. Get back to obsessing about your neighbour, saddo.'

Now Izzy's voice was in Mel's head as she looked up at the ghost's face, leaning over the balcony, a tight smile. 'So if you did need any jobs doing,' he said. 'Things aren't exactly busy at the moment.'

Mel wanted to laugh. What did Flynn think she needed doing, in her tiny flat? It wasn't like she had gutters to clean or a deck to sand or some other traditionally masculine odd job she couldn't handle. Taking the bins out, disposing of spiders and changing lightbulbs was about as handyman as it got at her place.

'Thanks, but we've got it.'

The ghost shrugged. As he straightened up, he said, 'You remind me of her.'

It caught Mel off guard. 'Who?'

'My mum.'

Mel laughed. Izzy would love this.

But then a picture flashed in Mel's head – the image of a woman who had been doing it alone a long time ago. Dom's mum, Gina, who Mel had met in an airport arrivals hall almost two decades before. A woman so delirious with delight to have her boy returned to her. She'd hugged Mel like she was happy to see her, too, although Mel knew Gina just wanted Dom to herself. This great big man, picking up his tiny, young mum and swinging her around the arrivals hall. Mel standing back, excited, nervous. Dom's mum had laughed with the joy of reunion and then grabbed both of Mel's arms, her eyes shining as she said, 'Welcome to Australia, Melanie. My son hasn't stopped telling me about you for an entire year. Now I get to see you in the flesh!' And she'd pulled tired, smelly Mel into her smooth, tanned arms and whispered, 'Thank you. Thank you for bringing him home.'

She hadn't seen Gina since the funeral. And now here was the ghost, talking about his mum, and Mel's head was full of Gina's face, twisted with the ugliness of grief.

'My mum used to yell a lot, too,' said Flynn. And he smiled a familiar, wonky smile, waved his hand and disappeared.

9

October: Mel

The ghost didn't know that Mel didn't yell at her kids as much as she used to. Before Simon left.

Only six months ago, the tension in the tiny unit by the sea was so thick it suckered itself to the walls and drew them in tight.

Every day back then Mel had started with an internal promise to do better. *Today*, she thought, when she woke up just before dawn. *Today I won't shout. Today I will breathe before I speak. I won't sweat the small stuff. I will pick battles. I will walk away.*

But every day, an hour later, her raw throat ached as she gulped down her cold tea.

'Why is this so hard?' she'd be bellowing down the hall, from the cluttered kitchen towards the living room. 'Every day we eat breakfast. Every day we get dressed. Why does it always come as a surprise?'

'Why are you shouting?' Simon would shout, as Eddie and Ava ran up and down the hallway, getting further from being ready to leave the house with every step.

This was in the days when everyone really did leave the house in the morning. When Mel went to an actual office, for hours and hours, to deliver presentations and brainstorm projects in small, glass-sided offices, creating slides at a desktop computer and eating lunch out of a plastic container at her desk.

Simon had to be gone, too, before 8 a.m., to open up the shop for the people who needed new school trainers, an emergency basketball or a pair of yoga leggings. He wouldn't be seen again until 6.30 p.m., when, drained from talking and selling and sorting all day, he was dead-eyed and clean out of words for his family.

And the kids – hustled into faded, over-washed uniforms, hair wrangled into something like smooth submission – were deposited to sit at their desks for six hours, and then on to the supervised carnage of after-school care for another three.

'We're never home.' It was the self-soothing statement used to end every conversation Mel and Simon ever had about moving house. About finding some more space somewhere where every square metre didn't come with a six-figure price tag. About the sanity-threatening proximity of apartment living with two growing children.

'We're so lucky,' they'd end up telling each other, as she poured another glass, on one of those evenings when they were meant to be having 'a talk', a future-planning session.

They'd bought the apartment with borrowed money and the optimism of young people who never imagined a time when they wouldn't want to live a chip-fling away from a glistening suburban beach, a busy strip of shops and two giant booze barns. Over the decade they'd lived there, the shops had become cafes all serving the same breakfast and the oversized pubs had morphed into 'entertainment precincts' that boasted kids' pizza parties, eye-wateringly priced fine dining with a view and footballer-friendly rooftop cocktails.

Mel and Simon didn't really resent these developments – who didn't like dukkah-doused avocado on sourdough, or pubs where ignoring your children while you sipped over-priced rosé was encouraged? – but the neighbourhood had left them behind in other ways.

The little-kid years had halved their income and extended their debt, and by the time Mel and Simon lifted their muddled heads and looked around, they found they were definitively priced out of the suburb they'd made their home. And then, just as they'd begun to lift their eyes further to the horizon, to see where the family roots might be replanted, they realised that, actually, those roots were pretty rotten.

But it also wasn't true that they were never home. Home was where every day began and ended, and no-one could argue that they were starting fresh or finishing strong. Not the way those mornings had played out.

For Simon, every day began with the intention to make every moment count. Every evening ended with his self-flagellation at having failed. He'd always been a man who put a lot of pressure on himself. When Mel met him, he had just given up on a professional tennis career, after years of training, travelling, disappointment and expense. He was done with it, but never defeated. Absolutely determined this would not be the beginning of a decline. Always practical, always busy setting new goals. Simon wanted to become a coach. And he did, but the tennis parents depressed him. Then he wanted to start a gym. He did, in a rented garage, with a friend. It went nowhere, so he switched dreams to having his own tennis store. And now, he was the franchise holder of a chain sports shop in a local shopping centre and he worked and he worked and he worked for every dollar that came in the door. It had all contributed, no doubt, to the shouting.

The yelling wasn't why she'd asked Simon to leave, but now that he was gone there was less of it. The chaos was a different shape. Partly because the days were different. Mel didn't have to go and brainstorm in her fifth-floor office every day now. She brainstormed at home, with her colleagues' faces in little boxes on her screen, everyone politely waiting for their turn to take themselves off mute.

She knew you weren't supposed to say so, but Mel didn't hate the new reality. Not the new mornings, at least.

So, Flynn, if you think there's a lot of noise floating up from down-stairs, you should have been here months ago, mate.

Mel replaced the empty recycling bin and rubbed at the marks on her long-sleeved T-shirt with a licked finger.

It was a home-learning day, and she knew that nine-year-old Eddie, sitting at the round family table in the sunroom with a borrowed laptop open, was not really listing all the countries that had hosted the Olympics since 1952. She knew he would be watching some pale, scrawny YouTuber playing video games and shouting excitedly into his headset mic. She knew that Ava would be writing lists in her scrapbook rather than working on the Pobble story her Year Two teacher had set through a static smile and gritted teeth via video this morning.

Ava was really into lists right now: *10 Things Ava Can't Live Without, 10 People Ava Thinks Are Awesome, Ava's Favourite Foods, Things About Eddie That Annoy Ava.* She was always neatly printing out misspelled columns of words, punctuated by tiny felt-tip drawings of cupcakes, doughnuts and milkshakes.

He smels like toe-jam. Werst brother ever. (Ice cream with sprinkles.)

If Mel checked on them she'd have to correct their course, and she wasn't sure she was up to it this morning. She had a confer-ence call about the new influencer strategy for a kombucha-infused immunity tonic in fifteen minutes and she needed a strong coffee to face that.

Families working together around messy tables – everyone on a different screen. That was now normal.

On her walks, Mel saw that every house was doing the same. Everyone was home. Everyone's worlds had downsized. Computers set up on ironing boards, on sofa arms. Couples sitting opposite each other with back-to-back laptops, Ugg boots touching under the table. Taking turns to talk. Kids chalking on front pavements, playing handball in the skinny, high-walled gaps between unit blocks.

At least she and Simon had never had to be together all day, every day.

The thought of it made her shudder.

When Mel was little her grandma had given her two gerbils for Christmas. Mel had loved them, at first. But two gerbils became sixteen in an alarmingly short space of time. And the cage, and then the additional fish tank, and then the other cage, weren't big enough for the ever-expanding gerbil family. One day, Mel, who must have been around seven, like Ava was now, had woken up to check on her furry friends and found that one of them had been murdered by his siblings. He was lying on the sawdust floor of the cage with his feet chewed off.

That's what would have happened to Simon and I, she thought, *if we had been forced to stay together in this flat, for months. I would have bitten off his feet.*

As it was, everything exploded about a week before the city's doors closed. The first days of isolation were also the first days of Mel's life as a newly single mother.

Single mother. The ghost had one. Mel reminded him of her.

She heard the ever-so-faint tinkling theme tune of one of Eddie's favourite YouTube jerks.

'Kids,' she yelled down the hall. *Take that, ghost.* 'I'm going on a work meeting in my room. I'll come and check your work afterwards. Twenty minutes!'

Eddie's immediate and enthusiastic 'Okay, Mum!' confirmed that he was doing something he shouldn't be.

Ava's silence meant her list-making was getting heavy. *10 Things Ava Wants To Do When The Virus Is Gone.*

Mel unscrewed her little mocha coffee-maker, the one she'd bought herself as a cheap present after Simon took the fancy espresso machine, the one she'd once bought him as a not-so-cheap present, two Christmases before the end.

She spooned the coffee into the tiny pan and pressed it down with the back of her spoon. Clicked on the gas. I should be making a list, she thought, as she headed into the bedroom to make sure the laptop was set up for the meeting.

10 Reasons Mel Needs To Get Her Shit Together.

It wasn't like her to be so unsettled by the ghost upstairs. To be rattled by his unfounded parenting critique, his over-familiar sharing, his ability to bring up all these feelings, these memories, that she'd almost forgotten she had. Gina, for God's sake. When was the last time she'd thought about Gina?

Everyone's losing it, duck, she knew Izzy would say. *You're not so special. Stop beating yourself up for being normal. Most people are.*

And when was the last time she'd thought about how, one hundred years ago, a young Australian man called Dominic had lifted his glass of English beer, swallowed a mouthful and put it down on the bar?

'Who are you?' he'd asked her. And Mel had rolled her eyes.

10

October: Mel

The bar had been busy, and she was moving on to the next person, and the next, and the next. People who needed their glass filled and their money taken and a smile from the bar person who was their equal in every way but this one, the way that they were drinking their way through college, and she was working.

But Dominic Rolff hadn't moved away from the bar. Oblivious, apparently, to the push around him. To the irritated looks from the undergrads who tutted at the man standing between them and their pint. He'd stood there and sipped his beer at a pace that marked him as different again. Not a guzzle, not a swig. A slow sip.

Mel kept moving but her eyes came back to him. He didn't look like the other men in the bar. He was sturdier, less pale. He was tall but not towering, broad-shouldered but not imposing. He had a strong, angular nose, high cheekbones, a full mouth. He looked, Mel would marvel many times in the coming weeks, months and years, like a beautiful woman and like a masculine man. Not for everyone, this unusual combination. Not for everyone, the way that he looked at her that night, his eyes appreciating and teasing at once.

He'd just stood there, at the bar, sipping his beer, watching Mel move from pump to till to bottle to till to wipe-down, rearrange, back to the pump, back to the bottle, smile, take the money, change, back to the bottle, back to the till. She must have walked thousands of steps a night in that job, all within a few square feet.

'I'd like to help you,' he'd called, over the noise of another incoming crowd.

'What?'

'I'd like to help you. Can I come back there?'

'No!'

Of course he couldn't come back there. The manager of the Student Union bar, Keith, would have a conniption if he saw a strange, adult man behind the bar.

'It's too busy for one.'

And Dominic Rolff had slid his hand underneath the counter, found the serving hatch and opened it, breaking the barrier between the controller and the controlled.

At the time, Mel hadn't known what the hell to do. The bar was packed because there had been an impromptu meeting to vote to change the name of a study hall, from its tribute to an old white benefactor to something more relevant, more 'now'. Tuesday was usually a quiet shift, but not today, not when there was a vote on.

'What can I get you, mate?'

Mel watched as this strange person stepped into a role he had no right to assume. She had never seen him before, and she had seen everyone who drank in the Student Union bar. There were never any surprises in the clientele, or their overtures, their problems, their stories. At least, that's how it had seemed to her. Even though a lot of the people whose drinks she poured daily were her friends, she wasn't like them. Mostly, because she lived two suburbs over, with her sister, Izzy, round the corner from their mum. She hadn't parachuted into another city to study, like most of these kids. She was a local. It set her apart, and it made her the perfect, incorruptible Student Union barmaid. Until now.

'Get out!' she'd hissed at him. He'd ignored her.

The stranger knew his way around a bar, though, that was clear. He knew to tilt a pint glass when you were pouring lager, how to pump a bitter to get a foamy head, how to tap-tap at the spirit measure to make sure you got the last tiny drops customers would complain about missing. And when he spoke, it was obvious he was most definitely not a local.

'What the hell do you think you're doing?' she asked him as he cheerfully took the money from a young woman who'd ordered a snakebite and black, and placed it next to the till, for her to enter.

'I'm helping. Rush will be gone soon,' he said, like he'd stepped off *Neighbours*. He smiled at her, sideways, as he turned to the next customer.

'I don't need your help.'

Mel laughed to herself every time she thought of her young self spitting that at Dom, simmering with anger as she grabbed a bottle of Sol from the fridge.

She didn't laugh because she'd been wrong to feel that way, bulldozed by a man with a saviour complex who might just cost her her job. She laughed because the man she thought Dom was that night wasn't who he really was.

He'd moved around that small space with the grace and wisdom of a hospitality professional. He never touched her, or 'accidentally' brushed her body, or let their hands collide. It had been like a dance. Like they were spinning around each other, choreographed. Destined.

When Keith had reappeared at the back of the room, Mel had muttered, 'My boss is back!' and Dom had ducked beneath the bar hatch and disappeared. Like he was never there.

A knock at the door and the smell of toasting coffee pulled Mel back to her kitchen, to where she was supposed to be.

The only people who knocked on her front door were already in the building. So it was likely to be Ainslie, who lived downstairs, and liked to complain about the kids leaving their bikes on the front path.

'Mum!' Eddie was yelling from down the hall. 'Door!'

Was it the ghost? Offering more of his services? Or another parenting judgement?

'Mum!' Ava was suddenly at her side, list in hand.

10 Reasons Why Mum And Dad Should Get Back Together.

'Sorry, darling,' Mel was pulling the door open as she spoke. 'Shit,' she said.

It wasn't Ainslie. And it wasn't Flynn. It was a young woman she'd never seen before.

She was short, and sort of honey-coloured. Frazzled around the edges, both in the way she looked and the energy around her. She was dusty, tangled, twitchy.

She was smiling a dazzling smile that was unfamiliar to her pink-edged eyes and she was sagging just a little, because over one shoulder she carried a heavy-looking, scuffed and muddy backpack. Her short denim overalls were faded. Her feet were bare, and her head was bobbing, trying to peer behind Mel, into the unit.

'Hello?' It was a question.

Mel had others. Where's your mask? Where are your shoes? Why do you look so scared?

'Are you okay?' she asked.

'Oh, yes.' The girl put a flat palm up to her forehead, as if she was feeling it for warmth, a motion that made Mel take a step backwards, her arm down across Ava's chest, gently pushing her backwards, too. Then the girl dropped her hand. 'Sorry to bother you, I'm looking for Flynn.'

Of course.

'He does live here, right?' Her accent, Mel had recognised a beat ago, was English. Southern. A little posh. Her 'sorry to bother you' had shown her manners. The tone of this question, and its expectation of a quick answer, had shown her privilege.

'No,' said Mel, wondering how this young woman might imagine that the ghost lived in the same house as her and this little girl at the door. She watched confusion, and then disappointment, pass across the girl's face.

'He lives upstairs,' said Ava, from two feet below. 'Right above us.'

The honey girl was inflated again, the smile spreading across her clear young face, her head turning to look up the stairs to her left.

'We can hear him,' Ava went on. 'Mum says we shouldn't listen too hard, that we might not understand what we hear.'

The girl smiled at Ava, and reached out a hand to . . . what? Pat her on the head? Mel instinctively batted the girl's hand away from her daughter's head. You can't just *touch* people.

The girl looked up at Mel, surprised. 'Sorry, I was just –'

'It's fine,' Mel said, but it clearly was not. The girl pushed her hair back from her forehead, a little flustered.

'I'll go find him,' she said, and immediately turned away.

Clearly she was so keen to get to the ghost she felt the backpack would slow her down. The girl abandoned it outside Mel's door and bounded up the stairs, two at a time. Those cute little overalls. Her smile. That hair. Mel could feel what the girl was feeling. Butterflies, fear, roiling excitement.

Upstairs, the click of a door and the ghost's voice saying, loudly, plainly, 'What are you doing here?'

And the honey girl saying, 'I came to find you. Thank God.' Something in her voice was frightened, shaky. Mel felt inexplicably queasy.

'Come here,' said the voice from upstairs. Firm. Hot. And then there was a silence that could only be a kiss.

11

October: Mel

Mel's work call was punctuated by the sound of the ghost and the honey girl having sex.

She sat on the bed in the corner she'd set up for maximum professional backdrop. Just in frame behind her was the rounded edge of a pleasing mid-century shelf – the bookcase was the only other furniture there was room for in the tiny space. A succulent – a money plant that had long failed to fulfil its promise – was visible behind her, next to a pretty book, a clever book, and a picture of Mel and the kids on a Queensland beach two years ago, in a tasteful metallic frame.

Mel had worked out that if she propped the cushions just right, and put her laptop on the weird little tray table she'd found on council pick-up day, she could sit here for thirty minutes until her back hurt, on a video call, giving the impression of a calm and organised working environment, just a quick dash down the hall from where the kids were bickering/bludging/scrolling.

But her tiny bedroom was directly below the ghost's. And a bed leg shoved an inch across floorboards by the body weight of two people falling on it, hard, made a sharp scraping sound across her ceiling. The gentle thud of a bedhead against a windowsill, once, twice, then rhythmically – it wasn't so loud that Alena from sales could hear it, but Mel could. She couldn't really hear anything else.

As she presented the list of influencers she thought would be a 'great fit' for promoting the immunity tonic, Mel could only picture the abandoned backpack at the bottom of the stairs. Lying on its belly with its straps up, like an upended turtle.

It was eight minutes since the girl had knocked on the door. And they were already . . . That kind of urgency was a very specific feeling.

Stop thinking about this.

With her out-of-sight hand, while Alena was discussing budget, Mel messaged Izzy.

Met myself at my front door this morning. Think ghost girlfriend. Listening to them fucking. It's 11 a.m.

Izzy would be asleep. When she got this, she'd roll her eyes and tell Mel to stop being a creep. She'd also, probably, laugh.

But the phone flashed back, while Mel took her turn to talk about a display strategy across health verticals. She looked down, quickly.

Saddo.

Two more minutes and the call was over – everyone waving goodbye politely from their little rectangle. Mel's back was already beginning to ache.

Why you awake?

Bad night. Tom not great.

Mel groaned. No. No. No.

No downturn. No crisis. No deterioration. Not while the world was closed.

Sure it's just a night, Iz. Treatment sucks when it's working.

Where did Mel get that from? It sounded like bullshit. As if her reassuring words could keep things on track.

There was a moment longer than usual before Izzy's reply.

Yep.

Fuck. Mel hadn't said the right thing.

'Mum!'

Eddie. It had been a long time between home-teacher shifts.

She sent her sister a deeply inadequate love-heart emoji and unfolded herself from the bed.

'Coming!'

Mel's walk down the hall was maybe twelve steps. As she took each one, she ticked off a list of what she had to do today. Another presentation to finish for tomorrow, this one external, the kind you had to tap-dance for, in lipstick. She had two one-on-one meetings with members of her team. Ava had a Zoom karate session that required a morale-lifting funny hat (morale lifting for who?) at 3.30 p.m. Eddie had an actual real-life 'walk' scheduled with a friend who lived a short drive away at 4 p.m. Since when did nine-year-old boys go for walks? She had a post-campaign report to write before five other people could weigh in on it, dropping their comments into little speech bubbles alongside, creating another cluster of jobs. Science projects, for both kids, were meant to be handed in on Thursday. Something about an island archipelago, and papier-mâché, and the life cycle of a frog. She needed to put in that supermarket order that wouldn't come for days, and go round to the local shop to get something vaguely healthy for dinner. She needed to order new contact lenses. She needed to call Fi about what kind of plans they could make for her birthday. She needed to exercise. She needed to call Izzy and she needed to stop her sister's husband from getting any sicker.

Back in her hundred-years-ago life, the cloud of student drinkers had cleared with the 11 p.m. last-orders bell.

Mel knew there would be one left, and there was.

'So,' said the strange man as she walked towards the back door. 'As I said, Who are you?'

'Who are you?' she asked. 'And why are you here?'

'So many questions.'

Australians weren't common in northern England in the noughties. This wasn't London, which, she would soon learn, had a large and loud community of Australians and New Zealanders, with a representative behind every bar. Until that night, Mel had never met anyone from so far away. Not that she was going to admit that.

He'd been wearing a T-shirt. In his hand was a denim jacket. It was pitifully inadequate for a northern winter. Mel knew that the night, outside the uni hall, was freezing and damp. She knew she had ten minutes before her night bus would leave from the bus stop five minutes away. She wondered if this person was worth missing the night bus for.

'My name's Dom. Dominic.'

'And why are you here? You're not a student.'

'I was meeting someone.'

'And she didn't show up.'

'*He* did show up,' he said, with that smile again. 'We had a drink, the chat we had to have, then he left.'

'The chat you had to have? That sounds interesting.'

'It's a long story. Do you need a walk home?'

'Long walk,' said Mel. 'I'm getting the bus.'

'Then let me walk you to the bus stop.'

Mel could still picture Keith's face, as he looked up from counting the till. 'Y'alright, Mel?' he called.

Mel could also remember the moment she'd taken to check her instincts, because she wasn't an idiot.

'Yeah, alright, Keith,' she'd replied. 'Just going to the bus.'

She could remember, even now, what a Manchester night in autumn smelled like, and how it felt to be walking with someone completely new, through the streets you'd walked on your whole life. 'You're Australian,' she'd said.

'Yes,' he'd said. 'And you're not.'

'I'm from here,' said Mel. 'Unlike almost everyone in there.'

'Really?'

'Can't you tell?' she said. 'The accents. Accents are big in England, haven't you noticed?'

'Oh, I've noticed,' he said. 'But we can't decode them, haven't got the handbook.'

Lots of times since, Mel had tried to remember exactly what they talked about that night. She wished she had a complete, detailed transcript, but there were only a few lines, tiny grabs, that floated back to her. Were they the important parts? How had her memory decided what to hold on to and what to let go of? Because some of it didn't seem so important.

Like the bits about the neon-signed takeaway boasting chips with curry sauce for 45p. That led, of course, to the predictable, culture-clash stuff, like how Dom didn't even know about chips and curry sauce, or cheese and onion pies, or the joy of a vegetable pastie from Greggs. But he was no cliché either, walking the streets of the big city with wide eyes or a Crocodile Dundee knife in his sock. He was three years older than Mel, he'd been travelling for more than a year, and he'd been living in London, and not loved it, so had headed north on a well-worn trail up to Scotland to see some castles and pubs. He wasn't sure how long he was staying. The date at the Student Union was with a cousin, a couple of times removed. They'd promised their mothers they'd meet. They did. The cousin had to leave for an actual date. That was that.

She couldn't conjure up their conversations in detail, but she could access the feelings in a moment. Because they had been entirely unfamiliar. Wary of men, both from experience and the cautionary tales that filled her female-heavy home, Mel felt safe next to Dom. It wasn't safety like she felt with the friends she'd made at uni, or with her own cousins, or even with the very few men she could call exes. It was a safety that came with the hypervigilance of attraction. *Intense* attraction. As he walked her the short way to the bus stop, and she pretended the first bus was not the one she was waiting for, and they sat and stood and stomped and walked and talked a little more, Mel knew exactly where his arm was in relation to hers, where his hand was, his thigh, his mouth. If any part of his body came close to a part of hers, flashes of adrenaline zipped between them. It was dumbfounding to her, really, that she couldn't see the zings, like tiny fireworks leaving smoky trails.

It had been the first time she had ever felt like that.

When the next bus came, Mel had to get on.

If there were hazy bits of dialogue in her recollection of that night – times when she could see their mouths moving but not hear what was being said – this part was as clear as a bell.

'I have to get this bus,' she'd said. 'My sister will be stressing if I am any later.'

'Your sister?'

'I live with her. She worries.'

'That's great.'

'It is?'

'We're lucky if we have a few people who worry about us.'

What a weird thing for a twenty-six-year-old to say. Even now, it seemed unlikely. Even though she'd learn, soon, that Dom said things like this all the time. That he was what her mum might term an 'old soul' and what Simon might call 'a pretentious prick'. Take your pick.

'Well, it's actually kind of annoying, but still, I've got to go.'

The bus, a big orange double-decker, came sliding up in the drizzly cold, lights blazing.

She'd looked at Dom, waiting for him to ask for her number or try to talk her into not going, and for a quick, mortifying flash, she thought it was just her, feeling this, not him. The bus driver opened the doors and she waited another beat before she stepped up and on.

Were there other people on that bus? Other people at that bus stop? Mel couldn't remember.

Because as she shrugged and stepped up and onto the bus, backwards, Dom followed her on.

'What are you doing?' Mel had asked.

'Seeing you home.'

A little exhale. She hadn't been wrong.

'You can't come into my house,' she said, as the bus driver sighed, and she clicked her pass in the ticket machine, twice. 'Izzy won't let you.'

'I don't want to come in,' he said. 'Not tonight. I just want to ride with you.'

Mel had laughed because that was another ridiculous thing to say, on a drizzly night in the pissy-pukey midnight streets of the inner city. She almost ran up the twisted steps to the top deck of the bus to take her favourite seat, the one at the very front, on the right, in front of the stairs. His footsteps behind her all the way.

She could still remember what it felt like, that next part, because he kissed her, or she kissed him, or both. Either way, it was almost midnight on an empty orange bus that smelled of contraband fried food and weed. They'd snogged in English and pashed in Australian all the way back to Izzy's street, the one right round the corner from her mum's.

Now, Mel didn't know how many more kisses she was going to get in her life. Proper ones. Passionate ones. A lot, she hoped. A few, she imagined. None she didn't want, that was for sure. But there wouldn't be another kiss as perfect as that. The kind of kiss people

69

wrote songs about. Poems. The kind of kiss fairytales promise but human people rarely deliver. Trying to untwist and untie the ingredients that make a kiss like that, as Mel had done many, many times over the years, in various stages of regret, nostalgia or inebriation, was futile. It was time, place, chemistry. Magic.

A kiss to change the course of a life.

He'd watched her walk to her sister's door and go inside. And she had watched him, from the glass panel beside the front door that Izzy was always saying needed to be frosted. She'd watched him walk from their door and, as he turned onto a street she hoped he knew how to handle, he gave a strange little skip.

It had made her laugh out loud, next to the pile of shoes and coats that never stayed on hooks. She had laughed out loud at the unexpected turn of a damp Tuesday night in Manchester.

He hadn't been for everyone, this strange man from far away, a mixture of confidence and vulnerability, of hard and soft, of knowing and unknowing. The man with the magic kisses. But he was for her. She knew it, that night. He was definitely for her.

12

October: Mel

Eddie was playing Minecraft. Ava was decorating the edges of her latest list – *10 People Who Should Just Go Away* – with an elaborate frame of cartoon doughnuts, flowers, cupcakes and puppies with their tongues out.

Mel stood in the doorway for a moment. Then she took a deep breath and yelled, 'School!' at the top of her voice, hoping it travelled upstairs. She watched her kids scramble – Eddie, switching tabs back to his spelling list quick smart, Ava pulling her reader book across to cover her doodles.

'Come on, you two. You have to *help me*.' It was the phrase she probably said more than any other, these days.

'I can hear them upstairs,' said Ava.

'Me too.' Mel went over to the sunroom window and closed it with a satisfying thud.

'Do you think he's hurting her?' Ava was looking up at her mum, her brow furrowed.

'No, darling, I think they're dancing.'

Mel followed Eddie as he grumbled his way into the hallway. 'Get yourself a snack,' she said, softly pushing him towards the kitchen.

Before she knew it, she'd slipped the front door onto the latch and was standing in the hallway, looking at the honey girl's backpack.

She bent down and picked it up, throwing the heavy load over her shoulder and then slipping her arms into each strap until they settled on her shoulders.

She was just taking it upstairs. That's what she'd say if anyone walked in the front door right now. Everyone knew it was very bad for your back to lug a pack over one shoulder.

Mel felt like she knew what would be inside it. Clothes, obviously, tightly rolled, and carefully selected from a different country at a different time. This many pairs of knickers, this many bikinis. This many T-shirts. This many cut-off shorts. A little dress, maybe two. How many pairs of shoes? That had always been Mel's packing downfall. You needed flip-flops, and trainers, and something to go out in – a strappy sandal, perhaps. Did young women wear strappy sandals now? She'd have packed something warm. Her mum would have told her to pack a waterproof . . .

The weight was pulling her slightly backwards. A couple of books, although maybe the girl just read on her phone, if she read. Not everyone did, anymore. A bulging washbag, shampoo wrapped inside a plastic bag, a rubber band snapped around its neck.

Mel started up the stairs, towards the ghost's door. She had to lean forward to stop herself from overbalancing. She'd forgotten how tiresome it was to walk around with everything that mattered on your back.

She turned at the landing and took the last few steps. Mel could hear music now from behind the ghost's door. Something she didn't recognise thrumming softly, a firm beat. She heard laughter and she wondered how many other people were in there, while the ghost and the girl were fucking in the bedroom. Mel could smell toast, and the sickly woody scent of incense. A cigarette. She realised, as she leaned towards the door, that she'd closed her eyes, that she couldn't really feel the heavy backpack straps on her shoulders anymore.

'Hello?'

The door swung. Mel's eyes flew open. It was the girl. She was wearing a singlet, and a pair of shorts that didn't look like hers, falling loose on her hips. Her wavy hair was a tangled mess, and her eyes looked different. She was smiling but confused.

'I was just bringing this back.' *Shit, you're so busted.* 'The neighbours don't like . . . clutter.'

'Thanks,' said the girl, after a moment. 'I was just coming to get it.'

Neither of them said anything for a second, and Mel wondered why. Then she remembered, and started shaking the backpack off her shoulders.

'Long time since I've worn one of these,' she said, in a tone that she hoped was jovial, light. 'I used to –'

'Thanks,' the girl cut across her, grabbed the heavy pack as Mel started to drop it. And then the hands of the ghost caught it. Mel looked up at him, so much taller than the young woman in front of him. Bare-chested, a towel around his waist. A bemused expression, his eyes meeting Mel's.

'This is Sal,' he told the girl, 'from downstairs. Thanks, Sal.'

'Mel,' said Mel with a sting of ridiculous disappointment.

'Mel, yeah.'

'We met,' said the girl. 'I knocked on her door by mistake.'

'And you dropped your bag,' said Mel, feeling silly.

'I'm Lori,' said the girl. 'Thank you, you really didn't need to.'

'No, you didn't,' said the ghost, and he looked like he was about to laugh. Mel needed to disappear, urgently. 'But thanks.'

'See you later.' Mel headed down the stairs as quickly as she could. She knew they'd still be there, the ghost and Lori, smiling at each other, her bare shoulder leaning into his bare chest, her head upturned to his, the big backpack with Lori's world in it loose and light in his big right hand.

Fuck, she was an idiot.

'Remember,' the ghost called out after her, 'if you need anything doing . . .'

'I won't!' Mel called back, disappearing to her door, and her crammed little home.

13

November: Lori

A day that started with an orgasm was a good day.
It was remarkable how that jolt of lightning energy made Lori care less about the state of the shared kitchen. How the sleeping bodies on the couches became less intrusive. How the numbers on the bank app seemed less terrifying. The spring rain less melancholy.

If she started the day shuddering under Flynn's hands, his fingers, his lips, his tongue and teeth, the big life panic of 'what's next' seemed more manageable. The ever-present low hum of fear subsided.

Set alight like that, she could handle anything. Lori was more confident, lighter, smarter, faster. She was better looking, she was sure of it.

It's the secret to everything, she wanted to tell everyone she knew, but in reality could only furtively text Jools. *Why doesn't everyone know that? Find someone who'll give you earth-shattering orgasms and the world's your lobster.*

It was their in-joke, *the world's your lobster.* She didn't remember why, some ancient school history.

Shut up, Jools texted back. *You're insufferable.* But she'd added a skull and crossbones emoji, so she was laughing.

I had no idea, Lori had replied, not ready to move on. *Don't tell Adam. Or Elise.*

It was a sign of her newfound lightness that she was invoking the name Elise, considering that relationship, and the fallout from its discovery, had been the thing that had started her running in the first place.

Really, Jools tapped back. *I can't deal with this level of sexual smuggery.*

Lori grinned and dropped her phone to the floor. Was it the orgasms that had made her stay, back in Broome, long after Jools had left?

Was it just the orgasms, or the love she whispered to her journal about, that were responsible for her lying on a futon on stripped floorboards in a wedding-cake-white block by the blue Pacific ocean, while Jools was back in her parents' house in Surrey, watching *Strictly* with her nan, preparing for a long winter and applying for a graduate degree that she'd never sit in a lecture theatre to complete?

It's true, she was lying on the futon alone, since Flynn had rolled off uncharacteristically early to meet some guy about something, but in the two weeks since Lori arrived, they'd never started a morning without sex of some description. And all those descriptions involved Lori, flushed, gasping, alive.

'Where did you learn how to do that?' she'd asked him, back in Broome, on the van mattress, after she'd orgasmed from actual 'penis and vagina sex', as she and her friends disparagingly called it, for the very first time. 'How did that . . . do that?'

Flynn had pushed his full mouth up against her ear and breathed, 'I just pay attention, that's all.'

Lori was gone. She saw that now. When he'd left, driving away from the red-dirt, cobalt-blue tourist town, she'd briefly pretended it changed nothing. That it was a closed chapter, an adventure to hold on to as she went on with her newly sensible life choices. But in the days and weeks between that farewell and this Sydney reunion, she'd decided it was love. With every kilometre between there and now, on buses, in cars with people she was trying hard to forget, she'd been more and more convinced.

Lying on these pale sheets in this pale morning sun, alone in a room with a door that closed, Lori knew that whatever made her feel like her body was a worthy home, like she was full, complete, swimming in a warm bath of enough, this had to be magic. And that magic had to mean something. Love.

Is he still a dickhead?

Jools.

She hadn't liked Flynn. Of course she hadn't. He'd changed their plans, and there was nothing more annoying than having your plans changed when you were the one who'd meticulously made them.

Jools, who'd spreadsheeted their journey, calculated their budget, booked their planes and trains and buses, Jools wasn't really up for, 'I'd just like to stay a while longer, see how things work out.'

Jools hadn't wanted to get a job changing fancy people's sheets to bolster the funds trickling away with every day they were staying in paradise.

And Jools hadn't liked the fact that she was meant to be sleeping in her single-sex dorm with her oldest friend, but was there most nights alone, forced into small talk with strangers while Lori slept – or didn't sleep – in a van parked in a very pretty car park, a few clicks out of town.

Not a dickhead. Just different.

Lori knew she'd been the one to derail the grand tour. She knew she was the one who had broken the code. She knew she wasn't supposed to let her friend go on without her, which is what happened when Jools had finally had enough of waiting for Lori and booked that next bus trip.

'Your friend is on her trip, you're on yours,' Flynn had said, on the floor of the van, kissing his way up her side.

Lying there, the sun fighting its way in through dirty windows, the doors open to the ocean breeze, Lori had felt like she felt now, like she'd been put back in her body. 'You don't need to go because she's done with this place and you're not. Stay and learn what you need to learn.'

What she'd learned was that ten days after she'd put her tear-streaked friend on a Greyhound bus, she was standing in that beautiful, desolate car park, next to the fly-blown toilet block, watching Flynn's van drive away from her, too. Flynn had learned what he had needed to learn from Broome and was ready to move on. Unencumbered.

'We'll find each other again,' he'd said every time Lori pushed for a plan. Or an invite.

And here they were. Lori was still convinced it was magic that had pulled her all the way to Sydney, even through the nightmare of Merimbula. And magic that had dropped her in this bed, stretching in the sun and feeling like every single cell in her body was alive, firing, singing in harmony. Magic, or orgasms?

We're living a normal life now, she typed. *Not even weird.*

Jools, on the other side of the world, didn't respond.

She knew Jools had made it to Cairns and the reef before the news got dark and the texts from home more urgent. *Come home while you still can.*

Lori, too, had been getting those messages.

Jools was sold. *We have to go*, she'd been texting Lori in those days when decisions needed to be made. *We have to go, or we might not be able to get back at all.*

It'll be alright, Lori remembered she had messaged. *I'm not scared.*
Jools got on a plane, and Lori did not.

Now, Lori didn't want to get out of bed. Beyond the futon, her contentment was more complicated, much less certain. But the sun was intensifying, and through the window, shoved open a crack, she could hear the kids downstairs shouting. She was meant to be finding a job today.

She sat up in bed, and the spell was broken. The fluttering in her stomach returned, settling in for the day ahead. She went to the wardrobe, where she kept her backpack, pushed underneath a rail draped with Flynn's T-shirts and wetties.

She instinctively knew this was the place to stash her bag – that it was best not to spread her things around, to make herself too visible.

Lori fished around for her towel, the one she was meticulously washing and drying outside so it didn't begin to fill the room with a mouldy, salty smell. And so it didn't get co-opted by anyone else.

She wrapped it around herself and went to the bedroom door, listening for signs of human life.

No-one officially lived in the apartment other than Flynn. Lori wasn't even sure how 'official' that was. But they were rarely alone. People moved through, stayed a few days, moved on. Or they popped in, for a beer and a 'yarn', and didn't leave until morning.

There was no noise. Lori stepped out and towards the bathroom. It was, of course, grim around the edges, more so than it had been last night. She hung up her precious one-woman towel and quickly bent to take out the spray cleaner and sponge from under the sink, where she'd put them a few days before. She squirted and wiped at the bathroom's grimy tiles and rims until she felt okay about sitting on the toilet.

Flynn would be glad he had her around, she knew, if she made no trouble and kept things nice. He'd wonder why he'd ever driven away from her in Broome. He'd never get that look in his eye that meant he was slowly moving away from her.

He had been happy to see her. She knew it. She just had to stop focusing on that first expression she saw on his face. Because it hadn't been irritation. It really hadn't. It had just been a surprise. Like when you see someone in a place you weren't expecting to see them and it takes you a minute to piece it all together in your head. It was just that.

'What are you doing here?' sounded bad, if she played it over in her head. But he didn't mean it like that. He meant it like, 'What are *you* doing here?' Like he couldn't believe it.

Lori rinsed the blue and white cloth under the tap, watching black hairs that weren't hers run down the drain. She remembered how that moment had turned and he'd looped an arm around her waist to pull her to him. Then he'd kissed her, his mouth on hers, the smell of him, his skin on her skin. It had felt like a great exhale, like a wave of anxiety was pushed away by the certainty of his response. Like she might be safe.

But to stay safe, she had to stay in his gaze. She turned on the shower and wiped down the tiles with the rinsed-out cloth. Stepped in and half-heartedly scrubbed the taps while the water pounded on her head.

Lori had never cleaned a bathroom before in her life. Well, not if you didn't count the ones at that fancy Cable Beach resort. There had always been a cleaner, at home, at college. She wasn't a neat freak. She'd never felt the need to primp the homes of any of the boys she'd dated back home. Her mother would laugh her loudest, most sarcastic laugh if she could see her independent backpacking baby scrubbing toilets for a man.

But her mum didn't get it. This was Lori's choice.

Flynn smiled every time she walked into a room right now. And she needed it to stay that way. Which meant a certain amount of compromise on her part. No objections to house guests, for example. Earning her keep in housework, for another. Not too many demands on him and his freedoms to come and go. That was definitely one.

Listen to his advice. Like the advice he was giving her about where to get a job. Flynn had a plan that involved the woman downstairs. The one who'd carried her backpack up here, the one who was listening at the door on that first day.

She wasn't really coping, Flynn said. He knew, because he'd had a mum just like her. All heart, all bravado. Would never ask for help. But she needs your help, Flynn had said. There's a job there for you, if you can just make her see it. She needs you.

Lori thought he was probably right. There was a job there she could do and like doing – looking after those kids, doing a bit of whatever around the flat. It must be lonely being a single mum when the world had closed down.

Today – Lori told herself, letting the cloth drop to the floor, letting the warm water from the shower pour hard on her head, pushing down her rising panic – *I'm going to ask the lady downstairs for a job.*

14

November: Lori

I *wonder what she looked like before.*

That's what Lori thought when the woman downstairs opened the door.

Lori had a favourite picture of her mum saved on her phone. She looked at it when she missed her. It wasn't from a familiar memory, it was from her mum's uni days, the early 1990s, before Lori was born. Her mum was wearing baggy jeans with a wide belt, and a skin-tight black top, which she'd told Lori was actually a bodysuit that did up with snap-studs between her legs. She was standing outside a pub in London, one of those chocolate-box-looking ones with hanging baskets and a swinging sign. It must have been summer because she wasn't wearing a coat. She was holding an uncharacteristic pint of beer, and laughing. Her lips were bright with a matte red, and she had big chunky boots on her feet. Lori loved the picture because her mum looked so happy, so cool, but every time she looked at it she thought, *I wonder if Mum knew that she was never going to look like that again?*

It's not that her mum looked old now. She just looked tired. Even on the days she wore the red lipstick, it was never enough to disguise the years of putting Lori and her brother ahead of herself. That shit, Lori was beginning to see, wore you down.

The lady downstairs looked fine, too. Something about her haircut and the way her working-from-home pants sat on her hips, and the fact her white trainers were still white, suggested that she used to be cool, too. And that she still cared. But still, she had that faded, distracted look about her, just like Mum.

When Lori eventually knocked, after standing outside for five minutes, the woman had opened the door only halfway, looked surprised, and then come out to the doorstep, holding the door open with her back.

'Hi,' she said, as if it were a question.

'I live . . . I am upstairs. With the backpack . . . I'm Lori.' She wished she had been able to text this exchange. Maybe she could just ask this woman for her number.

'I know. I remember,' said the woman. She didn't sound mean or sarcastic. She just sounded like she knew, she remembered.

'Good.' Lori realised she was twisting her hands together and quickly moved them behind her back. 'I mean, right.'

'Are you alright?'

It was the second time the woman had asked Lori this, and it was kind of irritating. Did Lori not look alright? She thought she was doing a pretty good job of looking alright, considering.

'Yes, of course, thank you.'

'Great.' The woman looked back inside the flat where, Lori knew, the kids were home. There was the sound of high-pitched, teasing voices, and the soft thumps of mess being made. It sounded like Lori's childhood, of the kind of 'playing' Lori had done with her brother. The kind that usually ended with her crying and him pointing his finger at her and hissing the words, 'cry baby'.

'Do you . . .?' The woman was asking Lori something, her eyebrows raised, impatient.

'Oh, yes.' Lori took a breath. 'I wondered if you needed any help. You know, anything done around the house.' She said it all quickly, the words chasing each other out of her mouth in one big jumble. And then she remembered to smile.

The woman didn't say anything for a second, then she grinned.

'Flynn said the same thing to me the other day,' she said. 'I must look like I'm not coping.' The woman laughed a little, but her eyes said it wasn't funny. 'I'm Mel, by the way.'

Mel sounded amused. And northern. Lori noticed for the first time that she was English. Clearly, last time, she hadn't been listening.

'What sort of help do you think I need?' she asked.

This was the problem with face-to-face conversations. You couldn't help but say the wrong thing.

'Oh.' Lori twisted her hands again, found herself scuffing a toe along the floor. 'Well.' Was this a trick question? A trap?

'You know, with the kids. I used to work with kids back at home.'

'Where's home?'

'Surrey. Dorking.'

'Oh.'

Lori could tell from Mel's accent that she wasn't from Dorking. She rushed to add, 'I worked at the school holiday club in uni breaks.'

'So you like kids?'

Lori nodded. 'Love them.'

That was a stretch. She didn't love them when they called her Beep-Beep Lorry, or when they ignored her instructions because she was young and a girl. She didn't love them when she was clearing up the 'accidents' that invariably involved bodily fluids. And she didn't love them when they blindsided each other with crushing insults, and then taunted the weeping child. But, you know, she probably loved them *enough*.

'Look, Lori.' Mel shifted her weight and held the door open with her hand, making her taller, firmer. 'Thank you, and Flynn, for your concern about me, but I'm fine.'

'Oh, we know you're —'

'I'm not a damsel in distress,' Mel went on, and her voice was getting stronger, and faster. Lori wasn't sure which part of being offered help would make you angry, but she knew anger when she saw it. 'I don't have money to burn. And I really, really don't like being sold to at my own front door. It's not Bali!'

Lori was confused about this reference, but she got the gist.

'If I need a babysitter, I'll come and knock. But, really . . .' It seemed the rush of indignation might be running out.

'Okay,' Lori said, embarrassed and exhausted at the same time. 'Well, if you ever do need a babysitter, text me.' She was very keen to walk away from this unwanted confrontation.

The butterflies were back, the wave of nausea.

'I don't have your number,' Mel said, her voice a little calmer, as if she'd taken a breath and was trying to remember what she was so mad about. There was an awkward pause before she said, 'I'll get my phone.'

While she did, Lori stood staring at the closed door, fighting back tears. What had she thought might happen? That Mel was going to welcome her in? Put the kettle on? Bundle her up and take care of her? It's not like she wanted that. She could have gone back to her mother for that.

Still.

'Here, put your number in here.' Mel was back at the door, with her phone, and a miniature bottle of sanitiser.

Lori squirted her hands, then tapped in the number. 'I'd love to help, but only if you need it,' she said, and she hoped the smile she was directing at Mel was enough to convince her she was a safe pair of hands.

'Look, I might need it, sometimes, but don't count on me.' Mel returned Lori's smile with her own, and Lori felt grateful for it. 'How long are you staying upstairs?'

'Oh, I don't know,' she said. 'No-one's really going anywhere at the moment, though.' She thought of all those bodies on the couches.

'True.' Mel moved as if to close the door. 'Take care.'

Lori nodded.

Then Mel said, 'Just be careful not to stay too long, hey?'

Before Lori could turn around to ask her what she meant, Mel had closed the door.

15

November: Lori

Paella.

Flynn was standing at the kitchen bench, chopping an onion, humming and buzzing to the music pumping out of his battered black tin speaker, alternating a flurry of chopping with a sip of beer from a dark brown bottle.

There was a pile of slime next to him on the counter. He said it was a squid.

'Des can jigger a squid with his eyes closed,' he was saying to Lori, 'you've never eaten fresher than this little guy. He was swimming around off Clovelly a couple of hours back.'

That seemed a little sad to Lori, but she didn't say so. Instead she murmured a 'wow' and went about trying to find a pan big enough for the flubber and a tonne of rice, while not clanging pans too loudly and killing the vibe.

'Who's coming?' she asked, using two hands to pull the biggest frying pan she had ever seen out of a low cupboard. Clearly, the woman who really lived here made paella too.

'Dunno,' said Flynn. 'I've put a little call out in a few chats, should be a crew.'

On cue, there was a knock on the door. Flynn didn't look up from wrestling the squid, and didn't say anything, so Lori knew it was up to her to scurry over and offer a welcome.

It was Des, of squid-jigging fame, a familiar face in Flynn's orbit, and his improbably beautiful girlfriend, Lea, who hugged Lori's shoulders. They were each offering a bottle in a paper bag, and smiling and aah-ing at the size of the squid. Lori had only just closed the door when there was another knock. Elva, the Brazilian, and his cousin Eldo. They were high, Lori could tell from their wide eyes and their licked lips and the way they overreacted to the smell of frying onions.

Another knock, and this time, as Lori let in Kianne and Lu – both 'old friends' of Flynn's from his time in Alice, who in her opinion spent a bit too much time hugging him hello, goodbye, and as many times in between as they could manage – she caught sight of their neighbour Mel's face looking up through the banisters from the landing below. Lori's stomach clenched, because she knew this many people in one apartment was probably against whatever rules they were supposed to be living by now. The rules that none of the people in this flat thought applied to them.

She gave Mel a smile and a small wave and went back inside.

Lori opened bottles and dug out glasses, and pushed her way through the bodies crowding into the kitchen to watch Flynn stirring the seafood into the rice, theatrically pinching the dried saffron in from a great height to send the pan golden yellow.

'A Spanish girl with the blackest hair you've ever seen taught me this dish in Madrid,' Flynn was telling them, wooden spoon in one hand, craft beer in the other. 'She learned it from her mother, and her mother's mother.'

'I bet that's not all she taught you,' said Des, eyebrows up. Nobody laughed, not Lea, not even Flynn, who just took a sip from the neck of his bottle, and Lori felt a small sweep of relief.

'Her old man was a fishmonger,' Flynn went on. 'And they'd make it with whatever he didn't sell at the end of the day. I stayed there a month and I never ate the same paella twice. Still,' he looked around, and Lori stepped forward into his space, 'I couldn't leave before I'd memorised the recipe.' With his spoon hand, he pulled Lori in and kissed her on the head. There was a rippled 'aw' from the guests, and Lori felt the glow of public possession she'd been searching for since Broome. 'You learn something from every season,' Flynn said, looking into her eyes, and Lori blushed, happily, her stomach calm for a moment.

Her phone buzzed in the pocket of her denim overalls and Flynn released her, a little flash of irritation across his face. The guests were beginning to spread out down the hall, and Lori needed to see if this kitchen, stocked with a stranger's things, had enough plates for everyone. She pulled out her phone and looked at it.

There are a few flights out.

Jools.

I just saw them on Travelmate. You know your mum would pay.

'What's up?' asked Flynn, taking his eyes off the squid rice to focus on her.

'Nothing,' said Lori. 'I've got to get some plates.'

'Must be something,' Flynn said, still looking.

'Just Jools.'

'Your sidekick from Broome?'

'My friend.'

'Bad news?' He went back to stirring, nonchalant, but his arm was tense on the pan handle.

'No, she's just telling me about some flights.'

'Why's she doing that? I thought you'd decided to stay.'

'Well, I did,' Lori fumbled. 'She's just rattling my cage, seeing if I've changed my mind. It's only going to get harder to get home.'

She stood on her tiptoes to reach the plates in the cupboard next to where Flynn was cooking. She grabbed as many as she could with one hand and for a second she swayed under their weight. Flynn kept stirring, eyes back on the pan.

'You're not going to take off, are you?' he said. 'I'm . . .' he took a swig from the bottle and looked at Lori sideways, 'getting used to having you around.'

Butterflies were back in her tummy. Along with a warm, soft feeling. He was asking her to stay.

Lori regained her balance, both hands on the plate pile. She could hear the loud talking and laughing, clinking and slurping, out in the lounge room. 'No,' she said. 'I'm not going anywhere.' A little step further, 'Not if you're happy to have me here.'

Flynn smirked, his full lips curling up a little. He nodded at her, slowly. 'Mmm.'

Another knock at the door. Lori half suspected it was Mel from downstairs. Surely someone was going to complain soon about this illicit gathering. She didn't much mind if everyone else had to go home and she and Flynn were left with a mountain of fishy rice, and him saying he liked having her around.

'Get that?' he said, eyes back to the pan.

Lori put down the plates and went to the door, pulling it open not to find Mel, or that grumpy old man from the basement flats, but instead someone who looked a lot like Des asking after Des. Another man was standing beside him, hands in pockets, and he saw Lori's face and looked down and away.

'Hey,' said the fake Des. 'We're here for the cook-up. Flynny told me to come early.' He pushed past Lori, heading for the kitchen with a swinging six-pack and an exaggerated swagger.

Lori couldn't move from her spot, even when the big guy pushed past her. She was firm as a statue as his shoulder bumped hers.

But if her feet wouldn't move, her arms would, and she pushed the door closed, leaving the second man outside.

But Rob lodged a foot between the door and the frame. 'It's okay, Laura,' he said.

'It's Lori,' she said.

Maybe remember the name of a woman you've attacked.

Rob had regrouped from his initial surprise and gestured to the door with his empty hands. 'Can I come in?'

Lori hadn't seen him since that night in Merimbula. George had thrown Rob and his bag out of the hostel cabin, pulled a mattress off a bed and laid it across the door in a gesture of protection. Kat had tried to hug her in the wide double bed, and Lori had just lain there for the rest of the night, hearing footsteps. She remembered now that Rob had howled outside the door for a while until the caravan park's security bundled him off, to who knew where. As soon as it grew light, she'd showered and packed her blasted bag and woken Kat to tell her she was going to find a bus. Kat had sworn softly and said, 'I'm coming, too.'

'Rob? Mate?' The Des lookalike was calling for his friend.

Lori stepped back from the door and Rob stepped inside, brushing past her as if she wasn't there, the very edge of him touching the very edge of her as he turned down the hall, away from the kitchen, where Flynn was tasting from his wooden spoon.

Flynn looked up and his face told Lori she must look shocked, or pale, or scared or . . . something.

'What?'

'Nothing.'

'Can you get the plates into the other room?'

'Yes.'

She headed back to the kitchen, the party getting louder and louder from the living room. A crowd of young people from many places, too close together in too small a space.

'The paella is officially ready, we can honour that freshly caught squid,' said Flynn, looking down at the heaped pan.

'Can I ask you something?' asked Lori, before she got to the plates.

'Of course.' He looked at her, steadily.

'That guy who just arrived . . .'

'Des's brother.'

'And his friend.'

'Didn't see him but sure.'

'Can they *not* stay over, please?'

'Why would you say that?' asked Flynn, his eyes still on her, irritation flickering.

Lori took a breath, and she had no idea if she was going to say this thing until she said this thing. 'I know that guy. And he's not a good guy.'

She hoped that her eyes were conveying to Flynn what she couldn't say.

There was a moment, then. A moment when Flynn considered what Lori was telling him and what she was trying to tell him.

'Did you . . .' Flynn started. 'Fuck him?'

Lori almost gagged at the question. Instead she just shook her head.

'No, I certainly did not,' she managed.

Lori could tell the exact moment when Flynn understood her non-words. Her non-disclosure.

'Would you like me to get rid of him?' Flynn asked. He seemed gentler, less in control. Sceptical. And a little bit afraid. *Afraid of my story*, thought Lori. *He doesn't really want to hear it.* 'Because if you do want me to get rid of him, it's something I can definitely do.'

Lori pictured that moment when Kat had punched Rob so hard his lip had split. When he'd had his foot in the door a moment earlier, she could still see the scab on his upper lip. Weeks on and still healing.

Lori put her hands on her stomach to settle it. She pictured Flynn going down the hallway and asking Rob for a quiet word. Or asking Des's brother for a quiet word, and talking to him about his dodgy mate. She thought about the questions that would come. The denials. She thought about all those eyes on her, and the confusion, and the raised eyebrows.

'After dinner,' she said, putting a hand on his back in the most possessive gesture she had tried outside the futon. Then she picked up all the plates she could lift and said, 'Let's just go.'

16

November: Lori

Lori stood in the sunroom of Flynn's borrowed apartment and watched as he leaned in close to Rob's face, his lips moving quickly, his eyes wide.

She was standing against the windowsill, the glass pulled open either side, the warm evening air at her back. She could smell sweet flowers, and cigarettes wafting up from Des and Lea and the Brazilians, who had all gone downstairs to smoke. She thought they should probably move a little further down the street, to not add to the annoyance of the neighbours. Clearly she was the only person who worried about such things.

For the first time in a while, she felt completely calm. Which was not how she was supposed to feel because all evening she'd been feeling sick about this very thing happening.

But here it was. Flynn had sent the others away – for cigarettes, for wine – it was remarkable, really, how he could move people. A touch on the elbow, a word in the ear, a nod, and they went where he wanted them to go. How did you get like that? wondered Lori. How did you go from being someone who was carried by the tide to someone who channelled the flow? Like Kat. How did these people happen?

Now there was only Flynn and Des's brother and Rob in the room. They were all standing around the coffee table that was strewn with wine glasses and beer bottles and rice-flecked plates. Des's brother was quiet, arms crossed, watching. Flynn was talking. Rob was looking down at his feet, like he was taking a telling off from the head teacher.

She had made out the first words Rob launched in defence – 'What, her?' – when Flynn had turned towards him, and started talking, fast and low. Rob had gestured towards where Lori was standing with a dismissive sneer, and Flynn's strong hand had shot out, quickly and grabbed his arm, pulling it back to his side.

Lori knew that any plan Rob had of smearing her, of painting her with words like *liar, drama queen, slut*, all the words that Lori had wondered were maybe true about herself whenever she thought about that night, none of them were going to stick to her. Flynn hadn't heard all the details but he knew it was true.

That was when the calm had set in. That was when she realised she was right.

'You need to go now,' she heard Flynn say finally, stepping back from Rob.

Lori pulled her phone from her pocket.

I'm not getting a flight, she typed. *I'm in the right place.*

'And, Joe, be more selective about who you bring into my house.'

Des's brother nodded quickly, turned to Rob and said, 'C'mon, fuckhead.'

You're stuck there, Jools wrote back. *Do you have any idea what you're doing?*

I really do, tapped Lori.

Rob didn't look at her as he left. He looked pathetic, beaten. Des's brother followed him, head also down, sucking his teeth. The word, she thought, was skulk. They skulked out.

Flynn shook his shoulders, pushed his hands across his head, and then turned to her. 'Did he hurt you, that guy?'

'He tried to.'

Why he didn't ask her for the story, Lori didn't know. Why he didn't question her, push for details, she had no idea. He walked over to where she was standing near the open window, put his arms around her, and said, 'You're safe now.'

Lori's face was in his chest and she took a deep breath in, smelling him. 'Thank you for believing me.'

'Of course,' he said, stroking her head, his hand then running down her neck towards the small of her back. She could feel him hardening against her.

Just as Lori thought Flynn was going to dip his head down to kiss her, he let her go with one arm, leaned his body forward out of the window and spat, a great glob flying down to where Rob and Des's contrite little brother Joe were leaving the building below.

Then he said, 'I protect what's mine.'

Part Two

17

January: Flynn

Flynn's legs were dangling over the edge of the cliff. If he looked, it was a long way down to where the waves were slamming into the base, their foamy white fingers reaching higher with every collision.

The sea was relentless but tonight the air was still. Flynn felt as calm as if he was sitting in a picnic chair on a flat paddock. No wind at his back, no whistling in his ears.

The police had suggested to him that this cliff was where Lori had come. More than suggested. Asked him why she did. But she didn't.

It had been a fucking day, really. And the absolute last thing he needed was all this drama. The cops and the neighbours and the regular pinging of his phone as word got around. *Lori's gone? UOK, bro?*

This is where he came, when he needed to clear his head.

It was easy to forget you were on the fringe of a city of millions of pushing, striving, shouting idiots when you were perched on the very edge of the continent, looking out to the vastness of the ocean, the power of the whole fucking thing. Sucking in, pushing out. All day, every day.

It was the only saving grace of this shitfight of a place – that its towers and malls and bridges and stadiums were all built here, at the ocean's edge. A city with beaches was the only tolerable kind of city. But still, the sooner he could get out of here the better, that was for sure.

He couldn't stay in the unit, not tonight. Des was there, as always, pulling bongs on the lounge, offering bullshit platitudes. 'She'll be back, mate. She's just trying to give you a bit of a fright. Teach you a lesson.'

Teach me a lesson? I don't think so.

Flynn closed his eyes, began to sway back and forwards, ever so slightly. With every forward motion he let his fingers, curled around the rock edge, loosen just a little.

He tried to picture Lori's face the last time he saw her. But that was too hard. So he tried to picture the first time he saw her.

In Broome. At that bar. There was only really one pub where everyone – backpackers and hospos and tradies and blackfellas – ended up, in that town, and it was a bit of a shithole, but it had this red-dirt beer garden strung with fairy lights and lanterns, and at night you couldn't see how much of a dump the place really was. The nights were so warm, the Kimberley air so sweet. It was an escape from the gossip of the van park. If you had the bucks for a couple of cold jugs you were almost always going to meet people there – people you knew from up and down the track, people you'd never seen before.

Flynn didn't really know why Lori. Yeah, she was pretty, but she wasn't the only one. Not in that crowd. Young girls in not many clothes, far from home. Easy to impress, most of them. They wanted their heads turning. Wanted a story to tell. Wanted something different from what they usually got.

Lori had been with that friend of hers who was always such a punish. Such a sour vibe of negativity about her. Always pissed off about something. Lori wasn't like that. She was light. That night she was laughing a lot. Some Irish guy at the table was telling terrible jokes and she must have been just drunk enough to appreciate them, because when Flynn found himself sitting at her table, it was her giggle he noticed first. And her smile, and her body under that loose white dress she was wearing, all floaty at the front and short on the legs, like a giant man's shirt. Sexy as all get-out, and she seemed to have no idea, which was exactly what he liked. Those try-hard girls, with all that stuff on their faces, did they have any idea how ridiculous they looked trying to pull that off out here?

Now, on the city's edge, eyes closed, legs swinging into a dark, blank space, Flynn could feel the moment Lori's attention had turned to him. When she'd focused that smile on him he'd thought, *Yes, this is why I came out tonight.*

But she hadn't come back to the van with him. That mate of hers shook her head and pulled on Lori's sleeve, mouthing 'No'. But by then he'd got the scent, it was something that happened to him sometimes, when he became a bit obsessed with getting what he wanted. And Lori, that night, with her giggle and her shiny skin and her soft, fancy voice, had become something he wanted.

Like a dog with a bone, his mum had always said.

He'd let it go, that night.

Flynn opened his eyes, looked at the moon over the ocean. Only a big cat smile tonight, smug as fuck next to the blinking stars, competing with the lights. Hard to know how anyone could disappear here, really. Or maybe not. Maybe this soup of humanity was the perfect mess to slip away into. He'd suggested as much to the cops, but they were convinced Lori had come up here. *She could be anywhere, mate*, he'd said to the woman. *Look around.*

Full moons were a big deal at Cable Beach. The tourist people had made up this bullshit thing about how the mudflats looked when a big one rose – a staircase to the moon. There were markets and after-dark camel rides and moon-themed dinners and, of course, doofs on the beach, all playing out across silvery slabs of mud. If you can turn mud into a reason to party, you've got it made.

He hadn't got her number. He hadn't really got her name, but he knew people who knew where to find a pretty young English girl who was scrubbing toilets at the Pearl Club. And so he could get word to her about the moon party, and the bonfire at the van park.

He could see her that night, laughing in the light of the flames. There wasn't much romantic about the smell of kero and pot, but he'd known it wouldn't take much. She was so eager to cut loose, he could feel it. He'd seen it before. Girls who'd been travelling just long enough to feel safe, but not long enough to be over it. They were just at the tipping point of wanting to try things they'd never tried. To take some risks, out of sight. To feel like they were finally fucking living. Lori was right there. Her mate wasn't, but it hadn't taken long to get rid of her that night.

Flynn heard a noise behind him. He was on the wrong side of the fence that ran all the way along the cliff line. Or the right side, in his opinion. If you couldn't be trusted to stand close to the edge without falling then you weren't very steady in the first place. It was the kind of thing his stepdad would have said. They put this fence here for babies and wimps, he would have said. Got to protect the weak from themselves, apparently.

Shut up.

Of course Lori wasn't the first, or the last, girl in the van. But he wasn't a dog, not like his stepdad. Flynn knew that about himself now, he was capable of treating women well. He enjoyed them. He'd enjoyed Lori. Back in Broome, her visits to the van park, rapping on the door, smiling up at him from the bottom of the steps, climbing up with that look on her face. She was an excellent addition to that chapter of the big trip.

But that was the thing with women. And sex. All of it. It never stayed like that. Like a fun chapter. Someone always had to push it to become a whole fucking book. It's not like you wanted things to go bad, but you wanted them to stay in that moment, and that moment was always being stretched, manipulated, hustled.

'Flynn?'

He turned towards the light of a mobile phone, couldn't quite see who was behind it, shining it over the fence, but he recognised the voice.

'I knew you'd be out here,' she said.

'Then you knew I wanted to be left alone.'

'You know people are watching what you're doing, right? With Lori . . . gone.'

'Piss off.'

But she didn't piss off. She climbed over the fence. Awkward in shorts that tight, he thought, and in shoes that stupid. Her long, dark hair swung across her face and she turned off the phone light and knelt down. Not wobbling, not shaking, steady as he was.

'I'll just sit here with you for a bit, I think.'

Flynn looked straight ahead. 'Aren't you scared?'

She laughed a spluttery little laugh. 'No, I'm not scared of you.'

He sucked in a breath of night air, and held it for a minute, then blew it out in one long puff. 'Yes, well, you always were pretty brave.'

'I thought you might want somewhere to stay.'

Flynn thought about that for a moment. 'What if Lori comes back?'

From the watery yellow light of the clifftop lampposts and the sliver of moon, Flynn could see her eyes, locking into his.

'If you think Lori's coming back, why are you sitting out here on this cliff?'

'Yeah.' Flynn's head felt like a buzzing wasps' nest. 'Well, maybe just for tonight.'

'Come on.' Kat stood up and held out her hand. 'Let's go.'

18

January: Flynn

Flynn pushed open the door to the apartment. The air was still, dead; it was clear no-one was there. 'Hey!' he shouted, to be sure. Nothing.

The sunroom and living room were flooded with sunlight by mid-morning. It washed over the hand-me-down furniture that Emily had collected and arranged. The stuff he was meant to be looking after, while she was stuck. It was all pretty dusty, pretty stained, pretty singed from the occasional candle and joint burn.

Two days of no Lori showed in the state of the place, too, Flynn noticed, dropping his keys on the coffee table among the empty cups and cans. How many keys were there to this place? Lori had a set, but God knew where they were. Des had one. He must get it back. He needed some space and peace now.

It was good to have not been here last night, to have spent what was left of the dark hours lying next to Kat, familiar and calm. If she was thinking shit about him, she didn't show it.

Flynn went to the sunroom and pushed open the windows, letting the heavy summer air slink in.

He was meant to do a job this afternoon. They were rare enough these days, with all the bullshit regulations cancelling events that would usually keep him going during one of these city stints – bumping equipment in and out of venues, connecting wires, blasting speakers, twiddling knobs. So he was just lending muscle to anything that needed it, which was proving more lucrative than he'd imagined, since bored people with money were knocking down and building things at an accelerated rate, and most of the transient workforce had fucked off back to wherever they'd come from.

But if he went to the Maroubra site today to clear out a block after the demolition had been through, if he turned up, like he'd promised, would he look like he didn't care? What was the right thing to do, in this moment? Were you meant to sit here, on the grubby couch, looking at your phone, twenty-four seven? Were you meant to be out on the streets, literally looking for her?

'You should put a post up,' Kat had told him this morning. 'People are starting to do that.'

Flynn didn't know what people did, but he felt an itchy, uncomfortable sensation at the base of his spine. That sounded like something that could quite easily spin out of control.

'I don't do that shit,' he'd told her. 'I haven't been on Facecrook for a year.'

'But people will think you should,' she said. 'That you should be doing anything you can to help find her.'

'And I have to care what people think? People who don't even know me?'

'Yes, Flynn, right now, you do.'

There were traces of Lori all around this room. Not traces that the cops would have seen, when they came yesterday for their half-arsed interview and stickybeak. But traces Flynn could see.

That was her lilac sarong, draped over the back of the couch. She'd got it at the night markets in Broome, worn it over her bikini on long beach days and longer party nights. She'd used it to pretty up Emily's dull brown lounge. Those wilting frangipanis in that tiny jar on the windowsill – well, that wasn't Des. Even the fading wipe marks on the glass-topped coffee table – Lori's hand had definitely made those. They'd lain on that couch together many times, her legs wrapped around his, her head on his chest. Her bare feet had padded in and out of here a thousand times, leaving little footprints on the floorboards. There were strands of her honey hair everywhere.

They'd fucked on the floor, quick and hard against the edge of this table, long and slow on that handkerchief rug. Every half-melted candle had been lit by her hand over these last months and blown out by her mouth. Tiny, invisible clouds of her spit settling on their wicks, no doubt.

Flynn got up from the floor and walked down the hallway towards the kitchen and the bedroom, trouble rising in his stomach with every step. There were more Lori traces here than anywhere else in the place.

Every pan stacked on the draining board next to the sink, her hand had put there. The dishwasher stood open and half-empty, that was Des for sure, but that cloth draped over the tap, that was Lori. That half-empty honey jar next to the kettle – Lori's. She had a weird obsession with hot water and honey. Pulling open the fridge, there was more of her everywhere – a quarter of a browning avocado, oat milk in the door shelf, a bowl of spicy stir-fry he'd made on the night that turned out to be the last. It was sitting on the bottom shelf, covered in one of those stretchy beeswax wraps she'd bought at the grocer. Those noodles had been great, but she couldn't finish them. She hadn't been eating much these past few weeks.

Flynn didn't want to go into the bedroom. It was the worst.

When the cops had been here yesterday, they'd had a pretty good look around. They'd taken her phone, which had been on the floor next to her side of the mattress. No, he didn't know her password, he'd told them. Why would he? But they'd left her backpack exactly where it was, in the crappy wardrobe. She'd always kept it there, all her stuff inside. She'd never unpacked.

At first, Flynn appreciated this. Recognised it as her being considerate of him. He didn't need her shit all over the place, he liked his stuff where he liked it. But, slowly, it began to annoy him. Wasn't she planning on staying? Where was she going to go? Who was she running to? Wasn't a bag, always packed and ready, a symbol of someone with an escape plan?

This is what he meant. Nothing could ever stay how it was. Shit always blew up. Messes always arose. He didn't ask for any of this.

Ironic, really, that she was gone, and the fucking backpack was still here.

The bed. The covers were pulled back, exactly how they were that morning, and you could still see the indent of Lori's body on her side. She was little, wasn't she? Compared to him. Compared to Kat. She was small. There was not much of her when she was trembling under his hands.

Her shoes were on the floor, the plastic sandals she slipped on every day, just there, one toe pointing to the other's heel. She might have kicked them off like that, or they might have been knocked by the people who'd been in and out of here since. Him. Des. The police.

Next to the bed, the book she was reading. The picture on the pink cover of a young woman lying on her belly, her knees bent and her feet up, looking at a phone. It echoed a pose he'd seen her in so often. A pot of some face cream her mum had sent her. Her hairbrush, the bristles pushed down in the centre, wisps of her everywhere-hair tufting out. A tiny pot of lip balm he'd seen her poke her finger into a thousand times, pulling it out all sticky and slick.

Flynn couldn't leave the doorway. Couldn't move forward into the space they'd shared that was now, what? Just his? Four more months of this arrangement with Emily. She wasn't exactly nagging him to get out. Maybe she would be, if she heard about this.

He looked, again, from the open cupboard with the raided bag, to the strings of fairy lights dangling across the picture rails, to the rumpled sheets, to the shoes with their shiny indented inner soles, worn smooth by her feet slipping in and out, forward and back, walking, always walking, as all the young travellers did.

Move, you idiot.

Flynn's brain still felt like it was buzzing, vibrating on a low frequency of frustration. He was suddenly furious at all of this – her bag, her shoes, the sheets. The pots. The pans. The mess. The pressure.

He turned to the kitchen, wrenched open the cupboards under the sink where there were cloths, and sponges, and detergents, and bin bags. All the things he'd need to put everything back how it was before everything went fucking tits up. Everything necessary to remove the mocking reminders of how badly he'd screwed this up.

It was hot now, and he pulled off his T-shirt and dropped it on the floor before he grabbed the bin-liners, the wipes, the soap spray. He'd start in the sunroom, the lounge room, with those marks on the coffee table, those sad fucking flowers, those messy melted candles.

He'd sweep up every one of those honey-coloured hairs, and wipe away every print from her finger and drop from her lips. He would reset this place.

But as he headed down the hall, there was a loud knock on the front door. 'Hello!'

He knew the voice, instantly. It was Mel, the mum from downstairs. Flynn froze, just a few steps from the door, his hands full with his cleaning plans.

Go away.

'Flynn! Are you there?'

Go away.

But the door wasn't locked. It was on the fucking latch, which is how he'd left it, no doubt. The moment he realised that and lurched towards it, dropping the Spray n' Wipe and the scrunched-up blue cloths and the roll of black bags with a thud and a clatter, must have been the moment that Mel, on the other side of the door, realised it, too, and she pushed it open just as he went to flick it closed.

'Flynn!'

He saw, in that second, what Mel saw. Flynn, bare-chested, flustered, sweating. At his feet everything needed to scrub a home clean. To remove every print and every drop. He saw her dark brown eyes registering him, flicking down to the bottles and cloths on the floor, flicking back to his face. There was a beat, a second, and then she looked him in the eyes. Concern, worry, that was what crossed her features. Not fear, not anger. Not suspicion. He could tell the difference.

'Flynn,' she said. 'You're home.'

'Yes.' What else could he say? His useless arms by his useless sides. He bent, started picking up what he'd dropped.

'Any news?' she said. 'I didn't sleep at all. Can't stop thinking about it. About her.'

'No,' said Flynn. 'No news. We're just . . . waiting.'

He saw Mel pick up on the 'we' and look up and down the hall for signs of life.

'Is there anything I can do?' she asked. 'You must be so worried.'

You've done enough, Flynn wanted to say. Why couldn't your life stay downstairs, instead of drifting up here and poisoning mine?

But he didn't say it. Instead, he found himself thinking of what Kat had said, about what he should be doing today. Something that would almost certainly distract from the cleaning products he was now holding again, and that Mel was looking at, pointedly.

'Actually, there is,' he found himself saying. 'You use Facebook a lot, right?'

19

January: Flynn

'I posted last night,' Mel was saying.

Flynn was gripping the edge of the chair, leaning forward. He hoped he looked focused, concerned.

He knew that his presence unsettled this woman from downstairs. In almost every encounter they'd ever had, she'd flushed and blushed, stumbled and stammered. He didn't think that's who she was, to other people, in other situations. It wasn't who she was when she was with her kids, or talking to Ainslie from downstairs.

She was one of the mask people. Always worrying about proximity, always taking a step back and away. But Flynn had a feeling that wasn't the only reason she didn't want to get too close to him. You got an instinct about this stuff. And apparently, today, she was anxious enough about the whereabouts of her babysitter that she had forgotten about the plague that was otherwise dictating her movements and choices. Today, she was inside his apartment again, sitting very close.

'Here,' she said, pointing at the screen. 'Quite a few are starting to pop up now, I think it'll get momentum.'

Please help us find someone very special! Lorelai June Haring (Lori) is 21, English, from Surrey, and lives upstairs from me. Her boyfriend reported her missing twenty-four hours after she was last seen. The police have been notified, but are not yet treating it as suspicious, because she's an adult, but this is very out of character for her. Lori has been my babysitter all summer, my kids love her and we're all very worried. This is a picture my daughter took of Lori just three days ago. We live in Coogee, and Lori didn't know many people in Sydney, nor was she familiar with many suburbs beyond our own. If you have any information at all about Lori, if you see her anywhere, if you hear anything, please let us know and we will pass it along to the police!!!!

Flynn looked sideways at Mel. So many exclamation marks.

He could tell this photo of Lori was going to end up everywhere. She was wearing the tight blue tank top she'd worn pretty much the whole summer. She looked great in it. She was posing for the kid, pouting a little, making big goofy eyes. The wholesome energy from that shot blurred all sharp edges, smoothed any raw underside. Lori looked like a pretty white girl who'd gone missing. This was going to be a podcast.

Her boyfriend reported her missing twenty-four hours after she was last seen.

Was that a dig at him? Mel was sitting just an arm's-length away, in a tank top and shorts of her own, scrolling the comments on her heartfelt post. She didn't seem scared. She actually seemed less flustered around him than she usually was.

'You know I called the cops as soon as I realised something was wrong, right?' he found himself saying.

'I know, you told me that yesterday,' Mel replied, not taking her eyes off the screen.

Flynn caught a couple of those scrolling comments. *Oh, Mel, so sorry to hear about this! Please be careful.*

Hoping Lori's found quickly, Mel! So scary women aren't safe anywhere these days.

'You should post,' Mel said, taking her eyes off the screen and turning them to him. 'The more posts, the more attention this will get, the more eyes will be looking for Lori and . . .' She looked a bit embarrassed for a moment. 'Her boyfriend posting will get more interest.'

'I don't do Facebook.' Flynn pushed a finger across the table as if trying to rub out a mark. 'I hate all that shit.'

'But you have an account, right?' Mel typed a couple of words into her laptop, and there was a picture of Flynn he barely recognised. 'Lori follows you.'

His hair was long, curly, sad. Surfer phase. He was sticking out his tongue, in what he remembered as the immediate, natural reaction to having a phone pointed at your face at the time. Hated having his picture taken then, hated it now. Girls were always doing it, documenting everything. Lori was always fucking doing it, no matter how much he pushed her away. God knew how many awful pictures of him were on that phone the cops had taken.

'Haven't used it in years,' he said to Mel.

'But you have a couple of hundred friends,' she said, scrolling. 'It will help. And people will share it.'

Flynn looked at the picture of himself, frozen in a little circle. This is who you are. This is what represents you. If Mel scrolled down – and he knew she already had – she would find some pretty nonsensical posts from beach breaks across the west coast. Blurry shots of waves where you could almost see who was riding them. A couple of pics of mates from back home. Kat.

'Okay,' he said, 'I'll do it.'

Mel pushed the laptop towards him, across the table, across the space where he'd been so busy trying to erase something with his finger.

'Now?' said Flynn. 'I can do this on my phone, you know.'

'Aren't you worried?' He knew she'd been wanting to say this since she'd come upstairs. The woman downstairs who knew way too much about him, and Lori, already. She'd come up here and clocked him about to tidy up and decided he definitely wasn't doing enough.

'Don't I look worried?' he said, holding her gaze.

'Not really.'

Flynn was tired of this. Tired of playing nice with the past-it mum from downstairs, no matter how helpful it would be to have her on his side.

'I think you should go,' he said. 'I'll do the post in a while.'

'People will find her, Flynn.' She closed her laptop and stood – thank God – to leave.

Flynn wanted to laugh at her faith in Facebook. But he didn't.

'Let's hope so,' he said, standing too.

Mel clearly had something else she wanted to say. But then the fluster returned, and she looked around awkwardly, turned to go.

'Let me know if you think there's anything else I can do to help,' she said. 'The police have interviewed me once, I'm sure they'll be back, but until then . . .'

Such a flex, thought Flynn. *Are you really trying to write yourself into this drama?*

Flynn didn't ask her what she'd told the police. He didn't want to give her the pleasure of telling him.

He began walking towards the door, knowing she had to follow him. He still hadn't put a T-shirt on. He still wanted to scrub this flat from top to bottom, and for everyone to leave him the hell alone.

'You know,' said Mel, 'I told Lori you reminded me of an old friend.'

'Really?' Flynn was only half-listening.

'He was handsome, sexy and incredibly seductive.'

Really, Mel? Flynn was listening now. *We're doing this now?*

'And he also could be a dangerous dickhead.'

Flynn stopped halfway down the hall. He turned towards Mel, blocking the hallway. 'Mel,' he said, 'I don't have time for this.'

His voice, he knew, left no room for misunderstanding. 'I can't have anyone around me who isn't one hundred per cent focused on bringing Lori back.'

He yanked open the front door. It was time for Mel to leave.

She walked past him, her mouth folded into a tight line as she headed towards the stairs.

Flynn closed the door, firmly, and resumed erasing Lori from the flat, scrubbing away every tiny reminder. He pulled out his phone.

I need to write a post, he tapped, to Kat. *Help me?*

20

January: Mel

'*If you know Lori, and you know anything about where she is right now, please tell the police everything you know. That is all I want, all I care about. There's an empty space by my side where she's been these last few months. Ever since her journey merged with mine under a pearl moon in red earth country, I knew she was on her own trip, and that I was a lucky son of a bitch to have her walk alongside me for as long as she has. Now, it looks like I'm walking alone again . . .* Can you believe this shit?'

Mel was reading out Flynn's Facebook post to Izzy, across the world. 'I mean, this guy. He's just . . .'

'Keep going,' Izzy said, her mouth full of something. Breakfast, probably.

'*Lori, if you're reading this, so many people are missing you. I would never want to tell you what you should do with your dreams –* HA! No, of course not *– A woman with a soul as light and beautiful as yours needs to let it float where it wants to go. But please, tell us where you are so we know you are safe. And if you don't want to tell me, for whatever reason, tell your mum. Or your brother. Or your friend Julie –* she's not called Julie, you tool – *Tell someone. Anyone. I am here, waiting. Always waiting.*'

'Well.' Izzy had finished chewing. 'That's . . . good?'

'It makes her sound like a flaky idiot.' Mel knew she sounded indignant.

'And she's definitely not?'

'No!' Mel was a little forceful with her 'no'. 'Would I leave the kids with a flaky idiot?'

'No comment,' said Izzy. 'I've left mine with the twelve-year-old from next door before when I'm desperate. And everyone knows she pulls the legs off flies.'

'Yeah, well, you always were the irresponsible one.' This, they both knew, was not even a little bit true.

'Are you okay? This sounds like a lot.'

'I am,' Mel said quickly, still staring at the screen. 'Should I share this post? I mean, Flynn doesn't have loads of followers, you know how the young people are about Facebook, but I feel like maybe I should put it in the local group.'

'To get more people looking, or to make him look like an idiot?'

Mel thought about it for a minute.

'He really does sound like an idiot, doesn't he? Does he also sound . . . dangerous?'

'Mel . . .'

'I know, I know, leave it.'

'He literally lives upstairs from you. You don't want to poke that bear.'

'Oh, it's already poked.'

'But the kids, and you . . .' Izzy sighed, sounded tired again. 'I just think you shouldn't push it any harder than you already have.'

Mel knew what Izzy was saying. And what she was going through. She didn't need anyone else to worry about. 'How's Tom today?'

'He's okay. Only two more sessions to go. Sleeping a lot. The girls and I are trying to give him as much peace as we can. It's . . . fine.'

'Not fine.'

'No, not fine.' Izzy sounded defeated. Mel sat there, phone to her ear, eyes still on Flynn's post, finger hovering over Share.

Izzy took a breath, changed her tone. 'This whole mystery thing you've got going on reminded me of that time you and Dom were in Thailand and you didn't get in touch for three weeks. Mum was losing her shit.'

'Vietnam.'

Izzy laughed. 'Mum was calling people, writing letters, ringing me every day and crying. And I was like, "She'll be fine." But then even I started to worry. Then you bloody resurfaced. You were just lying around having sex and smoking opium.'

'Two weeks, Iz, two weeks tops. And it wasn't opium.' They'd been on a river boat on the Mekong. It was exactly how Mel had imagined. A sticky, steamy paradise – a wide, endless river. Every shade of green, and brown. Every hot, sharp taste. This beautiful man who just wanted to be next to her, all day, every day. She and Dom were at the phase in their relationship where they barely came up for air. There were other travellers on that boat but they were only rough sketches of people, bit-part extras far from their tight focus on each other.

Dom told her he couldn't live without her. He said it wasn't a figure of speech, it was a fact. That if her feelings for him ever changed, he didn't know what he would do. It had shaken her.

In London, she'd had the occasional glimpse of what Dom's mum apparently called his 'intense side'. There had been a chaotic night when a man had pushed past Mel in a crowded pub, a drunken elbow bumping her breasts, and Dom's fury had been so instant and so misjudged, he'd copped a black eye in the scuffle that followed.

She knew he'd meant her to feel protected, but the escalation only made her feel unsafe, as did his flashes of hot jealousy whenever she was near other young, attractive men who could spin a story and tell a joke – hard to avoid in a crowded world of share houses and blurry parties.

She'd pushed away her wariness at this side of him, chalking it up to her inexperience, and their mutual passion. After all, she shared this all-consuming hunger to be together. But in Vietnam, his declaration scared her, because she realised, in that gently swaying cabin that smelled of cloves and diesel fuel, her head always on his chest, both of them slick with sweat, that she wasn't in control of any of this.

She wasn't in control of how she felt about Dom – which was, mostly, joyful, an overwhelming feeling of delight and possibility, like she'd found a partner in crime. But on that river she'd begun to feel herself disappearing, and it was scary. The intensity. The way he looked at her, like he wanted to eat her. Back then she couldn't have put it like that, but now, she knew. She knew that the reason she hadn't called home in that time was partly that she felt like she was floating in another world, far from everyone who tethered her. And partly that she was afraid. Afraid of what she would say.

'It wasn't opium,' she said now. 'It was a mind-boggling infatuation. I actually think I forgot you all existed.'

'Lovely.'

'I remembered you eventually.'

'That sounds like something we're all meant to experience, at least once.'

'Once is enough.'

Mel thought about Tom. Tom who was, right now, fitfully sleeping off the poisonous cure, upstairs from where Izzy was stealing bites of her girls' peanut butter toast. He never left Izzy's side, but he took nothing from her. Steadfast, but not demanding. Loving, but not consuming. Mel had thought maybe she'd found a Tom in Simon. But she hadn't. There was a difference between an effortless relationship and a facsimile of a relationship. You might not need mind-melting intensity to form a sure bond, but you needed a connection.

'I've got to go, talk later?' Izzy's tone switched to businesslike.

'You know,' Mel said. 'When I went upstairs before, he was cleaning. Who cleans when their girlfriend is missing?'

'Mel . . .' A warning tone. 'Don't take this too far.'

'I know, I know. Love you.'

Mel hung up the phone. She stared one more time at Flynn's post. And then, with a click of her mouse and a shot of adrenaline, shared it to Lori's Facebook page, to her wall, where hundreds of messages were expressing love and prayers and positive thoughts. Where everyone who loved Lori was coming together to will her back into sight. Where people were swirling in a melting pot of grief and hope and outlandish theories and anger and fear.

They were going to eat him alive.

21

January: Mel

Ava and Eddie were worried about Lori.

They'd been there the morning that the police had knocked on the door, and had probably heard everything the two young officers had said, even though Mel had sent them to their room when she'd realised she was meant to invite the police in. The officers had sat, awkwardly, on the lounge, among the detritus of family life.

The kids, with their big elephant ears, would have heard the young man and woman, in their masks and their sensible shoes, ask her about Lori the Babysitter.

She hasn't been seen for more than twenty-four hours.

When was the last time you saw her?

How did she seem to you, then?

What was your relationship with Lorelai like?

Did you hear anything unusual that night?

Did you see anything unusual that night?

Is there anything you think we should know about what goes on upstairs?

And Eddie and Ava would have heard Mel answer. Heard her lie.

That's worrying.

The day before yesterday, she looked after the kids for two hours while I went to the office.

She seemed exactly like she always seemed. Perky. Almost irritatingly so.

It was polite, professional. She's English, I'm English. Sometimes we'd talk over a cup of proper tea. We're both feeling so far from home . . . I felt a bit protective of her. Not like a mum though.

No. I hear quite a lot of what goes on upstairs. It was just the usual. I didn't see anything. I was down here with the kids.

Eddie and Ava's questions were harder to answer. Was Lori coming back? Was Lori dead? If people could just disappear, could you just disappear? What about Dad, could he?

Mel wanted to be one of those parents who didn't lie to their kids. She knew some of those, parents so righteous, so determined to earn their kids' trust that they wouldn't even go along with Father Christmas. But she wasn't one of those. She slipped in white lies to make life easier for everyone, especially herself, after a hard day.

The ice cream van plays that music when there's no ice cream left.

The beach is closed today, darling. They're cleaning it.

YouTube isn't working today. Everyone who works there is having a nap.

And so answers to questions about Lori also had to be carefully constructed. To do the least amount of damage.

Probably. But if she doesn't, she will be thinking of you wherever she is, because Lori loves looking after you more than almost anything.

No, people don't just disappear. It might look like that's what has happened, but it isn't. I'm not going anywhere. Nor is Dad. Just you try to get rid of us!

God forbid that children should understand the chaos and unpredictability of adult life before they absolutely had to.

Now Ava and Eddie were home from Simon's house after another weekend, and Mel's relief at them filling every corner of her too-quiet flat with their colour and noise was tempered by the endless confronting questions they'd brought with them.

Mel knew that this topic was about to surface in Ava's lists: *10 Things That Might Have Happened To My Babysitter. 10 Reasons Never To Trust Anyone At All, In Case They Disappear.*

'Why isn't it on the news?' Ava asked in the kitchen, as Mel dished up some red-sauce pasta into her daughter's bowl. 'It should definitely be on the news.'

'I know it feels like that,' Mel said. 'But just because something's important in your life doesn't mean it should be on the news.'

'But people should know. And the news would tell them.' Ava took a fistful of shredded yellow cheese from the bag on the counter.

'She might be on the news soon, darling, depending on what happens next.'

'What do you mean?' Ava stood in front of her mum, blocking Eddie from reaching the stove for his bowl of spaghetti.

'When Lori turns up,' Mel managed. 'Can you move, please, Ava?'

'Turns up?' There was nothing in Ava's determined little face that suggested she was moving on with this soon. 'What's "turns up"?'

'Tells people she's safe.'

'Wouldn't she have already told people she was safe if she was safe?' That was Eddie, elbowing his sister out of the way, proffering his bowl for dinner.

'There are lots of reasons why she might not have done that.' Mel dumped two big spoonfuls into Eddie's bowl. 'Let's go sit down and talk about something else.'

'What are some of the reasons she might not have told people she's safe?' Eddie kept pushing.

'Her phone is dead,' Ava offered hopefully, turning to walk down the hall, thank God. 'Remember when your phone was dead,

Mum, and you didn't call Dad to say you were late and he got really cranky?'

Yes, I remember.

'Or she's lost her voice and can't call.' Eddie was also heading away from the kitchen.

'But then she'd text. Maybe she's okay but she's trapped somewhere and can't move her arms.'

This was getting worse. Mel followed her kids down the hall, carrying her own bowl, a stomach full of guilt, and a glass of red.

'It's possible,' Mel said, carefully, 'that Lori doesn't want people to know where she is.'

'No way,' said Ava, firmly. 'That's not true.'

'Lori wouldn't want us to worry,' added Eddie. 'Or for Flynn to worry. Or for her mum to worry in England, like Auntie Izzy.'

They really did think Lori was pretty perfect. And, despite herself, Mel felt a prickle of irritation.

Seeing Flynn upstairs, lounging, shirt off, among the chaos that Lori had told her she righted every day, was infuriating. It had caused Mel to press that button and set Lori's friends and family on him.

It was his calm and then his dismissal of her. It reminded Mel of how Dominic could be when he felt threatened. He would be deliciously open, as relaxed as a dog exposing his belly, but then close so tightly as soon as he disapproved of something Mel had said, or done. The moment he felt he wasn't in control.

That boat trip hadn't ended well. It had been the first time the flashes of anger she'd seen directed at others were aimed at her. Dominic had decided that Mel had disrespected one of the boat crew – a young man whose job, it seemed to Mel, was to bring them fresh juices, and plates of seeping fresh watermelon. She hadn't understood the politics of river boat life, and she'd asked him one day if there were bananas instead of watermelon. Was it possible to change it today, please? Such a small, naïve thing to do. Dom told her she was embarrassing him. He called her ignorant – this man she spent her every waking moment thinking about, obsessing over, giving everything to. 'I can't look at you,' he'd said that night, the sky a dark navy, the air thick with the buzz and sting of insects. 'You're not who I thought you were.'

Mel had been stunned. It seemed such an overreaction, such a blindside. A pivot from the man who loved her more than anything to this man who had such blisteringly high standards she couldn't possibly ever live up to them. The man who thought she was wonderful, but also, apparently, awful. Lovable. Unlovable. On a few words. On a watermelon.

Where did that come from?

He triggered me, Mel thought. To use young person's language. *Flynn triggered me.*

'I think you should go.'

'I don't have time for this.'

Dominic had been dead for so long. And then this guy moved in upstairs and, just like that, brought him back to life. Triggered was the word.

Mel sat down at the table with the kids, all of them with their little bowls of plain pasta, red sauce and grated cheese from a ziplock bag.

'Lori wouldn't want you to worry,' she said. 'I'm sure she didn't want to leave. Maybe it wasn't her choice.'

The kids looked at her, their little heads turning in unison at these surprising words from Mum.

'You mean someone made her go?' asked Ava.

'Like, a bully?' asked Eddie.

Mel forked some pasta into her mouth and shrugged. 'She wouldn't want you to worry, darlings.'

22

January: Mel

It wasn't like there weren't enough pictures to choose from.

The Instagram feed of a twenty-one-year-old woman isn't short of self-imagery.

Lori last week, sitting on the stone wall at the beach, swinging her legs in little denim shorts, looking up from under her fringe, the ocean the same blue-grey as the sky behind her.

'Who took that, do you think?' asked Fi, who was looking over Mel's shoulder as she scrolled and screen-shotted. 'Upstairs?'

'I doubt that.' It was a flattering, beautiful image, taken with care. Flynn didn't seem like he ever looked at anyone for that long or that carefully. Except, perhaps, himself.

Selfies with predictable captions.

When you're exactly where you're supposed to be. Under a close-up picture of Lori's head, eyes closed, hair spread out flat on green grass, as if she were sleeping in the park. Except, in a pretty way.

'Not that one,' said Fi.

'Obviously not.'

There were other images – the palest pearl-pink shells in a rockpool. Her feet in the sand at sunrise. Flynn's smooth, dark back on the futon upstairs, Lori's hand in shot, staking claim. A vivid red milkshake studded with fresh raspberries from Melonfoot, just around the corner, and a radish-sprinkled poke bowl of brown rice and raw fish. There was a picture of a hand – Flynn's – thick fingers, freckled knuckles, one tiny tattoo of a circle on the middle finger, resting on Lori's knee, staking claim. There was a picture of her family – mum, dad, brother – around a table in a garden back home. Mel could tell it was England from the brick, bay-windowed house, the trees and the teeth – the caption just a crying-face emoji and the words, *My whole heart.* It was posted three weeks ago, this picture of the frightened people Mel had spoken to just this morning.

The grid told a story, one the police would be looking at now, if they cared enough to. A familiar story of a young woman who had been swimming in the Instagram aesthetic her entire adult life, who instinctively knew the soothing visual power of a photogenic milk-shake. A young woman who had a boyfriend who didn't want his face on her feed. Someone who was very far from her family back home.

Mel stopped, jolted, as she scrolled past a picture of her own children. The backs of their heads, at least. They were upstairs, she could tell. Little bodies in colourful T-shirts shot from behind. On a big, beige couch, watching a headless man in torn jeans play guitar. *Jesus, Lori.*

'That one's good.' Fi was pointing at the laptop. It was the best look at Lori's face. No flirting up through a fringe. No eyes closed on the grass.

Mel drew around it with her cursor, a tiny satisfaction in the click of the screen-capture.

Lori was looking at the camera, laughing, outside a pub in the city. She looked like herself. Wide open, smiling. Free.

'That'll do,' she said, and dropped it into the template she had on screen. 'Looks like her.'

Mel squared the shot and took a minute to go back and consider it. MISSING, she began to type. HAVE YOU SEEN LORI?

'She's so pretty,' said Fi. 'Such a shame.'

'She's so young,' was all Mel could really think to say, unable to break eye contact with the Lori in the picture.

LAST SEEN IN COOGEE ON 6 JANUARY. IF YOU HAVE ANY INFORMATION, CALL THE AUTHORITIES.

'Let's go stick them up,' said Fi, tugging at Mel's arm like an impatient child. 'Needs to be soon, right?'

Missing people on social media were one thing. But they were swimming in a soup of competing priorities, easily rolled past on the way to your cousin's new baby and the ten most sarcastic things Chandler ever said on *Friends*. The faces pasted to lampposts, and stuck to cafe noticeboards, were the people you remembered. The ones you found yourself staring at, creating stories for, while you were waiting for coffee.

'You know this will really put the pressure on him.' Fi pointed upwards. 'Her face everywhere.'

As if on cue, music started pounding on the ceiling.

Fi pulled a face. 'Is it wrong that I'm judging the distraught boyfriend for the fact that he's playing Kanye?'

'Well,' Mel snapped the laptop shut and stood up. 'The partying schedule does seem to have resumed.'

'I don't know how you live here, Mel,' said Fi. 'You know it's time to move?'

'It was time to move about five years ago,' Mel said. 'Let's go. Simon will be dropping the kids back in an hour.'

The music got louder.

'I don't know what Lori sees in that idiot,' said Fi. 'I don't get it.'

'I do,' Mel said, as casually as she could. 'He reminds me of Dominic.'

'Who's Dominic?'

Dom was so vividly present to Mel, so relevant to every thought and feeling that she had about what had been going on upstairs, that she forgot other people didn't know who he was.

'He's an old boyfriend.' On a day when the sunlight was blistering, pouring through the glass front doors of the building into the hallway, how was Mel meant to explain Dominic? 'He's who I came to Australia with. Why I'm here, I suppose.'

'What happened to him?'

What to say?

'He drowned.'

'That's terrible.'

'Yes.'

Fi was about to draw breath for more questions but the sunlight in the hallway was momentarily blocked by a man fiddling with the lock and pushing through the doors. The music was still blasting from upstairs, but this, without question, was Flynn.

He looked flustered, angry. And beautiful.

'Hey,' he said to Mel, not breaking stride, making it clear he was about to barrel into them if they didn't step aside.

'Hey,' said Mel, as she pressed herself up against the wall. He passed so close to her, she could smell him. His arm, his skin, almost brushing hers. She felt dizzy. Disgusted.

Fi hadn't stepped aside. She was blocking the hall, and Flynn had to stop in front of her.

'Excuse me,' he said, his voice a polite growl.

'We're just on our way to put some posters up of your missing girlfriend,' Fi said, full of authority. Mel's entire being prickled with anxiety. What was she going to say?

'Okay,' said Flynn, with a gruff shrug. 'Excuse me.'

But Fi still didn't stand aside.

'Would you like to help us?' she said. 'Would you like to do *something?*'

Flynn turned to Mel. He looked haunted and harried. Angry. She just knew Lori's friends and family had been bombarding him. That his phone had been fizzing with questions after that Facebook post.

'You've done plenty,' he said, towards Mel, and then turned back to Fi. 'Excuse me, please.'

Fi stepped aside. Mel wondered if Fi found it hard to breathe as he passed, too? Or not, because she didn't know about Dominic. She didn't know that Flynn was a familiar ghost. That this was a familiar story, playing out over decades. She just saw a villain stomping down the hall, turning upstairs towards the music.

'Well,' Fi said, as they finally stepped out into the sunshine of the street, her voice thick with sarcasm. 'Isn't he lovely? I totally get it now.'

Mel just nodded. 'Told you so.'

23

January: Flynn

Kat had raised her eyebrows at the cleaning. She'd turned up just as he'd finished scrubbing the bath. Every last long, fine hair gone. Every last splatter of sweet-smelling shampoo from the tiles. Every fingerprint smear of that sticky stuff Lori put on her face at night. All gone, all flushed down the sink. All spinning into the sewers and spilling out into the ocean, rolling around now, just past the breakers.

He'd shoved her bottles and potions back into her lilac washbag, and pushed it into the top of the backpack in the cupboard, closing that door hard. Vowing not to open it again until – probably, inevitably – the cops came for it. Why hadn't they already? Four days in, it was messing with him, it really was.

But Kat had looked around the flat with almost comical surprise. 'Wow. Have you ever cleaned up before?'

And he had snapped at her. 'Don't give me that bullshit, I've been looking after myself since I was fourteen. I know how to keep shit clean.'

Kat's raised eyebrows said, *Really?* But she didn't push it.

'What are you going to do?' she'd asked him instead, throwing herself onto the lounge.

'I'm going to wait,' he said. 'Something has to happen, right?'

'Something?'

'She'll come back. Or she won't. She'll turn up.'

Flynn noticed that Kat couldn't conceal a flinch at those words.

'You know what I mean,' he said. 'You know me.'

She did know him. He and Kat had been in and out of each other's lives since Year Seven.

Twelve-year-old Kat was a girl you knew not to mess with. Impressing her had been his first romantic obsession.

Flynn, who saw high school as a chance to build a world less fucked than the one back at his house, quickly decided that having Kat Howarth by his side would be a shortcut to the status he needed.

But it had never been that simple. Kat had the same issue that he did – dickhead parents. He had his stepfather to deal with, she had her dropkick of a mother. Slowly, he had been granted access to Kat's house and she his. A wordless acknowledgement that theirs weren't the families you saw on the TV, or even the ones their friends complained about. Their families were more like the ones you heard about on the news, when something went badly wrong.

After a while, Flynn saw enough to know that Kat's cool-eyed calm had been honed over years of being the only one who might know what to do with an empty fridge, the whirling storm of a violent argument, a dangerous man loose in your home, or your baby sister sick with a drenching fever and no-one around to care. Kat's cool was actually perspective and an unhealthy amount of experience in crisis management. As was his.

They were the same.

Too much the same to keep their childhood sweetheart status going for too long. The first time she slept with another guy – an older, all-blond meathead AFL type from the Catholic school at Burswood – it actually hurt. He remembered the confusion, the nausea, the bubbling fury. And he remembered how she'd looked at him, like he was soft, silly, to care so much. But then he did the same to her. And she to him. And he to her. By the end of high school, they were no longer Flynn and Kat.

Not being able to control Kat, to make her want only him, had changed everything. He could see that now. He had learned how it felt to care about someone, to really give a shit, and for it not to matter. Avoiding that same thing happening again was probably what had defined every relationship he'd had since, if he was honest about it. Not that he had any intention of being honest about it. Got you nowhere, that kind of bullshit.

At sixteen they'd gone in different directions – him to the road, moving all the time. Her into the city – different kind of adventures, a constant upwards momentum. Both leaving their domestic shit-shows behind and opting for reinvention. But they were bonded by what they knew about each other. There was a trust, a forever kind of connection, he was sure, as they drifted in and out of each other's orbits over the years.

'Some people might think it looks a bit dodgy that you've scrubbed the place,' Kat said.

'I needed to move on,' he replied. 'It'll be a mess again soon enough. Des'll be back.'

Flynn sat at the end of the couch, near Kat's bare feet. His phone was buzzing in his pocket. It always was now. 'I can't stay here,' he said, quietly.

'You can't leave, though,' said Kat. 'Not until this is all okay. The cops will be all over you.'

He looked at her, still cool, still calm. 'She just left, you know,' he said. It was the first time he'd said something so definitive, out loud, to anyone but the police. 'She was here, then she was gone.'

'It doesn't matter,' said Kat, not leaning towards him, not laying a comforting hand on his twitchy arm. 'It doesn't matter what really happened.'

Flynn felt heat rise into his cheeks, fizz through his chest, down his arms. 'I think it fucking does.'

Kat shrugged. 'Wasn't like you, really, to have someone living with you. That's not usually how it goes.'

'How would you know how it usually goes?' He was getting agitated, annoyed, but Kat smiled.

'Of course I know.'

Flynn found himself standing up, pacing around. 'She just turned up.'

'I know,' said Kat. 'I brought her.'

'And that's so wild,' Flynn said. 'Like, I've seen the world is full of coincidence, but that's pretty wild.'

Kat looked at her feet, wiggled them this way and that. 'Why did you like her so much?'

'Why are you talking about her like she's dead?'

'I'm not,' Kat said, quickly, finally looking up at him. 'I just mean . . . I thought you stopped liking her so much.'

Flynn rubbed his head, rolled his shoulders a little. He remembered Lori's laugh, the way she moved around the flat, a little sway in her walk, a little skip in her step. Lightness. He liked to shock her, sometimes, show her what kind of a man he could be. It was fun to watch her mouth form that surprised little O and her eyes widen when he did something that revealed the side of him Kat knew.

'I liked having her here. But then . . . she didn't like it so much. And I got a bit sick of her being so sooky about everything. You know how I am about sooks.'

Kat raised her eyebrows in a way that Flynn suspected was a little mocking.

'It just got a bit . . . hard, you know.'

Kat looked like she was about to say something. Ask something. But then she changed her mind. She sprang up off the lounge. 'Let's go,' she said.

'Where?'

'Anywhere. The pub. Lu's place. Anywhere where you're not so sad-sack, and anywhere you don't feel . . . watched.'

'I'm meant to be working.'

'No-one's working when their girlfriend disappears.'

'Don't say that.' Flynn flinched.

'Maybe she'll be back and all of this will blow over,' Kat said, unconvincingly. 'Sometimes things turn out fine.'

'When?' snapped Flynn, knowing if anyone could take the hard edges of his stress, his irritation, his guilt, it was Kat. 'Not a lot of sometimes for us, is there?'

Kat pouted at him, picked up her jacket and called back down the hall, 'Don't be a sook. You know how I am about sooks.'

24

January: Flynn

The police were back, with Lori's phone.

Another night had passed. Flynn had followed Kat to the beach for ciders, to the beer garden for bourbon, and back to the flat with a bunch of randoms for all kinds of things.

He didn't like to get so messy. Messy guys make mistakes. Messy guys get jumped. Messy guys get caught out.

But last night, he could feel the drinks dousing the relentless crackle of fear in his gut, soothing it, laying it down to sleep. So he'd kept pouring. Now he had a memory of people poking around the flat. People who shouldn't have been here. Some of them asking to see where the missing girl slept. A young woman, who looked a little like Lori, wanting to see the English girl's bag, her clothes.

Kat's arm on his arm, calming him. All night, Kat kept him close, nudging the party along but somehow holding herself apart from it. Had she even had a drink? Thank God she'd been here when the mum from downstairs knocked at the door. Who knew what time that was, but he could see Mel's eyes, even now, the way she'd looked at him over Kat's shoulder. He'd been coming out of the bathroom with that girl from . . . where was she from? No place came to his mind, but he could see her wide, hot mouth.

Did Mel's late-night visit have anything to do with the cops returning this morning? Was it a coincidence that they'd arrived early to poke around in his sludgy brain, to cast their eyes around the flat that – so spotless and ordered yesterday – was now a mess of bottles? Surfaces covered in a thin sprinkle of ash. Everything sticky.

'The thing is,' the woman cop was saying, 'we think there's a chance you know the passcode to this phone. And I can't overstate the importance of us getting into it. This is how we find Lori.'

She was good, this cop. He knew exactly what she was thinking, but nothing on her face betrayed it explicitly. She was thinking what Mel from downstairs was thinking: *Piece of shit.*

It made him jumpy. And fighting through the foggy thickness of his brain was a sharp point of fury. These women, judging him, pushing him, prodding him for answers and information that he didn't have.

Where did he think Lori would go?
Why would she want to leave him?
Was she depressed?
Did she have a history of self-harm, of suicidal ideation?
I don't know, he wanted to say. *I never asked.*

It didn't look good this morning. He knew he was being sullen, unhelpful. Sitting there, stinking of last night, rubbing his head, blinking in the reality of another moon rising and sinking with no Lori.

'Partners often know each other's passcodes,' the woman cop was saying. There was still a hint of a smile in her voice. He knew it wouldn't be there tomorrow. Definitely not the next day. 'My husband cracked mine first time. He knows me well enough to guess.'

'I don't know,' Flynn said. 'We weren't that close.'

The man cop laughed. A laugh without humour. He was short, shorter than a cop should be, Flynn thought. His stepdad had said that when they scrapped height restrictions for the police everything went downhill. 'How can you respect a dude with short-man-syndrome in a uniform?' he'd said. Not that Flynn agreed with most of what his stepdad said. But it did have a way of sticking in your head.

And now the short, silent man cop was laughing at him.

'That's a strange thing to say,' said the woman. 'You lived together.'

'She was staying with me.'

'She's your partner.'

Flynn put his head in his hands. He needed to hold his brain in place. 'Partner isn't a word I use.'

'You were in an intimate relationship, living under the same roof?'

Yes. Yes we were.

'I suppose so. Yes.'

'Flynn.' Her voice changed. 'Do you know Lori's phone passcode?'

'No.'

'So you never unlocked her phone yourself?'

Only every day for the last two months.

It was after their bubble was burst by Lori's annoying mate and her endless messages. They'd appear on the screen, and if he was around – and, increasingly, he seemed to be around – he would feel a pop of panic as the first two lines were there, and gone.

I've called the consulate for you . . .

It's going to be too late . . .

He'd been trying to pinpoint exactly when it was that his irritation at having Lori around had flipped into a fear she would leave. It wasn't that long after all the shit went down with Rob, maybe.

The night he'd made paella.

Lori was tougher than he'd thought she was. She'd been on her way to see him when this thing with Rob had happened to her.

She had kept coming. He didn't know all the gnarly details. He hadn't made Lori tell him, and had asked Kat not to. Because it surprised him, how much he felt about it. How much he wanted to kill that little idiot.

But also, he was surprised by how it changed the way he felt about her. Who else was looking at her like something to be taken? What else might she do? Brave enough to fight Rob off, bold enough to tell Flynn to get rid of him. This woman he'd looked at as lightness, as a soothing entertainment, making life that little bit more interesting for a while – he began to worry what she might be thinking.

See, it never stayed simple.

'There's a guy you should talk to,' he said, his tongue heavy and thick in his slow mouth. 'He attacked her once.'

The man cop stopped leaning on the wall and took a few steps towards where Flynn was sitting, hunched, on the coffee table.

'Attacked her? And you're telling us now?'

'I just remembered,' said Flynn, irritated. 'She embarrassed him here. You should go and talk to Rob.'

The woman cop spun the dead phone in her fingers. 'And you can't unlock this phone?'

'I told you, she didn't give me her code.'

Except that time she did. Under his hands, in his bed, gasping.

25

January: Flynn

Flynn woke up blind, the afternoon sun slicing across the bed and into his eyes.

He blinked, and blinked. There was someone standing at the end of the bed, a shape against the darkened door. A woman.

'Lori?' It couldn't be. But in that moment, it was the only name in his head.

'Get up,' said Kat, stepping forward. Taller, stronger. 'You can't be sleeping all day.'

'Fuck.' Flynn rolled back onto his stomach. He did need to get up. The cops had finally left and, this time, they'd taken Lori's backpack. God knew why they hadn't done that before. He could feel the space it had left behind in the wardrobe, behind that chipped door.

He'd sent the cops off after Rob and gone back to bed.

Now he needed to sort this place out. Take control of this situation however he could. He was getting sloppy.

'Des is here,' said Kat. 'And Lea. They're going to stay. Make sure you don't do any more stupid things.'

'What are you talking about?'

'The police,' she said. 'This place. This mess.'

'Hey,' Flynn sat up. 'You helped make this mess.'

Kat tutted. 'And I left you alone in it for half an hour.'

Flynn felt confused by Kat's irritated tone. Why was she angry with him? 'Have you spoken to them?'

'They spoke to me two days ago,' said Kat. 'They've spoken to most of us.'

Why wasn't she offering up what she'd said to them?

'And?'

'And nothing. I told them the truth, that I barely knew Lori.'

'Did you tell them about Rob? About what happened?'

'No. Why would I? It seems so long ago.'

Flynn decided to let it go. He needed to get up. 'Can you piss off and let me get out of bed, Kat?'

'I've seen it all before.' There was something almost sneering in her tone. He didn't like it.

'Just fucking go.'

She turned to leave. 'They have nothing, Flynn, don't worry about it.'

'I'm not worried about it.'

He fell back onto the bed. He could hear Des moving around down the hall, some kind of ska-bop playing. He could hear furniture moving, paper rattling, the chink of glasses. They were tidying up.

He could hear Lea talking to someone on the phone, telling them to come over. He could hear muted announcements over the beach loudspeaker system outside. Swim between the flags. Keep your distance. It felt like the space left by Lori was springing back, filling up. Could that happen? Could things just move on? Would Lori just fade away? Was that possible?

She was there, under his hands, in the bed. She was telling him a story about what she called her 'old life', and at first, he was laughing.

How could a twenty-one-year-old have an 'old life'? She was only a handful of years out of school.

He had told her a carefully selected collection of stories from his life, some true, some not so. Like a jump-cut reel of scenes, a trailer for a more complicated movie.

Here was young Flynn, labouring long days on a blistering Subiaco building site and working a bar to save enough money to leave.

Here was the first English woman he met in London. How she said his accent made her swoon and he didn't know what she was talking about because he didn't know he had an accent.

Here was Asia, blowing his senses, especially his mind. A Buddhist retreat. A yoga girlfriend.

Here was home, and enough money from his stepdad's last lucky streak to buy his van.

Here he was in Broome. At that table under the fairy lights, cracking onto another English girl who loved his accent, who was coming into focus as he spun his yarns and his strings of seduction. A gentle brush against skin here, a soft tease there.

And here was Lori, in his bed, listening and thinking it was her turn to talk.

But these stories from her 'old life' weren't entertaining, they were unsettling. Lori's life without him made him feel inexplicably angry.

She was telling him a story about why she'd left. Why she'd felt the need to get as far from home as she could. It involved her small hometown, the one that sounded damp, safe, beige. And a photo of herself and the girl she was secretly dating. A *girl*. She said it as if it was nothing.

He remembered the girl's name. Elise. She had a boyfriend, who Flynn imagined as a dumb, smug Englishman. A chinless wonder, like the ones he'd seen on TV. Flynn didn't know why he spent more time imagining the boyfriend than Elise, the girl in the picture that screwed Lori's pretty little life. A picture of the two of them, that she had meant to send only to Elise. Instead, a thumb-slip, Lori called it. A thumb-slip that posted to the Stories feed instead. An easy mistake, she said.

He could still hear her voice. That light, sing-song tone with just a hint of a tremor. 'I didn't realise for a while. Jools told me, first, and I deleted it, of course, but it was too late. The messages had started. From Elise. From her boyfriend. His friends. It felt enormous. It was all anyone in town talked about, for what felt like ever. Elise was so furious with me, she –'

She kept talking, and Flynn had put his hand over her mouth. 'Stop,' he'd said.

Stop.

Her eyes had gone wide, and momentarily frightened, until he'd pulled back his hand and kissed her. 'That's not a story I want to hear,' he'd said to her, here in this bed. And he knew, as he said it, that his words were leaving a mark.

'I don't want to know who you were before,' he'd said. 'I want you to start again.'

Now, Flynn's head was pounding. It felt as if Lori was here now, in that moment when he'd told her that she was no-one until she met him.

'We're erasing all that,' he'd said. He remembered, although at the time he didn't know why, that his mouth was almost on hers, as if he was saying the words into her, like they were going to snake inside her and coil around her tongue. 'It didn't happen. We're only here now. You're only mine. You were a virgin until I found you.'

He remembered that Lori, for a moment, had misunderstood him, and smiled, her eyes – so close to his – half-closing in a little laugh. 'Is this a game?' she'd asked, her hands linked around his neck. 'I can play along.'

'Not a game,' he'd said. 'Your new reality.' And when he'd kissed her again, he'd used all his weight to push down into her. He'd have known, although he had no recollection of knowing, that she couldn't really breathe then, and that his mouth would be bruising her mouth. He held it there for just a pounding beat too long, and when he'd let go, and pulled back up, she was looking at him differently. Afraid.

When was that? Not long ago. After the first time she tried to leave. Two weeks? Just before Christmas. The night Mel downstairs had seen them together outside.

Now Kat's voice was calling him.

'Your neighbour,' Kat was calling from outside the bedroom, in the kitchen. 'You should talk to her.'

'Why would I do that? She hates me.'

'She's put up all these pictures of Lori.' Kat was coming back to the doorway, a silhouette again. A silhouette carrying a hot cup of something for him. 'You know, wanted posters.'

'Missing posters.'

'Yes, those. On lampposts. At the cafes.'

'Of course she has.' Flynn sighed.

'You should talk to her, make sure she sees how upset you are. Make sure she knows you want to help.'

'I don't want to help.'

'Don't let anyone hear you say that.' Kat handed him the coffee. 'Not even me.'

26

January: Mel

It wasn't entirely clear to Mel how she arrived upstairs, drinking with the stranded travellers.

But here she was, sitting on the floor. Her middle-aged knees up around her chin, a can of something called a seltzer in her hand. There was music at a comforting mid-level throb, chatter all around her, and the smell of stir-fry in the air.

This is what happened up here. This is what she was listening to, night after night, the sound that lulled Eddie and Ava to sleep.

'You alright?' asked Kat, sliding into place next to her.

'I don't think it's me we're meant to be worried about.'

'This must all look a bit weird to you.' Kat tapped her hand on the floor, pointed downstairs. 'From down there.'

'It does.' Mel took a greedy gulp from the seltzer, which tasted like salty-sweet, dirty water, and not something a grown woman should be drinking. 'I don't know how he can be so . . .'

She leaned forward to look down the hall, to where Flynn was cooking something that smelled like Asia. Like crushed galangal and lemongrass. How did a labourer from Perth know how to cook like that?

'Yeah,' said Kat, whose drink looked a lot like water. 'Well, people deal with things in different ways.'

'But inviting all these people,' Mel gestured around with her can. 'For a party . . . who does that? When their girlfriend's missing?'

Kat shrugged. 'Maybe he thinks she's fine.'

Mel and Kat's eyes met for a moment and Mel wanted to laugh, almost. 'Yeah.'

The path that had led Mel to be sitting on the ghost's sticky floor and drinking this sucky seltzer was paved with dubious intentions. Her phone was pinging every few minutes with notifications from Facebook about Lori. Sympathy and concern. Theories and ideas. People were trading tiny nuggets of information about where she might be, who she might be with, where she might turn up 'one way or another'. It was making Mel feel sick.

Mel had wanted to get up here. She had wanted to see how the space left by Lori was shrinking every day, but . . . these people. The women were beautiful and confident in a way Mel never remembered feeling. Perhaps she did once have skin like that – a smooth, blank, shiny canvas – and eyes that weren't hooded with exhaustion's slow droop, retreating back into her face as if they'd seen too much. Perhaps her hair had been smoother and glossier than she remembered, and perhaps her thighs had been undimpled and her stomach unwrinkled, and perhaps she hadn't always had to wear a bra, even under pyjamas. But she didn't remember ever feeling it. It felt like these young women did. In their high-waisted shorts and their sloppy Ts, their bra tops and their scratchy tattoos. In their jackets over almost nothing and dresses that just brushed their bums. Their bare feet and their clumpy boots, their colourful trainers. They all just looked so *good*. She didn't remember that. She remembered unironic ugly sandals, cheesecloth sundresses and denim overalls.

Not one of the men had Flynn's presence, his charisma, but they all looked like slightly faded versions of him. Like they were straining with the mammoth effort of not trying too hard, not smiling too wide or laughing too loud, dressed in the uniform of slim denim shorts and T-shirts blasting colourful explosions of random graphics. They cradled craft beers in neon-candy cans. They had strangely retro beards. Dominic had had stubble. That was a thing then, too, to always look like you were a few days away from a good shave, and to never, ever look like you cared.

These people all care a lot, thought Mel, feeling like a munchkin in a sea of sunflowers. *Except about what's important.*

'What's the alternative?' Apparently Kat was reading her mind. Mel had forgotten she was there. 'What choice has everyone got but to get on with things? They're all stuck. They're all feeling sick about Lori.'

Mel had wrangled this invitation into the world upstairs by apologising to Flynn, earlier today.

She had been at the kitchen sink when she'd heard the front door slam in the very particular tone she knew to be Flynn's. It was a careless bang by someone who wasn't considering neighbours and noise.

She had gone out to the hallway, to say something.

She knew that if she wanted to get upstairs, to see what she wanted to see, hear what she wanted to hear, she needed to convince Flynn that they should be allies, not enemies.

She stepped out of her front door right at the moment Flynn looked up. He looked wretched. Sick. Toxic. His skin was pale, waxy. The circles under his eyes had become scooped-out trenches. His eyes were watery, lined with pink. But mostly, it was the way he held himself. The way his head was dipped as if in slight apology. The look he gave her was almost nervous, all traces of his trademark arrogance gone.

It took every steadying breath in Mel's body to say what she said next.

'I'm sorry, Flynn. I know you are under a lot of pressure. Maybe I can help you.'

At first the look that crossed his face was scoffing, incredulous. But he didn't walk on. He started, instead, to shake. And then, to Mel's absolute horror, he started to cry.

'I've been out,' he choked, 'on the cliffs. Looking . . .'

The barrier Mel had been so careful to keep between them, the one between her past and her present and the messes she'd made before and the ones that were still with her, fell away for a moment and she stepped forward and hugged the ghost.

He let her. His head dropped to the top of hers, and he shook with tears.

Mel had found herself putting her arms around his shoulders, as this tall, strong young man wrestled out sobs. He looked broken but he smelled clean. He had nothing more to say. She held him, as she might hold Eddie if he fell and scraped himself when he knew he had been doing something foolishly reckless, and she'd looked up to see Kat on the upstairs landing. Their eyes had met, and Kat had motioned with a backward tilt of the head that Mel should come upstairs.

Despite the intense churning in her stomach, Mel didn't need asking twice.

She'd stayed, and helped the young people clean up this strange, in-between space – a place of waiting, and questions. She'd spoken to the ghost in a way she hadn't before. About Lori, about the conversations they had shared. About how Mel knew how hard it was for Lori to be so far from home, but how she also knew she couldn't leave Flynn. 'She really loves you, you know,' Mel had said, careful to use the present tense.

He'd listened. Mel had watched his face closely as he'd nodded, and folded his arms and his lips. 'You should stay for some food,' he'd said, 'I feel like we should all be together.' Her stomach had leapt at the invitation. Then people began to arrive, two by three by two, from who knew where, answering who knew what silent call.

Now here she was, too many of these silly drinks in, sitting on the floor. She knew she needed to have a different conversation with Flynn now.

Mel stood up, pushing off Kat's restraining hand, and headed to the kitchen.

It smelled like Thailand. Mel hoped she was entirely steady on her feet as she leaned on the kitchen doorframe and watched Flynn cook for his audience of two young women in short shorts and neon hoodies.

She knew this spot was where Lori had stood. She knew the door to the left, slightly open, led into the bedroom where Lori had slept, just above her own. Flynn was telling the watching women that he had perfected Tom Yum Kung while he'd been working as a cook and handyman at a health retreat south of Bangkok, and he'd dated a masseuse from the nearby town who'd taught him how to make her mother's favourite comfort food.

'I couldn't leave before I'd memorised the recipe. This exact way of doing it has been passed down for generations.'

The women nodded and cooed and took pictures of soup with their phones.

Mel considered the likelihood that a small Thai spa would employ an Australian cook over a local one and stifled a laugh. She wondered if she had been as easy to impress when she was young and travelling, so keen to seem worldly, curious and interesting. The evidence would suggest definitely yes.

The Flynn she'd met in the hallway a few hours before – sobbing, vulnerable – had faded. In his place was the Flynn Lori had lived with: charming, confident – no, arrogant. 'We need prawns!' he was exclaiming, loudly, waving his beer hand. 'You can catch them down at Gordons at this time. Nothing like a night walk along the cliffs.'

The women looked uncertain about whether this was a joke from the man with the missing girlfriend. Was he really talking about walking along clifftops at night?

He squeezed past the girls to the freezer, and yanked at the ice-choked bottom drawer to pull out a bag of frozen prawns. 'No need!'

Mel knew Lori had bought those prawns. She pictured the young woman in Woolies, choosing the ginger and the lemongrass, the stock and chillies and the bag of icy blue, caught-in-Thailand prawns, almost a week before. Now, she was gone, but the shellfish she'd carried home were being tossed into a smelly soup by this man.

Yes, Izzy, she continued the imaginary conversation that she was always having with her sister inside her head. *I am getting indignant and rageful about home-brand frozen prawns.*

'Can I talk to you?'

It was her voice, as loud and forceful as she could manage. Heads turned, and she registered confusion on the faces of Flynn's friends. Who had invited the mum?

I used to be you, she wanted to say. *One day, you will be me.*

She had said exactly that to Lori, once. Infuriatingly, Lori had laughed.

Flynn nodded at the women. A dismissal.

They padded past her, smiling politely, heading for the living room, back to the people who were like them.

Now it was just Mel and Flynn in the kitchen, and the soft hiss and pop of a bubbling pot, and the slightly open door to the room where Lori had slept, and the bed right there, mussy, messy.

Flynn sipped his beer and turned his back on the stove, leaning against the counter.

He looked at her expectantly, shrugged his square shoulders in his faded grey T-shirt.

'Want to say something, Mel from downstairs?' he asked, in a playful tone that didn't match his expression.

'Who are they? Those girls?'

'Not girls,' he replied. 'Women.' His smirk was insufferable. Dom's had been too, at times.

'Barely.' As soon as she said it, Mel hated the way it sounded. Jealous. Mean. 'Who are they?'

'Friends,' he said.

'Are they even supposed to be here?' Mel put down the seltzer. She knew she'd had a little too much; her insides were warm and swimmy. 'Isn't it breaking all the virus rules?'

'The rules are bullshit,' said Flynn, sipping his beer. 'Designed to keep us in line. I don't buy into that narrative.'

'What narrative do you buy into?' asked Mel, feeling a little bolder. 'Because there's a pretty strong one going around that you should be acting a little more bothered about the fact your girlfriend has disappeared. That having parties every night isn't a great look when you're the key . . . witness.'

'Witness, is it?' Flynn turned back to the soup, poked at the flabby prawns with his wooden spoon. 'I thought you just told me Lori loved me so much. That we all needed to be together. Now I'm a witness?'

'It's not what I think. It's what everyone else thinks. They're watching you, and you probably need to take it seriously.' Her tone, imitating his earlier plea, sounded a little more taunting than she'd intended.

Flynn didn't say anything for a moment. Stirred at the soup, shook his head slightly. Then, he changed.

'Why don't you fuck off back downstairs?'

He spun around towards her and Mel felt like she was back in her body, decades before. Being growled at by a different man, in a different place.

'For a moment, I thought you were cool,' Flynn said. 'But you've gone back to being the busybody from downstairs. The old woman with not enough going on in her life.'

Mel snapped back into herself, embarrassed that she was embarrassed by Flynn's words. Old enough to know just how empty and ignorant they were. But still. *Old. Busybody.*

Who do you think you are? Up here, with these people?

She wanted to say something. Something to make her feel strong, especially later when she knew she'd be going over and over this encounter.

'Lori spoke to me, you know,' she said. Her voice was higher, smaller. 'I know a lot more about you than you think.'

'Is that because –' Flynn took one small step towards Mel. It was a tiny distance but it had the effect of him filling her vision. She could feel him again, smell him. '– you've been obsessed with me since I moved in?'

Mel wanted to throw up. It was an immediate, throat-burning feeling. She swallowed, hard. 'Are you threatening me?'

Flynn laughed. 'How am I threatening you? By saying something true, not all that bullshit you're spinning on Facebook about me?'

'I am not saying anything that isn't true. In fact, I wish I was saying a lot more. Lori has gone. You're not telling anyone the truth about what happened. And you don't care.'

'Don't tell me what I care about.'

Flynn's fury was rippling under his skin. He was clenching and unclenching the hand that wasn't tightly gripping his bottle of beer.

The noise drifting down the corridor from the living room was growing louder. Chatter, music, clinking cans, bursts of laughter.

He took another tiny step towards her.

'Why are you up here, anyway? Is this really all about Lori?'

Mel's chest grew tight. She needed to leave. Why had she thought this might help?

'I need to leave. You're not a safe person to be around.'

Flynn laughed again. 'Sure, I'm the bogey man. Lori was an angel. And that makes me the devil. You keep telling yourself whatever you need to believe to get through. I'm sure you've been lying to yourself for years. And to your poor fucking husband.'

His stare was forensic. Like it was stripping something from her.

'Or that old boyfriend of yours. *Dom?*'

Mel shoved past him, towards the front door. She could see Kat, standing at the door of the living room, staring. She looked so powerful. So serene and composed in the centre of this roiling storm.

'Flynn,' Kat called, her eyes on Mel. 'Is that food ready, mate?'

'Almost!' he shouted back. 'Our neighbour's just leaving.'

'Oh, shame.'

Kat kept looking right at Mel.

Mel grabbed the door handle and pulled. Flynn stepped in and leaned to her ear, his voice hot and close.

'You don't know anything. You're so sure Lori told you all about *me*. Well, she told me all about *you*. Don't you think people are watching you, too?'

27

January: Mel

Downstairs, Mel fell through her door and straight into the bathroom to be sick.

Kneeling on the black and white tiles she and Simon had picked out so many years before, delighting in their very adultness – *Look at us, we're choosing tiles and taps and plugs. Look at us, making our little home better. Look at us, renovating.*

Now, a few years down the line, among the half-empty bottles of kids' shampoo, topless toothpaste tubes and almost empty hand-soap, Mel was getting the grooves of these carefully selected tiles embedded in her knees as she knelt over the toilet, her head so close to the ceramic bowl, retching.

It was the seltzer on an empty stomach. It was fear. It was disgust. *What a terrible excuse for a grown-up I am.*

She pulled herself up from the floor, looked in the mirror, the one with the pleasing art deco edges, the one she'd told Simon was worth the extra money he hadn't wanted to spend. 'This is our home,' she'd said. 'Don't you want it to be nice?'

Who was it nice for, now?

Cold water splashed on her tired, lined face. Eyeliner applied in some sort of deluded hopeful state earlier – to look nice for the young people upstairs – now draggy-smudged down her cheeks.

Look at the state of you.

Words thrown at her, so many years before, when everything began to turn with Dom.

It was Bangkok. The weather was so heavy there. Like a hot, wet blanket you were always trying to shrug off. They had a fight about it. About air-conditioning.

By then, Mel had learned to be watchful for the signs that Dom's mood was shifting. The short flashes of anger she'd seen in London, the swelling irritation spilling into cruel words on the Mekong, were still outnumbered by the days she was certain that her person – the man she saw skip with joy on her sister's rainy street the night they met – was perhaps the only one she had ever met who truly saw her, loved her, knew her.

But at the hostel in Chiang Mai, the one between the old town and the new, rooms without air-conditioning were ten dollars a night. Rooms with a fan were a little more. Rooms with full air-con were fifteen dollars.

Mel wanted to spend the extra money. They'd been sleeping on boats and on trains. They'd been sweating into their clothes for days and days. She'd felt like the grime of the road was in every pore and crease of her body, and in every piece of clothing in her bag. The romance of the road, of bumping along beside her beautiful Australian man, falling asleep with her head on his shoulder on buses, at stations, was still tangible. But she also wanted to shower. In private. She wanted to wash all her clothes. She wanted to slip in between cool, clean sheets with damp hair. She wanted a cup of English tea.

The clouds began to roll in as she suggested this to Dom.

'This isn't a holiday,' he'd said at the reception desk of the hostel as they were checking in. 'This isn't a two-week package trip to Ibiza. This is life on the road.'

It was after the deep green bubble of the boat trip, where he'd told her he couldn't live without her. It was after him holding her face in his hands and diligently, softly, kissing every part of her face. 'Because I want to have kissed every inch of you.' It was after he'd licked her until she came, over and over, in a narrow bunk on a rattling train carriage as an unfamiliar world flashed past the windows and she had barely believed this could be her life and that he was in it, telling her she deserved to be honoured like the goddess she was. She had giggled at that, even while it felt so wonderful, so perfect, and pulled him up to her face and kissed him, tasting herself on him, not caring. Loving him and herself, and feeling like any doubt she had was only her insecurity talking, because this man loved her, loved her, loved her.

And here he was, the rain tipping down outside the reception shack of an unimpressive hostel. Morphing, as she watched, from the man who needed to kiss every inch of her face into the man who found her an embarrassment. It was shocking.

'What do you think people think about you?' he'd asked her, too close and too loud. 'When you're whining about wanting air-conditioning, and clean sheets, and tea bags?' His hand around her arm was gripping much harder than it should have been. 'You're embarrassing me.'

'It's just a fan, Dom,' she remembered saying, but tears were coming, because she was confused, and exhausted, and a little bit afraid. Strangers' faces turned to them, curious, uncomfortable. 'It's only two pounds. I can pay for it.'

'*You* can't pay for it,' he said. 'Your money's my money, here. We've been on the road for three weeks. How long do you think we can last if you're going to be a fucking princess at every stop?'

HOLLY WAINWRIGHT

She didn't want to cry in front of strangers. Or in front of this man, who she'd believed, only hours or minutes before, thought she was wonderful. It was the first time she truly felt that poisonous soup of uncomfortable emotions she would become so familiar with over the next few months. *Don't talk to me like that. Please don't stop talking to me. Leave me alone. Please don't leave me.*

Now, eyes closed in front of the art deco mirror, Mel could see herself, as if she were a stranger, standing next to a wooden counter with propped-up signs for banana pancakes and temple tours, a small queue of other grimy travellers straight off the night train behind them. She saw young Mel, looking down at her feet, in those stupid Velcro sandals that were back in fashion again now, seeing her own ugly toes. Her throat had been burning and a man leaning against the wall near the door had been smoking one of those cigarettes that smelled like cloves. His face had been twisted in a smirk. She remembered feeling the straps of her pack cutting into her shoulders and the smell of herself, and that her tears had tasted salty but dusty as they dripped onto her lips. She had felt like she was a woman of power, until that moment when she realised how foolish that was.

'Look at the state of you,' Dom had snapped, and yanked her towards him with that forceful grip. 'You're pathetic.'

Then he'd let go of her arm, but she could still feel his fingers there as he turned back to the counter and paid with the cash he kept strapped under his shirt, along with her passport and her money. Safer that way. Then he'd turned, wearing his huge, battered backpack and walked out of the reception.

Mel remembered pushing the tears away with the flat of her hand. The face of the young woman behind the counter, who smiled at her, but nodded towards the door, keen to move on to the others who needed a bed, needed a fan, needed to hand over their hidden notes.

The room, when she found it, had air-conditioning. But no Dom. Only his pack, discarded on the floor, ripped open, his dirty shirt crumpled next to it, a different one, presumably, pulled out. More tears in the shower. More tears in the damp, smelly washroom as she'd shoved her clothes and his into the giant, rusty washing machines. The sheets, when she'd crawled between them, alone, were scratchy on her skin, the whirr of the fan was loud and no sleep came. At midnight, she'd pulled on a T-shirt and shorts and gone to look for him in the guesthouse restaurant, but it was closed up. He wasn't among the travellers sitting drinking Singha in the courtyard. She went to the gates of the guesthouse and looked up and down the street. So many cafes, so many bars, he could be in any of them. What if he didn't come back? Was that possible? Might he leave her here? Would he do that?

She'd gone back to the room, back to the sheets and the whirr of the air-conditioner and the drone of the mosquitos. She'd felt punished.

Some time as the night crawled towards morning and she lay there, wet with tears, she heard him shove the door open and bump into the room. Her relief was so enormous, so complete, that she'd launched herself from the bed and onto him, into his arms, and he'd pulled her up and around him, and she'd kissed him and kissed him and he'd pushed her up against the wall, and the sex that they had that night, sex that she didn't think she had the strength to have, was, even now, one of the most memorable fucks of her life. Why was that?

Stop it, Mel.

Where are these memories coming from? Mel stared at herself in the mirror. The version of young Mel in her head looked a lot like Lori. Was she getting herself confused with the young woman who lived upstairs? Was that how all this had begun? Why it had gone so very far?

She rubbed away the dark eyeliner with a cotton pad, drank some water, thirstily, straight from the tap, and undid her dress, letting it drop to the floor in a tangled pile. There was no-one else here, she didn't have to keep the bathroom nice.

The unit's silence was familiar to her now; weekends without the kids were no longer a novelty. Mel grabbed her robe from the back of the door and threw it on, walking out through the empty hallway, the door to the kids' room wide open, the darkness signalling its emptiness.

No question, she'd seen Lori stepping where she had stepped, decades before. And it had poked at her, and poked at her, as she'd lain there, listening, night after night. As Lori had drunk her English tea in the kitchen with fingers that trembled slightly as they closed around the mug, eyes that darted with any sudden small noise.

'Were you always like this?' Mel remembered saying to her, one of those afternoons when Lori came downstairs to be with the kids, but stayed a little longer than she needed.

'Like what?'

'Jumpy? Nervy?'

'Am I?' Lori had pushed the comment away, lightly, but her eyes stayed on her tea. 'It's a bit of a nervy time, isn't it?'

But Mel knew.

Now she went to the lounge room, lay down on the couch, her head still swimming. Blurry around the edges. She picked up her phone, scrolling, scrolling.

So many good wishes for Lori. *Wherever you are.*

There was a story on a news site. *Fears grow for backpacker missing in Sydney's eastern suburbs.*

Mel clicked, suddenly very sober.

Lorelai Haring, twenty-one years old, was last seen in Coogee on 6 January. Reports suggest her boyfriend, Flynn Strout, assumed she had gone for a swim at the beach when he woke to find her missing. He sounded the alarm when she hadn't returned home later that day. It's believed all her belongings were left at their Bay Street apartment.

'Lori loved the water, often went to swim at the beach or Gordons Bay early in the morning,' said a friend of the missing girl. Ms Haring, originally from England, had been in Australia for eight months, and was believed to be looking into returning to her family when the borders were closed. 'It's not at all like her to not come home or call,' said the friend. 'She really doesn't know very many people, so it's a bit worrying.'

Which friend was that?

Police say they are following several lines of enquiry, and haven't ruled out either accident or foul play. 'We are talking to everyone who's close to Ms Haring,' said Detective Inspector Gray. 'We're dealing with a transient population in extraordinary circumstances during a pandemic, so we're not discounting anything at this stage.'

Anyone with any information about the whereabouts of Ms Haring is urged to call Crime Stoppers.

Mel put her phone down and swallowed hard.

She copied the link and sent it to Izzy. *It's in the news.*

Of course it is, her sister wrote back, quick as anything. And then. *Why are you awake?*

How to answer? Because these virus-bound summer holidays had begun to feel like a strange hiatus in time, when days and nights were long and blurred. Because she was being haunted by the ghost upstairs and the chain reaction of terrible decisions his arrival had kicked off. Because her kids were at Simon's and she had too much work to do to feel ready to face it. Because she just couldn't seem to tether herself to a time period these days, and kept on slipping back, all the way to Bangkok.

Bit out of it, she messaged back to Izzy. *Strange night.*

You need your kids to come home.

I do. I do. I do.

Mel stood up; time to go to bed. Time to get some sleep and wake up in the morning and get on with making everything more normal again, for Eddie, for Ava. For herself. For Lori.

Mel clicked off the lamp and moved through the darkness towards her bedroom, aware of a pulsing beat from upstairs, the murmur and hoot and occasional thud of people moving around up there.

But as she passed her front door, turning to the bedroom, there was a sudden knock, and a hiss. 'Mel?'

At the very same moment, her phone buzzed in her hand, vibrating, illuminating the hallway.

'Mel?'

It was a number, not a name, and one she didn't recognise. But she knew, immediately, to answer.

'Mel?'

Two young women, saying her name at the exact same time.

On the other side of the door, it was Kat.

And on the phone: 'Mel?'

It was Lori.

Part Three

28

November: Lori

'**W**hat happened to the van? I miss it.'

'I bet you do.'

Lori looked to her right, at Flynn, who said this with a closed-lip smile that made her stomach lurch. He had one hand on the steering wheel of the old Corolla, the other out of the window, tapping on the outside of the car in time to the music – something she didn't recognise. Something she knew she should. It sounded old, and cool. Important.

The moment, like the music, felt like it was from another time. Who loved the messy blast of open windows in the age of air-con? Who drove along with one arm out, like one of the American road-trip movies Lori had absorbed as a kid, lying on her mum's bed when there were people downstairs, mouthing the words to *Thelma and Louise* along with her friends on sleepovers? Those women were her mother's age, her mother's generation. That freedom, even the freedom to drive straight off a cliff, was intoxicating when you were living in a world where the punishments for stepping out of line, even the tiniest bit, seemed so swift. *Posted the wrong thing?*

Liked the wrong thing? Followed the wrong person? Unfollowed the wrong person? Used the wrong word? How embarrassing for you. How basic of you. How dumb. I hope you're ashamed. I hope you're going away now. Lori's chest tightened at the thought, then released, with a big blowy gasp, when she looked ahead at the highway, and to the right, at the man.

'I sold the camper,' he said. 'Got a solid few grand for it from some Irish kids who want to live in it until this shitshow blows over.'

'So whose car is this?' Lori's toes were up against the dashboard, her bum low in the seat. It was exactly how she'd imagined, driving along the highway in a country of wide, open roads. Music playing, handsome man beside her.

'Some mate of Des's.'

Ownership seemed fluid in Flynn's world.

Even the ownership of the unit, the place where Lori lived, was mysterious. There was a woman called Emily who Flynn had known back in Perth. It was her lease, but she was stuck in Victoria. The man who owned the place was her uncle, or cousin, or something, and he was stuck in Norway, or Sweden, or something. The place was in limbo, the people moving through it, too. The car was just another thing that belonged somewhere else, to someone else, that Flynn had picked up and was using as his own.

Lori wriggled her toes, watched the silver toe-rings she'd bought at the moonlight markets back in Broome shimmer and twinkle. She hoped Flynn noticed them, noticed who she was now – the kind of girl who had her feet up on the dash, who wore toe-rings, and had tousled hair in beachy waves. An easygoing girl who didn't care about who owned what, either.

Looking up from her twinkling toes, Lori saw they were driving through trees, trees, trees, on both sides of the highway.

The Corolla had stopped and started through suburbs of Sydney she was sure she'd never seen before, ones that seemed to trickle on forever with their chicken shops and car dealerships and sprawling pubs with neon signs for pokie lounges.

But the suburbs had finally stuttered out, giving way to all this bush, all this green.

'We're nearly there.'

Where, Lori didn't know, but Flynn had told her it was going to blow her mind.

Anywhere with you, Lori thought. Anywhere just us.

They turned at a big green sign for a national park. Lori felt the familiar tiny thrill of seeing yellow road signs with images of koalas, of kangaroos – wildlife on road, be careful. How far from home she was. What a long way she'd come from the signs of her streets – Boots, Oxfam, Ladbrokes – from squirrels and Costa Coffee and *Match of the Day* to this winding road through soaring trees towards the ocean.

It was an ordinary Tuesday afternoon and all the world was doing ordinary Tuesday afternoon things. But Lori was here, pulling into a bush car park with this man, joining the handful of other cars belonging to people who had nowhere to be midweek that would stop them being right here.

'Come on.' Flynn pulled her out of the car by her hand and she giggled into the sunshine. 'Where are we going?'

He reached into the back for a towel, threw it over his shoulder and began to walk, in his five-dollar thongs, towards a scrubby beach path.

Minutes later they were out the other side, on the edge of a huge stretch of glistening blue water, then sand, then the waves of an ocean beach.

'It's a lagoon,' Flynn said, as if that were obvious, as if lagoons were ten-a-penny, basic as hell, and not a word only associated with palm-fringed tropical paradises.

He dropped his towel and launched himself into the water with the confidence of a person who never thought about submerged rocks, sharks, rips, or any of the other things that Lori was trying hard not to consider. Did lagoons have those things?

The clear signal was to follow, and to do so without hesitation or fuss. The girl with the silver toe-rings did not enter the water cautiously, shivering and tentatively placing each foot down with care. The girl with the silver toe-rings ran in and leapt, and didn't even think about the beachy waves she'd put in her hair in the bathroom this morning.

Some days in Broome she'd channelled that version of herself, and here she was again.

The lagoon looked like blue-green heaven and felt like icy slush. As her head hit the water Lori felt the tightness in her chest return for a second. She pulled up, coughing. 'It's freezing!' she said, before she could stop herself.

'It's spring,' Flynn called, from where he was now kicking around on his back, ten metres away. Even from there Lori could see the slight wash of disapproval that crossed his face. 'It makes your fucking neurons fire! Don't be a wuss!'

Lori gulped a big breath of air before she ducked back under to swim towards him.

There was a family on the edge of the lagoon, playing in the shallow water, the mum in a bikini and sarong, kids in sun-safe one-pieces and bucket hats, the dad sitting further up the sand, looking at his phone. The children were too little for school. Lori pictured herself in the mother's swimsuit for a moment, spending her days chasing toddlers around beaches and waving sunscreen in the air. There were two older blokes, over on the far side of the water, fiddling with fishing rods and unpacking sturdy plastic boxes of stuff.

Flynn saw her coming and reached out under the now-cool water to pull her in to him.

'You look perfect here,' he told her, 'like a fucking mermaid.' Lori was certain her smile was wider than her head.

Flynn's fingers slipped inside the pants of her red bikini – the ones her mum had bought her at Marks & Spencer on a grey and rainy, hot chocolate–fuelled shopping afternoon as a going away present – and his fingertips brushed against her while he maintained eye contact, treading water, smiling at Lori like she was an adorable kitten, or a delicious meal – she couldn't tell which.

Lori gasped as Flynn's hand kept moving. She looked around. Was this who the toe-ring girl was? Someone who could have a man's fingers inside her just a few feet away from a toddler rolling around in the shallows, spitting water into the air? She leaned into Flynn, into both his fingers and his lips. Apparently the answer was yes.

'Come on.' His hand was now out of her bikini and he was pulling Lori out of the water, towards the beach and the bush beyond it, the breeze hitting her wet skin and bubbling it into goosebumps. The eyes of the family and the fishermen were searing her as she grabbed at her towel and her dress and was pulled along behind Flynn's confident stride. *They all know where we're going.*

'Flynn, I –'

'Come on. It's Anything Can Happen Day.' He threw a smile back to her as he pulled her up the sand. Soon they were in the dunes, out of sight of the lagoon group but no doubt discoverable by any bushwalker. Lori didn't have time to spread the towel out, as she'd imagined, before Flynn was pushing into her, hot despite the chill of his board shorts and his skin, his mouth, his hands, on her. *My hair*, Lori thought, just before the back of her head hit the sand.

Afterwards, they pulled the towel over themselves, burrowed into the dune. She was now sand, and sand was now her.

'This is like Broome,' she said, her mouth next to his ear. 'Just us. The beach.' Not the flat. Not the friends. Not the mess.

'I like who you are at the beach,' Flynn said.

So you don't like who I am elsewhere? Lori thought. But what she said was, 'Yes, me too.'

He wanted them to wash off the invasive sand in the surf. The waves were small but terrifying enough for Lori, who stayed in the shallows, trying to rinse herself in the saltwater with her feet firmly on the bottom, while smiling and nodding to Flynn, who had ducked under the surf and was swimming with strong, confident overarm strokes beyond the breakers.

Lori waded out of the shallow surf and sat on the towel that, this time, she had spread carefully across the sand. This was better. This was okay. She lay back, feeling the sun burn her goosebumps smooth, listening to the waves.

Sometimes she didn't know what to say to Flynn. There were the conversations they could have about Broome, about meeting, about travelling and the road. She could listen and ask the right questions about his time overseas, about the women he met, who he loved to bring up, as if daring her to show any discomfort or envy when he spoke of them. She didn't. Lori was much too familiar with toe-ring girl for that to happen.

But she didn't talk to him much about her pre-Flynn world, and he didn't ask.

Two people didn't have to be the same to be in love, right? To be compatible? To be happy?

It was better with minimal talking, Lori knew, as she burrowed down a little further in the sand to catch some of its warmth on her back.

Suddenly she felt a spray of rough sand and water. A hand grabbing her wrist and pulling her up.

'We're not sunbathing, princess,' Flynn said, his big hand around her small arm. 'It's Anything Can Happen Day. We're not sleeping through it.'

Lori had a second to grab her dress, the towel, her sandals and to follow Flynn as he headed to the end of the beach where the water lapped up against a path that climbed from the rocky outcrop along the side of the grassy cliff.

'Today,' he said, 'we're going to fly.'

29

November: Lori

On the drive in, Lori hadn't noticed the devastation.

She hadn't clocked the fact that so many of the trees flashing past were black-trunked, hollowed out by fire. She hadn't noticed because, if you looked up, you only saw the comeback, the greenery, the tentative shades of an infant leaf, spreading like a pretty rash across the rough black of the tree stumps. But if you looked down, you saw it. The trees were black, the ground was black. It was a tough job, resurrecting this forest.

She would ask Flynn about the fire – how long ago and how fast and fierce it was – but it was obvious, from the set of his mouth, by the tapping of his fingers on the wheel, by the rolled-up window, he wasn't talking to her.

Not since the cliff.

'Come,' he'd demanded, at the top of the path, standing so close to the edge it made her nauseous.

He had one hand outstretched to her.

'I don't want to,' she'd said. 'I'm afraid of heights.'

The walk up had been long, and hot, and her skin burned and prickled. She'd been trying to keep pace with Flynn, who was bounding up the cliff track barefoot, but she couldn't, and he'd reached the top a good few minutes before her, leaving Lori to appear red-faced and panting.

Then, she waited while she got her bearings and her dignity back, for the sweating to stop, before she approached Flynn. But, also, there was the cliff.

'I'm close to the . . . edge . . .' he sang, doing a wobbly strut right where the rock disappeared into sky and ocean.

'Please, Flynn.' Lori wanted him to step towards her. She did not want to step towards him. 'Come back.'

He outstretched his arm again. 'You come here,' he said. 'I need to show you something, you won't believe it.'

Lori had shaken her head, pulled her arms tight around her, shivering again, from the wet of her swimsuit, the wet of her cotton dress, the wet of her long, bedraggled hair. The wind that was now whipping up around them was cold and bitter.

But Flynn had kept his hand outstretched, with his best smile, full-beam blazing. 'Come on.'

Lori hadn't wanted to. But she did. Reluctantly, stomach churning, she reached out her hand, and took a step, and then another, until she and Flynn were holding hands at arm's-length on the top of the escarpment.

'Do you trust me?' he asked, smiling.

Lori giggled, hoping to deflect whatever was coming.

'Do you?' Flynn's voice got stronger, louder. 'Do you trust me?'

No.

'Yes.' Her voice was small.

Flynn whipped his arm down hard and yanked Lori towards him at the same time, so she rolled and stumbled, winding up coiled in his arm like a tango partner, her face so close to his face, his arm around her chest, tight.

'Do you trust me?' he asked again, except this time his voice was different. Quieter, deeper, firmer.

Lori was looking into his eyes and she was afraid. What was happening? Why was he doing this?

She nodded slowly.

'Let's dip,' Flynn said, and he spun her round his body in a single, sweeping move, and dipped her, like Fred Astaire dipped Ginger Rogers, only over the edge of a sheer cliff face. In thongs.

For a certain, dreadful moment, Lori had felt that she was going to slip, and fall. That Flynn was going to stumble and they would both go spinning in slow motion to the rocks.

'Flynn!' Lori had shrieked. 'Let me go.'

He'd dummy-dropped her, so she slipped through his hands, as if she was going to fall towards the rocks. Lori screamed. Her head was hanging right out over the edge of the cliff, her body contorted into some approximation of a bride's first dance. Both her feet were almost off the ground. The terrible wind snatched at her hair.

'You asked me to let you go,' he hissed into her ear. 'I could have dropped you. But I didn't, did I?'

'Please, Flynn.' Lori was almost whimpering now, but she didn't care. 'Please.'

He laughed, a full-throated laugh, and straightened up, pulling her with him. 'Please what?' he asked, mimicking her voice. 'Is something the matter?'

Feet back on the ground, Lori had twisted away from him and had almost run away, away from the edge, away from Flynn. She was so angry and frightened in that moment, so sick of being a victim and a plaything, that she did the most un-toe-ring-girl thing she could do. She shouted.

'What's *wrong* with you?' she yelled, leaning towards him, her hair in sea-soaked tangles, the sundress she'd chosen so carefully for its length and style and colour just a soaked and patchy sea-rag now. 'Why would you think that was funny? I was terrified. I could have *died*. That was absolute bullshit. You are a *bully*.'

It was the last word that stung him. It flew out of her and hit his face, changing it from an amused, teasing leer to a furious, closed book.

'Please!' She kept going, her heart banging, banging, banging in her chest, her breath in ugly gulps. 'That was horrible. You shouldn't –'

'You need to calm down,' Flynn said, and his voice was calm, authoritative. 'That was nothing. Just a joke.'

'It wasn't fucking funny.'

Lori turned to walk away. Away from him, away from the cliff edge and the fear. But Flynn put his hands on her shoulders, stopping her from moving any further.

'Lori,' he said. And she realised how infrequently she had heard him say her name and how, even here, with the panic rising, it sounded so good in his mouth. 'As if I would have let you fall. I know what I'm doing. Always.'

They had stood there for a minute. His hands on her. She dipped her head. He let her go.

They had walked back down the cliff path. Flynn in front, her behind, trying to get her breath to return to a regular rhythm. She saw herself through the eyes of the family and fishermen as they passed them again, on their way back to the car that belonged to who knew who, toe-ring girl, bedraggled and reduced, walking behind the young man she'd been kissing in the lagoon only a short time before.

Flynn hadn't looked back towards Lori even once. She felt like a scampering puppy, ten steps behind, head down, ragged dress, wet hair.

Now, in the car, travelling through the black trunks of the burnt-out trees, Lori asked herself why she had reacted like that.

Flynn was never going to drop her over a cliff. Flynn loved her. Didn't he?

You're nothing like the cool girl you're pretending to be. You're uptight, afraid, buttoned up. Boring. He hates you now. He's questioning why you're even together. You're not the girl for him. That's what he's thinking right now. He's going to kick you out. Then what are you going to do?

Lori put her head against the window, closed her eyes. Took a deep breath. Then exhaled, ran her hands through her salty hair and twisted towards Flynn, who was driving, staring ahead. Stone.

She leaned forward and put her head in his lap.

He swerved, the tiniest bit. Corrected. 'What are you doing?'

'You know what I'm doing,' Lori said, in the primmest, most English of voices. And she unlaced his stiff board shorts.

30

November: Lori

'**M**ilk? Sugar?'

Mel from downstairs had PG Tips. And she did need a babysitter, after all.

She made a cup of tea just the way Lori's dad used to. Big mug. Bag in, water straight off the boil, steaming hot. It was important that the milk did not touch the bag. Sit to steep until dark and strong. Bag out, splash of milk in. Bag in bin.

'Oh, thank you.' Lori closed her hands around Mel's big mug and cradled it. 'Thank you, thank you.'

Mel had looked at her sideways. 'You don't have tea upstairs?'

'Not proper tea,' Lori said quickly. 'Too many people for good tea bags. Milk's always finished or off. Oh,' she stopped. 'That makes me sound bad.'

'It's alright.' Mel laughed. 'I know. There's a lot going on up there.'

'I hope we're not too noisy.'

Mel shook her head, although it was not necessarily a no. She picked up her mug and motioned for Lori to follow her down the hallway. She was wearing a loose, white, linen button-through dress, the kind that was in the window of the too-expensive surf shop around the corner where Lori had tentatively asked for a job. The dress was a bit nice to be wearing for an afternoon at home with your kids. Was Mel going out later? Maybe she had a date? Maybe that's why she needed a babysitter.

In the living room, the children were staring at a video game they didn't appear to be playing. A man in a box in the right-hand corner of the screen was wearing headphones and shouting. YouTube. Of course.

The kids didn't look up. Mel took the remote control off the coffee table, turned the volume down. The kids looked up.

'Mum!'

'Monsters, this is Lori.'

Two sets of eyes turned her way.

Ava was just like Mel. Wavy dark hair, dark skin, big brown eyes. She looked at Lori the way little girls looked at big girls, with interest bordering on study. Lori knew little girls. If she was kind to Ava, if she was interested, gave her compliments, the young girl would be her champion. Little girls were easy to impress, you just had to notice them.

'You must be Ava! Nice to meet you properly. Gosh, you have beautiful hair.'

Ava's face broke into a big comfortable grin.

Eddie was more circumspect, much less interested in this person blocking his view of the TV. He looked different, too. Fair and pale, unsmiling. He flicked his gaze towards her, returned it to the screen. 'Hi.'

'Not cool, Eddie,' said Mel, crossing in front of them to the big round wooden table in the sunroom. 'Be polite.'

This table, it was clear, was where life happened. Laptop open, kids' scrawl in notebooks, felt-tip pens strewn everywhere, an empty plate with Vegemite smears, two plastic cups. The unit was a perfect copy of upstairs, but scattered with a very different kind of mess.

'Lori is going to look after you sometimes this summer,' Mel said, in a deliberately slow, loud voice, the signal that the kids should be listening to her. 'Daddy's got to go away for a bit, and I've got to work.'

'Dad's going away?' Eddie's attention was caught and he looked at his mum, his eyes narrowed in suspicion. Lori took a sip of her tea and walked around Mel to sit down at the table.

'Just to visit Grandpa, while he can, nothing to worry about.'

'But the borders –'

'Borders, schmorders,' Mel said, and Lori observed the way she stayed loose and relaxed, giving nothing away. 'Grandpa doesn't live that far. And things are fine for now. Put your worry away, Eds.'

What a weird little world for kids, Lori thought. Their normal was so abnormal.

Mel raised her eyebrows at Lori and the kids. 'Worries a lot,' she mouthed to Lori, silently.

Lori nodded, took another sip. *Who doesn't?* she thought. *Smart kid.*

'So, how are things upstairs?' Mel asked, again.

'Good,' said Lori. *Today*, she added, silently. *Good, today.*

'You and Flynn seem happy,' Mel said, in a tone that Lori immediately recognised as the one her mother used when she was fishing for something specific. *Elise seems like a nice girl. You seem to be sleeping a lot lately. You seem to really like that Adam boy.*

'Yes, we are,' Lori said, keeping her smile as light as possible. She raised her mug in a tiny cheers motion. 'Thanks again for the tea.'

'Is he working at the moment?'

'Oh, you know, this and that. Weird times, but he's keeping busy.'

Lori wasn't really sure what it was that Flynn was working at, exactly. Some days he seemed to leave to go to a building site that one of his friends – Des, perhaps, or Rich – was the 'gaffer' for, down at Maroubra. Sometimes he was working in the apartment block that was being gutted just a few doors down from here. What he did on these sites exactly was unclear, undiscussed. But he came back shining with sweat and dust and sometimes with envelopes of actual cash. Other times he gave a pleasing nod at his phone's pinging bank app. It was rare to hear Flynn talk about money, or work, or anything so ordinary, so basic. Which was annoying, really, when someone had to pay for the bread, the milk and the beer. All too often it was her, and her dwindling savings.

She did know that he would like to be doing something else. Something about music, and engineering, and equipment that he would like to be able to afford. Lori heard him talking about that with other people, but never with her. That work, which seemed to rely on gigs and artists and venues and dates, was on and off, on and off, with the unpredictability that was becoming predictable. Living with him for several weeks now hadn't given Lori any firmer impression of his purpose. Only that if he didn't feel like getting out of bed and going to work, he didn't, and no-one seemed to have a problem with that.

'Yeah.' Mel was looking at her. 'Seems that way.'

Lori wasn't sure what Mel wanted from her. Did she want to know if Lori was reliable? Was she fishing to work out her financial status? Sometimes Mel seemed cool. Other times, like now, she seemed irritated, suspicious.

Let's get on with it, thought Lori. 'So when would you like me to start?'

Mel broke her study of Lori's face. 'Simon's dad's really unwell,' she said, in a hushed whisper, her eyes flicking over to the TV-hypnotised kids.

'Simon?'

'Their dad.' Mel looked down at her tea. 'My ex.'

'Oh, okay.'

'We're usually sharing stuff that comes up with the kids, after school, holidays . . . But he's got to go to his dad and so maybe I do need to take you up on your offer . . . Pick the kids up and drop them off from some activities. Maybe give them dinner if I'm working late.'

A job downstairs. Exactly what Flynn told me to do. He's going to be so pleased. Ever since their day at the national park, she'd needed new ways to please him.

Also, hanging out with a couple of kids was going to be easier than scrounging for shifts at the juice bar again.

'Of course,' said Lori, smiling and setting her tea down. 'I'd love to. I think that me and Evie –'

'Ava.'

'Ava.' *Shit, that would cost her.* 'And Eddie, are going to get along great. Don't you, kids?' She threw that last line loudly towards the children, and then quietly, back to Mel, 'Sorry, there was a little girl at the care club I worked at called Evie. She and I were great friends.'

That was almost true. There were about twelve little girls called Evie at the school holiday club, and one of them followed her around and told Lori her shoes were ugly.

Mel nodded once and took a glug from her tea.

'There will be a few rules, of course.'

'Of course.'

'If you're picking them up from school, please don't let them have ice creams, even if they tell you that's what they do every day.'

'Oh, I don't do dairy,' Lori reassured, realising as it came out of her mouth that this was not entirely relevant.

'They do,' said Mel, her gaze steady. 'But still. No ice cream unless I say so. Their dad,' she mouthed the word *dad*, as if, even if the kids were listening, they wouldn't be able to guess who she was talking about, 'gives them way too many treats already.'

'No ice cream.'

'And screen time –'

'Is not allowed,' Lori jumped in, certain she'd got it right this time.

'*Is* allowed,' Mel said. 'But only for half an hour when they get home from school. If you end up doing bedtime, I'll tell you how it works, but they're allowed screen time just before bed.'

Isn't that what every doctor says you shouldn't do?

I should say something about this, thought Lori. *Show that I know stuff, that I'm knowledgeable about kids.*

'Did you hear,' Lori leaned in towards Mel, 'that in Silicon Valley, all the guys who invented iPhones –'

'Don't let their kids touch them, yes, I heard,' Mel interrupted, eye-rolling. 'But the guys who invented iPhones also have French-speaking nannies and housekeepers who do all their domestic labour so excuse me while I don't take real-world parenting advice from those men.'

Lori chuckled, nervously. *Aren't you about to hire me to do your domestic labour?*

'Where did you say you were from?' asked Mel. She was looking at Lori in that intense way again, and Lori remembered this was a job interview. Not a done deal.

'Dorking. It's in Surrey.' It sounded like such a silly word, and so far away. 'Bit different to here, hey? As you know.'

'Do you miss it?'

'Nope.'

'You didn't have to think about that for very long.' Mel was smiling. 'But you will.'

Why were old people so patronising? Did Mel want to argue with her about her own feelings?

'I wanted to come away. Dorking isn't going anywhere.'

'You think that,' Mel said, looking into her tea. 'But if you stay away long enough, it will move on without you.'

'How long have you been here?' Lori didn't really want to get deep with Mel from downstairs. There was a lot to be said for keeping this relationship at arm's-length. She didn't need Mel knowing any more about her than what she was overhearing from upstairs. Even that was too much. Much too much.

'Almost twenty years.' Mel looked up again. 'Long time now.'

'Did you always know you were staying?'

Mel shook her head. 'Life happened. But I love it. If my sister lived round the corner, I would never even think about home. There's nothing else I miss.'

Home. After decades and a family made here, that's still what Mel called the place she grew up.

'Only PG Tips,' said Lori.

Mel smiled. 'You can get them here now. World gets smaller every day. Until, of course, this happened,' she gestured around, sweeping hands that Lori knew took in viruses, borders, grounded planes. 'Doesn't your mum miss you?'

'Pardon?'

'Travelling. Being so far away. Doesn't your mum miss you?'

The kids in the next room shifted a little. They had been listening, Lori could tell.

'Well, yes, she does,' said Lori. 'But she also wants me to live my life.'

Mel snorted. 'She does not.'

'I think she does.'

'She has to say she does,' said Mel, and her demeanour had changed, she was leaning forward, animated. 'Just like my mum did.

But she doesn't mean it. She would like it a lot better if, during a global pandemic, you were upstairs in your room, where she can see you and feed you and know that you're safe.'

An image of Jools watching *Countdown* with her nan in that little blond-brick terrace came into Lori's mind. 'I think she's okay with it.'

Mel smirked. Lori decided it was time to go. She drained the last of the delicious, hot, strong tea.

'Your mum probably also isn't wild about Flynn,' Mel said.

'Oh, she doesn't know about Flynn.'

'She does.'

'Mel, I'm sorry, but I don't think this is –'

'She knows there's a love interest, believe me. Why else would a young woman decide she's going to strand herself on the other side of the world from everyone who knows her, for God knows how long, with a virus on the loose?'

Jesus. 'That's not how it is.' Lori's face was getting hot. 'I just don't want to go back.'

'Would you want to go back if it wasn't for . . .' Mel pointedly looked upwards.

'With all respect,' Lori said, digging deep for a smile, 'you don't know me, Mel.'

The little girl, Ava, was suddenly standing next to her mum. 'Mum, you sound a bit rude.'

'Do I?' Mel laughed, reached out to stroke her daughter's hair and then looked back at Lori. 'Sorry, Lori, I don't want to sound like the worst kind of old lady.'

'Oh, no, you –'

'I just see a lot of myself in you,' Mel rushed on. 'I've been a bit homesick lately, and I'm projecting.'

Ava was crawling onto her mum's knee and sitting down. She was a bit too big to do that, but maybe she was used to being her mum's comforter.

Lori was still shaking, just a little, from saying what she said. *You don't know me, Mel.* It had flown out of her mouth.

'Do you have brothers and sisters?' Mel was resting her head on her daughter's now, softer.

'A brother.' Her brother's face, big smile, sad eyes.

'Do you miss him?'

'Not really, he's doing medicine in London. Our parents are doctors. It's kind of . . . expected.'

'And you?'

'Not interested,' Lori said. 'I didn't get that gene.'

'Girls can be doctors,' said Ava. 'Girls can be anything.'

Lori laughed. 'Yes, Ava, they can. But I don't want to be a doctor.'

'So what do you want to be?' It was the little girl again, fixing her big brown eyes on Lori with curiosity.

The laugh was still in Lori's mouth.

'Right now,' she said, 'I want to be your babysitter.'

*

Outside Mel's door, in the cool hallway, Lori added up the number of dollars the hours she'd just agreed to would get her. It wasn't bad. She wouldn't need to ask Flynn to pay for anything for a little while, which was ideal. The fewer ripples the better.

The front door opened as Lori started on the first steps up to Flynn's apartment.

The fresh breeze from the street carried in a young woman's voice. 'I know. It's crazy here, too.'

The voice was familiar, but it took Lori a moment to place it. Long car rides. Fish and chips by the water. That hostel, in the dark, adrenaline pumping.

'Kat?'

It was her. Dropping the phone from her ear, looking up at Lori. 'Oh, hi. Of course, Lori.'

Kat looked different. Her hair was shinier, smoother, redder. She was wearing clothes that weren't for sitting in cars all day. Fitted, smooth colours that showed every mark. Kat was dressed as if she belonged, not like she was passing through.

'This is such a weird coincidence.' Lori had forgotten, but was quickly remembering, how Kat didn't rush to fill a silence, didn't hurry to make anyone feel comfortable. 'I live here. What are you . . . what about you?'

Kat flipped her hair over her shoulder. 'Visiting an old friend. He lives here, too.'

'Flynn?'

The way Kat looked at Lori then – her gaze steady, her shiny mouth just ever so slightly turning up at the edges – made Lori feel like there was something that she didn't understand. A joke she was missing.

'Flynn.'

Lori's stomach started its familiar churn. Of course. *Of course.* Perth. Rob. They were all from the same place. A city that was really just a big country town.

'That's wild,' she said, her voice flat. 'I'm with Flynn.'

Kat's turned-up smile broadened. 'Oh, yes. The shirtless guy from Broome.' Her tone didn't match the smile, unless the smile was mocking. 'I should have guessed.'

'Come on up.' Lori motioned. 'I have keys.'

'Great.'

Kat stepped past Lori on the stairs and started climbing, her long strides leading the way. Lori found herself following along behind, two steps to every one of Kat's, her door key jangling its quiet power in her pocket.

'Oh look,' said Kat, at the top, her hand pushing the door. 'It's unlocked.'

And she walked right in.

31

November: Mel

'**M**um's home!' Mel had pushed the door open with her shoulder, arms full of bags.

It was Lori's voice, as it so often was now. Signalling loudly for the children to stop what they were doing, and make a fuss of Mel.

Back in the office was a thing. After months and weeks of everybody doing their desk jobs just as well from the desks in their actual homes, it felt pointless, punishing, to waste two hours a day getting to and from a place where you sat down, took your computer out of your bag and did what you'd been doing at home the day before. Even the foyer's posters, huge pop-art representations of health and vitality befitting a company that sold vitamins, felt oppressive, hanging above thin trickles of masked, resentful workers.

'It's bullshit,' Mel had told Izzy, phone pressed to her ear on her walk back from the bus stop.

'I thought you hated working from home,' Izzy replied, not unreasonably.

'I do not!'

'You told me you miss people, and brainstorming, and lunch from the cafe downstairs. The kids are always around. You miss the separation of work and home. You miss the different identities you can adopt in each physical space.'

'Izzy, am I not allowed to be complicated?'

'You're allowed to be insufferable. I'm just keeping receipts.'

'*Someone's* been listening to the way the kids talk,' Mel huffed. 'I just hate getting the bus. I forgot about standing up all the way home.'

'You're forty. Drive a car.'

'That's deeply stereotypical and offensive.' Mel knew Izzy would pick her tone of mock outrage. Not something you could count on for everyone, anymore.

'Okay,' Izzy was almost yawning now. 'Sounds to me like you just want to complain.'

'What's your point?'

Now Mel pushed open the door to her flat with the weight of the day on her back. The company she worked for was grappling with a sticky storm around their 'wellness' brand. Mel was paid to convince people to take supplements to improve their health. But in pandemic times, they were walking a fine line of separation from the anti-science brigade, the wellness warriors, the food-is-medicine people. It meant vigilance and caution around every message, every meeting, every piece of communication.

Until Eddie was born, if you'd asked Mel what she did for a living, she would have said, 'I work in events'. Parties and launches and festivals and conferences – Mel was great at them. She knew how to listen to the ill-informed rambling of a C-suite manager who was certain they had the answer for how their company party, launch, conference should look, feel and taste.

She knew how to nod and smile and realise what was actually possible on a budget that was always, always tighter than the aspirations. She knew how to hit deadlines and plan schedules and find the right people to make the results of hours of negotiation and slog look easy, effortless, simple. Mel had no idea how she knew how to do all that, but Izzy did. Her sister's theory was that it was part innate – that Mel's hand-me-down dolls were always going to the most fabulous parties – but that it was also a control mechanism, that when they were kids 'making things nice' and 'smoothing things over' those were the tactics little Mel used to cement her role in the family and make life easier for Liz, a mother being pulled in many directions, with very little help. If Izzy was the sensible one who remembered it was Nana's birthday, Mel was the one who plotted how to celebrate. Even at ten. 'Nana loves biscuits. We should get everyone to give us 10p to buy a giant tin of McVitie's and then lay them all out in a big love heart.'

Of course, Mel's stoic Nana Nina said she thought this was a terrible waste, but Mel noticed the secret smile she gave Liz, the tiny tick of approval. Making things nice for people made them happy, and Mel had wanted everyone to be happy. 'Your curse,' Izzy called it.

Then she'd fallen into a career that suited her perfectly. Those early days in Sydney. Licking her wounds after Dom. Deciding whether to stay or go. Needing work. A friend of a friend was a caterer. Wanted to make a good impression at a wedding for an artist friend of another friend who had impeccable taste but no money.

If Mel thought about that wedding now, she wondered how the hell she'd had the guts, the confidence, to say yes, she would do that. How she'd thought it was perfectly reasonable to experiment and wing it through a day two people would remember for the rest of their lives.

She had no experience then, no contacts, no spreadsheeted budget. But she did remember standing at the back of the room at the end of that wedding, more than a little bit drunk and extremely relieved that there were now only minutes, rather than hours, left when things could go wrong. A feeling of calm rising from her toes upwards as it became clear that nothing terrible had happened, and actually it had been rather fabulous, and people complimented her on pulling off something unexpected. Her caterer friend had recommended her for an events job at a venue in Kensington that wanted to attract 'young people' to celebrate birthdays, weddings and parties in their cavernous warehouse space, and almost without realising it was happening, Mel had something like a career. And she'd stayed.

Then she met Simon and she'd kept on staying, and kept on jumping around between events companies, working evenings and weekends, until her first pregnancy wrought her so sick and tired that looking at sample menus made her stomach churn. Eddie arrived, and never slept and rarely ate, and for a while her life became as small as the rooms she paced around, patting a colicky baby's back.

It was clear that 'events' weren't compatible with tiny children. In fact, almost no work was.

What Mel had needed was a job that played to her strengths but didn't require stupid hours or involve crises over the wrong-coloured crockery or a tipsy MC saying the wrong thing to the wrong crowd.

So she studied, with Simon's vocal support, and by the time Ava was almost one, Mel was newly qualified and talking to people about jobs 'in marketing'.

Seven years later, it was in Mel's job description to convince as many different kinds of people as possible that they needed the vitamins and tonics and detoxifying potions that she spent all day selling. But the virus had brought with it an awkward friction, one that was giving Mel a headache as she pushed herself against the door and into her apartment.

Lori almost knocked her over as she barrelled down the hallway to the kitchen, carrying a couple of sauce-smeared plates.

'Hi Mum!'

I'm not your mum.

Lori put the plates down near the sink and turned, smiling. 'How was it today?'

'It was fine.' Mel managed to return the smile.

'Kids have been great,' said Lori. 'I only let Eddie have twenty minutes of Minecraft when we first got home.'

'Thank you, not an easy task.'

'Hi Muuuuum!' came Ava's sing-song voice from down the hall, along with the sound of canned laughter from the TV.

'They're having a bit of Funny Fails time,' Lori said. 'But I gave them dinner. Sausages.'

'Thanks.'

Mel and Lori stood for a moment in the kitchen, Lori's Birken-stock-ed foot jiggling, clearly impatient for something. 'I have to go,' she said, after the silence clocked over a beat or two too long. 'I'm planning something special for Flynn tonight.'

Mel could tell Lori wanted to elaborate. 'Oh?'

'I'm packing him an English picnic and we're going to have it on the cliffs.'

Mel had a vision of white-bread cucumber sandwiches cut into little triangles, crusts off. She imagined one, slightly limp, hanging in Flynn's thick, blunt fingers.

'Strawberries and cream?'

'How did you guess?' Lori flashed her full-beam smile, her whole body vibrating slightly with anticipation.

Dorking. That's how I guessed.

'And I'm going to make gin and tonics in a little flask.'

'Take a lemon.' Mel nodded towards the fruit bowl, where tiny flies buzzed around the apples Ava and Eddie weren't eating. 'You should go, I'll get the kids sorted out.' *Bath and bed. No clifftop cocktails for me.*

'I just wondered . . .' Lori looked sheepish. 'Could you pay me?'

Shit, thought Mel, *haven't I paid you?*

'I know we said end of week, but it would be really helpful to me if we could make it a little more regular.'

'Of course.' But Mel was irritated. Even the tiny act of finding her phone and opening the bank app and finding Lori's code felt like another bloody job, an imposition, when she'd agreed to do it once a week, on a Friday.

Lori didn't move, just nodded, smiling.

Mel rummaged around in her bag for her phone.

'Mum!' It was Ava again. 'Are you coming?'

'You could come here, darling,' Mel shouted back, as brightly as she could manage. 'And say hello to me and goodbye to Lori.'

'I think Flynn's going to love it,' said Lori. 'I think we need a little bit of time doing something special together.'

Despite herself, Mel's eyes flicked up to Lori's. 'Things okay up there?'

'Oh yes.' Lori's eyes moved away just as quickly. 'We've just got a guy on the couch and a lot of visitors.'

'I know.'

Lori was moving now, eager to get off to her picnic, almost skidding down the hall to wave at the kids and grab her tiny canvas backpack. It was familiar to Mel, this fluttery panic. It brought it back to her, in an unsettling rush. Never feeling safe. Never feeling enough.

'Hey, Lori.' The young woman was on her way back down the hall and out of the door. 'Enjoy your picnic. It's very thoughtful of you, I hope Flynn appreciates it.'

Lori looked at Mel as she pulled the door open. 'Thanks. He will.'

Like hell he will, thought Mel.

32

November: Mel

The banging on the door woke Mel at 1.56 a.m.

It took a few hazy moments of half-consciousness to mentally tally the things that usually woke her and pick which one it was this time.

A sudden surge in noise from upstairs? One of the children, calling out in a tone that could mean fear or sickness, bad dreams or buzzing insects? A spike in her own anxiety about work, money, Simon? Dom's ghost? Hot legs?

No. It really was someone knocking at the door. Banging. Loud, fast, urgent. Mel rolled over, looked quickly at her phone to see the time. Shit. Whoever that was, they were going to wake up the kids. *Shush*.

'Coming!' she shout-hissed as she fell out of bed and grabbed her robe that was – for once – hanging where it was supposed to be, on the hook near the door.

Bang. Bang. 'Stop it. *Coming!*'

'Muuuum?' Ava's voice. Shit. Shit.

'It's okay, baby, just someone at the door. Just getting to it.'

'Muuum.'

'Hold on, hold on.'

Ava's call turned into a wail.

'Coming, coming!'

To the knock. To the kids. *Coming*.

Hold on. Who the hell *was* that?

Mel couldn't ever remember having used the old-fashioned peephole in the door of her apartment in the ten years she'd lived here. Those things had a creepy, horror-movie vibe and there wasn't a single time she'd thought about it without picturing her eye finding another eye on the other side. However, this seemed like the moment to test that phobia. Mel leaned in, and the fish-eye view of the hallway revealed Lori's face, close, very close, pink and white, tear-streaked, straining.

'Lori?'

Mel opened the door and Lori fell through it, onto her.

'Lori, what the hell?' Mel's arms were full of the girl. She was hot, alarmingly so. And she was slightly damp, the short, white jumpsuit she was wearing sticking to her skin. She looked up at Mel, her wet face flushed and shining and her breath, hot and fast, smelled of alcohol. Gin.

'I called you,' Lori said in a slurry tumble. 'I called you and called you.'

'Muuuuum?' Ava's voice had escalated to something like a scream. And then Eddie's voice. 'Mum, I'm scared. Mum!'

'Stay there! It's all fine. Lori's just not well. I'm looking after it. Everything's fine.'

Mel called this behind her as she tried to pull Lori away from the open front door and the kids' bedroom.

'Come on, Lori, let's get you in here.' Mel pushed the front door closed with one hand and pulled Lori under her other arm. 'Come *on*, Lori.'

'I called you,' Lori said again. Her voice was slow, thick, wet.

'I was asleep.'

Everything about this moment was nuts. Mel felt like she was observing the story she would tell Izzy later. A middle-aged woman in a Sussan knock-off kimono shushing her frightened children as she tried to drag a semi-conscious young woman down the hallway towards the family room. The girl's long, bare legs trailing while two small kids sat up in their bunks, calling for their mother. For fuck's sake. She had to get up in a few hours.

Finally, in the living room, Mel managed to half-drop, half-throw Lori onto her couch and crouch beside her. 'Lori, are you . . .?' Feeling Lori's hot breath on her face, Mel remembered the virus, and pulled her kimono over her nose and mouth.

'Lori,' she said through the thin cotton, as the young woman's eyes blinked open and closed, and her mouth moved noiselessly. Jesus.

'Lori. Are you sick? Have you taken something?'

Lori let out a long breath, lifted her head ever so slightly off the pillow and opened her eyes wide. 'I couldn't call my mum.'

'Mum.'

'Mum.'

Mel turned to the door. It was Ava. Of course. And Eddie. Of course.

'Mum. What is it? Is Lori okay? Is everything okay?'

What was the right thing to do in this moment? Was it to call an ambulance? Was it to get her kids away from this distressing sight and back to bed? Was it to make sure Lori wasn't going to choke here on the couch? Was it to march upstairs, which was, Mel only now noticed, unusually silent, and demand to know what had happened?

'I wanted to call my mum.'

The kids first. That was the first right thing, as long as Lori wasn't dying, and it didn't seem like she was, this minute. But if she could kind of tip Lori onto her side . . .

As Mel started to roll Lori onto her side, Eddie appeared beside her. And so Mel found herself and her nine-year-old son pulling at a near-unconscious twenty-one-year-old on the lounge she and Simon had bought with the baby bonus they'd banked when Eddie was born. Yet another scenario she'd never imagined when they'd stood arguing about beige versus brown on the garish showroom floor of Fine Enough Furniture.

'What's wrong with her?' asked Eddie, as Mel stuffed pillows at Lori's back to stop her rolling. It seemed like Eddie was always clear-eyed, even at 2 a.m. with a limp invader in his family apartment. 'Is she going to be alright?'

'Yes,' Mel said automatically. 'She'll be fine, she needs to rest. Let's get you and Ava back to bed. I'll make sure she's okay.'

'Why is she here?' Eddie asked as they walked back to the doorway where Ava was standing, her hands over her mouth, her eyes wide, like an artist's impression of a shocked person.

'She knows it's safe here,' said Mel, not knowing where that came from. She knelt to pick Ava up. Ava was too big to be carried, and it made standing up again difficult, but Eddie steadied her and the three of them moved slowly back down the hallway, towards the bedroom, like one bulky, clumsy ship.

Mel heard her steps echoed by another pair of feet, walking down the hallway upstairs. Ghost feet. Instinctively, as she turned into the kids' room, Mel looked at her front door to make sure the latch was down. It was.

It was 2.34 a.m. when Mel came out of Ava and Eddie's room, after spending a few minutes lying awkwardly between the kids on the double lower bunk, stroking Ava's head, whispering to Eddie, assuring them both of things she had no idea were true.

'Does she have the virus?'

'Is Lori drunk?'

'Is she going to die?'

'Did someone do something to her?'

They were all reasonable questions from her children, really. And Mel's answers were the ones any mother gives. A mixture of white lies and half-truths and hopeful stabs in the dark.

'I really don't think so.'

'Maybe.'

'No.'

'No, no-one wants to hurt Lori.'

Finally, they drifted close enough to sleep for Mel to leave them and tiptoe out of the room to check on the status of the babysitter.

But something stopped Mel as she left the bedroom and passed the front door. The bone-tired exhaustion she'd felt on the kids' bed, the prickling anxiety rolling in her stomach, all stopped, just for a moment, as she stood next to the door and heard – no, felt – a person on the other side. Mel found herself leaning in towards the tiny round golden peephole.

And as the blurry hallway came into view, a slow creak made Mel freeze, and she looked down to see the door handle being pushed down from the other side, tested, tried, and clicking against the lock. Mel jumped back from the door, afraid that the person trying to open her front door could see her.

Shit. That's why peepholes were creepy bullshit, and this was why troubled young women shouldn't bang on your door at 2 a.m.

The sound of Mel stepping back and away from the door must have startled the person on the other side, too, because the handle snapped back into place the moment Mel's foot hit the floorboard.

Mel, sensing a retreat, quickly leaned in to look through the cursed bloody spyhole. All she saw was the swing of some long, dark hair, and the flash of a blue dress, and the back of a woman moving down the hallway, towards the front door and the warm, soupy night.

33

November: Mel

Seven thirty and the ghost hadn't floated downstairs to check on the whereabouts or wellbeing of his girlfriend.

Even the kids thought this was weird.

At the table in the sunroom, Eddie and Ava were picking over toast and Vegemite, a pale and drowsy Lori still on the lounge under a blanket. Embarrassed but not making any moves towards leaving.

Ava went and stood in front of her with a piece of green paper, edged with felt-tipped daisies.

'I made you a list of how to get better,' Ava was saying. 'Number one: hugs. Mum's hugs always make me feel better when I'm sick.'

Mel put a hand on her daughter's head as she passed with the breakfast plates.

'Number two: orange juice. Dad says Vitamin C can cure anything. Even monster bites.'

Lori gestured weakly with the glass of OJ Mel had given her ten minutes earlier.

'Number three: exercise. Dad says moving your body –'

'Okay, okay.' Mel had put the plates down, was at Ava's back. 'Time for a bit less of Dad's coaching wisdom. Go and eat some breakfast please, Ava.'

'Number four: healthy food.'

'Go.'

Lori smiled but didn't make eye contact. Mel looked at the time. She had about forty-five minutes before she had to start work. She sat down on the couch, and Lori moved her legs to make just enough space.

'Lori, what happened last night?'

Lori's face was pasty beneath her tan. There were pink half-circles under her eyes, smudged with wispy black flecks of that mascara that made your lashes longer. Extending but not tear-proof, clearly.

'I think I just had too much to drink,' she said, her voice small.

'You think?'

'Gin and tonics were too strong, obviously.' She tried to smile and cast her eyes upwards, signalling to Mel that this was a little, silly thing.

Mel was tired. Her plate was full. She didn't need another human's wellbeing on her list. But Lori was still here. She hadn't crept back upstairs in embarrassment or retreat.

'Lori, you were frightened when you came down here.'

Lori didn't say anything to that. Pursed her lips and shook her head very slightly.

'You were. That's why you were banging on my door at two in the morning. That's why,' Mel pulled her phone out of her robe's pocket, 'I have about eight missed calls from you. And it's hard not to notice that Flynn hasn't come looking for you this morning.'

'I'm sure he's calling me,' Lori said, looking around. 'I just don't know where my phone –'

'I think he knows you're here.'

The kids, just a few steps away at the round dining table in the sunroom, were eating their toast in front of iPads. The sunlight was pouring through the front window, even at this hour. Birds were squawking, bus brakes were squealing on the corner. The day was getting into full swing. But this young woman looked frozen on Mel's couch.

'You know,' said Mel, dropping her voice to a level that slipped just under the sound from the iPads. 'You remind me a lot of me, when I was young. I went travelling with my first proper boyfriend, my first love. He loved me, I know. But,' she chose her words carefully, aware the kids were close, 'he didn't always seem to like me that much.'

Lori made eye contact, then quickly looked down again.

'We fought a lot. Little things I did seemed to make him furious.' Mel sucked in her breath. Just talking about this made her chest tighten, even now. 'I thought that's what love was. But . . .' What to say? 'Really, it just made us both pretty unwell.'

'Flynn's not like that,' said Lori, her voice a little stronger. 'We're not like that. I just drank too much last night and made a bit of a fool of myself.'

'And you ran away down here because . . .'

'I don't know. I was drunk. I just lost it.'

Okay. The kids had finished breakfast. Mel had to get them moving, or they would never get to school, and she would never make her first meeting about the new ad script. Today was going to be hard enough after only three hours' sleep.

She felt a surge of irritation. At Lori and at herself. Why was she offering up pieces of her story to this young woman who clearly had no interest in hearing it? Who had no idea what it cost Mel to share these memories? Who was refusing to learn from Mel's mistakes? Why were young people so self-obsessed?

'Okay. Lori, I just have to tell you then, it's not really okay to come down here and bang on the door at 2 a.m. because you're drunk. It was scary for the kids.'

'I know.' Lori's eyes started to fill up again. 'I'm sorry. I shouldn't have –'

'I'm not saying I'm not going to help you if you need me, of course. But –'

'Thank you. I'll be more careful.'

There was a silence but for the pinging of video games and the squealy thrum of an unboxing soundtrack.

'I know you don't want to talk about it, Lori, but I'm just going to ask you three things before I get on with my day.'

Lori nodded.

'You don't have to answer, just think about them.'

Again, a little nod.

'First – are you sure that was just booze last night? Because you seemed pretty out of it. Second – why didn't your boyfriend look after you when you were . . . upset? And third – why did a young woman with dark hair try to get into my place last night, looking for you?'

Lori looked up. 'What?'

'She didn't knock, but I saw her. Why her, and not Flynn? Just think about those things before you go upstairs and pretend that everything's okay.' Mel stood up. 'I've got to get ready. And get the kids ready. Why don't you lie there while we do all that, then you can have a shower and clean up in peace if you want.'

'Thank you. Thank you so much. I promise this won't happen again.'

'I do have one more question for you,' said Mel, taking the orange juice glass from Lori's hands.

'Go on, then.' Lori smiled.

'Why don't you look into going home? Last night you said you wanted to call your mum, and you couldn't. Maybe, with all that's going on in the world, it's time to go back to Dorking.'

Mel's words stayed in the air for a moment, before she looked over at the table. 'Come on, you two. Tech off. Teeth!'

'You didn't go home,' said Lori.

Mel didn't want to think about the last time she saw Dom, but the memory barged in, elbows out, conjured by her clumsy attempts at counselling Lori.

A bedsit in Wollongong. She had found him there, after his mum, Gina, had called Mel. 'I think he's having a bad time,' she'd said. 'I can't get there before the weekend, but could you?'

It had been about three months after Mel and Dom had broken up. Again. About a year since that day in the arrivals hall, when Dom was the triumphant returning traveller, bringing his English girl back to begin a fresh chapter in a life full of promise. Almost two years since Mel had poured him that beer.

Mel had caught the train to Wollongong, an hour or so south of Sydney. By that time she was sharing a house in Coogee, tentatively figuring out what a life in Australia without Dom looked like. She was bruised, tender, stepping through her heartbreak with caution. Gina's call felt like a little landmine, fatal to recovery. But there was no way she could refuse. No way she could say, 'Thank you for telling me, but I don't think I can help Dom anymore.' Her misery and happiness were still intertwined with his. So, she'd gone to him.

Mel remembered the wait on the platform at Central Station. It was June, it was cold. She didn't have a proper coat yet, because she'd come to Australia thinking it was always warm, always golden, like on *Neighbours*. The wind was whipping around her as she'd got off the train at an unfamiliar station, and she'd felt exposed, vulnerable, as she'd climbed into a cab with the address Gina had given her written on a piece of paper, scrunched in a pocket of her skinny jeans.

The taxi smelled of cigarettes, as if the driver smoked between paying customers, and the cab had one of those thick plastic shields between the back and front seats, the kind that were there to protect the driver from violent passengers but, actually, would be perfect for these pandemic times. She'd had to shout through the barrier to tell him where to go, and, she discovered when she walked back later, he had taken her the long way.

Dom was staying in an old brick terrace with a crumbling, rendered facade, and when she'd pressed the buzzer to flat six, her stomach had been flipping, like it always did when she knew she was going to see him. Maybe, despite every scrap of evidence to the contrary, things would be different. Perhaps Dom would be in excellent form, in gregarious, cheerful form, and he would be so delighted to see her, he would pull her into a kiss and tell her that he needed her in his life. And this time things would stay that way. Mel swimming in the glow of Dom's adoration and approval, Dom allowing her to love him back. Dom loving her exactly as she was.

Of course she had known, as she pressed the buzzer, that wasn't what was going to happen. Over the course of two years, a pattern had been established that was not about to miraculously change direction. Sunshine and storms. Adoration and fury. *It's the hope that kills you*, Mel's dour Lancastrian grandmother had always said. And she was right.

Dom had buzzed her in and he'd opened the chipped wooden door at the top of the stairs and stood there, trying to smile. He seemed thinner and paler than when she'd seen him last.

'My mum said you were coming,' he'd said, and he didn't sound happy, but he didn't sound sad either.

'I tried to call you,' Mel had said, as she reached the door. 'You didn't call me back.'

Dom had shrugged. 'Didn't look at the phone. I don't want to be a slave to that thing.'

She had hugged him because she couldn't not. Couldn't not put her arms around his waist and bury her head in his familiar shirt – a checked lumberjack flannel he'd bought in London at one of those cheap warehouse places where everything was discounted, if you were prepared to dig through mountains of what you didn't want to find one little scrap of something you did. They'd done that together, laughing and eye-rolling and feeling guilty about just how these cheap clothes could be so very cheap.

Mel remembered that Dom had smelled musty. Not dirty, not fresh. And that his arms, when they closed around her back, had held her loosely, politely, without urgency. 'It's good to see you,' she'd said. 'I was worried.'

'Don't worry about me,' he'd said, flatly. 'I'm not worth worrying about.'

It was an infuriating response from someone who Mel had spent almost two years thinking about every second of the day. Whose wellbeing was so linked to hers that she couldn't sleep without knowing he was sleeping, couldn't eat without knowing that he was full. If he wasn't worth worrying about, what was she? The person who loved him? If he was worthless, she was worse.

'Shut up,' she'd said into his chest, into his limp embrace. 'I will always worry about you.'

He'd stood aside to let her in, and immediately she could tell that a woman lived here, too. There was a mattress on the floor that had been cheered up with a brightly coloured Aztec bedspread and too many cushions. There were jars with burnt-down incense stubs balancing on the edges. There were neatly piled dishes by the tiny sink, a hairbrush and an apricot scrub-cleanser on the shelf above it. Dom's bag – the same battered holdall he'd brought from London, the same one they'd hauled on and off buses and boats and planes and trains – was at the foot of the bed, spilling his familiar, faded clothes onto the floor.

'Whose place is this?' she'd asked, standing just inside the doorway in her inadequate jacket and her imitation Adidas trainers.

'A friend's,' Dom had said. He sat down on the only place to sit other than the mattress – a two-seater, leather-look lounge that was peeling on the armrests. In front of it was a coffee table – wiped clean, but scattered with half-drunk teacups. 'She's at work.'

'And what are you doing while she's at work?'

I was so young, Mel thought now. *I had no idea what I was dealing with. Gina should never have sent me there.*

Dom had gestured at the teacups. 'Just hanging out,' he said calmly, although with just enough edge that it was clear the question irritated him. 'Trying to figure out my next move.'

'Your next move?'

'Thinking of getting a job on a boat.' Dom had looked at his bitten fingernails. 'Import–export. Guys are always looking for skippers.'

This diminished man in front of Mel was not talking his way onto a boat. Was not finding his sea legs. He was not skippering anything. This man couldn't finish a cup of tea.

'Your mum's worried about you,' Mel had said, shifting from foot to foot in the doorway. 'She thinks you should go home to Grafton so she can take care of you. She thinks . . .' *Careful, Mel, you've been here before.* 'You're having a bad time.'

Dom smiled. But it wasn't a good smile. It was the smile he'd given her more than once when he found what she was saying ridiculous, naive, patronising. His mood was shifting.

'Everyone's so worried,' he said. 'It's so *nice* of you.'

'Dom, I –'

'My mother and my ex getting together and talking about my mind behind my back. So *supportive*. So *kind*.'

Mel remembered that, even then, talking to this barely there man in another woman's bedsit, the word 'ex' felt like a wasp sting.

'It's not like that.'

'Oh? What is it like, Mel?' Dom had asked. 'What is it like now you've washed your hands of me? Having gone back on every promise you ever made me. What is it like?' The words were awful but his tone was worse – loud, but completely flat and emotionless.

'That's not what happened, Dom, you know that.' Mel's butterflies had turned to stones.

'I *don't* know that,' Dom said. 'I only know when everything was good you were there, and as soon as things got difficult, you ran. You ran like a toddler. You *toddled* away from your childish fantasy.'

Dom had selected words that would particularly pain her. The childish fantasy that she had shared with him, that her destiny didn't lie in her hometown but came in the form of love from far away. A bullshit idea of destiny she had decided Dom embodied. She knew there was no truth to what he was saying. She hadn't run away from anything. Them being apart hadn't been her choice but his, over and over.

But Mel was battle-weary enough to know not to argue with his version of events.

'Why are you down here?' she said. 'Away from the people who care about you?'

'Who says I'm away from people who care about me?' Dom replied, quickly. And then he rubbed his eyes, and yawned. 'I'm staying with someone who loves me.'

'*Loves you*? How long have you known her?'

'You're jealous and petty.' Dom was looking at her steadily now, through his tired, hooded eyes. 'Did Mum really tell you to come?

Or did you just hear about Bridget and decide you couldn't help yourself? You couldn't let me be happy.'

'Dom, you know your mum told me, she told you she did. I had no idea about Bridget.' *And you don't seem happy.*

'You and my mum are two witches muttering over a bubbling pot,' he'd said. 'And your spells have been fucking with my head for too long.'

'Now that's just cruel.'

'I am cruel. When the person you love most in the world abandons you, you get meaner.'

'Dom,' Mel had said, through tears now. 'Please stop.'

'I can't just stop, Mel,' he'd said, his teeth gritted. 'Not like you, who stopped caring about us when it was no longer convenient. Not like *Gina*, who stopped wanting me around, cluttering up her new life.'

Mel knew not to argue with his version of history but, also, she couldn't let it stand. 'None of that is true. Your mum loves you and wants you home. And I am here because I love you. I never stopped. And I know that you need us, no matter what you say.'

'You don't know anything. You should go. Fuck off.'

She should. She would. But even all these years later, Mel remembered what it felt like to stand there, feeling destroyed by the terrible choices before her. She could insist that Dom came with her, back to Sydney. She couldn't make him, of course, not physically, but she could refuse to leave. She could wait for whoever Bridget was and reason with her that this man needed help.

She could leave, and tell Gina that, yes, Dom was having one of his bad times, but there wasn't anything she could do about it.

She could lay her head in his lap, and tell him she would never leave him.

But the one choice she desperately wanted was not available to her. Choosing to will the old Dom back to life, to love him into being the way he was when she met him, when everyone looked at her in envy – such a handsome, clever, charismatic, funny, sexy boyfriend. Such a catch.

He was right. It was a childish fantasy.

But standing in that doorway, Mel knew she was going to take the easiest option. There was no putting this dream back together and she couldn't look after this man. Unlike Gina, Mel had a choice about that.

'Dom. If you need me . . .' she started.

He looked up, something like triumph in his eyes.

'You know where I am. You have my phone number. You have my address. I mean it. I will be there for you. Always.'

Did she mean it? As she said it, with one eye on the door?

'Sure you will,' Dom had said, as if he could hear her thoughts. 'You'll go running back to your family as soon as you realise you can't torment me anymore.'

'I promise –'

'I said fuck off, Mel.'

And she did. Mel turned and walked through the door, leaving it open, almost running down the narrow stairs. The front door had opened and a woman pushed through it, in a great big Aztec coat, carrying a cloth shopping bag filled with tins. She was young, like Mel, and clean-faced and tired-looking around the eyes. She looked up at Mel in surprise, and said 'Hello' as if it were a question, but Mel pushed past her, choking a sob. Before the door swung shut behind her, she heard the woman calling, 'Dominic? You alright? Who was that?' and then the door slammed and Mel was on the street, running away, jacket wrapped tightly around her.

Eight minutes, she'd been in that bedsit. The last time she ever saw the man who completely changed the course of her life.

'You didn't leave,' Lori said, back in the living room, with the kids grumbling about turning the iPads off and the clock ticking down to Mel's first Zoom meeting of the day.

'No,' said Mel. 'But maybe I should have. There was a window, and it closed, and I wouldn't change it now. But . . .'

'Well, there you go.'

I promised someone I'd be here if they needed me.

Mel didn't say that. She didn't need to share any more with this hungover young girl on her lounge on a morning when she was already behind on her to-do list.

'Let's get moving, kids,' she said, instead.

Ava appeared at Mel's side, offering her list to Lori. The daisies had multiplied and spawned sprinkled doughnuts.

'Ways to get better, number five – lie on our couch and watch TV. Hide from the bad germs.'

Lori smiled at Ava, her eyes still watery, and Mel pushed her daughter gently towards the door. 'Let's brush our teeth.'

As they walked down the hall to the bathroom and toothpaste, there was a fast, firm rap on the door. A man's voice, Flynn's voice, calling loudly. 'Lori?'

'Oh look,' Mel said, hopefully quietly enough for her daughter to miss it. 'The bad germs are at the door.'

34

November: Lori

'**W**ell, that was embarrassing.' Flynn was behind Lori as she walked into the flat, and turned right to go straight to bed.

'I don't think —'

'I mean for you. That was embarrassing for you,' he said firmly.

Yes, it was. It really was. Lori's head felt heavy and muddled, her arms and legs ached, and she felt certain she could sleep for a week if she could be assured of good dreams. She fell face first onto the futon, reaching around for a sheet to pull over her head.

'What are you doing?' Flynn asked, his voice spiky and rough.

'I need to sleep,' said Lori. 'I need to rest.'

'Are you sick?'

'I don't know, am I sick?' Lori pulled the sheet up over her face. 'Or was there something about last night that's made me feel like death today?'

'You knew what you were doing.'

'I really didn't.'

Flynn sighed heavily and turned to leave. He didn't ask her if she was okay. He didn't ask her if she needed anything. He didn't ask her if last night had scared her. He just walked out of the room and said, 'Those sheets are going to need changing, I reckon.'

Lori lay there, drifting in and out of something like sleep, but every conscious moment brought with it an instant plunge of dread. She was alone. Safe ground felt completely out of reach, a shoreline receding every time she opened her eyes. And every time she closed them, there was her mother's face, looking up from a phone screen, worried.

'Lori.' It was a woman's voice. Kat's voice, poking her awake. The light pushing into the room through the faded sheer curtains said that it was afternoon now. Lori opened her eyes and saw that Kat was close, on the edge of the bed, and she was holding a cup of something.

'Lori.' Kat said. 'Come on, wake up.'

Kat's face pushed Lori back to the night before. A frame of her, close focus, smiling broadly.

'I think you should drink this.' Kat was holding out the cup. 'It's tea. It's herbal. I swear by it when I'm sick.'

If these people think I am sick, Lori thought, *why are they near me?*

Lori's mouth was dry and she felt shivery, despite the high sun. 'Thank you,' she said, as she pushed herself up and took the cup. 'I'm sorry, I don't really know what happened last night.'

'You just had a bad time, that's all.' Kat's words came out dismissive and gruff. Yet here she was, offering tea. Not sighing. Not leaving. 'It happens.'

'It happens when?'

'Psilocybin.'

Lori knew that word.

'Mushrooms.'

'Something like that. Des had some. You all drank some after your picnic. You were already pretty out of it, Lori, to be honest, from the booze.'

'Gin and tonics.' Lori could see the blanket on the clifftop, the sandwiches with the crusts cut off. The English chocolate she'd travelled two suburbs to source. Flynn's beautiful face, on the blanket next to hers, nodding and smiling at her effort, approving of the lengths she'd gone to for them, for him. He couldn't taste the difference between the Euro Cadbury's and the Aussie Cadbury's, but he'd laughed indulgently as she'd made him blind-test the bites of melty, gooey goodness.

'It's a myth they're any different,' she remembered him saying, as she kissed his chocolate mouth. 'A Swiss girl told me that.'

The ocean was a silver-grey blue. The sky orange-pink. The time of day influencers called the Golden Hour. It was so pretty, she had managed to convince Flynn to pose with her as the light changed, and dimmed, and dropped altogether. He'd kissed her ear as he sat behind her, lifting a cocktail to her mouth. Her whole body had tingled and she'd sunk into a warm, sunny sensation as she felt the argument, the chill that had been hanging around ever since the national park, melt away. She was back in the evening sun of Flynn's attention.

And then. They'd come back to the flat, and there were people. Of course there were. There was Des, and Kat, and some others whose names she couldn't remember. And she'd felt her warmth fading as the night set in, but she was giddy, happy, sitting on Flynn's knee on the dog-eared armchair she'd covered with her Broome sunset sarong.

'I was tripping?'

'You were tripping. It was mixed with water in a Sprite bottle. I'm sure you knew.' Kat sounded casual, off-hand.

Did she know? Things were hazy from the gin, but she could picture that bottle, she could picture everyone giggling, taking their turn for a sip. She must have known.

'I'm a bit hazy about it.'

She remembered, suddenly, taking the gulp, and then Flynn jolting his knee so she fell right off, with a bump, onto the floor, and the room was laughing at her. Her stomach had gone cold, and she'd taken another sip.

'Well, I'm not,' said Kat. 'I was there, but I didn't drink it. I don't trip.'

Nor do I, thought Lori, although that wasn't strictly true. There had been a time, in her first year at uni, when she'd taken a corner of some papery tab with Jools and they had just lain on the bed in her grandma's house, giggling and giggling until Lori had vomited, and it had been horrifying, for both of them. They'd spent the next hour googling how to sober up and both swore, after drinking a gallon of orange juice, and more vomiting, never again.

'Good call,' she said to Kat. 'Me neither. Until last night, obviously.'

'I like to be in control,' said Kat. 'It's important to me.'

The way Kat said that heavily implied that it should also be important to Lori.

The green bottle, the fall on the floor. The next memory was laughter. Hers, and others'. Music. Someone had a playlist for the occasion, she couldn't remember who. She'd laid her head against Flynn's knee, and closed her eyes against the wave of sound. She felt like she'd never heard music before, like she could hear every string plucked, every breath drawn.

'You really shouldn't mix that stuff with booze,' Kat was saying. 'Flynn should know better. It wasn't fair, really.'

'Fair?'

'You were fine, and then you weren't. A song came on that made you cry.'

Oh, shit. Yes. It was that song Elise used to play. Taylor fucking Swift.

'And you didn't stop.'

Oh, God.

'And you kind of ran away, and I came to find you. You were in the bathroom, looking for your phone. Which was in your hand.' Kat was almost smiling.

Lori remembered sitting on the closed toilet seat. A wave of panic.

'You said you didn't know anyone, that you needed to go home, but you couldn't call your mum to come and get you. Which,' Kat was definitely smiling a little bit now, 'is really cute.'

'Not cute,' said Lori, putting down the tea and lying back. 'What about Flynn?'

'What about Flynn?' Kat's tone shifted and she pushed herself up off the bed, walked over to the wardrobe. Her office clothes of yesterday were gone; she was in short denim shorts and a crisp white shirt. She must have gone home, at some point, to change. Where did she live? Why was she back here?

'I shouldn't think this will shock you, but Flynn isn't really the type to sacrifice his trip for someone else.'

Someone else.

'You were afraid of me,' Kat went on. 'Which is ironic, because I feel like this isn't the first time I've rescued you.'

'Rescued me?'

'You were afraid. You kept saying something about a cliff. And your mum, of course.'

'And then?'

'You ran away from me. I was trying to keep you away from the front room, where everyone could see you.' Kat fingered the fairy lights Lori had strung up between the door and the window. Warm white. Sprinkling magic.

'And?' Lori got a flash. She had run into that room, had run to Flynn.

'You were shouting at him. You wanted him to take you home.'

'And he . . .'

'Was a bit angry, to be honest. Like I said, Flynn's not the selfless type. You were killing his vibe.'

Lori remembered. Flynn had stood up, and he seemed enormous. Like a giant, towering over her, holding both her hands down with one of his, talking in her face. 'Chill the fuck out.' Faces swivelling to her, frozen smiles, laughter stopped on lips.

'I ran away,' Lori said.

'He threw you out.' It was delivered matter-of-factly.

'He didn't.'

'He did.'

He did. Flynn, who only hours before had his head in her lap, mouth full of Galaxy, who only hours before had been kissing her ears, giggling. He held her hands behind her back and pushed her out of the door. He'd hissed in her ear, 'Fuck off until you calm down.'

'You were ruining everything.' It wasn't clear if Kat meant this was a fact, the way Flynn saw it, or was just offering her opinion.

Lori looked up at her. Who the fuck was she? This woman who was around these men? Who seemed, at times, like she was protective of Lori, but at others like the devil herself.

'How do you know Flynn?' Lori asked, pulling the sheet up around her neck.

Kat shrugged. 'Known him forever. He's like a brother.'

'So you're not . . .'

'No, not for years.'

'Oh.'

Kat came back to the bed, sat down. 'Lori, I have to tell you this. He's not your boyfriend.'

Lori closed her eyes. She was on the top step, her phone magically in her hand. She was calling her mum, over and over. But it wasn't her mum. After what felt like a million tries to get through, she'd heard the door open behind her and, convinced that Flynn was so furious he might just push her down the stairs, she finally stumbled down them, towards Mel's door.

'I don't say that to be a bitch.' *Oh, really?* 'I say it to help you.'

'Why didn't anyone come to see where I was?'

'I did,' said Kat. 'I mean, I always have Flynn's back, but that was cold, shoving you out like that.'

'And?'

'I saw you go downstairs, saw that woman let you in.' Kat slid her hand into the back pocket of her shorts. 'Found your phone on the top step.'

Lori grabbed it with both hands. 'Oh my God, thank you.'

'Old mate took it off me for a while, mind,' Kat said. 'Don't know why.'

Lori unlocked it, checked her phone calls. Had she called her mum? Please, no. And no, there were only eight calls to Mel's number, all unanswered. She flicked to the photos, desperate for evidence of the night before it had turned into a nightmare. All the pictures of Flynn on the golden cliff were gone.

'He knows your passcode?' Kat asked.

'He does.' Lori stared at the photo roll, the pretty pictures of the sunset, the food, her feet against the grass. 'He made me tell him. To prove I trusted him. It's no big deal.'

'That sounds like him.' Kat's voice had an edge to it. A harsh streak of disapproval, but it wasn't clear who with. Lori or Flynn? 'Clever, because if you change it now, what are you hiding?'

And that would make him so angry.

'Lori.' Kat put a hand on Lori's leg. 'I don't know what you're thinking, but I'm thinking you should leave.'

It sounded, like everything Kat said, half like advice, half like a threat.

'I don't think this is going to end well.'

And in case there was any doubt about what she was saying, she added, 'For you.'

35

November: Lori

Through the thin cotton of her T-shirt, Lori felt the warmth of the rock on her back. If she closed her eyes it felt like it was sending golden rays right through her. Light and strength, the hippy travellers she'd encountered on the road would say. Mother Nature sharing her power.

Just a few minutes' walk along the cliffs from the shouty heave of a late spring Coogee Beach was the quiet beauty of Gordons Bay. Flynn had brought Lori here, more than once. He pointed to the spot, high on the cliffs, that you could scramble to on the right night if you were young and dumb enough, where tiny raves disturbed the local multi-millionaires in the small hours before the cops came. He'd showed her how to avoid the scummy flotsam of the beach by climbing around the edges of the rocks to a place where steps were carved, by a very old hand, or nature, it wasn't clear which, and you could step down to a smooth flat rock that was the perfect sun-bed when the tide was right. 'This is the best spot on the bay,' he said. 'Locals only, a secret shared with me by the boys.'

And today it was hers and the kids'. Ava and Eddie had trailed along the cliff-line on their scooters and scampered around the rocks, and now they were fishing around in the shallow pools while she lay here, one eye on them, one eye on the water.

Right now, the magic rock was the most perfect place to be. It was late on a weekday afternoon. There were only a few other people scattered around the bay. Some keen Speedo-clad swimmers. A group of young vapers giving off a distant tinny thump from a portable speaker, the occasional peal of laughter reaching Lori when the wind blew a certain way.

The kids were happy to splash in the water, but Lori was nervous about swimming here. There were no lifeguards at this beach, no reality-TV hunks to save you.

But she really should dive in. After all, she was saying goodbye.

I'm transferring the money today, the text message had read, just as Lori had settled down on the rock. *Pay for the ticket and get on the plane now. Before it gets any harder.*

Mum.

These last few days, as Lori had allowed life in the apartment to drift back to some kind of normal, she'd started sending her mum the kind of messages she'd been waiting for.

She could picture her mother, sitting at the table in the heated conservatory, grey morning all around, sipping her giant morning cup of café au lait, flicking from the *Times* crossword online to the little blue bubbles of messages arriving from Australia.

Mum, I think you're right. I think I need to come back before things get any worse.

The night of the gin and mushrooms had changed everything, and so had Kat's words. Whatever her reason for saying them, she was right. This wasn't going to end well.

Lori could imagine her mum smiling and nodding, and lifting her expensively blonde head towards Richard, Lori's father, and saying, 'Looks like Lorelai is coming to her senses, darling.'

And her dad would nod and make little skyward fist-pumps with his increasingly mottled hands. 'Good for Lolo! Smart girl!'

They might not get their Verbier ski trip for Christmas this year, but they might get their daughter back. Worth celebrating with a pain au chocolat, perhaps, even though it was only Thursday. And Dad would go off and check the freezer for that Waitrose packet Lena the housekeeper knew to keep accessible for just such wild diversions from routine.

Lori watched Ava trying to prise a limpet from a rock while her brother dug a moat around her feet, and she imagined pulling her backpack out of Flynn's wardrobe for the last time, pushing her travelling clothes down into it, pulling it on and walking out of the apartment. Not saying goodbye to Flynn, just leaving.

It's not as if he had been awful to her since that night. Kat had suggested an apology was in order – 'don't think about whether it's fair, think about whether it will make your life easier' – for making a scene, for ruining Flynn's night, for dragging Mel into his business. And since Lori had delivered it, he had seemed quietly pleased with her. Lori had gone back to keeping the peace. Morning sex, clearing away the detritus of the party each evening, providing a rapt audience for Flynn's stories and songs, or being an attractive and smiling foil at his elbow, or sitting, attentive, at his feet. Retreating when the signals were clear he was done with her for now, not drinking too much, neatly passing on the joints, the suspect water bottles.

But it was a fractious peace. Kat, so often finding a reason to be around despite apparently having a home of her own, had begun to look at Lori with something like urgent concern. Flynn's moods were unpredictable. Sometimes the flat felt like it was littered with broken glass, and she was trying to pirouette through it. A stumble was inevitable.

The money was coming, an end was in sight. Tonight she could go upstairs and the flat, hopefully, would be empty. Kat gone, Flynn working. She could shower, find something in the fridge for dinner, and think about how many more days she wanted to stay, being the new Lori, on this side of the world, before she headed back to pull on the warm sweater of the old Lori, in her parents' over-heated home. Then she could figure out who she was, after Elise, after Australia, after Flynn.

Lori watched a white plastic bag swim past the magic rock, billowing like a grace-filled jellyfish, and decided swimming was off the agenda. It would be a dry goodbye. 'Come on, kids!' she called towards the rockpool. 'Let's go.'

Lori had been relieved that she hadn't been fired after turning up at her boss's door at 2 a.m., wild-eyed and hysterical. Mel, it seemed, would prefer to keep Lori close.

'I don't think you're careless enough,' Mel had said, 'to let whatever's going on upstairs affect the kids.'

And she was right. Lori liked who she was through Mel's children's eyes. Ava's, wide and impressed, gave her the view of herself as a grown-up girl with an adventurous life. Eddie's, more discerning, doubting, gave her the chance to woo and win over. She was good at that, always had been. A big smile and a skip in your step, as her brother would say, has got you a long way.

Not that far, really, Lori had thought at the time, but here she was now. A very long way away.

'Top three worst things about the beach,' Ava called over to Lori, not looking anything like a child getting ready to leave.

'Go on,' she called to Ava.

'Sharks!'

'Too obvious.' Lori laughed.

'Jellyfish!'

'Not today.'

'Itchy sand!'

'I'll give you that one.'

'Sluts in bad bikinis.'

It was a man's voice, familiar, behind Lori. Low enough for Ava not to hear, loud enough that Lori definitely could.

She turned around, and instantly wished she hadn't.

'Where's your boyfriend?' Rob was on his own, just a few feet behind her on the rocks. How he'd got there without her seeing him she didn't know, but perhaps he'd been with that group with the portable speaker. He was wearing a pair of brand-name baggy shorts that sat low on his hips, more for running than swimming, but they were dripping wet. He had a T-shirt over his shoulder, running shoes in his hand.

'Please go away, I'm working.' She felt a strong surge of adrenaline, but Lori was more irritated than frightened. After all, there were some people scattered around and surely even Rob wasn't dangerous in front of little children.

'You've cost me,' he said, crouching down and putting his shoes on the rock, as if to put them on. 'Friends. Parties. Kat. Des.'

'That wasn't me.'

Ava had stopped splashing in the rockpool, had turned to look at Lori and the stranger talking to her.

'That was you.' Lori hadn't turned around again.

'If Flynn wasn't so cuntstruck, you'd be out,' he said. 'And you will be.'

'Oh please.' Lori felt a surge of frustration at this ridiculous man. 'They all think you're a joke.'

'Who's that, Lori?' called Ava, from the rockpool. 'Who you talking to?'

'No-one,' Lori called back. 'Come on, let's get going.'

'Yeah,' said pathetic Rob, straightening up. 'You'd better run.'

'No.' Lori turned to him. '*You'd* better run.'

He sneered at her, a curled-lip growl that Lori wondered now why she never saw coming, back in Adelaide, when she'd agreed to get in a car with him.

He gave her a light shoulder-barge as he huffed past her towards the steps out of the bay, turning a few heads as he did.

'You okay, Lori?' asked Eddie, abandoning his moat, pulling a towel around his shoulders and coming over to her.

'I'm fine. Let's go.' Lori smiled widely as she handed Ava a faded paisley towel, and started gathering up goggles and suncream and discarded clothes. 'Let's get home for Mum.'

It was so exhausting. It was so fucking exhausting. Smiling. Being okay. Constantly second-guessing and fighting off and forgiving and forgetting. If she needed another sign that going home was the right decision, it was the sight of that *boy's* back, with his exaggerated swagger and his bogus bravado retreating along the path. It was time to go. She had proved her point.

Back on Bay Street, Lori delivered Eddie and Ava to their tired-looking mother. Her T-shirt air-dried against her salty skin, hair crunchy from the sea air, Lori climbed the stairs to Flynn's apartment, swinging her beach bag and humming with the relief of a decision made. When she got to the door and turned her key, it flew open. She wasn't going to be alone, then.

'You're leaving?'

It was Flynn. He was, of course, shirtless, standing in the doorway in his cut-off boardies and bare feet.

'Flynn, I . . .'

'You're fucking leaving.'

For a moment, Lori's adrenaline spiked again. Was he angry? She gripped tightly to the ropey handle of the beach bag. She could run downstairs, she knew Mel was there. And then, there was movement behind him. Kat, her hand on Flynn's shoulder. 'C'mon, mate.'

He shrugged Kat's hand off, not with aggression, with something softer. Resignation.

Lori's eyes met Flynn's. They were full. He wasn't angry. He was upset.

'Lori,' he said. 'Please don't leave.'

The shock of hearing her name in his mouth stopped her. Lori stood there, frozen for a moment, until he stepped forward and pulled her into his arms, his head dropping to hers, his voice a rough whisper in her ear. 'Don't go.'

The smell of him, the feel of him firm against her, and the unfamiliar rush of pleasure and power.

Lori had the briefest sense of Kat sighing in something like disgust as she buried her head in Flynn's shoulder, and breathed him in, so deeply. Every part of her was alive, every cell firing.

'Please don't leave.'

Her mother's conservatory. The coffee, the croissants. The talk. The questions. The expectations. It all fell away as her beach bag hit the ground.

36

December: Lori

Ava was writing Santa a special list.

The very idea that it could be nearly Christmas was ridiculous to Lori. She wasn't sure why people in the Southern Hemisphere bothered, really. After all, wasn't the whole point of Christmas – if you didn't, you know, buy into the 'birth of Jesus' bit – to bring light and celebration and some semblance of joy to the darkest, coldest dog-end of the year?

Who needed fairy lights when the sunshine lasted well into the night? Who needed a clogging feast of roasted bird and steamed pudding when the sunshine and ocean would wash over you with sparkle and fizz?

She was saying as much to Flynn before she went downstairs to help Ava with her list and coax Eddie into writing one, as per their mother's instructions, so Mel could get some work done.

Flynn was lying on the bed, naked, the sheer curtain flapping above his head at the open window, giving anyone who happened to be looking, from, say, the building next door, a full view of his dark, lean, firm form. He was fiddling with something Lori didn't recognise – some sort of plug, or pedal. He had made a patchy return to some kind of studio work, the details were vague – but he was, apparently, listening.

'You have a very narrow view of an Australian Christmas,' Flynn told her, his long fingers picking at an invisible wire he was trying to get a hold on. 'Believe me, we need cheering up as much as the next miserable Pom.'

'But you live in paradise!' Lori tweaked his toe. 'And it's summer!'

'Clearly, I have taught you nothing.'

'You mean all those conversations I sit in on every night about how screwed this place is? This under-populated gigantic continent bursting with beauty?'

'Yup, those.' Flynn grabbed the little wire with a small triumphant grunt and yanked it. 'There are many Australias, Lori, and white-bread beachside suburbia is not the only one.'

Lori loved it when Flynn said her name. He'd been doing it more and more lately.

'I've seen other bits of Australia,' she said, waggling the toe she'd grabbed, hoping it was a playful, sexy gesture, rather than an irritating, suffocating one. 'They're all more interesting than Dorking. And better looking.' She bent over and kissed his toe.

'My family Christmases did not look like barbecues on the beach,' Flynn said, sliding her a little smile. 'No lifeguards in Speedos and Santa hats. No fucking –' he was pulling and pulling at the wire now, and it gave, '*prawns*.'

Lori stopped toe-waggling. Flynn never really talked about his family. His childhood. He talked about his travels. His adventures. The skills he'd picked up, the characters he'd met. He could talk and talk and talk about those. And did, almost every night, with his lightly rotating appreciative cast as audience. It didn't really matter what everyone else was talking about, Flynn could bring the conversation back around to that time he was the only one hiking the Camino without a tent. Or that time he lived hand-to-mouth on a Vietnamese island that you wouldn't find in any guidebook. Shellfish and seaweed will only get you so far without explosive diarrhoea, he'd learned.

At first, Lori loved the stories, despite often struggling with the logistics. And the maths. 'When were you there?' always elicited a vague response, a wave of the hand, a dismissive 'A while back'. And why were so few of his friends people he'd met overseas? Almost all of the people sleeping on the floors, on the lounges, were from Australia, collected on more prosaic adventures.

'What did they look like?' Lori asked.

'What?'

'Your family Christmases.'

Flynn looked up, as if surprised. 'They didn't look like much,' he said. If Lori hoped he'd elaborate, which she did, he sensed it, and went back to his wire. 'That's my point. Australia isn't postcard paradise for most of us.'

'It's pretty good for you now though, right?' Lori got up. Sharing time was clearly over.

'Stolen land,' Flynn muttered, 'has bad karma.'

'Well, that bit's true.' Lori grabbed her hairbrush. 'Although I don't see anyone around here suffering too much.'

'That's because,' Flynn said, 'you're looking in all the wrong places.'

'Well, I'm going to look downstairs,' she said, brightly, pushing the discomfort away, again. 'I'm going to try to be Christmassy with those two little Aussie kids who have no idea what Christmas is *meant* to look like.'

'Just because it's your way, doesn't mean it's the right way, Pommy,' said Flynn. But his voice was playful, and when she looked back at him, he had put down the plug, and he was hard, and smiling. Lori looked quickly at the time on her phone. Five minutes.

'I have five minutes, Flynn,' she said.

'If we have to, three's enough,' he said, hand outreached to her, eyes flashing.

And it was. It could be three, it could be thirty. His desire for her was elastic. And addictive, all over again.

*

Mum, calm down, there are hardly any flights, Lori was texting, twenty minutes later, downstairs, while Ava looked for exactly the correct colour of metallic marker to use to write a letter to the most important person in the world. *They are costing up to $30,000! I'm fine. I'll wait it out. I'll send you the money back.*

It was true. Well, it was kind of true.

I've got whiplash, her mum returned. *I can't keep up with this.*

Over in England, Lori's parents had just woken up. After a few days of avoiding questions about flight bookings, return dates and requests for the first home-cooked meal, she'd had to tell them she wasn't coming home by Christmas after all. *Sorry, Mum, things have changed*, she'd tapped, knowing the reception her messages would be getting, over in a detached stone home in Dorking. How cold the conservatory would feel, now.

Sorry, Mum, I've changed, she should have written. *Again.*

There's no price tag too high for me to have you home. Such privilege, such bravado. A pause. *That's Australian dollars, yes?*

Ava returned brandishing the perfect silver pen and Lori pushed her vibrating phone under a cushion. Mum wanted to FaceTime. Lori wasn't ready for that.

'I know exactly what to put at the top of my list,' Ava was saying.

Eddie, over at the sunroom table, hunched over his iPad, let out a little snort. 'She's going to say "Daddy to come home",' he said, dismissively.

Lori often forgot this was the first Christmas since their father had left. The father Lori had never met, or even seen.

'Was not,' called Ava, apparently unperturbed by her brother's – actually quite mean – taunt. 'I was going to ask for a Nintendo Switch.'

'Yeah, right.'

Ava looked at Lori. 'Do you think Mummy will get us a Nintendo Switch?'

'I know they're expensive,' Lori said, gently. 'And Santa has to share all the presents around between all the children in all the world, so . . .'

'As if Santa's elves are making Nintendos in the workshop in the North Pole,' Eddie huffed. 'If they were, Ava, there would be more than enough to go around. I don't think Santa pays the elves.'

Smart kid. Cynical kid. Tiring kid, when you just wanted him to do something simple, like write a shopping list of toys.

'Your mum wants you both to make a list,' Lori said, sitting up straight on the couch and using her most teacherly voice, 'so that you can send it to Santa, the elves and your nana in England and between them, they'll work out what you can have.'

'The magic of Christmas,' sighed Eddie. Sarcastic kid, too.

'And you, Lori,' Ava was saying. 'You have to write one, too.'

'Sure. Go give your brother a piece of paper.'

'Eddie's going to be in Year Four,' Ava said, as she twirled over to her brother, fluttering her sheet. 'No-one believes in Santa in Year Four.'

'It's just a phase,' said Lori, picking up one of Ava's sparkly markers. 'They come around again by Year Five.'

Eddie looked up, despite himself, a little smile on his lips.

Ava and Lori lay on the lounge-room floor working on their lists, both carefully illustrating the borders of the page. Ava with snowmen and Christmas puddings – clearly, rampant Northern Hemisphere indoctrination – Lori with the kind of meaningless, artful squiggles the people upstairs had as tattoos. An ironic ship anchor. An ace. An empty triangle. Three wavy black lines. A smiley face. A thistle.

Eddie, over at the table, was listing every computer game he'd seen played by the pale-faced YouTubers who shouted from his iPad daily. Printing neatly, with no illustrative flourishes.

'These are in order, tell Mum,' he said, seriously. 'Santa can start at the top.'

'Don't you have most of those?' Lori asked. 'You seem to have lots of games already.'

'Nah,' Eddie said. 'Only the crappy free versions.'

Ava's list did, indeed, start with a Nintendo Switch, although Lori had a feeling her heart wasn't in it. The most glorious cartoon embellishments were reserved for *Nion model clay* and *rainbow fedgets* and *LED lites*. 'Do you think Santa cares about spelling?'

'Very much so.'

'So what's on your list?'

Lori read. 'Cake for breakfast. A swim. A good book. A call from my brother.'

'Those aren't presents.'

'They are, to me,' Lori said, smiling at Ava. 'Anyway, I'm not really around anyone who might help Santa get my presents this year. It's a different kind of Christmas for me.'

'What about your boyfriend?' It was Eddie, over at the dining table. He was pointing upstairs with his pencil. 'Won't he buy you something?'

'Flynn is not my . . .' Lori stopped. She didn't have to carry on that exhausting schtick to primary school kids, surely. 'I don't know,' she said. 'We haven't talked about it.'

'You know what I'd like . . .' Eddie had finished his game inventory and was looking at Lori and Ava expectantly. 'I'd like to go upstairs and see his guitar.'

Lori was surprised. Eddie barely ever gave the impression that he was registering anything going on around him – even when they were outside this house, he would break away and occupy himself in a solo activity. He never asked Lori anything about herself, never spoke about her, or Flynn, or upstairs, or his dad, or his mum, or anything really, beyond his immediate needs and interests. *Is there any more food? Is it iPad time yet? Do we have to watch this stupid kids' movie?*

'You would?' Lori asked. 'Really?'

'Mummy doesn't want us going upstairs.' Ava had stopped drawing her baubles on tiny, pointy Christmas trees. She looked as surprised as Lori. 'She'd be mad.'

'Would she, though?' asked Eddie, in an imitation of an adult phrase he must have heard somewhere, often. 'I might want a guitar for Christmas. Which,' he waved over his list, 'Mum would like a lot better than all these *games*. How will I know unless I go and see Flynn's?'

It was bullshit logic. Even the seven-year-old in the room could see that, judging by Ava's exaggerated eye-roll. But Lori liked the idea. She didn't want to miss another minute of the mood Flynn had been in when she left, all glowy and open. And the idea of him seeing her in her work-mode – Ava's big eyes adoring her, Eddie somewhat obeying her instructions – well, it was seductive. She knew he'd get a kick out it. And God knew, he loved a new audience.

'You want to go up and see Flynn's guitar? Really?'

Eddie nodded.

'You know, usually,' she did a mental stocktake of what was going on upstairs, who was there, who wasn't, the state of the flat. She'd done a sweep through earlier this morning, and there hadn't been any interlopers on any furniture when she'd left. 'He has more than one lying around.'

'Please, Lori?' Eddie was out of his seat, looking at her directly, another very rare occurrence. 'Can we?'

She laughed. Ava clapped her hands. 'Naughty!' she said, but she looked delighted.

Lori looked at her phone. At least half an hour until Mel got back. Quick trip.

She opened her texts.

Are you decent?

He replied immediately.

Silly question.

He must still be lying on the bed.

Put clothes on. The kids are coming up.

37

December: Mel

'What percentage of our customers do you think will be actively anti-vax?'

Mel was tired of dancing around the houses, as her gran would have said. Time to open the door, barge right in and pull up a chair. She was, as she always seemed to be, 'on a call', but this one included the international head of marketing, dialling in from an early start on the American west coast. Knowing the delicacy of what she wanted to talk about, knowing the clear headspace it was increasingly difficult to find in her ever-shrinking flat, Mel had asked Lori to watch the kids, and headed to the office.

She was sitting in the empty boardroom alone at the massive wooden table, a handful of her peers on the giant screen in front of her. She thought she deserved some recognition for the fact she'd travelled in for this conversation, but instead she felt like she was being interrogated by superior beings, beaming in from more pleasurable planets.

'Pro-choice,' corrected Jake, Northern Beaches Man, from the top-right-hand corner of the screen.

'They are not –'

'A small percentage,' said the international lead, a woman called Julia who spoke like she was born somewhere in the mid-Atlantic. She spoke at the pace of someone who operated in at least three time zones simultaneously. Mel was slightly in awe of Julia, a little bit terrified of her, and one hundred per cent exhausted by her. 'Especially in Australia. We're talking about a loud minority.'

Just as Mel felt she might be getting somewhere, her phone began to vibrate.

Shit, it was Lori.

'I have to . . .' Alone in the boardroom, Mel waved her hand vaguely. Be truthful. 'Take this call about my kids.'

'Good luck, Mel,' Northern Beaches Man said, in a tone that suggested he meant exactly the opposite. 'Such a busy time of year for mums. I mean, parents.'

Fuck. You.

Mel left them talking about third quarter projections as she answered the call. 'Lori? Everything okay?'

'I hate to call you,' Lori's voice was cheerful, lilting upwards, as always. 'But I knew you'd want to know.' Just a tiny touch of panic in those sped-up words.

'What? Want to know what?'

'The kids –'

The children's school secretary, if she ever had a reason to call Mel, started every interaction with, 'Hi, Mel, Eddie's absolutely fine, just calling to tell you . . .' It was smart, because every parent's stomach dropped when their phone flashed up the school phone number, and in order for you to hear anything the caller was about to tell you, the worst case scenario had to be eliminated first. This was a lesson that Lori had not yet learned.

'What about them, Lori?' Mel was leaning on the boardroom door, looking out at the empty office, the ghost desks and chairs.

'Well,' Lori was choosing what to say next, Mel could tell.

'Please, Lori, just say it.'

'Well, Simon took them.'

'What do you mean, Simon took them? He's in Lennox.'

'He came back, I suppose. And he came to the flat. And we weren't there.'

Often, Lori took the kids down to the beach, the rockpool, the ice cream shop. All permitted, all fine, they couldn't spend their afternoons locked in the flat, after all.

'And . . .?'

'And when he saw we weren't there, and then he saw the kids . . . He got kind of . . . angry. I mean, I've never met him before, but he seemed angry and he kind of took them.'

'Lori. None of this is making any sense. How did he see you if you weren't there? What are you actually talking about?'

The line went silent for a moment. 'I know you won't be thrilled about this,' Lori started again.

'Just make some sense, would you, Lori? I'm meant to be in a meeting and I need to understand if this is serious or not.'

'Well, we were upstairs.'

'Upstairs, at Flynn's?'

A picture of her kids playing with the ghost flashed into Mel's head. That familiar face, those familiar hands. Doing what? Saying what?

'Yes. Eddie wanted to see Flynn's guitar. For his Christmas list.'

More words that didn't make any sense.

'And we were up there, and Eddie and Flynn were playing music, and . . .' Lori faded out, and back in. 'Ava saw her dad out of the window, and she was waving and calling to him.'

Oh Jesus. The picture was coming into focus, now.

'I guess he came to see you, and he saw us upstairs and he came up and –'

'And he lost it and he took the kids.' Mel finished the sentence for Lori. She could picture it now. Simon, fresh off a long, long drive from his dad's. Coming to surprise the kids. Seeing his little daughter leaning out of the open window of a unit that's not their home. Music pumping, chaotic young people he didn't know.

Simon liked rules. He liked order, and for the kids to be where they were meant to be as per the big, colour-coded calendar that hung in both their kitchens. So did Mel.

A sigh. A rub of the temples.

'Lori. What the fuck? Why were the kids upstairs?'

Why hadn't Simon called her? Just as Mel was forming that question, her phone started to vibrate. He *was* calling her. Now.

Through the glass panel of the empty boardroom, Mel could see the meeting going on without her. She could see Northern Beaches Man talking animatedly, Julia in San Fran looking tired.

'I have to go, Lori. This really isn't great.'

'I'm very sorry, Mel, I didn't know what to do.'

Mel hung up on Lori, pressed accept on Simon's call and kept one eye on the screen meeting as he said, 'Melanie, we have to talk.'

Suddenly, Mel was so tired. So very, very tired. 'Simon. I know. I just spoke to Lori.'

'Your babysitter,' Simon said, his words very clear, very loud in her ear, 'is not responsible enough to be looking after my children.'

'Your children?'

'Ava was dangling out of a first-floor window, there were strangers up there, no-one's distanced, Eddie was playing guitar with some guy who looked like he was –'

'Simon. I don't have time for this right now, I am at work. Which is why the kids were with the babysitter. Well, that and the fact that you have been away for weeks now, and someone has to help me, and she's really, usually . . .' Julia from the west coast was speaking, inside the boardroom, and Mel could tell the meeting was about to end. She'd missed it. She also didn't know how to end the sentence about Lori.

'I'll have them tonight,' he said. 'We can talk tomorrow.'

'They're not prepared for going to you tonight!' Mel said, thinking of the meticulous schedule, the plans, the number of times they'd been advised to stick to the plan. The kids needed their expectations met. They needed to feel safe. Routine was everything. Simon knew this. 'We didn't even know you were coming back.'

'I wanted to surprise them,' Simon said. 'But turns out it was me who got a surprise.'

The call in the boardroom was ending. Jake from the Northern Beaches was smiling, waving at the Americans. God knew what had just been agreed to.

'Please don't overreact, Simon,' said Mel. 'I'm doing my best. You know I am. Where are the kids now?'

'I'm just outside my place.' He sounded a bit calmer. He always had been quick to wind up, quick to come back. Not a sulker or a grudge-keeper or a drama queen. He was even. It was one of the reasons she'd married him. 'They're inside.'

'Well, I hope you brought them presents,' said Mel, breathing out as the screen in the boardroom faded to black. 'Take them for ice cream, or something nice now you're back.'

If Simon was irritated at Mel telling him what to do with the kids he didn't show it this time. He wasn't in a rush to hang up, though. What else?

'I missed them,' he said. A simple truth. An important thing to say. 'I just want things to be normal.'

'Whatever that is, now.'

'Right. That guy upstairs,' said Simon, eventually, the sound of cicadas kicking up in the background. It must be almost dusk. 'He looks a lot like –'

'I know,' said Mel. 'I've noticed.'

Another beat, heavy with sadness and thoughts not shared. 'I really don't think the kids should be up there, Mel.'

'I know.' She sighed, again. 'Me neither.'

38

December: Mel

'It's our first divorced Christmas, I need it to be okay.'

'You're not divorced, yet.' Izzy was out walking in an icy park and Mel was wrapping presents in her underwear on the lounge-room floor.

Mel could picture her sister and the dog, a scrappy yappy little thing, making their way along the edges of the park she and Izzy had played in as kids, the grass crunchy with frost, the paths slippery with invisible ice. The football posts without their nets. The empty, creaking roundabout.

'Be careful out there, it must still be dark,' she said.

'No, the glorious December dawn is breaking.' Izzy snorted. 'It's pale grey. And freezing.'

'Watch out for black ice.'

'Yeah, thanks, Mum.' They were both quiet for a second. Each other's mum, now.

'Anyway, we've decided to do it together, Christmas Day.'

'Ambitious.'

'Perhaps. But why change absolutely everything when we can stand to be in the same room together for a few hours? We can handle it.'

'Watch out. People get weirdly sentimental at Christmas.'

Mel was in her undies because it was too freaking hot in the unit to be wearing clothes while figuring out how to wrap squishy unicorn toys and Razor scooters. If anyone saw her through the window, all flesh and sticky tape, brandishing scissors, she might just go viral.

Another festive first. Christmas as civilised separated people. Well, she hoped they were civilised. She had some ground to make up, since the whole 'upstairs' thing yesterday. She knew Simon would be more obsessed than usual with her work hours, the kids' schedule, the babysitter, everything now.

Unfortunately – or fortunately, depending on how you looked at it – if you ran a sports shop, the lead-up to Christmas didn't really give you a lot of time to obsess about your co-parenting arrangements. Kids wanted Santa to bring them cricket bats, skateboards, tennis racquets, expensive trainers with pointlessly large soles. Well, most kids. Not theirs, much to Simon's eternal disappointment.

Sticking a strip of tape to her thigh as she pondered stocking stuffers, Mel asked Izzy the question she'd been considering for days. 'Do you think Simon and I get along well as exes because there wasn't a lot of passion in our marriage? I read that somewhere. On Instagram, maybe.'

Izzy gave a small snort. 'Since when have you decided you and Simon get along well?'

'Well we do, comparatively. My friend Fi can't be in the same room as her ex. Not even the driveway for handover. Do you think she loved him more?'

'Didn't you tell me that Fi's husband cheated on her while she had cancer? Would *you* be in the same room as that guy?'

'No.'

'Maybe you and Simon are *starting* to get on well because neither of you did anything horrific to the other.' Izzy stopped, a little abruptly.

'What?'

'What?'

'You sounded like you just thought of something horrific one of us had done to the other.'

'Well. Maybe you shouldn't have married him in the first place. Considering you were still in love with someone else.'

'Oh, Izzy, come *on*.' Mel slashed at the untidy edges of her unicorn wrap with the scissors. 'If I hadn't met Simon, we'd have no Ava, no Eddie. It was definitely not a mistake.'

'I didn't say it was a mistake.' Izzy was walking vigorously again. 'Fuck, it's cold. Not a mistake, just, perhaps, a tiny bit unforgivable, on the cosmic scale.'

'Excuse me, who even are you?' But Mel remembered how Simon's voice had sounded when he said that Flynn looked like Dom. Wounded. Even by a memory.

'Cancer does funny things to your perspective.'

Oh, Izzy. 'What's Christmas looking like for you?'

'Tom'll be on a treatment break. It's a longer hiatus than usual because . . . the virus.' Izzy sniffed. Tears, or the cold? 'But at least that means he'll feel alright for Christmas. Might manage some pudding. And the girls are planning a big fuss. The tree's the size of a house.'

Mel could picture it. Twinkly, coloured lights, not white ones, heaped presents under the tree, wrapped in messy, warming colours.

'I wish I was there.'

'I know. Me too.' Silence. The sound of her sister's footsteps, crunching lightly on frost.

Mel shook herself.

'Instead, I will be having a more civilised divorced Christmas than Gwyneth.'

'Right. Good luck with that.'

'Iz.'

'What?'

'Even Simon thinks the guy upstairs looks like Dom.'

'Oh, man. Please. Stop it with upstairs.'

'I can't. She's my babysitter.'

'Get another one.' Izzy was as sharp as the crisp morning. 'And stay away from them.'

There was an impeccably timed knock on the front door. A voice, slightly coy, calling, like Lori often did. 'Mel? You there?'

Yes, I'm here, in my pants. Mel said goodbye to Izzy, dumped the scissors, grabbed her threadbare kimono and headed for the door, and an apology, she hoped.

Lori, pleasingly, launched right in. 'Mel, I'm so very sorry about what happened with the kids, and Flynn, and your ex-husband.'

'There are people, Lori, quite a lot of people, actually, maybe even most people,' Mel had rehearsed this part of the conversation a few times since yesterday, when she'd been a bit too furious to have it, 'who would consider a 2 a.m. crisis visit and then an unauthorised second location as grounds to just not use you anymore.'

'I know, and I'm sorry. I promise it won't happen again. You know, if you don't . . .'

'Fire you?'

'Fire me . . .' Lori's eyes were wet. Had she been rehearsing, too? 'Things have been so much better. And I think the kids really like me, and . . .'

Mel had a suspicion Lori might be about to pull the 'they don't need any more disruption' card. Or maybe that was just echoing around her own head. It was true that, lately, even Eddie had looked something like enthusiastic when he was told Lori was coming over.

But the bottom line was, whether the kids loved Lori or not, Mel needed her. Between now and the endless school holidays, she had to deliver the revised strategy for the new immunity campaign, Simon would be up to his ears in Santa's sporting grotto, and she had little choice, really, other than to enlist Lori's convenient and affordable help.

'So you're not going home?' Mel asked. 'You're sure? For a moment there –'

'I'm not going home,' said Lori, firmly, wiping her nose with the back of her hand. 'I can help as much as you need.'

'She's so helpful, isn't she?'

A woman's voice, loud, confident, slightly mocking. It was the dark-haired girl who had come to Mel's door the night Lori had turned up in a state. Mel had seen her around the building a lot lately. She was so different from Lori. Australian, for starters, with a broad, optimistic accent. But also more assured. In the clothes she wore, which clung to her in a way that Mel knew she wasn't supposed to notice or judge. In the way she held herself, tall and still, not a touch of apologetic fiddling or jiggling. Now she had come to stand next to Lori, at Mel's door, as if she'd been invited. Mel noticed the way Lori dipped her head, ever so slightly, the way a dog submits when it meets an alpha, making itself smaller with a tiny bend of a leg.

'Hi, Kat,' Lori said, as cheerfully as she could manage, Mel guessed. 'This is Mel.'

'I met your husband yesterday.' Kat spoke without pause, without apparent thought, as Lori cringed beside her. 'He wasn't very friendly.'

Who opened a conversation like that?

Mel knew who. Someone who was oblivious to other people's signals. Or someone used to confrontation, someone who wasn't afraid to stir pots.

'Not my husband anymore,' said Mel. 'And I think he'd had a bit of a shock that day.'

'Nice kids, though,' said Kat, as if Mel hadn't said anything. 'Lovely little girl you've got.'

Jesus. How many people did Eddie and Ava meet upstairs yesterday afternoon? Did Kat live upstairs too, now? Did Flynn have a *harem* up there?

Kat registered Mel's expression, shrugged and turned to Lori. 'Have you finished being told off now? Do you want to come shopping with me?'

'I was not *telling her off*,' Mel said, with a flush of indignation. She could see Lori looking at Kat with surprise – a little smile on her lips at being defended by this prickly creature, probably.

Another shrug from Kat. 'Sorry,' she said, without a hint of apology, then she turned back to Lori. 'Flynn wants to make a goat curry tonight. Something about his time in India.' There was an eye-roll in Kat's voice which Mel, despite her irritation, enjoyed. 'Des knows a butcher out near Rosehill who'll have the meat. Apparently, I need to drive.'

'Why does Lori need to go?' Mel wasn't sure why she felt defensive about the way this girl spoke to Lori. The way they all ran around after Flynn. This was all so very far from the things she should be thinking about right now, her sister was entirely right about that.

'Sorry, Mum,' Kat said. 'Didn't know she needed your permission. You know how the man upstairs is, though, right? He's feeling the need for some performative cooking, so we can't hang around.'

This girl really was extraordinarily rude. But also funny. And clearly had Flynn's measure. Mel couldn't help but like her, just a little.

Lori jumped in. 'Kat! It's fine. I'll come. You don't need me today, right, Mel?'

'No, I don't.' *Because the kids are on an unscheduled stay with their father, thanks to you.* 'Tomorrow, I think.'

'Okay. Thanks for . . .' Lori ran out of words, looking instead at Mel with something like an apology in her eyes. Kat continued with her steady stare, a slight smirk on her full lips.

'Let's go,' Lori said, turning away and touching Kat's arm, ever so lightly.

Back inside the flat, Mel headed for the window, and hopefully a gasp at some cooling air in this syrupy heat. She could hear Flynn's music drifting down from upstairs, some trance-like 'vibe', as Eddie would call it. She briefly heard Kat's voice calling out as the girls gathered themselves for the goat mission. Tonight would be another party, more noise. Mel needed to be out. The silence of the flat was too heavy. If something could be empty and heavy at the same time. No need to be here, tormented by the scent of sizzling spices and the thought of Lori making all Mel's old mistakes.

There would be Christmas drinks somewhere. Socialising was making a tentative return, outside, in backyards and in parks, and down at the beach. Groups of people starved of interaction were learning how to reconnect, assisted by alcohol sipped surreptitiously from coffee KeepCups. And not just young people. Grown-up people, parent people, retiree people.

Mel grabbed her phone and messaged Fi. *Kidless – what you doing?*

And before she'd even put her phone back on the table, Fi replied.

You wdnt believe it if I told you.

Mel tapped back: *???*

You should come.

The wrapping could wait until tomorrow.

39

December: Mel

The rooftop bar was packed with the people who'd bought all the houses that Mel and Simon could never afford. A middle-aged, middle-class, gym-honed, highlight-flecked push of bodies chattering at a high volume, gently pulsing to the retro remix a DJ in an ironic flat cap was playing over near the bar.

Mel mentally checked her outfit to ensure she looked like she was in the right place – a white linen A-line dress, sneakers and a colourful cross-body bag. Most of the women there were wearing a variation on the exact same thing. Some were showing shoulders, some were showing knees, depending, Mel knew, on which bit of flesh they still had faith in around forty. This was, after all, an occasion to show off, a meat market.

These were the people – she knew them from the kids' school, from the gym, from Saturday morning soccer and Sunday morning surf club – who could be held responsible for Mel still living where she lived when really, *really*, she should have moved on a long time ago. Moved away from the status of beachside living, away from noisy neighbours and toxic memories and ghosts of younger selves, and headed west,

west towards suburbia and peace, a back garden and an oodle of some description.

'Mel! You came.' Fi popped out from between two men Mel vaguely recognised but wouldn't be able to tell apart. Fi's arms were wide, rosé in hand. Beaming.

'Fi.' Mel stood back, not going in for the hug, hoping her friend didn't judge her for it. 'I have not seen this many people in one place for almost a year.'

'I know! I know!' Fi was giddy, eyes darting. 'But you know they just changed the rules and we,' she flung her arms out again, 'jumped on a last-minute booking for the terrace. Can't let the young people have all the fun, right?'

'We?'

'We call ourselves the Swingle Parents. It's a joke, of course. You can't swing if you're single, not really. Yet another thing we're not allowed to do.' Fi's words were fast, erratic. 'We just thought, why the fuck not? We've all been on our apps for months anyway, what if we all just invited who we've been talking to and see what happens?' She threw her arms out to the crowd. 'It's wild, right?'

It sounded risky to Mel, who still only had a tentative toe in the app world but was already aware of the relatively small pool in their five-kilometre radius. 'But what if you've all been talking to the same people?'

'We have! Who the fuck cares?' Fi put an arm around Mel, who tried not to flinch at the strange sensation of adult touch. 'You know people here, we're not going to auction you off or anything. Come and have a drink.'

Mel and Fi pushed past the lookalike dads, towards the familiar, delighted faces of Roland and Tess, who had been the third and fourth points of Mel's safe single-parent square since Simon left.

'Mel! You came!'

'Why are you so surprised?' asked Mel. 'Fi said the same thing. If I hadn't come, it only would have been because I didn't *know*.'

'Oh, you never come out,' said Roland, faux-frowning. 'Always got the kids, always working, always talking to your sister, always sad.' He stuck out his bottom lip in an exaggerated sulk.

Mel got one of those jolts that came when you saw yourself through someone else's eyes. *Oh, that's what they think of me.*

'Screw you, Rolly.' She decided to push past it, as doing otherwise would confirm their opinion. 'You've all had a lot longer to get used to this single-parent stuff than me. It's been six months.'

'I fucked my way through the first five months,' said Tess, loudly. 'I think I wore the apps out.'

Oh, they were definitely drunk. It was 6 p.m., and only an hour since Mel had called Fi. This was clearly an afternoon session and they were already heading for the messy ending. Was this what dating in your forties was like? Everyone back in their own beds by 9 p.m.?

'Your first five months probably weren't during a global plague.' Mel laughed. 'I need a drink. I need to catch up.'

Fi produced a glass of white wine for Mel as if she'd had it up her floaty caftan sleeve the whole time. 'Start here,' she said. 'And I'll scour for possibilities.'

Mel had a gulp of the wine and, as Fi headed off towards the DJ and what might loosely be described as a dancefloor, scanned the room. It was true, she did know some of the people here. There was Lainey, whose daughter was one of Ava's favourite frenemies. There was Lucas, who had helped her that time she was meant to be hosting reading groups in Eddie's class but had, instead, been a sobbing mess outside the school because she'd just hung up the phone from Izzy after a particularly shitty doctor's appointment. There was Lexi, the trainer who took all the mums through their paces at a blisteringly early bootcamp. And there was Simon. Of course. There was Simon, standing over by the bar, light beer in hand, talking to another man who looked like his natural state was Lycra and cleats.

Hold on. If Simon was at the swingle parent party, where were the kids?

The moment Mel saw Simon was the same moment Fi saw Mel seeing Simon, and she turned to catch Mel's eye and signal, 'Doooooooon't.' But Mel was already on her way over.

'Hey.'

'Oh, hey.'

Simon looked genuinely surprised to see Mel. In the split second that their eyes met, Mel read him, this person she knew so very well. He was thinking, 'You're not meant to be here' and Mel was thinking, *Why is Simon here when I'm not meant to be?*

'I thought you had the kids?'

In the unfamiliar hum and push of an almost-busy bar, Mel's ex-husband looked guilty, just for a moment.

'The kids are with my mum.'

The man next to him, who Mel had sworn she'd never seen before – and she thought she knew *all* of Simon's friends, old and new – turned away with raised eyebrows, embarrassed. He lifted his glass as if to say, *going to get another.*

'I should know that, shouldn't I?' she asked. 'Where my kids are?'

Simon laughed, took a sip of his drink. 'I don't think you're in a position to say that. Not today.'

Fair enough. 'It's just, you've been away and you might want to . . .' Mel trailed off.

How many times had she been told – or told herself – that the trick to making this whole new world work was to keep judgement out of it? She had a babysitter. Simon had his mum. These things were allowed. You both want the best for the kids. Every piece of divorce self-help literature on the internet had told her this.

'Mel, let's not do this,' said Simon. 'I just wanted to catch up with some friends, blow off a bit after being with Dad.'

You're a bad person, Mel.

'Of course. How is your dad?'

'Not great. But still with us.'

Mel expected she would have heard if otherwise. After all, Simon's family had been the closest thing to her own for a good few years. She squeezed his arm. 'I'm sorry, Simon.'

He smiled a straight-line smile.

'So Fi finally got you to come to the party.'

Finally? Mel laughed as if this were true. 'Yeah,' she said. 'But I'm just here for a quick drink, really. Needed to get out of the house.'

He looked at her. A familiar, concerned appraisal. 'Everything okay?'

Simon was tall, blond, broad. He was exactly the right fish in this sea of eastern-suburbs parents, who all looked distantly related. Anglo, fit, sun-kissed, greying and thinning now around the temples, but still – always – in good shape. Taking care of himself had always been Simon's thing.

The benefit of distance – and Izzy's constant narration on Mel's life choices – painted it obvious that choosing Simon had been an act of not choosing Dominic. A rejection of chaos. A pivot towards order. And also, a swing to hope. A vote that things could change.

It was almost painful to think that a romantic relationship, which had existed, in the real world, for only two years of the God knew how many she'd be granted, had changed everything.

Simon's relentless optimism was one of his best traits, and one of his more insufferable ones. More than a decade ago, he had won Mel over with his sheer competitive drive and his unfailing ability to be counted on. He was where he was meant to be when he said he was going to be, doing the thing he said he was going to be doing, showing up. It was a relief. And, she saw quite clearly now, it was also going to be very appealing to this next-time-around dating crowd.

'Everything's fine,' she said. 'Well, as fine as it can be a week from Christmas when the world's gone to hell.'

'Well, you look good,' Simon said, 'whatever's going on.'

'Thank you,' said Mel. It felt good to hear him say that.

'No, no, no.' Fi was by their side. 'No talking to exes. It's a rule. And if it's not, I'm making it one. It is not in the spirit of the occasion.'

Simon rolled his eyes. Mel couldn't imagine that sober, sensible Simon had a great deal of time for Fi, for her fuck-it energy. He had never had much time for that side of Mel.

'It's okay, Fi, we're just checking in,' she said. 'I'm going to go soon, anyway.'

'You are not!' Fi screeched. 'You just got here. Have some fun!'

Simon nodded. 'Don't go. Have a drink, enjoy it.'

Another glass of wine appeared in Fi's hand for Mel. The music seemed to notch up, just a touch, and seeing her ex-husband smile, give a little nod of approval, made Mel's insides relax for what felt like the first time in months.

'Okay,' she said. 'I will.'

40

December: Mel

Two hours later and Mel was outside the pub, leaning against the sea wall, head back, feeling the salty wind on her face, through her hair. The sickly sweet warmth of two-too-many wines swam in her stomach. She felt squishy, happy, silly. The sky was only just darkening, but it felt like midnight.

'Let me walk you home.'

'Oh no, no, no.' Mel shook her head. 'Dangerous.'

'Since when?'

How many of these sessions – the ones Fi had never told Mel about – ended up with exes indulging in old-times-sake trysts they would regret the next day? she wondered.

Plenty, she was sure. She and Simon couldn't be the only ones to suddenly see each other differently outside the usual surrounds of school-gate handovers and doorstop swaps. There must be occasions when circumstances conspired to show off new, single selves to the people who'd watched someone they once adored become something else – tired, stressed, dulled and distracted, weighed down by the responsibilities parenthood brought.

'You look great,' Simon said, again, moving to stand in front of her.

'I look exactly the same,' Mel replied.

'No, you look . . . alive.'

It was such a peculiar, telling choice of word. Mel laughed. She was tipsy, but Simon wasn't. He didn't let himself get tipsy. Everything he did was intentional. So it was intentional that he was now leaning in, as if he wanted to kiss Mel, the ex he'd barely spoken to, let alone looked at, for half a year.

'Can I kiss your neck?' he asked. 'I know how much you love that.'

She did love that. And Simon, pushing against her as the sky behind him turned that delicious inky navy it took on just before dark, had kissed her neck many, many times. But why did she love that? Was it the movies she'd watched, growing up? Was it Dom, that very first night, on the top seat of a wobbly double-decker, pushing back her hair with his hand, and leaning in with that broad, soft mouth in that hungry smile, not for her lips . . .

'We're too old to be making out at the beach,' Mel said, pulling herself back. 'And too divorced.'

'We're not divorced, yet,' said Simon. 'And it's only sex.'

Sex, now? 'There were a lot of women on that roof you could have only sex with,' she said, feeling a little less fluid, like she was coming back to her senses. 'I'm not one of them. Sex can't only be sex with someone you've been having it with forever.'

Simon shook his head, but the look on his face told her that his pragmatic side was kicking in. If this effort wasn't going to yield the desired result, maybe the effort wasn't worth it. 'But we know it would be . . .'

'Easy?'

'Good.' Simon laughed. 'God, Mel, we know it would be good.'

Her cross-body bag vibrated, and she pushed Simon away, gently, to lift her phone out. It was habit, when you had children, not to let a ringing phone go unglanced.

I can see you, Fi had texted. *From the roof. This why no exes.*

Mel looked up. The party was still going, the music pulsing gently out over the high rooftop, soon to be shut down by millionaires' curfew. Some faces were leaning over the tasteful, whitewashed railings. Fi's was one of them. She raised an arm, waving Mel back in.

'I'm going home,' said Mel. 'You should go back up there, Simon, all is not lost.'

'Let me walk you.'

'No, it's around the corner. Go back upstairs, or . . .'

'Or?' He looked hopeful.

'Home to the kids,' she said, trying to sprinkle as little judgement as she could manage.

Simon took her hand and pulled her off the wall. 'This was fun, though. Maybe we needed it?'

He meant the talking, the dancing, the flirting. Maybe, Mel thought, she was looking at this the wrong way. Maybe Simon was testing out his new moves on a comfortable target. That wasn't such an affirming thought.

'See you tomorrow,' Mel said, 'when you drop them off. Good luck in there.'

Did she mean it? Maybe. The primary reason she'd finally asked Simon to leave their marriage was that she realised she didn't care anymore. That they didn't have sex. That they'd become tetchy colleagues rather than lovers. That the idea of any repercussions – 'If he's not getting it at home' – didn't bother her. All the clichés about long-term love were alive and well and living in her crowded flat and she didn't even mind. She cared so little that it had taken a pandemic and a sister staring down losing her life partner to shake her into action. Suddenly the idea of upending her children's lives wasn't a choice. It was an urgent necessity, to prove she wasn't dead yet.

So yes, clearly, the fire could be restarted in the right Sunday-session circumstances but it wasn't what she was craving. What Mel was craving was . . .

Flynn and Lori. She rounded the corner onto Bay Street and there they were.

At first she thought they were having sex, right there, in the street, at twilight. They were in silhouette against the streetlight outside their building, shining through the trees that could really do with a prune. The two figures were so close together there was no light between them and they were moving, back and forth, ever so slightly.

Mel saw the lights on in Flynn's flat above her own, the chatter of a crowd drifting down along with the sweet smell of a coconutty curry.

Were they serious? Were they really out here fucking, in a street where children played on summer evenings, among unit blocks festooned with festive fairy lights and solar-powered twinkling trees? With buses flying past and people – like her – pootling home from the pub?

For fuck's sake. *It's not all about you*, she wanted to scream at them. *We all have to look at you!*

Two buildings down, Mel stopped, partially hidden by the fran-gipani no-one at number fourteen ever thought to trim. Still a little woozy from the wine and the weirdness of the evening, her irrita-tion gave way to something else. Arousal? Curiosity? She stopped, shielded by the dark green leaves. Now that she could focus she realised she wasn't looking at what she thought she was looking at.

They weren't having sex.

Flynn's hand was twisted tightly through Lori's long, honey-coloured hair, pulling her head back, so her face was tilted up and towards him. His mouth was close to hers, but not actually on it, and it was moving fast. The expression on his face, even in darkness, was cold and hard. Lori was trying to pull away but her back was up against a white stone pillar. Flynn's other hand was gripped tightly around her other arm. If it wasn't getting so dark, Mel was sure she'd be able to see that his knuckles were white with the effort. The movement she'd thought was love-making was actually a delicate struggle, as Lori tried to move away, and Flynn tightened his grip.

Mel couldn't see Lori's face with any real clarity but she knew, she just knew, that there would be fear there. Her lips, so close to Flynn's, were trembling.

She hadn't stumbled across lovers in a passionate clinch. She'd found a vampire, tormenting his victim under moonlight.

Stop staring and do something, Mel told herself.

She stepped out from behind the bush, purposefully made her footfall hard on the pavement and coughed, to drive the point home.

Flynn looked up first. Immediately stepped back. 'Hi,' he said, with that deep, ghost voice. He shrugged a little. *Nothing to see here.* 'Nice night.'

Lori peeled herself off the pillar, but stayed back, out of the light. Her hand went straight to her arm, to the place he'd been holding her. She lifted her face just a little, so the streetlamp caught it. Tears. She tried a small smile. 'Hi, Mel.'

'Are you okay?' Mel asked, her eyes on Lori. Lori nodded. 'Everything okay?' Mel asked again, looking towards Flynn.

'Everything's fine,' he said. And Mel looked, pointedly, she hoped, towards Lori. 'Are you sure?'

'Yes,' the girl said in a small voice.

Mel looked between them. She knew everything Lori felt. The desire and the confusion and the excitement and the need and the shame.

She walked towards them, the couple upstairs she thought about too much, too often, and she looked right at Lori and said: 'You need to get away from him. Right now.'

Flynn laughed. Lori looked at the pavement, strewn with leaves and dried-on chewing gum and a few Macca's wrappers that had escaped the bins on garbage day.

Mel was emboldened by the wine, and her anger. Flynn was right there, but his body language was pulling back, not pushing forward. He didn't feel like a threat. He felt like a dog who'd had its snout slapped for sticking it where it shouldn't.

'I have stood where you're standing,' Mel said, before she knew she was saying it. 'I have felt how you feel. And one day, you'll wonder why you spent so long letting someone destroy all the things about you they say they love.'

Now Lori laughed, which stung more than it ought to.

'Turn it up, Mel,' Flynn said, his voice trying hard to be dismissive. 'Come inside, Lori.'

'You can come to my place if you want,' Mel said to Lori. 'Again.'

'No,' the pair of them said in unexpected unison.

'I'm fine, Mel,' Lori added. 'Flynn and I were just talking.'

He took her arm, more lightly than before, this handsome, horrible man, and started to move her inside.

'Are you sure, Lori?' Mel called after them, as they pushed the front doors open.

'I'm fine, Mel,' Lori called back again, her voice stronger than before. Flynn gave a little nod and a smile. Mel thought she might explode. With frustration and fury at the injustice of this shit.

'I know what I'm doing!' Lori said. 'I promise.'

Fuck her. Fuck him. Fuck him, the most. But also, fuck her.

Still standing out on the street by the rogue frangipani, Mel pulled out her phone.

What was the point of all the lessons we learned? she typed furiously.

All the words written and stories told. All the consciousness raising. All the awareness training. What was the point of any of it if we're just back here, playthings for monstrous men. No more able to get away than we ever were.

Mel shoved her phone back in her bag and looked up at Flynn's window. Heard the muted noise change shape as the missing couple re-entered the flat.

Woah. What are you doing? Izzy tapped back.

A shape appeared at the window. A woman. Taller than Lori, square shoulders, long hair.

Kat stepped close to the window, so the light from the street showed her whole face. And she shook her head, slowly, at Mel, staring directly into her eyes. And then she pulled the window closed, and dropped the blind.

Part Four

41

January: Lori

The sound of the waves had been soothing at first.

Now the constant *swoosh-woosh* was just invasive, relentless white noise. How did anyone stay sane here, when there was never, ever any hope of silence?

Rich people problems.

Lori was under instructions not to raise the blinds and not to approach the windows. But on day three she'd begun unfolding one of the deckchairs out on the garden veranda – slowly, cautiously, as if its very creak and clunk might betray her – to feel some air and sun on her face. No-one could really see this back deck, edged by the tangle of bush, trees and fin-shaped rocks of the national park. The front faced the ocean, and in between were two streets of sparsely populated, oversized holiday homes. She could hear families arriving, unloading, loading, leaving, but back here, surely, it wouldn't be noticed that there was someone staying at number seventeen.

The problem with the back deck, though, was the screaming cockatoos. They sounded terrified, yelling from the trees all morning as if warning her to get back in the house. Jesus. Was this what stressed-out Sydney people considered a peaceful retreat?

'I don't think I can stay here anymore,' she'd said to Mel last night on the forbidden phone call, after more hours spent lying on the clean, crisp sheets of the impossibly comfortable bed, tortured by sleeplessness. And she meant it. Solitary confinement was a punishment, not an escape.

'I know I'm not meant to call you, but I just can't do it. I have to come back. I'm going a bit mad.'

Mel had sounded terrible. It hadn't been even a little bit reassuring to hear her voice, thick with panic. And she was sure she'd heard Kat, too, in the familiar landscape of Mel's narrow hallway. An anxious whisper. 'Is that Lori?'

'Is that Kat?'

'I can't talk now, Lori. I can call you in the morning, but, please, just *hold on*.'

And then the phone had gone dead and Lori wasn't sure if Mel had hung up, or if the dumb pre-paid phone had just crapped out on her, but she'd been left, a small person in a big room in a dark house, staring at the phone's tiny screen with just the blasted sound of those non-stop waves smashing into her head. 'Thanks a lot.'

Now it was morning again and Lori had to decide what to do. Day six.

More *Love Island*? Or just leave? Abandon this insane plan and walk to a train station – was there a train station? Or try to use the stupid phone to call a taxi and use this pile of notes to go somewhere, anywhere else.

Her pretty prison was Mel's friend Fiona's house. Actually, officially it was Fi's family's house. The holiday home 'down the coast'.

And the idea to stay here, the idea to stage this whole, elaborate mess, had been born on Christmas Day.

Everything had changed after the goat curry.

After that night, it had become impossible to hide. Fingerprint bruises would do that. Tiny, blue-black signs that things had got out of control. And she wasn't the only one who knew. After pushing Mel away, assuring her that things were fine, nothing was fine.

The morning after, she had turned up downstairs, a little embarrassed by what her neighbour had seen the night before, but mostly feeling like a faint shadow of a person. Walking gingerly, holding herself carefully. After the glow of being back in Flynn's good graces, that sunny spot she'd been indulging in for days, everything had shattered. Again. His fury at the story she'd felt she could finally share – the story that, she'd imagined, told him how strong she was, and why she'd made the choice to come here and start again. He had been so dismissive, so furious, so terrifying.

She remembered smiling, as she walked into Mel's place, trying to show her that things were fine, she was fine, she was there to do her job. But Mel was completely different that day. She looked like she hadn't slept. She looked like what had happened to Lori had happened to her.

And she'd demanded that Lori tell her everything about what was happening upstairs. Some of it had felt like a welcome release. But it also felt irreversible.

'You have to leave,' Mel had said, more than once. 'You need to get away from him. You need to go home.'

Lori had only just returned all the money for the unlikely plane ticket to her parents. A gesture of independence that now seemed reckless at best.

'I don't think it's going to be okay,' she'd admitted, that morning, to Mel.

'We'll find a way,' Mel said. 'I promise.'

After that, perhaps the countdown to the plan was inevitable. Mel's flat became a safe retreat. Cups of tea and cuddles from the kids, their innocence and excitement about Christmas became a twinkly light shining into the increasing darkness upstairs.

On Christmas Day, Lori woke on the futon to discover Flynn had disappeared. Just a text: *Christmas not my thing. Gone fishing.* Nothing more.

And it was like Mel had known, as Lori's self-pity and her avoidance of her vibrating phone had been interrupted by a knock from little Ava, sent upstairs with a home-made card, a mince pie and an invitation to join Mel, Simon, Fi and a gaggle of kids down at the beachside park for a Christmas dinner that looked nothing like Christmas dinner. No turkey, no potatoes, no boozy pudding. But salad and prawns and quietly sweating ham.

Salty children were drenching each other with freshly unwrapped super-squirters as Mel handed Lori a plastic wine glass of warm prosecco and a proposition to do something radical. Why not give Flynn a taste of his own unsettling emotional warfare while buying a little time to try to find a flight, a way out?

'Aren't you angry?' she'd asked. 'Aren't you sick of being scared?'

And Lori was angry. Angry and shaken and bruised, literally and figuratively.

It was the birth of the plan that saw her here, now, in Fiona's refuge.

'They're not renting it this summer – because of the virus,' Mel had told her, on Boxing Day, as the plan morphed into a tangible, touchable thing. 'It's just empty. Perfect place to lie low while we get you sorted out. And Fi gets it. She's been there, in a way, herself.'

'What will I *do* there?' Lori had obviously known filling these hours would be a problem, since that was her first question.

Mel had looked at her like she was a little bit stupid. Probably because, Lori could see now, it was the least concerning part of this whole plan. A week alone in a beach house also likely sounded like a fantasy to Mel, whose time was never her own.

'There's Netflix,' Mel had said. 'And we can make sure there's a bag of supplies. It's a holiday house – there are books, and puzzles . . .'

It was true. There were books. Holiday house books that visitors had churned through on a sandy towel or across a damp weekend but not felt compelled to hold on to – thrillers, romances. Lots of murder, lots of sex. She'd started one by an English author whose name she knew from those twisty TV dramas everyone was obsessed by for one week a year, but it had felt too familiar, too close to home, when she considered the surreal quality of where she was and what she was doing. So she dropped it, and picked up a racy romance. But the sex scenes unsettled her, the hero's hands made her think of Flynn, and that was confusing, upsetting.

My life is imitating the art of a holiday-house book no-one liked enough to keep, she thought. And the thought made her laugh, but there was no-one to tell her little joke to.

Lori missed her phone. That was the dumbest part of this plan.

'You can't disappear with your phone,' Mel had insisted. 'You are instantly trackable as soon as you use it.'

'I can turn Location Services off.'

'You don't think Zuckerberg has thought of a way around that?'

The frustrating thing was, this would have made an incredible Instagram Story. Definitely worth saving to Highlights. How to fill a day somewhere you were pretending not to be.

Lori entertained herself thinking about that.

There was food preparation. As promised, there were two green, recycled bags, bursting with groceries in the elected getaway car.

It had touched Lori a great deal when she'd unpacked them on that first morning. The thought put into what a young woman would want on a week's non-holiday; there was no doubt that this bag had been packed by a mum. Chocolate biscuits – English ones, McVitie's digestives. But also fresh strawberries, and yoghurt, and honey. Gluten-free pasta and jars of sauce. Sprouted sourdough, for her gut health. Tea. Of course tea. PG Tips. And chamomile, for relaxation. Popcorn. Baked beans. Tampons. Naprogesic. Vegan cheese, because too much dairy could trouble her tummy, and one bottle of low-alcohol wine, with a message scrawled on the label in one of Ava's metallic sharpies – *Don't drink this all at once.*

There was muesli, which was the first thing Lori prepared every morning, and what would have been her first Insta frame, if she wasn't living this monastic screen-free existence. She'd spent time making it pretty in one of the plain IKEA bowls that filled the kitchen cupboards, sprinkling the frozen berries, and dribbling the honey in a juicy 'O'.

She even pretended to take a picture of it, with the dumb phone.

Being #missing is no reason not to give yourself the best start to your day! she would have written. Too dark?

The problem was there was too much time to think. Too much time to consider where she was and how she'd got there. She knew she should be feeling grateful. Safe. But what she actually felt was guilty and embarrassed. Mostly, she felt sick.

Sick at the thought of that night when Mel had stepped out from behind that tree where she had been spying – and she was undoubtedly *spying* – and Flynn's anger had bubbled back to the surface after that brief, golden period of safety and warmth. Of lying around, talking. Of intimacy and even praise. When *Don't leave me* had become *I don't know what I'd do without you*, embellished with *You make me a better man.*

But on goat curry night, everything began to curdle. After weeks of observing Kat drifting in and out of the flat around Flynn, Lori saw that her relationship with him was completely different from hers. Kat was able to poke Flynn, with a gentle but sharp point, about some of his stories, some of his attitudes, some of his habits.

Lori watched Kat circling Flynn with ease, not fear.

Want to take your feet off that table while someone else wipes it clean for you?

Tell us that story again, please? We definitely haven't heard it enough.

Yes, I'm sure Lori loves pulling your pubes out of the drain every morning.

Lori envied that. More than Kat's height and grace and confidence.

Kat wasn't afraid of Flynn.

Lori was. She hadn't been ready to admit it before, but she was now.

It had been good there, for a while, after he'd said *Don't go.* He'd even laughed off that awkward afternoon when Mel's husband came upstairs and made a scene about the kids. Such an overreaction, honestly. Lori guessed that Simon hadn't seen many hookah pipes like the one on the coffee table that day. And she knew that Mel wouldn't leave the downstairs windows open quite so wide as the one Ava was leaning out of, standing on a chair she'd dragged there while no-one was looking. Not ideal. But no-one died. And the kids were delighted.

No, that hadn't been the trigger for the very particular and peculiar turn of events that saw her here, now, pretending not to be the sole occupant of an oceanside house that smelled of damp emptiness, completely isolated, entirely unaware of what, if anything, the small world of the Bay Street block was making of the fact that she had been there, and now she was gone.

The trigger had been that fucking goat curry. And her attempt to be more like Kat. And Mel's busybody tree-lurking. And what happened afterwards, in bed with the man whose sun she just couldn't seem to stay in for long.

No, she wouldn't give up on the plan today. Mel would call the bloody burner phone back soon and tell her what was happening, and when she could leave. It wouldn't be long. A glimmer of hope at the end of this strange iso-week. A timeline for the reunion with her phone and the rest of the world. And an update on Flynn.

Was he missing her? Was he insane with worry? Was he angry? Was he sorry?

Mel would tell her. So it was *Love Island USA*, then, to keep the spookiness at bay for another day.

Lori crept to the big window in the front bedroom, the space she was mostly confining herself to as the rest of the house felt too big and too empty. She lay on the floor, as she had done before, and pulled back the bottom corner of the blind to peer out onto the street.

Through the tiny triangular view, the street looked as sleepy and lifeless as it had the last time she'd peeked. Two lines of red roofs before the blue and white of that crashing ocean. Boats in driveways, surfboards on balconies, plastic chairs pulled out onto lawns. Other closed blinds, locked-up homes, buildings that only saw life on long weekends and summer holidays when a virus wasn't infecting every damn plan.

A car on the street at the end of Fi's driveway was parked with its nose sticking out just a little. That wasn't there yesterday. With a startling panic, Lori realised she knew that car, and it wasn't the one she'd been spirited down here in.

Rushing back to a moment months ago. Waking with a jolt against a window. Green and blue. Green and blue. The irritation with the phone charger. A peeling private school sticker on the back window. George, his head in his phone. Snapchat.

It was Rob's car. And it was parked across the drive of number seventeen.

42

January: Flynn

'She knows something.'

'You sound paranoid.'

'I'm not paranoid. You might have noticed there's a problem around here.'

Kat sighed. She sounded far away. He didn't like it.

'Where are you?'

'I'll come over later, Flynn. I've just got to do something today.'

'Something more important than being here with me?'

'Yes.' There was just a spike of exasperation in Kat's voice. 'Today, yes.'

Flynn was watching his bare feet on the floorboards of the hallway. He was walking up and back, up and back, and he felt, as each flat foot hit the wood, like every step was being traced from below. Like the barrier between the apartments was dissolving. Like Mel, down there, was looking straight up at him. Straight into him.

'I can't explain it, but after last night . . .' A flash of what he'd said to Mel in the kitchen, so close to her face. So angry.

'I don't even know what happened last night. I just saw the neighbour leaving, looking dark as hell.'

'I . . .' Flynn clenched and unclenched his fist, curled and uncurled his toes. 'Lost it at her a bit.'

'Well, that's not going to help, mate,' Kat said, her voice softening. 'I thought I said to keep her onside. Downstairs is your biggest problem.'

It was annoying how Kat said that. Flynn didn't have a problem, except for these women. 'What happened to "Don't worry about it"? Now I have a big problem downstairs?'

'Flynn, I don't know what to tell you. Just . . . don't do anything. Just stay put.'

The call went dead and Flynn looked at his phone in disbelief. *She hung up on me?*

He walked back down the hall and pushed open the door to the living room, to an assortment of bodies on the couches. He slammed the door back, hard, opened it again. 'Get out!' he shouted. 'Get the fuck out, now.'

At exactly that moment, he heard windows downstairs being pushed open, the particular noise the old wooden frames in this building made as they slid up or down. *Good morning, Mel. Hope I didn't wake you.*

He pictured her, nursing a tender head, stepping gingerly around her apartment, in that big white shirt he sometimes saw her running out to the rubbish bin in. Bare feet, strong legs. Women looked good for much longer now, he noticed. His mum never got to get very old, but her friends and his aunties had all seemed ancient. Loose and lined, shapeless clouds of ciggie smoke and complaints, most of them. Not like these together eastern suburbs women who must be – what, *forty?* – but spent all day at the gym and marching up and down the cliff path, and were never out of those clingy leggings.

From the back, at least, they looked like a different species to the women he grew up with.

Mel wasn't one of those stringy women though. She looked like she could have been quite a good time, once, if she wasn't so sad all the time. And if she wasn't so weird about him. Seriously, every time he passed her in the hallway it was like she was going to explode and he didn't know – or he hadn't known – if she wanted to fuck him or fight him.

Or if it was just about Lori? A protective mama-bear act? She'd answered that, the night she'd yelled at them in the street that she used to be them, or some shit. They were somehow caught up in whatever midlife crisis she had going on down there. And it was ruining everything.

'Come on!' Flynn called towards the lounge-room door, where he could hear some scrambling, some floor-scraping, some movement. 'I've got things to do! Get out!'

'C'mon, mate.' It was Des, appearing from the little bedroom, the one with the mattress on the floor. 'No need to scream the place down.'

'Actually, there fucking is,' said Flynn. 'I need you all out of here. Today. For good.'

He needed them gone. He needed this unit packed up. And he needed to go. It was clear as day.

Nothing good was coming for him here.

Flynn pushed into the bedroom and grabbed a T-shirt, pulled it over his head, shoved his phone into his back pocket and banged back towards the door. 'You've got an hour, Des,' he yelled as he pushed the door and started down the stairs. He trotted at pace, holding his breath as he reached the ground floor. *Don't come out, don't come out, don't come out,* he repeated silently, over and over, towards Mel's door.

But as he came level with her door, of course it opened. He didn't stop moving, but there was a shout. 'Flynn!'

It wasn't her. It was the lady cop.

He kept going, through the front doors out onto the tiled path, then he stopped, turned around. 'Hi,' he said, as calmly as he could, aware his hands were shaking, that he was barefoot, that he probably looked like shit. Again. 'Any news?'

'Maybe,' she said, stopping a few steps ahead. This is how far apart we stand now, in public, he thought, yelling at each other, across the divide. 'There's been a development, I was just telling your neighbour.'

'Why are you telling my neighbour?' Flynn hadn't meant to ask that, quite like that, but he couldn't help himself.

'I'd be happy to explain,' she said. She pushed her hands in her pockets. It was a hot day, but her shirt was white crispy cool. She was younger than Mel but older than him. She had this very cop-like way of saying things, calm but firm, pushing but not shoving. 'Maybe you could come and talk to us at the station, later today? We could take you through it? I just have to clear up a few details first.'

Going to the station did not sound like a good development. Flynn knew that. He hadn't been told, or strongly encouraged, to go there yet, but it was only a matter of time, he knew, if Lori didn't turn up first.

He caught sight of Mel, fiddling with a blind in her window, pretending not to watch. She wasn't in her nightie shirt, looking fragile. She was dressed, tidy, together.

'Have you found her?' Flynn asked. 'Is she okay?'

'No.' The lady cop's eyes didn't leave his. 'We haven't found her. But we do have some new information.'

'Is it to do with Rob?' Even as he'd fed them that name, he didn't believe it, not really. That little shit? Dangerous?

'I can't tell you, Flynn, you know that.'

'And her bag?'

'What about her bag?' Eyebrow up.

Was it wrong to ask?

'You took it yesterday.'

'We did.' She looked down at his bare toes. 'Where are you off to, Flynn?'

'The beach.' Did that sound flippant? 'Clear my head. This has all been . . .'

'I can imagine.'

She didn't seem that worried, the lady cop. If they thought he'd done something to Lori, why was the detective woman walking around on her own, gossiping with his neighbour, talking to him out in the sunshine? Why hadn't they pulled his apartment to pieces by now? It must be because they believed what he'd told them, the very first time he'd spoken to them. Or, at the very least, they'd found nothing that disproved his account.

He woke up, and Lori was gone. He had been irritated. It wasn't usual. Lori never got up before him. Mornings were their time. In bed. She was always all over him, first thing, no matter what. Then she would get up, start sorting out the flat, make him a tea and they'd shake off whatever the night before had brought with it. Sometimes, he'd go to work. Sometimes, she would. Sometimes she'd go for a walk, or a swim. But he'd woken up, and she wasn't there, and she hadn't told him she was going anywhere.

So, he was a bit shitty that morning. Maybe she was pissed off with him, about how the night had ended. She'd been a little bit more pissed off than usual, lately. Not that he could tell the police that. They'd ask why and then . . . well.

He'd thought about it a thousand times since, but Flynn was sure Lori had been there while he slept. He was used, after all, to her weight alongside him in the bed, the sound of her breathing in light little snuffles, her smooth skin pushed up against his, one leg thrown across, then rolling away. It wasn't something he'd talked about, ever, but *sleeping* with girls was almost the best bit. Someone next to you, all night long. Someone there when you woke up. Someone who chose to stay.

He hadn't felt her leave the bed. The picture he conjured in his head now, had he actually seen it? Her stepping, naked, three foot-falls across the floorboards, picking up the blue cotton dress she'd been wearing the night before. Pulling it over her head and just, what . . . leaving? Pulling the bedroom door closed behind her? It was shut when he woke up, and it was hardly ever closed. He hated closed doors, blocked exits. Had she pulled it tight so he didn't hear her next five steps to the front door and the click of that closing behind her? Was that it?

He'd told them all of that, the first time. But now the lady cop was standing on the tiled walkway and asking him something else.

'Your neighbour says there are often a lot of people staying at your place,' cop lady said. 'But on the night Lori –'

'There was no-one else there.'

'You're sure?'

'I'm sure. She'd asked me . . .'

'She'd asked you?'

'To have a night with no-one else in the house.'

'What did she say?'

He couldn't really tell her what Lori had said. Even now, with his back against the wall, it revealed too much.

Or maybe it was more how she'd said it that was so telling. With every breath of courage and spunk that she could summon. It was almost cute to watch. Since the night she'd told him about her past, about the thing that happened in her boring, prissy English world that had pushed her out of that nest with an unforgiving shove, things had been a bit tense.

As in, Lori was tense.

Flynn was wondering why he'd done this thing again – humiliated himself begging this woman to stay around, only to feel so fucking angry every time he looked at her. What was wrong with him that he couldn't just let her go? Fly off back to the life her parents had planned for her? Seeing her little pinched, sad face around the flat those last couple of days had made him feel like shit. He liked sunshiney Lori. He needed sunshiney Lori. But he had pushed that sunshine out of her. Again.

He watched her turn it on, dutiful little thing she'd been moulded into, when she went downstairs to look after those kids. Or when other people turned up, looking for a bed and a party, like everyone was at this shitful, stuck moment.

He'd checked her phone a few times in those last few days, to see if she was talking about plane tickets again. She wasn't, but he also wasn't entirely sure what he'd do if she was, this time.

'Flynn,' she'd said, the morning before she'd vanished, when she had brought him a cup of tea and an orgasm, like every morning. 'Tonight, can it just be us?'

She didn't ask for things, Lori. So he knew, when she chose to use her courage to ask him that, sitting on the bed beside him, the sounds of the other people in the unit starting up – groans and chatter and a low, pulsing beat of music – he knew she was trying to make things nice.

He'd smiled at her, raised his eyebrows, nodded, and it had made her braver.

'I want you to cook for me,' she said. 'Just me.'

And Flynn had felt a wave of affection for this tiny ask of hers to have a piece of him to herself, just once.

'She asked me to cook her dinner,' he told the lady cop. 'Just us. Like a date, I suppose.'

'That's nice,' she said. 'You a good cook, Flynn?'

Stop bullshitting me, lady.

'Yes,' he said. 'I am.'

'What did you make her?'

'Does it really . . . I made her a prawn stir-fry.'

She was messing with him. Just the latest in the chorus of women messing with him. He would prefer the short man cop right now, really he would.

'Why?' he'd asked Lori, on the bed that morning, although he knew. 'Why do you want me to cook for you?'

She'd pushed her honey hair back off her face, the sun lighting up her smooth, long neck. Only a faint blueish echo of a fingerprint visible now, beneath her ear.

'I just want us to have a nice night together,' she'd said, in that pretty, prim voice of hers, the one that turned him on so much. 'Feel special again.'

'Okay,' he'd said, and he'd weaved his thick fingers through her long thin ones and looked at their hands together, on the bed. 'I'll cook for you.'

'Even Kat,' Lori had said, her eyes also on their hands. 'Not even Kat here?'

'No-one,' Flynn had said. 'Just me and you. She can hang at her place. About time.'

He'd felt warm. He was going to give this girl what she wanted. He was going to do something for her and her only. So he lost his temper with her, sometimes? Not today. He was a good man.

'Prawns! Fancy,' the cop said, smiling. Light, fake.

'Frozen.' Flynn looked down at his feet. 'Can I go now?'

The cop's fake prawn smile was gone. She was back to a serious face.

'Yes. I'll call you later about coming in.'

'Right.'

Flynn spun on his bare feet and headed towards the ocean with the eyes of the lady cop at his back. It took every bit of willpower, every muscle, every fibre in his body, not to run.

43

January: Mel

'Mel, they're going to think it was me.'

'It *was* you.'

'Stop it.'

Mel dropped the blind, her phone pressed close to her ear, as if to keep the words close. Flynn and Elaine had stopped talking now. He'd pretty much sprinted off towards the beach, and the police-woman had climbed in her car, poked at her iPad for a while, and driven away.

'You're saying that someone told the police they saw Lori getting into my car?'

'Yes.'

'And there's a proper investigation now? A *missing persons* investigation?'

'Yes, but –'

'You need to call the police right now and tell them everything.'

The source of the nausea swelling inside Mel could be the know-ledge that he was right. Or it could be last night, those seltzers, that sickening encounter with Flynn, the memories assaulting her on the bathroom floor. Or Lori calling her, or Kat at the door. There was a lot to feel sick about this morning and the urge to vomit was definitely a symptom of being out of your depth. Way, way out. The comforting sight of the shoreline was a thousand unreachable strokes away.

But Elaine had just left, and if there was a moment to confess, she had just let it slip past when the policewoman had asked her if she was familiar with a blue Subaru Forester with a numberplate beginning with B-something-something in the street. A car that Lori had been seen climbing into, carrying nothing, at 5 a.m. on the morning she got out of Flynn's bed and never returned.

A sensible, family car.

Simon's car.

'This is ridiculous, Mel,' he said. 'I did you a favour. I didn't ask for this. Just call them.'

'You did a good thing.'

'They'll find out it's my car in about twenty minutes and I will tell them everything,' Simon said, firmly.

Mel knew he was in the car park of the store, the special part, cordoned off for employees. The bit that the kids always got a little kick out of being allowed to park in, when they had to go shopping. He would have dropped Eddie and Ava at their sports vacation camp this morning, the one that was only going ahead with masks and distance and the signed agreement that the kids would not hug, touch or shout encouragement at each other. He would have driven them to the oval, with badly packed lunchboxes and apples that would remain untouched. Had he remembered hats? And water bottles? This didn't seem like the moment to ask.

'Mel.'

'Yes?'

'This has gone too far. You know it has. I was happy to help a girl in trouble.'

'Woman. Lori's an adult.'

'Mel. Focus.' A phrase she'd heard him say a hundred times over the past ten years.

On Christmas Day, Mel had watched Simon, flimsy paper party hat pushed down around his ears, wrestling with Ava in the grass over the predictably sporty present he'd given her under the park's festive pine tree. Mel had watched him patiently, gently talking Eddie through how to use his new snorkel, how to clear the mask and hold your breath so you could take a long, swooping dip to the sandy bottom of the ocean pool. She had looked to Lori, pale and shrinking, being literally erased by a man she couldn't trust. And Mel had known Simon would help realise this crystallising plan. He was a good man. A man who, when asked if he would be part of a strange idea with a good intention at its heart, would trust Mel, and say yes.

But what he didn't know – how could he, Mel didn't, either – was how messy it was going to get. How much Mel had, apparently, been willing to risk . . . for what?

'Mel? I'm worried about you,' Simon said, now. 'This hasn't gone too far, yet. They'll understand you were worried about a young woman in an abusive relationship. But you have to tell them, you have to tell them now.'

Clear-eyed Simon, speaking the truth.

Mel couldn't swallow to reply. This was not a conversation for a car park. Not this bit. Not the reason why there was no such thing as going 'too far' now.

'You don't understand how it feels,' was all Mel could say. 'When someone else is taking you over, bit by bit. And you love them, but they're your enemy. And they just think they're entitled to every piece of you.'

Simon took a beat.

'Mel. Are we talking about Lori? Or are we talking about you?'

'It's not changing,' said Mel. 'Something should have changed, between twenty years ago and today. But it's the same shit. We have a daughter, Simon. Don't you want it to change for her?'

'This isn't going to change it, Mel. It's not going to make anything better for Ava, or Eddie.'

The breeze was blowing up outside, as it usually did mid-morning. Mel was picturing Flynn, down at the beach, smashing himself into the foam and froth, trying to release the anger and frustration from his head. The anger and frustration that, until now, he'd been taking out on Lori.

'Mel, I have to go to work. If you don't sort this in the next two hours, I'm going to call the police. I can't not. And you . . .' He sighed heavily. 'You need to talk to Izzy. She will tell you exactly what I'm telling you but maybe you'll listen to her.'

Mel heard the phone click.

Simon didn't know that Izzy didn't need to hear Mel's grand confession. He might understand how highly she valued her sister's opinion, but he clearly didn't realise that she would never have done this without Izzy. Without her big sister's knowledge, without her help.

Izzy knew all about that night Mel had seen Lori and Flynn on the street, the night she saw him holding Lori by the hair as he hissed into her face. The night something broke in her. When she'd sent Izzy that furious text about monstrous men, she could barely hit the keys with her shaking fingers.

How can I help? Izzy had replied. *I want to help. I need to do something. Something positive.*

And so Izzy had joined the plan. The group of people who were going to make a difference. Along with Fi. And Simon. And yes, Kat. Izzy's role was Lori's family liaison. *See, Simon*, thought Mel. *There's some well thought-out insanity to this plan.*

Even thinking about that night made the skin behind Mel's ears actually throb with a memory she'd scoured from her life.

No wonder she felt so wildly out of control. The ghost upstairs' possession was complete. Dominic was back inside her head.

His beautiful face and the smile that no-one could resist. His thick, deep voice and the reassurance of his solid, smooth body. He was her anchor, in this country. In this city. He was why she was here, then and now.

But he was also the man who had betrayed her. Not in the way people understood betrayal, by flirting with someone else, sleeping with someone else, cheating, lying. He had betrayed her by convincing her that she was everything to him, and that her heart and soul and body would be safe in his hands. And then he had slowly removed those safeties until one night, just a few months after their travels had landed them here, by the eastern beaches of Sydney, the Emerald City he had always wanted to conquer, he had instead shown her that she was nothing.

Dom had been away for two years. He'd talked about his return from the moment he'd met Mel. The return to the homeland, the great, big, fresh start.

And a great, big, fresh pressure. Mel had listened to Dom talk, and talk, about all the things that were going to happen for him. He wanted to start a surf brand, he wanted to film his mates on waves and pull in advertisers. But friends from up the coast who had also settled here were muttering that it might take some time. That Sydney, for all the sunny, gold and blue glamour, was a small city obsessed with the old school tie, that networks were hard to break into, that it wasn't easy to get things started. Narratives that Mel couldn't imagine in a place that seemed so new and optimistic, and that Dom had shrugged off until he couldn't.

His frustrations, building from an occasional comment to a bad day to a dark week, seemed to be growing. The kind of explosion she'd first seen in a hostel reception in Chiang Mai had become more frequent, always sparked, it seemed, by Mel stepping out of line. Asking for something, wanting too much. Being too much.

On the night she could no longer ignore, they had been to see a band at a pub in the city. A friend of a friend knew the singer. Their names were on the door. It was quiet, acoustic, the music was stunning, fragile, quiet. After a song that soared with sadness and grace, Mel, enraptured, had clapped and clapped and whooped until Dom, stone still beside her, grabbed her hands and pulled them to her sides. 'Stop it,' he'd said, in the kind of voice you might use on a puppy who hadn't learned to walk to heel and required a firm yank back to your side. 'You're embarrassing me.'

'What did I do?' Mel had asked, too excited and distracted to have realised that the eggshells she had studiously learned to avoid were scattering everywhere.

'You're clapping too loudly. Everyone's looking at you, you idiot.'

Mel had felt instantly sick. She knew she must have flushed scarlet-red from her neck to her scalp. She'd looked around the crowd. People *were* looking, although it wasn't clear if they'd just started, since Dom's voice wasn't quiet.

'How is it possible,' she'd asked, her voice trembling as hard as her hands, 'to get clapping wrong?'

'Shush!' Dom's face, his open, generous face, was screwed tight, furious.

'Why do you hate me so much?' Mel knew she should stop. But she was emboldened by the public space. The music was about to start again, she knew no-one could hear her, not really. 'Why is everything I do so terribly wrong?'

The next thing she remembered from that night was being outside that pub, dragged there by her wrist and pushed up against the wall, Dominic's hand around her neck, her back against the bricks, the feeling of the rough, broken surface scratching up her bare shoulders. She could picture it so clearly now, the image she'd pushed away for so long. She'd been wearing a flippy little cotton skirt and a singlet with thin straps. Her favourite, slightly beaten-up ballet flats. She'd thought she'd looked cute when they'd left the beaches on the bus that night.

'Don't ever talk to me like that,' the man she loved hissed at her. 'Don't humiliate me like that.'

And she'd started crying. Hot fat tears that she knew, instinctively, would only make Dom angrier, but there was no way to stop them coming.

'Don't fucking cry,' the man she loved shouted. But she couldn't really cry, because even as her eyes made the tears, her throat couldn't make the sobs. Because he was holding it too tightly. 'Don't be so pathetic.'

When Mel had seen Flynn and Lori in a pose that mirrored the one she had found herself frozen in, so many years before, all of the emotions she'd held on to poured back through her. Fear. Confusion. Shame. And fury.

Even back then, powerless in a new place, beholden to this man for everything, Mel had been full of fury. Fury at the total lack of control she ultimately had over her life, her actions. She could be yanked around like a rag doll, ordered when to speak and when to shush, told where she should go, where she should sleep, what she should spend. All by the man she loved.

She was furious back then. And she was furious now. Because of that fucking ghost, and all he'd brought back.

She didn't need to tell Izzy she'd become obsessed with history not repeating. But she needed Izzy to tell her what to do next, now that this rescue, or revenge drama – she wasn't sure which anymore – was spinning out of control.

Izzy, she typed into her phone. *I need your help.*

44

January: Lori

Lori was making herself small by the holiday house front door. It was a giant wooden slab with a glass panel on both sides. If she squatted with her back to it, she could crane to peer, ever so slightly and quickly, to either the left or the right, and see if anyone was coming up the gravel driveway.

The tiny white stones crunched, too, she remembered that from the murky dawn when she'd been dropped here, by Mel's closed-book of an ex-husband, who had said about five words to her as they'd driven the almost three hours from Sydney. The pretty pebbles didn't make the driveway perfect for a stealth approach. Thank God.

She was clutching the burner phone in both hands, ready to dial . . . who? Mel? The police?

If that was Rob's car, and she was almost certain that it was, where was Rob? It had been at least fifteen minutes now since she'd first seen it from the upstairs window, and still nothing, nobody. So where was he? Should she just open the door and run away? Maybe he was down there? Why would he be? Who would have sent him?

What would he want? Lori thought of the last time she'd seen him, at Gordons Bay with the kids, and what he'd said.

'You'd better run.'

For fuck's sake. Lori bent for another quick look. Nothing.

What about the back door? Had she locked it after she came in from her illegal trip to the veranda? Of course she had. She must have done. *Don't be ridiculous.* But now all Lori could see was that door handle, with the inadequate little button in the centre. Was it up, or pushed down? It probably didn't even matter. How effective was one tiny button? But it mattered. It mattered a lot.

Even as she started her crawl from the front door to the kitchen, Lori was viewing herself from above and thinking, *How am I scrambling across the floor of a stranger's home on the far side of the world? How am I suddenly the main character in a fucking true-crime thriller?* And also, as her heart kept bang-banging and her stomach kept flip-flipping, Lori could only think, *I am so sick of being afraid.*

She made it around the corner of the kitchen entrance, out of sight of the front door, and stood, panting, bent over just a little, still clutching the stupid phone in both hands. The door to the back veranda was in sight, and she rushed towards it, eyes on that handle. Was the lock pushed down? Was it?

Lori reached the door, saw that the silly little button was up, and in the exact moment she put out her hand to push it inwards, the handle turned, decisively, to the right.

Lori dropped the phone and screamed.

This is the sound I make when I think I'm about to die.

The door was pushed open. Despite Lori's panic – the adrenaline rushing through her at the most ridiculous of speeds – she couldn't stop that quick, shoving movement. Despite both her hands being on the door handle, pushing with as much force as she had left, she tipped backwards, in what felt like slow motion. And she fell back into that room, in that musty hostel by the sea, months before.

'Lori! For fuck's sake.'

It wasn't Rob.

It took Lori's muddled brain a moment to realise it, but it definitely wasn't Rob. From the kitchen floor, Lori was looking up at the same saviour she'd had that night back at the Merimbula hostel. It was Kat.

Kat's golden Birkenstock sandals, Kat's long legs, Kat's strong arm reaching out to her.

'Come on, drama queen,' Kat was saying, in that deep strong voice of hers. 'Up you get.'

'You were Rob.' Lori was finding it almost impossible to hold on to a thought, to loop together a story of why Kat was here, standing in the kitchen in the holiday house. 'I thought you were Rob. I thought you were him. The car . . .'

'I borrowed it.' Kat's hand was smooth and her grip was firm as she pulled Lori off the floor until she was standing in front of her. 'That dickhead owes me a few favours.' Kat smiled at her, a big, indulgent smile that made Lori burst into tears.

'How did you . . .' Lori gestured to the door, to the deck, to the back of the house.

'I was told not to come in the front door. Nosy neighbours. So I did a little off-roading round the back.' Kat flexed a golden foot. 'Copped a few scratches.'

As the connections began to fuse in Lori's mind, another possibility formed. 'Are you alone? Is Flynn . . .'

'Flynn? God no. He has no idea.' Kat was looking at Lori like she was trying to work out just how much of a mess she was in. And, clearly, the answer wasn't a good one, because she grabbed both her hands and, in the most uncharacteristic of gestures, she pulled Lori into a hug. 'Come on, let's get you sorted out.'

Twenty minutes later Lori and Kat were sitting on the bed in the giant master bedroom, Lori's home for the last five days. Kat had made Lori a cup of tea, had sat guard outside the ensuite while she shakily showered, and then produced some fresh clothes for her to put on. Lori recognised them, the heavy cotton neutrals. They were Mel's.

'So, this little escape plan has got a bit out of hand, yes?' Kat was saying. 'Judging by the state of you.'

'How did you know?' Lori had many questions, but this seemed like the right place to start. 'How did you know where I was?'

Kat's smirk was back, but softer, kinder. 'Mel asked for my help, on New Year's Eve.'

Even the words made Lori flinch. Flynn didn't do Christmas. But he did do New Year's Eve. It had been a night of booze, of Lori being pulled, like a limp trophy, from party to party, being increasingly ignored at every stop. She tried to remember seeing Kat that night, back at the flat. Talking to Mel? How did that happen?

'She's not stupid, Mel,' said Kat. 'She could sense something, pushed on it.'

Lori hadn't sensed it, though. Despite Kat stepping in to help her again and again, it had never occurred to her that Kat was anything other than one hundred per cent on Flynn's team. That she only had his back.

'I can't stay here, Kat,' she said. 'It's solitary confinement. I feel like I'm being punished.'

'That's interesting, isn't it?' Kat had said, looking up at Lori from where she was lying back on the bed. 'How this whole thing was about saving you and punishing him, but you still feel like the victim.'

Was that comment a criticism of her? Or a criticism of Mel and this bonkers plan?

'I need to know what's going on back there,' Lori said. 'And what's going to happen next. Because you can't leave me here.'

And so Kat began to tell her. About Flynn calling the police, on the second day. About the social media campaign. Posters on lamp-posts. About the article online. Every small piece of information felt like a stone dropping into Lori's stomach.

And then Kat stopped, at last night, and Mel and Flynn's clash in the kitchen.

'I need to go back,' Lori started saying before Kat had finished. 'My parents. My friends. Oh my God. I had no idea.'

'You had no idea that people would notice you were gone? Or would care? Of course they did.'

'I just didn't think everyone would know.'

Mel had made it sound easy, like a sensible, almost inevitable choice. The photos, the evidence, the time they needed to get the money together for a flight. The escape.

'I don't think I thought about it enough.'

'Lori.' Kat put a smooth, golden hand on hers. 'Mate. You didn't think anyone would care you were gone because he'd convinced you that you weren't worth caring about.'

Was that true?

Lori did know Flynn was looking at her phone. Watching her. He knew about the money that came and went. He knew about the ticket. He knew about it all, and he'd needed to see the money had been returned to believe she was serious about staying.

Flynn's 'Please don't leave me' had turned from a request to an order with the niceties deleted. After that night, it was very clear that any attempts to evade him were not going to be tolerated.

She really had been trapped. She had not imagined it.

'It sounds so serious when you tell it like that,' said Lori, as the images of her family flashed in her head. Of Jools. 'It feels like I overreacted. I should have just . . .'

'Just what?' Kat said, with that clear, challenging gaze.

'Stayed. It wasn't that bad.'

'Really?'

'It wasn't like he was . . . beating me.'

Lori thought about that night, the weight of his body on hers as he'd pushed into her, his hands on her shoulders, her neck. *Not a game. Your new reality.* She felt that crushing gasp for breath, the panic that came with it.

Kat rolled her eyes. It felt cruel. 'Of course he wasn't, Lori. That's not what he does.'

'What he *does*?'

She rolled onto her belly. 'Why do you think I helped Mel?'

'I didn't know you did.'

Little pieces of a picture were coming into focus.

Kat arriving and never really leaving. Kat on the stairs with her the night of the mushrooms and gin. Kat on the bed with her the next day. Kat at Mel's door.

I always have Flynn's back.

This isn't going to end well. For you.

'I didn't think you even liked me.'

'Who said anything about liking you?' Kat's smile was sly and slow, like a cartoon cat's, her hand still on Lori's. 'This isn't about you.' Then she blinked and looked away. 'Not entirely, anyway.'

'I don't understand.'

'I've been helping Mel all week. We share a certain viewpoint on what should happen. We've been watching him.'

'Watching him?' Lori couldn't help it. 'How is he? He must be worried . . .' *about me*, she wanted to say. *He must be worried about me.*

'He's Flynn.' Kat rolled onto her back, threw her arms up above her head. 'He's worried about himself.' She gave the slightest of shrugs. 'I'm sorry, but he is. You need to understand that.'

If Lori had felt in over her head, crawling across the floor, fearing a furious Rob was going to break down the door and destroy her, a slow realisation was now dawning that maybe her role in this entire, bizarre story was smaller, less significant, than she'd thought.

'So who is this about?' she asked. 'For you?'

'It's about him.' Kat propped her head on her hand. 'And all the fuckers like him. I've known Flynn forever. He's like my brother. But he's like a brother you know is dangerous. There's a point where you have to stand up. And I didn't know I'd ever get to it. Until I saw you.'

'Me?'

'You don't deserve it, Lori. You don't deserve him. Or fucking Rob, or any of them. None of us do, but that night I saw Flynn bump you onto the floor, and everyone laughed . . .' Kat blinked again. 'I don't know, I just couldn't watch it all happening again. I'm sick of it. For all of us.'

Again. Despite everything, a sting. Lori was just another girl. Kat was trying to tell her that Flynn's possessive obsession had nothing to do with her. That she was just an avatar, standing in place of . . . who?

'What about you two?'

'What about us?'

'You're so close. Are you saying he did this to you, too? How are you still in his life if that's who he really is?'

Kat laughed. 'Oh Lori, mate. Every superhero has his origin story. And every abusive narcissist has theirs, too. I'm afraid I was there for the early stuff.'

Lori felt something like jealousy at the intimacy of this statement. *Ridiculous. Get a grip.*

'He trusts me,' Kat said, clearly reading the conflict on Lori's face. 'He trusts me. That's why I can help.'

Lori shook her head. 'So, do the police think he *killed* me?'

Kat shrugged again. 'Maybe. Maybe they did. I don't know if they do now, but he's scared. For the first time, I think.'

'That's not right. I can't let them think that. I can't let anyone think that. It's horrific.'

Kat grabbed Lori's hand again. 'But didn't you think he might? For a moment? Didn't you think that, when he put his hands on you, his weight on you, when he put his hand around your neck, when he hissed at you with that look on his face? Didn't you feel like he might? Honestly. Think about it.' Lori had never seen Kat animated. She was always cool, detached, distant. 'Isn't that why you're here?'

'But, Kat,' Lori said, enjoying the feeling of a comforting hand, of someone tethering her to this moment, to this bed. It was perfectly possible she could spin away into nothingness at any moment. 'He didn't.'

'So, he didn't this time,' said Kat. 'But consider the future. Yours, or someone else's. Do you really think Flynn's not capable of worse?'

'I just can't stay here, Kat,' Lori said, the tears spilling over again. 'I'm going mad. And now I know . . .'

'I get it,' Kat said, holding her hands tightly, keeping her steady. 'We'll get you home. Just one more day. He's almost there.'

Lori didn't have the energy to ask where 'there' might be.

45

January: Flynn

Flynn was cleaning again when the phone started buzzing.

Des hadn't been happy about clearing out, but he'd gone, Lea delivering championship side-eye on her way out the door.

'You don't know what's good for you,' Des had said, huffily, as they left. 'You'd think you'd know who your mates are.'

And he'd heard Lea, just outside. 'Is anyone surprised Lori fucked off? *If* she fucked off.'

Whatever. The surf had cleared his head. Today was the day. He was gone. But first, this place needed to be clear. Not a trace of him left behind. If Lori could vanish, so could he.

His backpack was down from the top of the wardrobe, his stuff grabbed from all corners. What did he need to take, really? Flynn knew a lot about travelling light. About not letting stuff weigh him down.

He should have stuck to what he knew. No question about that. When Lori turned up here, that day back in spring, he should have told her there was no place for her here. He should have closed that fucking door in her face. Resisted that prim little voice. He should have known. He was going to get pushed back to the place he'd promised himself he wouldn't go again.

His phone started buzzing while he was packing his guitar case with the strings Des had left behind.

LORI.

The phone was flashing Lori's name. Flynn dropped the paper packets and grabbed it. Where was she calling him from? And why? To tell him it was all a massive mistake? To tell him . . . what?

But the police had Lori's phone. So what did that mean? They had unlocked it? They were using it to call him? Why wouldn't the lady cop just call him herself? Or just turn up here, like she always did, as if she owned the place?

Maybe it really was Lori. Maybe she was back. Maybe she was at the police station. Maybe he was off the fucking hook.

He pressed the green button. 'Hello?'

It was the sound of the ocean calling. Nothing else, just waves.

'Hello?' Flynn said again. Immediately, a tickle of fear, a pinch of frustration. 'Lori?'

These weren't the waves at the end of the road, these were crashing, loud, dramatic, not the waves that lapped harmlessly at the bay's edge five minutes away.

Flynn hung up. What was that? Some kind of automatic redial, some kind of robo cold call he didn't understand?

For a moment, alone in the flat, looking at the cracked phone in his rough, lined hand, Flynn felt unsettled. That was too weird.

The last of his clothes – a jumble of shorts and jeans, op-shop Hawaiian shirts, faded Ts, the uniform of a man who never had to dress for anyone but himself – were in a heap near the door. He was bending to scoop up his last few faded greys and blacks and blues, when he saw something new, lying on the carpeted floor of the built-in wardrobe, exactly where Lori's bag had been.

It was a polaroid photograph, but a tiny one. It looked like it was for children, or mice, not adult-sized people with ordinary-sized hands.

Flynn stepped back from the picture, as you might back away from a growling dog.

He knew that wasn't there before. He had been through Lori's bag, more than once. He'd taken the bag out of that spot in the wardrobe where it lived, and put it back in there, also more than once. There were no polaroids in that bag. There were no photographs littering the floor of that crappy old built-in wardrobe. There had been nothing there.

The phone in his hand rang again. LORI.

'Hello?'

Again, just the smashing anger of the waves. Not the bay, but it could maybe be the cliffs? The place he liked to sit in the dark?

Flynn put a hand to the top of his head. 'HELLO!' he shouted, so loudly he heard movement downstairs, registering the disturbance.

He hung up, threw the phone onto the bed, and went to the wardrobe. He picked up the tiny polaroid, gingerly, by its white edge.

The shiny square was white, and black, with a smudge of blue, and a light purplish-green.

It took Flynn a moment to realise what he was looking at.

A woman's neck. Long, pale, just the glimpse of the very edge of a hand holding back dark honey hair. Fingerprints. One, two, three, under the delicate earlobe with the trio of piercings. A tiny sun, a tiny moon, a tiny star. Lori's constellation.

Bruises.

Fuck. Flynn felt vomit rising in his throat. He dropped the photograph and bolted to the bathroom where he fell on his knees and retched.

He'd put those fingerprints there. He'd marked her, but when? More than a week before. On the day Lori evaporated, those bruises were no more than a sky-blue memory. He knew. That photo was old. Or brand new.

He retched again. Nothing came. *Breathe, mate, breathe.*

The phone, again, barking from the bedroom. He knew, if he went to it, what it would say.

Breathe.

When was that photo put there? Yesterday? This morning?

Surely it wasn't there when the cops came for Lori's bag? Because if it was, they would have taken it. And he would have heard about it.

Cops didn't mess around pulling blokes in if they had any evidence. And a photo like that, well that was evidence.

The cop this morning. She wouldn't have been so chatty about prawns, so 'come in and chat, yeah?' if they had that nugget. No. He had to remember, like Kat said, they had nothing.

They had nothing because he'd done nothing wrong. Not what they thought, anyway.

Where was Kat? Not that he could show her that picture. His mind was going too fast, running right ahead, refusing to settle anywhere. He needed to think.

He couldn't show that to Kat. Unless . . . Unless he told her it was a set-up. After all, it could definitely be a set-up. Kat would believe that, right?

The phone. Again.

Fuck. This.

He was being tormented.

Flynn stood up. Went to the sink. Splashed water on his face. Bent to wrap his lips around the tap and slurp at the cold water.

How did that photo exist?

The night Lori disappeared, he did make prawn stir-fry. He did what she'd asked him to do, told Des and Lea to disappear, didn't answer when Kat called, turned down any offers pinging on the phone.

He shaved the ginger and garlic so thin it was almost transparent, he'd crushed that red chilli until it was almost a paste, like he'd seen on those cooking shows his nan played on repeat.

When he thought of the little kid he was then, escaping the clatter and shout of his own house for hers a bus ride away, he felt contempt. Sneaking into Nan's flat, curling up on the peeling vinyl lounge, feeling soothed by the rhythm of the TV, stuck on the Food Channel. What a piss-weak attempt at escape it had been, before he was old enough, strong enough, to mount a real retreat from that whole mess. Nan, who never made him anything other than toast, or maybe mince on toast, watched the cooking shows because they were the only thing on TV that didn't upset her. The news was awful, she said. Those soaps reminded her too much of reality – 'I could tell *them* some stories' – and she hated sport, with its sweaty clash of angry men. No, the well-spoken people cooking all day were soothing. Little Flynn had to agree. The sizzle and hiss, the round, calm words. This thing makes that thing, do this and that will happen. Some smiling person was always travelling to some full-colour place, full of possibility. There was always someone else's nana there, with some impossibly exciting perfect recipe. The overflowing bowls of everything sitting pretty on kitchen counters, nothing in a packet, nothing in a bloody tin.

'Look at that,' Nan would say, when he turned up looking pinched and hungry. 'Purple garlic. Who thought of that?' And she never asked him why he was there or how long he was staying, or when he was going back. He'd just put his head on her knee, and they'd watch the food.

He should have been a chef. Maybe he still bloody would be. Not that he was interested in getting yelled at by some old pervert in a kitchen for years, scratching at pans and de-shitting prawns. Still, there must be an easier way. He'd head back up north. Tourists would come back soon, and they'd need people who knew their way around a chicken. Maybe he should go on one of those reality TV shows.

That night, just the two of them, prawns and rice and enough chilli to make Lori's eyes water. She'd told him it was delicious, this feast he'd made just for her, even if he was clearly trying to burn off her tastebuds. It was pretty nice. He didn't always know what to say to Lori, when they were alone, once he'd spun her his best stories, true and false. Sometimes the space between them was obvious in the silence, in the missed beats. But it was never like that in bed, and they'd got there, quickly, after dinner, after some cheap pink wine Lori had found somewhere, left behind by someone, from some party, some other night.

But now he knew, from that tiny scrap of blue-white-black film, that she was lying to him that night. Playing him. Someone else had taken that photo. And they had taken it for a reason. And even as she sighed and moaned under his hands, his mouth, with the windows open and the night air mussing up her hair as she moved on him, she was betraying him.

Because she said it was alright, that he'd got a bit out of hand. She said his sorry the next day was enough. She said she knew she shouldn't have told him those things, that she should have known it would make him jealous and angry. And she had said sorry, too. She said she wouldn't leave, she knew he didn't want to hurt her. She said it was okay. That he was still a good person. That she knew he was. That she knew he just couldn't help himself sometimes.

She said all that.

But she had already had someone take that picture. And now she was haunting him.

Flynn walked back into the bedroom. He looked at the photo on the floor. *If I wanted to see you*, he thought, *I could look at one of the thousands of pictures you took of yourself every fucking day, the ones you plastered all over the internet for every bastard to ogle at.*

Stop.

This was exactly who he didn't want to be. Again.

He crouched next to the picture and picked it up again, lifted it close to his face. It was such a tiny frame, there were no clues to be found in a background. But he knew where this picture had been taken. He knew who had taken it, too. As the phone started to vibrate again, with the ghost call from wherever that endless wave was smashing, he walked back over to the wardrobe, past his bag, past his box, past his guitar, lying open in its case.

Flynn very carefully put the polaroid back where he found it. On the wardrobe's carpeted floor, face up.

He picked up the guitar, moved to the bed, pushed the old wooden window frame open wide and sat on the bed. He started picking and playing, nice and loud, that Nick Cave song he knew downstairs was so keen on. The one that always made his mother cry.

46

January: Mel

The ghost upstairs was singing Mel's wedding song. To her.

Mel, due on a work call, her sister's voice still in her head, sat on the edge of her bed for a moment, then lay back and let the ships sail over her.

He had a beautiful voice, her ghost. Unfortunate, but true. Smooth with a sprinkle of spiky stones. Deep and warm and rough.

This summer she had slipped into the past. Little parts of her she'd abandoned had snaked upwards, slipping through the cracks in the floorboards, spreading through the upstairs apartment, attaching themselves to places they didn't belong.

'I couldn't stand it,' she'd said to Izzy. 'Watching it play out all over again.'

Dom had charmed everyone they'd ever met. The privilege of being handsome, of being deft with words, of being able to see, quickly, what other people needed, and of having a confidence gifted to him by a mother who put him before all else.

It was one side of his coin. The shiny side.

'Isn't Dom great?' said everyone they met, wherever they went, on three continents. It was intoxicating to be the woman who went home with that man. When all the eyes in the room were on them, she felt invincible.

But when the eyes inevitably turned away, she became invisible.

She shared it with Lori, across decades.

'It's like I was inside Lori. Like I could feel her feelings.'

'But you weren't. And you can't.' Izzy was unmoved.

Dom had loved this song. Sailing ships. Burning bridges. Making history. It was the kind of love that Mel, on the dirty-shiny black streets of Manchester, never imagined for herself. But Dom did. It was fated, he told her, that he should be in that completely random bar on that night. That of all the people in the world, she would be serving the drinks. It was written that bizarre circumstances – a vote, a rush, an absent boss – would conspire to see them collide and then their lives spin off in a new direction. Particularly hers.

If Dom hadn't walked into that bar that night, Mel's life was unknowable. She may never have lived in London, never have even visited Australia, a place so far away it might as well have been Mars. She wouldn't have discovered what happened when the other side of Dom's shiny coin was flipped. She wouldn't have retreated to the safety of Simon. Not have little Australian children with little Australian accents. She would not be living here, in her beautiful, chaotic, too-small flat by the sea. Not have just risked almost everything to repay some kind of cosmic debt.

But Dom? He would likely have done exactly the same thing. Without her, maybe alone, maybe with some other girl from some other place. He would have backpacked through Asia on his punitive budget. He would probably still have come to live here, by the beaches. Still have struggled. Still have left. And in all likelihood, he would still have died that day, in that place, at that time.

Mel was a bit part in Dom's story. He was a main character in hers. And it still felt unjust.

'Something triggered this mess,' Izzy had said, when Mel had called her for help today. 'It didn't just appear. The split. The virus. You manifested the ghost. You know that, right?'

'We're manifesting now?' A weak attempt at humour.

'What you have to do is work out what it's really about so that you can sort this shit out and move on,' said Izzy. 'I care about you more than I care about the rest of it.'

Dom was still alive when Mel married Simon. He wasn't yet a ghost. He was just the ex-boyfriend.

That's why it had been wrong, unquestionably wrong, just as Izzy had said, to choose that song for the wedding. Mel and Simon weren't about burning bridges, about sailing ships, about making history. Mel and Simon were about Wednesday night touch footy and Friday in the pub, Sunday morning runs and cups of tea in bed. About crosswords and weekends down the coast and meal prep for the week. They were about lifestyle and routine, they were about agreeing to disagree. They were about reasonable voices and considerate sex, and all of it was beautiful. And safe.

On the morning of the wedding, Mel messaged Dom. Her hair was done. Her face was on. There were people, everywhere. Except for in the toilet, where, in the white ribbony slip that was unlike any other underwear she would ever wear before or after, Mel took a seat and found the number she'd resisted using for so long.

I'm getting married today.

I thought you should know.

What did she want the reply to be? That's what she would ask Eddie, or Ava, when they were telling a story about some action of theirs that had ended badly. Well, what did you want to happen?

She had sat there on the toilet seat, manicured fingers holding the phone in front of her, tapping her bare toes on the tiles.

Why would he answer? It had been two years since that day in Wollongong, since the very last time she'd seen him, since she'd had to tell his mother that yes, it did look like Dom was in a bad place right now but no, she couldn't help and no, she wouldn't be able to do this again. He never had reached out again. After six months, a year, she even stopped thinking that he might.

Dom didn't do social media, but she knew, through scraps of shared acquaintances and Gina's occasional Facebook updates and messages, that there were some good times, and some not so good times, since that day.

A picture of Dom in something like a suit at a family party: *So lovely to have my boy home and doing so well.*

A picture of a beaming Gina and a tired-looking Dom, metallic balloons floating above his head like thought bubbles outside a riverside restaurant. *When your son turns 30!*

No photo, only words. *You're only as happy as your least happy child.*

A Melbourne tag, a skyscraper, Gina holding a cake. *When your baby starts a BIG job, but still needs his mama bear.*

He was probably busy, she'd thought. What did two-years-later Dom do on a Saturday morning, down in Melbourne? Had he become a bike guy? Was he making single-origin coffee in a stark, stylish city flat? Or waking in a hungover haze in a traveller house under a string of peace flags? It was unlikely that he was sitting around waiting for a message from an old girlfriend.

Mel remembered the buzz outside the bathroom, voices asking, 'Where's the bride?' and she'd got up, looked at the airbrushed version of herself in the mirror. The one with the smooth hair and the even skin and the wide, fluttery eyes. She blinked, once or twice. *That's me*, she remembered thinking. *That's me getting married today.*

Buzz.

Even now, she could still feel the rush of excitement as the phone had lit up.

It was still his number. He was still there.

Happy you happy.

Then, another buzz, a separate message.

Lucky guy.

Mel held the phone so tightly to her. And she thought, *I could press this button and he might answer.* He would probably answer. It would be that simple. We are connected, in this moment, looking at the same thing at the same time. Thinking about each other.

Why didn't she? Mel, lying back on the bed, a lifetime later, tried to remember which bit of reason had stopped her from hearing his voice for the very last time.

It was because she had worked so hard to move on, yes? It was because she had dragged herself, literally, it felt, out of the wreckage of that relationship, towards something better. It was because she knew, even then, if she did hear him, his voice eerily like the ghost upstairs' voice right now, she might not be able to put on that dress and walk out into that crowd.

Back in this bizarre summer, Mel's work computer started to buzz. She was meant to be in a meeting. She was meant to be talking about campaign flighting and renewed assets and post-campaign effectiveness measurement. She was not meant to be losing herself in this time loop. She had been slipping in and out of it for months, and if she let herself truly go, she might never come out.

The ghostly Nick Cave stopped. The twisted serenade was over. Mel heard the window upstairs close.

'Simon is right,' Izzy had said. 'We've taken this far enough. It's not too late to back out right now. Tell him you're going to sort it out.'

'I will,' she'd said. And she'd meant it. But. 'I want to make sure he knows what he did.'

Dom never did.

'Mel,' Izzy had said. 'I will fight every fight with you. But you have lost sight of something here. Is this about saving a young woman from an abusive man, or is it about Dom, and your midlife crisis? Because, you know, some of us have real crises to deal with.'

Mel sat up now, looked over at her pinging computer. It was time to join that work call, and then to set things straight.

Izzy's last words to her this morning were still pounding in her head.

'I know that, Izzy.' But. Mel's voice had caught when she said, 'I'd stopped thinking about him. It's like I'd forgotten him.'

'You've also forgotten that *you* left *him*,' Izzy had said. 'You found that strength, on the other side of the world, with no-one around you, and nowhere to go. You left him. The man you have always claimed was the love of your fucking life. You left him.'

'And I never saw him again.'

A phone call from Gina. Mel pregnant with Eddie, her belly round and smooth and scribbled with veins. She'd been lying on the lounge, in this flat, wearing only her sensible, stretchy maternity underwear, as the heat climbed towards unbearable. Simon was out, playing a sweaty game of tennis. The moment she saw Gina's name, Mel had known.

I thought you should know. Dominic died yesterday. Gina's voice. Like she was reading from a script. *I'm calling people. Before, you know . . .*

Mel's belly, rising and falling with the writhing baby. The weight of the heat on her neck, her shoulders, as she swung her legs around to the floor, put a hand to her head.

It was an accident. The doctor . . . is she a doctor? I don't know, the woman who looked after him. Says definitely an accident.

Gina's voice broke. *But it's funny, Melanie, because you know Dominic. He's a surfer. Such a strong swimmer. So confident in the water. Ever since he was a little boy. But he drowned.*

'He died, Izzy. He went swimming at a beach where no-one goes swimming. And I never saw him again.'

'But that's not your story, Mel,' Izzy had said. 'You had saved yourself long before. You need to remember that. Maybe, by thinking you could save Lori, what you've taken from her is the chance to save herself.'

Mel smoothed her hair with her hands, fastened the top button of her shirt and pressed join on the work call. She would do all the things she was meant to do. She would turn up for work, be the good provider her kids needed her to be. She would set things right with Simon. She would help Lori find her own way home.

She just needed one more day. One more day.

47

January: Lori

'**F**uck me, the birds are loud here.'

Kat woke up beautiful. She'd appeared in the room from God knew where, wearing a white robe she'd dug out of who knew what, and walked straight to the windows, pulling back the curtains with a decisive yank. The whole holiday suburb was laid out below, looking up.

'Kat! You can't do that,' Lori called, from her bed, where she'd spent the night not sleeping. 'The neighbours.'

'Fuck the neighbours,' Kat said. 'I think it's time we stopped hiding and started people talking. It's almost over.'

Kat hadn't meant to stay last night. She had meant to drive back to Sydney, to keep an eye on Flynn. The plan was coming to a *crescendo*, Kat had said, dramatically, as she raided Fi's family drinks cabinet for vodka. Which had led to a toast, which had led to Kat proclaiming that Lori had suffered enough, and that misery needed company. Lori hadn't really known what that meant but was certainly very happy to keep Kat around. The holiday house didn't seem so echoey and terrifying, with someone to share it with.

'You know, Lori,' Kat had said, as they lay on the back deck in the pitch black, clinking glasses and looking up at the improbably numerous stars. 'You are in a very unusual position.'

'Understatement.' Lori had laughed, taking a slow sip of the burny booze.

'You are in the unusual position of knowing what people would say about you if they thought you were dead.'

'Stop it,' Lori moaned. 'You almost had me not thinking about that.'

'The thing is, no-one says anything unkind about dead people.'

'I am not dead.'

'But they still have to pick very specific good bits, so they can show off that they knew you well.' Kat sighed. 'Proximity to drama equals relevancy. We all know that.'

'How depressing.'

'You want to know though, right?'

'Know what?' Lori was confused. The vodka. The dark. Kat. Everything.

'What they're saying about you.'

Lori thought about it. Of course she wanted to know.

So she and Kat had spent the next hour lying on the floor of the master bedroom in the darkness, scrolling Kat's phone. Being reunited with the blue glow of an iPhone screen made Lori feel calm. But seeing an outpouring of anxiety and sympathy from people whose faces she could barely picture made her feel queasy.

I travelled the West Coast with Lorelai. We shared sunrises and secrets. I will never forget her shy smile and sad eyes.

The name, the photo, completely unfamiliar.

A girl she'd shared a bus ride with from Exmouth to Useless Loop: *Lori was very pretty. I hope she is okay.*

'Jesus.'

'Said you were pretty, though.'

One of her high school English teachers, Mr Hinman. *I never forget a student, but I'd almost forgotten Lorelai Haring until now. Now I've remembered her, I just want her to be safe. Godspeed, Lorelai.*

'I had almost forgotten her? Are you *allowed* to say that?'

I can't stop thinking about Lori. As if the virus hasn't taken enough from us already. This might break me.

This from the girl in Dorking who had screenshotted Lori's mistakenly shared photo and scorched three months of her life. The catalyst to her escape. *This might break me. Really, Anna?*

'This is bullshit, I don't feel so bad now.'

'Maybe it's the vodka.'

'Most likely.'

The people closest to her, though, were nowhere to be seen on the Find Lori page. Kat had told her that Mel had 'handled' her parents and Lori didn't need to worry. Was that why?

'I feel a bit like a lost dog.'

Kat showed Lori Flynn's message, the one she'd helped him write. 'Think of it as a trick,' Kat said. 'We're playing an elaborate trick on him. To teach him a lesson.'

This morning, Kat was throwing light on everything. She had lain at the end of the big bed, stretched, relaxed. And she'd asked Lori what she wanted to do today.

'What's going to happen to Mel,' Lori asked, 'when the police find out she helped me, and didn't tell them?'

'It depends. Adults go missing and turn up all the time,' said Kat. 'It depends . . .'

'On?'

'What you tell them, when it's time.'

Mel. Jealous, angry Mel. Loving, selfless Mel. Lori had noticed that every time she bounced downstairs to play with the kids, Mel sagged just a little. It was as if her very presence threw Mel off, just as Flynn's did, upstairs. She remembered that first day, when she'd found Mel at the front door. Mel had been listening. Mel had been wearing her pack. It was strange. Sad. But at the same time, Mel left no space for pity. She was together, strong – defiant even. It was like she missed something about herself. Lori could feel it, in the way Mel looked at her. Half disgust. Half adoration.

'You can tell them it was your idea,' Kat went on. 'No-one's going to be mad with a frightened woman hiding from her abuser.'

'Did you know,' she asked Kat, 'that Mel took pictures? With Ava's little toy polaroid. Of my neck, after Flynn . . .'

'Yes, I knew. I think Flynn knows now, too.'

Of course she knew. This was their plan.

'Really? He'll know it's Mel.'

Kat shrugged. 'He's not stupid.'

'What if he does something to her?'

'He won't.'

'How do you know that?'

'He just won't.'

Lori looked at Kat, so untroubled she was inspecting the ends of her hair. Lori felt foolish around her, but also safe.

'I feel like I should have known you were part of this. I think I would have felt better.'

Kat looked up from her hair. 'It was better you didn't.'

'When did you . . .'

'After goat curry night,' Kat said. 'I saw you and Flynn out there. And I saw her watching you, shouting at you. I thought I'd go see her on my way home. I didn't like that I had to leave you there that night.' She looked up. 'I knocked on Mel's door on the way out. She was a bit wild, but we spoke.'

Lori remembered the next day, at Mel's, sharing the secrets of upstairs. Mel had already known. Already heard it from Kat. When she'd asked Lori if she could take the photos. When she began to talk of escape.

'And then, on New Year's Eve,' Kat went on, 'it came together. Fi could give you a place to stay. Simon could be transport. Mel's sister could deal with England. And I could manage Flynn. You had a team.'

A whole team. But only half the plan.

'Mel didn't tell me about framing Flynn. And I can't believe I just said *framing*.'

'It's not framing. We just want him to understand.'

The 'we' wasn't just Kat and Mel, Lori knew. It was a bigger we. 'You want him to understand how it feels to be scared.'

'Scared, and out of control. And we couldn't tell you that. You were still too vulnerable to him.'

Lori looked at Kat. 'I was scared of *you*, you know. I thought you were terrifying. You seemed so . . . hard.'

'I am hard.' But her face wasn't hard. The way she put out her hand and pushed Lori's hair from her shoulder wasn't hard. The fact she was here, keeping Lori from being alone, wasn't hard. The way she was struggling to decide whether to say what she was about to say, that wasn't hard either. 'I've just had enough. Looking after myself has meant letting go of a whole lot of terrible shit other people do. It's survival. But, it's . . .' She looked at her hands. 'Exhausting. I'm done.'

Lori leaned across the bed and hugged Kat, who shrugged it off with a cry of disgust. But in the moment before she did, she'd squeezed Lori back. Tightly.

'Thank you,' Lori said. 'Thank you, for not just letting it happen.'

'Not just me,' Kat said, quickly. 'You had a crew.'

*

Lori stood out in the sunlight, her feet, in Mel's too-small sneakers, crunching the little white pebbles in the driveway. It was hot, but a heavy day, like the air was wet.

After a day in the presence of Kat's remarkable energy, she felt like her focus and faith was leeching back into her body. The fear was fading.

The station wagon was waiting, and Lori climbed into the passenger seat of Rob's mum's car, the seat she'd never been allowed to take, pulling the giant front door closed with a satisfying thunk.

'I know exactly what I want to do today,' she said. 'I think I know how to tie this whole mess up.'

'Mel and I thought –'

'I think I need to do it myself,' she said. 'I don't want to be rescued again.'

'Okay, I want to hear your plan. But first I think it's time for you to call the police.'

And Kat handed her the iPhone.

48

January: Flynn

*O*ne last dance, Mel.

Flynn knocked hard on the downstairs door. Three times.

Everything upstairs was ready to go. Yesterday was the day for it, but Kat had let him down. He hadn't been able to leave, not without seeing her.

I'm stuck somewhere on a job, she'd texted.

I'm out of here, he replied. *It's time. Shit's getting weird.*

I think I know why. Hold on.

So he'd waited. The flat was spotless now, everything he needed crammed back into his bag. Everything from the van he couldn't carry left behind.

He knew what to do. He'd done it before. A bus to a place where the travellers gathered, usually by the sea. Then fire up the pre-paid phone for a ride-share, a van sale, a new adventure. The virus had knocked numbers down, but the great moveable mass was still out there, trying to outrun what passed for reality. He'd be right. Big country.

But the polaroids. He had found another, in the afternoon, on the fridge. How had he walked past it, held there by a magnet boasting the number of a local plumber. 24 HOURS. NO CALL OUT.

No eyes, pale and pink and purplish; there was a red mark on the slightly swollen edge of Lori's lower lip. It was him who had bitten it. But it could easily have been her, right? All of this, easily refuted. If only she'd come back and tell the truth. He'd never hit her. Never raised a hand to her.

That's what he'd been piecing together, last night, as he lay, not sleeping, looking at this picture, the one of Lori's face and neck, the lips whose laugh had got him into this fucking mess in the first place. Whatever they were trying to pin on him, it wasn't true. Couples argue. Shit happens. The man cop would understand that. He imagined the moment where their eyes would meet as it all became clear. *Chicks. Am I right?*

Mel opened the door. He was surprised. Not a tentative crack, a wide-open throw. She would have known it was him. She had a peephole.

'Flynn. It's six a.m.'

It was. And yet, she was up and dressed. Yoga leggings, of course. Ponytail. The uniform.

'I'd like us to talk.'

'You would?' Her face gave nothing away.

'I don't want to do it here. Can we go for a walk?'

He'd been rehearsing this, too. The smile that would go with the offer. The upturned palms, showing vulnerability.

'You want to go for a walk, at six a.m., with me?' Her voice was teasing. It shat him no end. *Stay calm, now.*

'You know that it's like Central Station down at the beach at six a.m.,' she said. 'If you were thinking of pushing me off anything, there'll be plenty of witnesses.'

'You're funny.' Flynn leaned against the doorframe. Brought back the smile. 'Come on.'

Mel looked back over her shoulder. He knew her kids weren't there. He always knew. She heard his life, he heard hers. And there was nothing quiet about a mum and two kids who needed instructions to wipe their arses and brush their teeth. She was alone.

She reached out to grab her keys, her phone. 'Okay.'

She was right. They hit the end of the road and the beachfront was as busy as it was at midday. The smell of the day's first freshly brewed coffee. Groups of women dressed like Mel, walking vigorously, talking at speed. At least two gangs of exercisers on the beachfront grass, pulling ropes, swinging weights. Men in Speedos and swim caps, running on the sand, all facing the same way, like seagulls. A few old birds doing yoga on the steps, their brightly coloured mats rolled out towards the sun that had just popped up, like a big old egg yolk, over the ocean straight ahead.

'Fuck me,' he said. 'Well, that settles it. No chance of knocking you off here.'

Mel didn't smile. She nodded towards the path at the closest end of the beach, the one that led up towards the cliffs. She started walking that way, and he fell into step alongside her, moving close enough so that his voice would carry without shouting, and so their arms were close, but not touching.

'The photographs,' he said.

Mel didn't say anything. Didn't look at him.

'I know you took them.'

She kept walking, along the path stamped with stingrays and jellyfish, the jolly seaside walk for families to do together. For these eastern suburbs idiots to kid themselves they lived in nature.

'I want to know what you're planning on doing with them,' he said. 'I understand what you must think.'

'You do?' Her first words but still no stopping, no looking.

'You're protective of Lori. We had an argument. I just . . .' He reached for the script. 'I don't understand why you've waited till now, when we've been looking for her all week.'

'Waited till now to what?'

'To tell me you had those photos.'

'I didn't tell you that.'

'The other night, upstairs. Why didn't you say?'

A group of men passed them, jogging purposefully, sweating, shouting to each other about the virus.

'It's really just a cold at this point!'

'Has been all along, brother!'

Flynn waited for them to pass. They were reaching the place, near the top of the cliff, where he would usually stop, climb the fence and sit with the waves. He stopped. He wasn't sure if she would, too, marching away as she was. But she did. 'What?' she asked him.

'I think you know where Lori is. I think you've been faking it, the posters, the campaign, the Facebook page. I think you've been trying to fuck with my head.' That language, the last bit, wasn't what he'd meant to say. It sounded too aggressive. He'd slipped up there.

Mel's expression didn't change. She stepped towards him, her face tilting up. 'Why would I do that?' she asked. 'That seems like something a crazy person would do.'

'You tell me.'

These people going by, these power-walking, jogging people, if they were looking away from their feet, from their smart watches, from their phones, they would wonder what these two mismatched people were doing, standing still on the clifftop thoroughfare, at six in the morning. Standing so close, talking so intently. Flynn wondered if you could tell, from a distance, that there was tension between them, that this wasn't a friendly conversation. Not a normal Wednesday morning chitchat.

'Because you're an abuser?'

'I swear,' Flynn breathed. 'I never hit her.'

Mel was looking at his mouth. It was an intimate shift. And confusing as fuck.

'I think you got it wrong,' he said. She was listening, after all. Whatever was going on here, she was listening. 'And I'm sure it came from a good place. But, you know, Lori and I –'

Mel kissed him. The script crumbled as she did it, this woman, this mum, right out here on the cliff at rush hour, she put one foot forward and reached up on her toes to press her lips against his. Her mouth was slightly open, just slightly, and the pressure was firm, like she meant it, and his arms instinctively reached out to pull her in as a tiny green light clicked on inside him. That's what this was about. It was going to be okay. He could make this woman do whatever he wanted. Just as he was tripping through those thoughts, Mel stopped kissing him, she pulled back, pushing his arms down, and she looked down at the path.

'Don't be embarrassed,' Flynn started, his body relaxing for the first time in what seemed like days. He knew what to do. This was familiar territory, he was fine.

'I'm not embarrassed,' Mel said. She looked back up at him and it was true. She didn't look embarrassed, or even worried. 'I needed to do that. To check something.'

Flynn tried to reseal the distance between them, to step back into that closeness. Mel stepped right out of it, again. A group of women power-walked past, their heads and ponytails swinging towards them as they did. An illustration of their intense visibility. Flynn stepped back.

'Check what?'

'That you really weren't him.' Mel said it as if she was talking to herself. 'I mean, of course you're not, but I had to check.'

'Mel, it's okay.' Flynn knew he had to give her permission for her desire. Women always wanted that. To be told it was okay to want. He'd noticed that in high school. The boys often needed permission to not want. The girls, always, to be reassured, you're normal, go ahead, take what you want. Flynn had been an expert in convincing the girls that what he wanted was what they wanted, they were just too timid to know it.

'I don't know what you're talking about right now, Mel, but it's okay if this is what you want. If this is what all this has been about.'

'It's not what this has been about.' Mel laughed. A big laugh. 'I just needed to do that. Now, you can get fucked.'

It was shocking, that line, coming out of this woman's mouth. More shocking than the kiss. 'Mel?'

'I put the photos in your room yesterday morning when you were at the beach. I took them with my daughter's camera.'

Mel's voice was loud now that she was standing further away. With the wind coming off the ocean, she almost had to shout. 'Which is fucked up, to have to use my little daughter's camera to take a picture of what a so-called man did to her babysitter.'

Flynn was trying to retrieve the script from the scattered debris of his mind. This is what he'd wanted her to admit, to say. The whole kiss thing had thrown him off. He needed to get back on track.

'I knew it,' he said. 'I knew it was you. How the fuck have you been getting into my apartment?'

'It's not yours,' Mel called across the wind. 'Nothing in there is yours. Nothing here is yours. I have Lori's keys. She's safe, in case you give a fuck, which I know you don't.'

Flynn felt a rush of relief so intense it made him wobble. He was off the hook. This crazy bitch had screwed everything for herself.

'I also have her phone,' Mel said. 'In case you were confused about that, too.'

'But . . . I gave the phone to the –'

'Not hers. Same model, same case. I swapped it.' She sounded proud of herself, this delusional woman. She seemed to have no idea she had just screwed herself.

'I'm going to call the cops, tell them I've been harassed by the crazy woman downstairs.'

'I've already called them.' Mel was smiling now. It was creepy, almost. 'So has Lori. It's all done. Kat is bringing her home now. I suggest you go.'

Mel started to walk away down the hill towards the beach and the house. Flynn's relief was interrupted by that one word flung at his feet.

'Kat? What do you mean, Kat?'

She kept walking, and Flynn couldn't help it, he started to run after her. Just a few big strides and he was ahead of Mel. 'Kat?'

'Who do you think helped me get Lori away from you? Who do you think knew exactly how dangerous you are?' Mel kept charging along, forcing Flynn to run backwards in front of her. He stopped, went to grab her arm.

'Don't touch me, I'll scream,' Mel shouted. Bootcamp heads turned.

'Kat?' It was the only word Flynn could say. High school. Blind with fury about seeing her talking to that fucking Andrew King that very first time. He could still see King's head, bent towards Kat in the canteen, her glossy head thrown back, laughing. The sight of it burned. He'd been so angry he'd punched Andrew King out at the school gate, and got suspended. He was so angry he'd cried, red hot tears stinging and his stepdad had told him to be a fucking man about it. So angry he'd pushed Kat up against a wall, called her a slut, shook her by the arms. He'd been so angry at the look of betrayal and shock on her face. What about *his* betrayal, his shock? He thought she understood him, that she knew how precious she was to him, how far he would go to protect that. He also thought she'd forgiven him. All these years, watching him with other girls. She had forgiven him, surely? Just as he thought Lori had forgiven him.

Mel started walking again. 'Also, the police have the rest of the photos,' she said. 'So don't leave the country. They'll be coming for your passport.'

'I don't have a passport.' Flynn felt physically winded. He bent over.

'World traveller like you?' Mel threw the words over her shoulder with a sarcastic laugh.

'I thought so,' she said, and she kept walking.

49

January: Mel

Eddie and Ava wanted to ride in the police car.

Mel was watching them from the flat, seeing Simon gently trying to distract Eddie from leaning in the open front window, Ava from trying to open the back door. Eddie's little face was serious, concerned. 'If Mum's going, I'm going.'

Ava started waving at Mel, stretching up on her toes. 'Hey, Mum!'

'It wasn't you who reported Lori missing,' policewoman Elaine was saying to her, 'so that's something. And Lori has informed us that this was all her idea. That she was in danger and needed to escape. But you have lied to police more than once about this matter. There is the possibility of a public mischief charge for wasting police time.'

'I know,' Mel said. It was all she could say. 'I'm just so sorry.'

She could apologise, but she could offer no convincing explanation for her actions, beyond the fact that, this summer, something slipped away from her, and she was only now getting it back.

Simon was looking in from the street, his face a picture of worry that mirrored his son's. He smiled encouragingly at her as their eyes met. She smiled back, weakly.

'The other thing that concerns me,' Elaine said, 'is that you had knowledge that this relationship was abusive, possibly violent, and you didn't disclose that in our conversations.'

'That's because I knew she was safe.'

Suddenly, Ava's voice, calling out Lori's name. The station wagon was pulling up behind the police car, Simon standing back as Ava threw herself around Lori's legs.

'It's possible Strout could decide to press charges against you,' Elaine said, but she was pulling her things together, her sensible little black handbag, her iPad case, her keys.

'I don't think he will,' Mel said. 'Although I'm sure I deserve it.'

'I don't think he will, either,' Elaine said. 'I doubt we'll ever see him again. Which probably isn't a great outcome for Lori. Or for women like her.' She stood up. 'We're going to talk to her now. See what she wants to do.'

'Will she be in trouble?'

'Running away from an abuser is certainly not a crime,' Elaine said. 'Lori's an adult, she can go where she wants, visa permitting. We just have to make sure she's okay.'

As Elaine headed down the hall, her male counterpart followed. Mel watched him for signs of judgement. What did he think about what this crazy woman had done? There was nothing, a blank face.

She remembered what Kat had said to her, on New Year's Eve, when she had slipped away from the crash of music and bodies upstairs to conspire, out of sight of a drunk and distracted ghost, with the boring old mum downstairs, watching the Sydney fireworks on the ABC and plotting an improbable heist. *You'll get away with it, if they find out. White, middle-class lady trying to help a young girl? They'll probably give you a medal.*

Mel had rankled at that, but she knew it was true. Her privilege protected her, could cast this as a victimless crime. *It's not how things go down where I'm from*, Kat said. *But here, I think we'll be okay.*

Today, Mel felt like she deserved punishment.

'We always suspected it wasn't her phone, by the way.' Elaine turned at the door. 'It was one of the reasons we didn't rule out a planned disappearance. Why this hasn't got a whole lot more serious before now.'

Mel followed the police outside, a few steps behind like a scolded child, to the nice street in the nice beachside suburb. The neighbours were stirring, leaning out of windows to look at the commotion.

There she was. *Missing Backpacker Found Safe and Well.*

Lori looked up from Ava's thigh embrace to Mel, and smiled. 'I'm back,' she said.

Lori was wearing Mel's clothes. Linen shirt and shorts that were definitely too big and too old for her. They made her look fragile. But she wasn't, not really.

Mel joined the hug. 'Good to see you,' she said, before Elaine stepped in.

'Lori, we'd love you to come with us and have a chat, if you're feeling up to it.'

It made sense. Couldn't let the meddling old lady downstairs cause any more mayhem.

Kat. Smiling more broadly than Mel had ever seen her smile. 'I'll come with you,' she said to Lori.

And Lori said, 'I'd like that.'

'Will you come back?' Ava asked. 'Will you come back and look after us again? I have so many lists to show you.' She started ticking off her fingers. '*Things I Miss About Lori, Reasons Lori is the Greatest Babysitter of All Time* and *8 Reasons Why Life is Better When You're Here.*'

Everyone was about to cry. Simon, standing back, his hands on Eddie's shoulders, was biting his lip. Lori's face was streaming. Even Elaine was smiling at Ava in a way that told Mel she was a mum, too.

One of the people watching from a window whooped.

Kat, of course, was the one who still had everything together, the one who looked at Mel and asked, 'Where is he?'

Mel shook her head. 'I don't know. He left, right after I told him. I saw him go.'

She had rushed into the flat, closed the door, locked it, leaned against it. She had lied to Flynn. She hadn't told the police. She'd called Kat, still out of breath from marching away from Flynn at speed, her lips still stinging from her ridiculous kiss. Then she'd heard him, crashing through the front door, running upstairs, two at a time. She heard him yelling up there, but it wasn't clear what. He'd sounded like a wounded, wailing demon. Like a terrifying, maleficent ghost. But only for a moment, before the upstairs door banged again, the stairs began to pound. Mel had instinctively leapt back from the door as he passed, almost expecting him to burst through it. But he didn't.

She'd run to the sunroom, phone in hand, ready to dial Elaine's number, and watched the ghost, with his backpack, his guitar and his box, exactly as he'd arrived, walking away from the building. Getting smaller, less impressive, disappearing from view.

'I was on the phone to you when he left,' she said to Elaine, who nodded sharply.

Kat shrugged. Reached out for Lori's hand. 'Come on, let's get this out of the way.'

*

'The ghost has gone.' Mel was lying in her bed, listening to the sounds of upstairs, the strong eucalyptus smell of a nit treatment in the air. She'd spent the evening settling the kids, which included baths, comb outs, something for dinner that didn't come on the back of a delivery bike. One day, she'd have to tell them why she'd let them suffer through a week of worry. But not today.

'Exorcism complete,' Izzy said, from the other side of the world. 'How does it feel?'

'I kissed him.'

'You *kissed* him?'

'I had to. Just to check.'

'Check?'

'That he wasn't Dom.'

'Of course he wasn't Dom.'

'Bear with me, it's been a rough summer.'

'Apparently.'

'The thing is, Izzy, as soon as I did that, it was like a spell was broken. Suddenly all I could see were the differences between him and Dominic. They just had this . . . toxic intensity in common. And that's when the ghost disappeared. That moment.'

'Sounds legit. Have you been smoking something from upstairs?'

From above, the familiar soft sound of clinking glass, music playing. The smell of a fancy candle, the faint whiff of Thai. It was the girls.

Lori and Kat had come back from the police station and come in for a while, while the kids whirled around them. Kat told Mel it looked likely to be over. Lori had told the police it was all her idea. Six days. A misguided Good Samaritan. Better to let it go.

'So the obvious question,' Mel had said, 'is what now?'

Lori and Kat looked at each other. 'We're going to hang out upstairs for a while,' Kat said. 'I called Emily. She's hoping to be back in a month, but until then . . .'

'You won't be scared he's going to come back?'

'We think he's long gone,' Lori said. 'I was hoping . . .'

'What?'

'To see him. To say something. I'm angry.'

Kat had her hand on Lori's hand again. 'We can use that. For good.'

And Lori's smile was back.

'Okay, you two,' Mel said. 'But we're getting you home. The whole bloody point of whisking you away was to find a flight while Flynn was freaking out. I've been talking to your mum, and to that travel agent who knows how to game these limited outbound trips. Costs a fortune –'

Lori had put a hand on Mel's leg, firmly. 'I don't want any more help,' she'd said. 'Thank you, but I can handle it, Mel. It's time to back off.'

And Ava and Eddie had laughed so hard at this that Eddie fell off the chair where he'd been picking at vegetables, and Ava, curled up in Lori's lap, echoed it. 'Just back OFF, Mum!'

'Smart girl,' Izzy was saying now. 'She's got to be the one to work out what to do next, just like you did.'

Mel could hear, in Izzy's house, the familiar hum of breakfast TV, faint in the background. The girls banging plates, making toast, whirring smoothies. The stuff and grind of the endless family routine.

'Don't *you* ever wonder what happened to the old you, Iz?' Mel asked. 'Where's your midlife crisis?'

The moment she said it, Mel knew she shouldn't have. There was a crisis going on in Izzy's house. But it was a crisis of life and death, not of regret and longing.

She heard Izzy draw breath.

'I'm sorry,' Mel said, before her sister could say anything. 'I'm sorry, Izzy, I know that's a fucking stupid thing to say to you.'

The family soundtrack became muffled, Mel could tell that Izzy had moved into another room. A quieter one, to say what she was going to say next.

'Tom's dying, Mel,' she said, as matter-of-factly as Izzy said everything.

'Izzy . . .' Mel, for once, didn't know what to say to her sister. The number of times in their lives that had happened she could count on one hand.

'It's fucking bullshit, Mel. It's bullshit that Dominic died so young. That you have been flipped back into grief shows you just how cruel that was. But this is different. This is our life. This is two decades. A family. My . . . person.'

'Izzy . . .'

'I'm proud of you, Mel, for doing what you did for Lori. It was stupid and kind of selfish, but I'm proud of you for it. It shows you still are that person, the one you've been wondering where she went . . . that's her. Brave.' Izzy's voice was shaking now. 'But it's time to put away childish things, as that famous fucking play or whatever says. This is serious. We've only got the time we have. Don't talk to me about midlife crises when every single year is everything. It's *everything*. Every day, every hour . . . it's everything.'

'Izzy, it's okay,' Mel, so far away, so very, very far away, felt every one of her sister's sobs. 'Izzy, I'm here,' she said, over and over, until the heaves began to slow. 'Put me in your pocket, take me with you today.'

And Izzy, on the other side of the world, slipped her sister in the pocket of the sensible coat she wore to her sensible job, and took Mel along with her as she blew her nose, splashed water on her face, and called the girls for the school run.

Mel, lying on the bed on a hot Sydney night, the lazy buzz of a mozzie in her ear, the ghostly sounds of young women making love drifting down from upstairs, stayed with her sister, hearing her, feeling her, right up until she fell asleep, right about the time Izzy made her ham and mustard sandwich for lunch.

Epilogue

In late January, Perth shimmers with an intense, dry heat. Adrian Junet liked to complete his morning cycle before the sun was truly up, before peeling off the Lycra for a shower and changing into his crisp cotton shirt. He aimed to minimise the time between the kitchen, where Kim made him an espresso and reminded him to stay away from a mid-morning croissant, and the air-conditioning of the Lexus, which was waiting in the three-car garage to transport him from Peppermint Grove to the CBD.

The office was cool, too, although the glare could be something fierce as the day cracked on. It was Adrian's morning ritual to have another coffee and a pastry while he got across his morning emails. His assistant, Alex, knew to have the treats on Adrian's desk by 8.25. He also knew to have scanned the boss's emails before he sat down, to weed out junk mail, nuisance and begging letters.

This one, he didn't know what to do with, so he left it at the top of the email list, for Adrian to get to first. In the tearoom, he would tell the other assistants that he wasn't that surprised by the subject line, considering he'd been drafted in as security at Rob Junet's eighteenth last year.

ATTN: ADRIAN JUNET
RE: YOUR SON, ROBERT JUNET, ATTEMPTED RAPIST
Dear Adrian,

I am writing to alert you to the very poor job you have done in raising your son.

I know you sent him to the finest of schools. I know he went skiing every season. I know he played in the first eleven, that coach 'Finny' Finster is an excellent influence on the lads, and I know that 'boys will be boys' was a mantra good enough for your generation.

But on 23 October 2020, your son tried to rape me while I slept. We were in a shared room at a youth hostel in Merimbula, NSW. The name of the hostel, manager and attending staff are included here. They can confirm that in the early hours of the morning, they were called to a disturbance in a room. Your intoxicated son had tried to forcibly remove my clothes, assaulting me in the process. Another witness to this attack was your son's former travel companion, George Fable, who, despite having the same upbringing and influences as young Rob, does not appear to be an attempted rapist, nor an apologist for one. I've been told you know the Fables, and I think you'll find they are currently enlightening the rest of your social circle as to why their son and yours are no longer close.

Your son's behaviour after this attack was as disturbing as the event itself. He repeatedly harassed and threatened me whenever our paths crossed, which was never at my urging or arrangement. What this behaviour suggests is that he is highly likely to repeat the attack, as it seems Robert has missed a crucial piece of human-being training – the part where you treat others with dignity and respect. Indeed, the part where you treat others as human at all.

Who can know the ongoing repercussions of this gap in your son's education? Perhaps you can guess at what they might be? At just how much 'worse' this could be, the next time.

Copies of this letter have been sent to your wife, Kim, to Robert's former school, to the university he has been selected to attend, and also posted in all the relevant social media spaces.

I'm sure you will rail against this attempt to 'ruin a young man's life'. 'Ruin' seems like an overreach, but yes, perhaps I might put a momentary kink in his chosen path. Perhaps a detour long enough for reflection, for pause.

The aim is simple. Your son shows no remorse for his attempted attack on me. He is highly likely to repeat this action, over and over, until someone stops him.

Perhaps that person is you. Perhaps it's me.

Thank you for your time and attention. Thank you also for the use of the family station wagon. You will find it parked outside the Sydney head offices of FullStop Australia, an organisation that supports the victims of sexual assault. The keys are under the wheel arch. I am afraid the tank is empty.

Lorelai Haring

*

The Travelmate Facebook page was again roiling with a constant chatter. Hard borders were dissolving, plans were being remade, and a generation were reigniting their profiles to find each other, and plan their escapes.

On their phones, in their hundreds, in their thousands, they were all finding the same notice, pinned to the top of the chat by Admin, just as it was in RoadMates, TravelTalk, and in group chats and on message boards where women shared intel about men to be avoided, reported and blocked.

WARNING

This man – Flynn Strout, also known by his birth name, Darren Strout – is currently being sought to assist NSW Police in a potential criminal investigation into intimate partner violence.

He is twenty-five years old, 180 centimetres tall, with dark hair and green eyes and several distinguishing tattoos, none of which are original, or interesting. He rarely wears a shirt.

If you see him, please alert authorities. Also please know that any story he tells you about that time he was a guru at a silent retreat in Kathmandu is one hundred per cent bullshit. He has never played semi-professional soccer in France, never sold socks at Everest base camp and he has certainly never practised tantra with a high priestess in Ubud.

Darren/Flynn does not hold a passport and has never left Australian shores.

Feel free to believe any story he tells you about exploiting vulnerable women, controlling behaviour and barely veiled violent tendencies. Those ones are likely to be true.

Do not be fooled by the fact a man can cook, can feign a listening face, and, yes, is a decent lover. There are ways to obtain both food and orgasms that come without existential risk to your body and your soul.

Please feel free to share this notice with anyone who will be safer for seeing it.

Lori

ori and Kat stretched out on a big patchwork blanket on the clifftop grass. On the right side of the fence.

For Lori, these last few days had been cleansing, restorative. Friends of Kat's knew for certain Flynn had left the city. They deadlocked the door every night just in case, but there was a distinct lifting of pressure, an absence of fear, that Lori was beginning to settle into. She felt the freedom she'd been looking for was finally here. But the cost was not self-sacrifice. And that was new.

Her mother's constant calls were background, wallpaper, to this new blossoming. Kat was its fuel.

She rolled over towards her beautiful, fearless friend, and put her hand on Kat's hip.

'I feel invincible today,' she said. 'I feel like I caught it from you.'

Kat smiled her slow, cartoon cat smile. 'It was there all the time,' she said. 'It's what brought you here.'

Flynn

'**A**ren't you that guy?'
    If one more person said it.
'Haven't I seen you somewhere?'
He would lose it for fucking good.
'Didn't I read something about you, brother?'
Come on, just keep your head down. Move through.
'I don't think so, mate.'
It was really starting to affect the efficiency of the journey.
'Are you dreaming? I've heard you're a complete deadshit.'
And certainly ruining his chances of finding a bed for the night
with a warm body in it.
'Can't have you working here, friend, it's not worth the aggravation.'
I've been cancelled. Flynn had read about it, but now it was real.
Of course, there were still corners of the country where you could
find people who weren't on social media. But they weren't places you
wanted to be. Or places a man like Flynn could work.
Kat will make this right, he'd thought. She's got a game going on
here, for sure.

Only she didn't.
He'd only heard from her once since.
He'd called and texted and called, like a desperate man.
And one day, Kat had actually replied.
Who is this? And it had hurt. Sounded just like her, but cut deep.
I can't believe this. You know me, he wrote.
Exactly, she wrote back.
And then she'd changed her number.

Mel

The airport felt like a foreign country, complete with forgotten languages and exotic traditions.

This is how we used to live, before. Rushing through this vast, echoey hall could be a normal Monday morning thing to do. And in the snaking queue for international check-in, the only thing worth remarking on was the length of the line, how few check-in staff were on duty, the extortionate price of coffee, and whether the child-distracting iPads were within easy reach.

There would be no children to distract on today's flight.

They were quite the party, in the departures hall today. Lori, of course. And Kat, who these days was wherever Lori was. Simon in his Attack Sports uniform, still insisting on being the dad who wheeled the trolley, stacked with heavy bags. Ava and Eddie, dragging at the brake handle, trying to jump on for a ride. All noisy, all excitable, all feeling the possibilities that an airport gives anyone who walks through the automatic doors. Escape and adventure, homecoming and connection.

It was time. No matter what Lori said. For Mel, it was time.

Sometimes, this summer, Mel had felt like she'd caught a glimpse of her young self, walking beside her. Another ghost, stepping through a parallel life to her own. This was the same airport where she had taken her first steps on Australian soil, almost two decades before, the giddy companion of a flawed man she loved madly. She could picture that version of Mel, downstairs from where she stood now, standing next to Dom in the arrivals hall, watching him embrace his mother, who was rippling with relief. With love.

Mel had called Gina last night. If she was surprised to hear Mel's voice, she didn't say so. She sounded older, tired. Sad.

After inquiries about health, and kids, and about the weather up there in Grafton, Gina had asked, gently, 'Why are you calling, Mel? Is something wrong?'

Mel told Gina she was calling because these past few months, for reasons too strange to relay, Dom had been in her mind every minute. 'I just wanted to call you,' Mel said, 'to let you know you're not the only one who thinks of him every day. To let you know you're not alone. That he's not forgotten.'

It had felt like a long time before Gina said anything. 'Thank you, Mel, that's lovely of you,' she said, eventually. 'I know he was difficult. I know you suffered.'

Mel didn't rush to correct her, as she once would have, as she did at Dom's funeral. She swallowed hard, and held her breath, saying nothing.

'And I know you loved him,' Gina said. 'So, thank you.'

Now, that ghostly Mel in the arrivals hall, so young and nervous and full of possibility, just like Lori, was fading out, and Mel was standing, in full focus, at the departures gate, ready to fly.

'Mum, I've made you a list,' Ava was saying. '*Top Six Reasons You Shouldn't Worry About Us While You're Gone.*'

Mel pulled Eddie to her, his worried little face pushed into her side. 'Hit us, Ava,' she said, her voice not wavering too much, she hoped.

Ava's list was unfurled, decorated, Mel could see, with meticulous love hearts, aeroplanes and ice creams.

'Number one: Lori and Kat will help Dad ALL THE TIME, including sleepovers and making sure we get treats and not just Dad's boring sport food every day.

'Number two: Auntie Izzy needs all your attention right now, but Eddie and I know that doesn't mean you're going to forget about us, like your memory has been wiped by zombies like in Eddie's video game that he will definitely be playing all the time while you're not around to tell him off.

'Number three: We love you more than the whole world and all the ocean and Daddy says distance is nothing in the face of such Big Love. Right, Dad?

'Number four: The food in England is horrible, so we know you'll come back.

'Number five: Except for chocolate, and we know you'll want to bring lots and lots back to us, because you love us so much.

'Number six: Family. You told us it's a word that means lots of things. And ours is in lots of places. And that makes us lucky.'

Tears ran down into paper masks. Mel had an arm for each child and her eyes on Lori. And Simon, a calm centre among strong women who had decided their own next steps.

For Mel there was no choice than to go. Police clearance and quarantine, red tape and many, many tests, whatever it took.

Lori was determined her future was here and not at home. Mel had realised that, right now, the place she had to be was at home, not here.

With her sister. With her nieces. With all the deeply painful mess and joy of a life lived well. And next time she was in this place, walking through this hall towards her family, Mel could go back to not believing in ghosts.

Acknowledgements

A bottle flying through an open window sparked the idea for *The Couple Upstairs*.

I lived in an apartment building in Sydney's Coogee for thirteen years. It's where this book is set. A white, beachside art deco block, with sliding sash windows that could be generously shoved open to let in laughter and music on a frangipani breeze, or crashed shut, to close out techno at dawn, the screams of arguments or uncensored sex. The slammed window was the first passive-aggressive sign that lives being led metres apart were getting too damn close and too damn loud. A hurled bottle was the last.

We came to know a lot about our neighbours as we slowly outgrew that flat, cramming a couple of kids and a dog into an almost-two-bed perfect for a pair. The people who lived above, below and alongside us weren't kept up by late-night paella sessions but by the clatter of children's stomping and us, yelling after them about shoes and teeth and hair.

The Couple Upstairs is set in that wedding-cake apartment block by the sea, but it's not about our lives there. What unfolds between

Mel, Lori, Flynn and Kat is a set of events inspired by an entirely different part of my life, and, of course, by the stories of women everywhere who know what it's like to love someone who makes you sick.

Which means my first acknowledgement is going to Brent McKean. We came together with enough experience under our collective belts to be certain of the kind of relationship we didn't want – and we built one that we did. It's not perfect, but it's right. And his support is everything to me.

And, of course, to our kids, Matilda and Billy. At times, work you love will take you away from the people you love and the cost of that must be acknowledged. Thank you, Brent, and to our excellent children, for being just fine without me. I love you all to bits.

Writing during these last two pandemic years has been a lot. Lockdowns, home-school, a major move, anxious children, closed borders, sickness and health. Lucky for me the anchoring constant in my life is my work at women's media company Mamamia, and the large group of talented people I get to work alongside, for and with every day.

Specifically, over the last few years, the Outlouders, who offer the best possible reason to show up and try your best. Top of that list are Mia Freedman and Jessie Stephens, the two people I love to argue with more than any other (actually, the only two people I love to argue with). They are generous and funny, encouraging, inspiring and clever, just like the army of women who listen to the three of us many times a week. They are the bedrock of so much. And to the extended Out Loud family of Lize Ratliff and Emma Gillespie and the entire team, thank you so very much for everything you do, every day.

Thank you to the tight army of women writers who understand how it is, trying to live a creative life as well as a family life and a work life. Tori Haschka, who has been a new blessing, my south coast saviour. Sally Hepworth, who is so generous with her advice on the big things and the little things, including how to transfer my post-it addiction to Scrivener. Also Jess Dettmann, Fiona Higgins, Suzanne Daniel, for conversation and wisdom and walks.

I don't have anything without my mates. Notably Penny Kaleta, my Coogee family, providing me with a bed in the big smoke, constant support and unconditional love. There are a lot of lucky women who call Penny when they're wobbling, and may we all return the favour. Also to my tight crew of Karen Flanagan, Angie McMenamin, Sally Godfrey, Helen Campbell, Katie Hodkin and Tara Nicholson. May we laugh together much longer. My Mothers' Group sisters (the kids might have started high school but we are forever bonded) Mel Ware, Rebecca Rodwell, Sam Marshall, Leanne McLaughlin, Ciara O'Neill and Sarah Sutton. My treasured 'old' friend Miranda Herron. And my genius posse of Lucy Ormonde and Monique Bowley, whose priceless pump-ups save me regularly.

Moving to a whole new place in a lockdown would have been a lot harder without the welcoming generosity of Ali and Art Lidbetter, Jo Willesee and Steve Ball, Heidi Fletcher, Mel Farr and others who texted 'do you want to go for a walk?' Answer: Yes, yes, I do, and thank you so very much for asking.

Shaun McKean and Kieran Fox, who provide our whole clan with a template of long-term love done right. Lindsay Frankel and Ian McLeish, who are my people, always. My family – Tom, Lila and Louie Wainwright, and of course my parents, Jeff and Judith – I can't do without them, even if I really haven't seen enough of them these last few pandemic years.

Which brings me to the virus. There is a lot of teeth-gnashing among authors about whether to include it in our work. For me, with this book, I wanted it to be the oppressive force hovering outside Mel's apartment block, keeping everyone trapped in such close proximity. But I had no interest in writing a 'Covid Book', so the exact timings of regional lockdowns and specific health regulations are painted in broad strokes. It's designed that way, rather than having us all relive those days of morning press conferences, schools opening and closing, fences in front of beaches, tape around playgrounds. It was enough, then.

Lastly, thanks must go to all the people who help a book become a book. Cate Paterson, whose belief in me was transformative. My wise agent, Catherine Drayton. My publisher Ingrid Ohlsson, warm and strategic – an excellent combination. Editors Brianne Collins and Deonie Fiford. Thank you for making me much, much better. Publicist Allie Schotte. Designer Christa Moffitt, who makes the most beautiful covers in publishing, the end. It's a pinch-me moment to hold a book you wrote in your hands, but the story of how it got there is a whole lot bigger than the person who wrote it.